Down Under

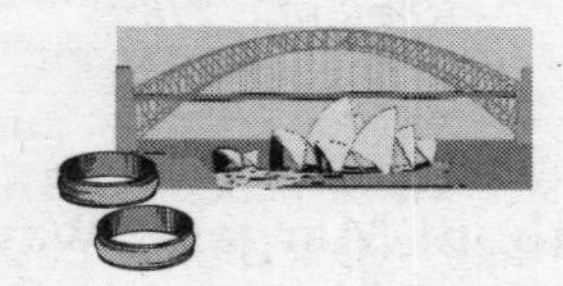

Red-hot Husbands!

Praise for three best-selling authors –
Helen Bianchin, Margaret Way and Jessica Hart

About AN IDEAL MARRIAGE?

'Helen Bianchin pens a sexy tale with vibrant characterisation and lively scenes.'
- *Romantic Times*

About Margaret Way

'Margaret Way uses...descriptive prowess to make love and the Australian Outback blossom brilliantly.'
- *Romantic Times*

About Jessica Hart

'Jessica Hart keeps readers on the edge of their seats...'
- *Romantic Times*

Weddings Down Under

AN IDEAL MARRIAGE?

by

Helen Bianchin

GEORGIA AND THE TYCOON

by

Margaret Way

OUTBACK BRIDE

by

Jessica Hart

MILLS & BOON®

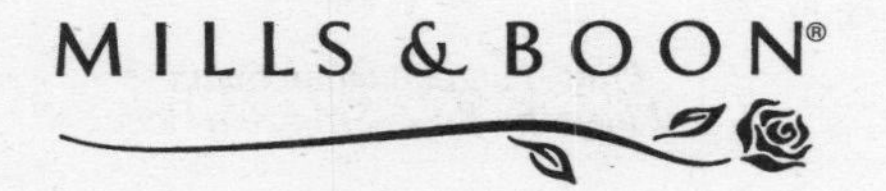

DID YOU PURCHASE THIS BOOK WITHOUT A COVER?
If you did, you should be aware it is **stolen property** as it was reported *unsold and destroyed* by a retailer. Neither the author nor the publisher has received any payment for this book.

All the characters in this book have no existence outside the imagination of the author, and have no relation whatsoever to anyone bearing the same name or names. They are not even distantly inspired by any individual known or unknown to the author, and all the incidents are pure invention.

All Rights Reserved including the right of reproduction in whole or in part in any form. This edition is published by arrangement with Harlequin Enterprises II B.V. The text of this publication or any part thereof may not be reproduced or transmitted in any form or by any means, electronic or mechanical, including photocopying, recording, storage in an information retrieval system, or otherwise, without the written permission of the publisher.

This book is sold subject to the condition that it shall not, by way of trade or otherwise, be lent, resold, hired out or otherwise circulated without the prior consent of the publisher in any form of binding or cover other than that in which it is published and without a similar condition including this condition being imposed on the subsequent purchaser.

MILLS & BOON and MILLS & BOON with the Rose Device are registered trademarks of the publisher.
Harlequin Mills & Boon Limited,
Eton House, 18-24 Paradise Road, Richmond, Surrey, TW9 1SR

WEDDINGS DOWN UNDER
© by Harlequin Enterprises II B.V., 2001

An Ideal Marriage?, Georgia and the Tycoon and *Outback Bride* were first published in Great Britain by Harlequin Mills & Boon Limited in separate, single volumes.

An Ideal Marriage? © Helen Bianchin 1997
Georgia and the Tycoon © Margaret Way Pty Ltd., 1997
Outback Bride © Jessica Hart 1997

ISBN 0 263 82779 8

05-1101

Printed and bound in Spain
by Litografia Rosés S.A., Barcelona

Helen Bianchin was born in New Zealand and travelled to Australia before marrying her Italian-born husband. After three years they moved, returned to New Zealand with their daughter, had two sons and then resettled in Australia. Encouraged by friends to recount anecdotes of her years as a tobacco sharefarmer's wife living in an Italian community, Helen began setting words on paper and her first novel was published in 1975. An animal lover, she says her terrier and Persian cat regard her study as much theirs as hers.

Look out for
THE HUSBAND TEST by Helen Bianchin
In Modern Romance™, December 2001

AN IDEAL MARRIAGE?

by
Helen Bianchin

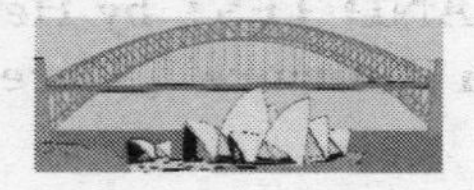

[illegible] traffic [illegible]
[illegible] in [illegible].
A [illegible] her fantasy [illegible]
[illegible] as [illegible]
[illegible]ed.

She [illegible] however,
[illegible] her hair [illegible]
and [illegible] The [illegible] of ten
minutes [illegible] of
her [illegible].

Her eyes [illegible] of the [illegible],
and she dwelt momentarily on the fact that [illegible] spent
on their [illegible] had [illegible] her lunch.
An apple at her desk that afternoon could hardly be
termed an adequate substitute.

The car in front began to move, and she followed
its path, picking up speed, only to depress the brake
pedal as the lights changed.

Damn. At this rate it would take two if not three
attempts to clear the intersection.

She should, she admitted silently, have left her office
earlier in order to miss the heavy early evening
traffic. Yet [illegible] single [illegible] had prevented
her from doing so.

As James Sheldon's daughter, she had [illegible] used to

CHAPTER ONE

GABBI eased the car to a halt in the long line of traffic banked up behind the New South Head Road intersection adjacent to Sydney's suburban Elizabeth Bay. A slight frown creased her forehead as she checked her watch, and her fingers tapped an impatient tattoo against the steering wheel.

She had precisely one hour in which to shower, wash her hair, dry and style it, apply make-up, dress, and greet invited dinner guests. The loss of ten minutes caught up in heavy traffic didn't form part of her plan.

Her eyes slid to the manicured length of her nails, and she dwelt momentarily on the fact that time spent on their lacquered perfection had cost her her lunch. An apple at her desk mid-afternoon could hardly be termed an adequate substitute.

The car in front began to move, and she followed its path, picking up speed, only to depress the brake pedal as the lights changed.

Damn. At this rate it would take two, if not three attempts to clear the intersection.

She *should*, she admitted silently, have left her office earlier in order to miss the heavy early evening traffic. Yet stubborn single-mindedness had prevented her from doing so.

As James Stanton's daughter, she had no need to

work. Property, an extensive share portfolio and a handsome annuity placed her high on the list of Sydney's independently wealthy young women.

As Benedict Nicols' *wife*, her position as assistant management consultant with Stanton-Nicols Enterprises was viewed as nepotism at its very worst.

Gabbi thrust the gear-shift forward with unaccustomed force, attaining momentary satisfaction from the sound of the Mercedes' refined engine as she eased the car forward and followed the traffic's crawling pace, only to halt scant minutes later.

The cellphone rang, and she automatically reached for it.

'Gabrielle.'

Only one person steadfastly refused to abbreviate her Christian name. 'Monique.'

'You're driving?'

'Stationary,' she informed her, pondering the purpose of her stepmother's call. Monique never rang to simply say 'hello.'

'Annaliese flew in this afternoon. Would it be an imposition if she came to dinner?'

Years spent attending an élite boarding-school had instilled requisite good manners. 'Not at all. We'd be delighted.'

'Thank you, darling.'

Monique's voice sounded like liquid satin as she ended the call.

Wonderful, Gabbi accorded silently as she punched in the appropriate code and alerted Marie to set another place at the table.

'Sorry to land this on you,' she added apologetically before replacing the handset down onto the console. An extra guest posed no problem, and Gabbi wasn't sufficiently superstitious to consider thirteen at the table a premise for an unsuccessful evening.

The traffic began to move, and the faint tension behind her eyes threatened to develop into a headache.

James Stanton's remarriage ten years ago to a twenty-nine-year-old divorcee with one young daughter had gifted him with a contentment Gabbi could never begrudge him. Monique was his social equal, and an exemplary hostess. It was unfortunate that Monique's affection didn't extend to James's daughter. As a vulnerable fifteen-year-old Gabbi had sensed her stepmother's superficiality, and spent six months agonising over why, until a friend had spelled out the basic psychology of a dysfunctional relationship.

In retaliation, Gabbi had chosen to excel at everything she did—she'd striven to gain straight As in each subject, had won sporting championships, and graduated from university with an honours degree in business management. She'd studied languages and spent a year in Paris, followed by another in Tokyo, before returning to Sydney to work for a rival firm. Then she'd applied for and won, on the strength of her experience and credentials, a position with Stanton-Nicols.

There was a certain danger in allowing one's thoughts to dwell on the past, Gabbi mused a trifle wryly as she swung the Mercedes into the exclusive Vaucluse street, where heavy, wide-branched trees added a certain ambience to the luxurious homes nestled out of sight behind high concrete walls.

A few hundred metres along she drew the car to a halt, depressed a remote modem, and waited the necessary seconds as the double set of ornate black wrought-iron gates slid smoothly aside.

A wide curved driveway led to an elegant two-storeyed Mediterranean-style home set well back from the road in beautiful landscaped grounds. Encompassing four allotments originally acquired in the late 1970s by Conrad Nicols, the existing four houses had been removed to make way for a multi-million-dollar residence whose magnificent harbour views placed it high in Sydney's real-estate stratosphere.

Ten years later extensive million-dollar refurbishment had added extensions providing additional bedroom accommodation, garages for seven cars, remodelled kitchen, undercover terraces, and balconies. The revamped gardens boasted fountains, courtyards, ornamental ponds and English-inspired lawns bordered by clipped hedges.

It was incredibly sad, Gabbi reflected as she released one set of automatic garage doors and drove beneath them, that Conrad and Diandra Nicols had been victims of a freak highway accident mere weeks after the final landscaping touches had been completed.

Yet Conrad had achieved in death what he hadn't achieved in the last ten years of his life: His son and heir had returned from America and taken over Conrad's partnership in Stanton-Nicols.

Gabbi slid the Mercedes to a halt between the sleek

lines of Benedict's XJ220 Jaguar and the more staid frame of a black Bentley. Missing was the top-of-the-range four-wheel drive Benedict used to commute each day to the city.

The garage doors slid down with a refined click and Gabbi caught up her briefcase from the passenger seat, slipped out from behind the wheel, then crossed to a side door to punch in a series of digits, deactivating the security system guarding entry to the house.

Mansion, she corrected herself with a twisted smile as she lifted the in-house phone and rang through to the kitchen. 'Hi, Marie. Everything under control?'

Twenty years' service with the Nicols family enabled the housekeeper to respond with a warm chuckle. 'No problems.'

'Thanks,' Gabbi acknowledged gratefully before hurrying through the wide hallway to a curved staircase leading to the upper floor.

Marie would be putting the final touches to the four-course meal she'd prepared; her husband, Serg, would be checking the temperature of the wines Benedict had chosen to be served, and Sophie, the casual help, would be running a final check of the dining-room.

All *she* had to do was appear downstairs, perfectly groomed, when Serg answered the ring of the doorbell and ushered the first of their guests into the lounge in around forty minutes.

Or less, Gabbi accorded as she ascended the stairs at a rapid pace.

Benedict's mother had chosen lush-piled eau-de-nil

carpet and pale textured walls to offset the classic lines of the mahogany furniture, employing a skilful blend of toning colour with matching drapes and bed-covers, ensuring each room was subtly different.

The master suite was situated in the eastern wing with glass doors opening onto two balconies and commanding impressive views of the harbour. Panoramic by day, those views became a magical vista at night, with a fairy-like tracery of distant electric and flashing neon light.

Gabbi kicked off her shoes, removed jewellery, then quickly shed her clothes *en route* to a marble-tiled *en suite* which almost rivalled the bedroom in size.

Elegantly decadent in pale gold-streaked ivory marble, there was a huge spa-bath and a double shower to complement the usual facilities.

Ten minutes later she entered the bedroom, a towel fastened sarong-style over her slim curves, with another wound into a turban on top of her head.

'Cutting it fine, Gabbi?' Benedict's faintly accented drawl held a mocking edge as he shrugged off his suit jacket and loosened his tie.

In his late thirties, tall, with a broad, hard-muscled frame, his sculpted facial features gave a hint of his maternal Andalusian ancestry. Dark, almost black eyes held a powerful intensity that never softened for his fellow man, and rarely for a woman.

'Whatever happened to "Hi, honey, I'm home"?' she retaliated as she crossed the room and selected fresh underwear from a recessed drawer, hurriedly donned briefs and bra, then stepped into a silk slip.

'Followed by a salutatory kiss?' he mocked with a tinge of musing cynicism as he shed his shirt and attended to the zip of his trousers.

She felt the tempo of her heartbeat increase, and she was conscious of an elevated tension that began in the pit of her stomach and flared along every nerve-end, firing her body with an acute awareness that was entirely physical.

Dynamic masculinity at its most potent, she acknowledged silently as she snatched up a silk robe, thrust her arms through its sleeves, and retraced her steps to the *en suite.*

Removing the towelled turban, she caught up the hair-drier and began blow-drying her hair.

Her attention rapidly became unfocused as Benedict entered the *en suite* and crossed to the shower. Mirrored walls reflected his naked image, and she determinedly ignored the olive-toned skin sheathing hard muscle and sinew, the springy dark hair that covered his chest and arrowed down past his waist to reach his manhood, the firmly shaped buttocks, and the powerful length of his back.

Her eyes followed the powerful strength of his shoulders as he reached forward to activate the flow of water, then the glass doors slid closed behind him.

Gabbi tugged the brush through her hair with unnecessary force, and felt her eyes prick at the sudden pain.

It was one year, two months and three weeks since their marriage, and she still couldn't handle the effect he had on her in bed or out of it.

Her scalp tingled in protest, and she relaxed the

brushstrokes then switched off the drier. Her hair was still slightly damp, its natural ash-blonde colour appearing faintly darker, highlighting the creamy smoothness of her skin and accentuating the deep blue of her eyes.

With practised movements she caught the length of her hair and deftly swept it into a chignon at her nape, secured it with pins, then began applying make-up.

Minutes later she heard the water stop, and with conscious effort she focused on blending her eyeshadow, studiously ignoring him as he crossed to the long marbled pedestal and began dealing with a day's growth of beard.

'Bad day?'

Her fingers momentarily stilled, then she replaced the eyeshadow palette and selected mascara. 'Why do you ask?'

'You have expressive eyes,' Benedict observed as he smoothed his fingers over his jaw.

Gabbi met his gaze in the mirror, and held it. 'Annaliese is to be a last-minute guest at dinner.'

He switched off the electric shaver and reached for the cut-glass bottle containing an exclusive brand of cologne. 'That bothers you?'

She tried for levity. 'I'm capable of slaying my own dragons.'

One eyebrow lifted with sardonic humour. 'Verbal swords over dessert?'

Annaliese was known not to miss an opportunity, and Gabbi couldn't imagine tonight would prove an exception. 'I'll do my best to parry any barbs with practised civility.'

His eyes swept over her slim curves then returned to study the faint, brooding quality evident on her finely etched features, and a slight smile tugged the edges of his mouth. 'The objective being to win another battle in an ongoing war?'

'Has anyone beaten *you* in battle, Benedict?' she queried lightly as she capped the mascara wand, returned it to the drawer housing her cosmetics and concentrated on applying a soft pink colour to her lips.

He didn't answer. He had no need to assert that he was a man equally feared and respected by his contemporaries and rarely, if ever, fooled by anyone.

Just watch my back. The words remained unuttered as she turned towards the door, and minutes later she selected a long black pencil-slim silk skirt and teamed it with a simple scoop-necked sleeveless black top. Stiletto-heeled evening shoes completed the outfit, and she added a pear-shaped diamond pendant and matching ear-studs, then slipped on a slim, diamond-encrusted bracelet before turning towards the mirror to cast her reflection a cursory glance. A few dabs of her favourite Le Must de Cartier perfume added the final touch.

'Ready?'

Gabbi turned at the sound of his voice, and felt her breath catch at the image he presented.

There was something about his stance, a sense of animalistic strength, that fine tailoring did little to tame. The dramatic mesh of elemental ruthlessness and primitive power added a magnetism few women of any age could successfully ignore.

For a few timeless seconds her eyes locked with

his in an attempt to determine what lay behind the studied inscrutability he always managed to portray.

She envied him his superb control…and wondered what it would take to break it.

'Yes.' Her voice was steady, and she summoned a bright smile as she turned to precede him from the room.

The main staircase curved down to the ground floor in an elegant sweep of wide, partially carpeted marble stairs, with highly polished mahogany bannisters supported by ornately scrolled black wrought-iron balusters.

Set against floor-to-ceiling lead-panelled glass, the staircase created an elegant focus highlighted by a magnificent crystal chandelier.

Marble floors lent spaciousness and light to the large entry foyer, sustained by textured ivory-coloured walls whose uniformity was broken by a series of wide, heavily panelled doors, works of art, and a collection of elegant Mediterranean-style cabinets.

Gabbi had just placed a foot on the last stair when the doorbell pealed.

'Show-time,' she murmured as Serg emerged from the eastern hallway and moved quickly towards the impressively panelled double front doors.

Benedict's eyes hardened fractionally. 'Cynicism doesn't suit you.'

Innate pride lent her eyes a fiery sparkle, and her chin tilted slightly in a gesture of mild defiance. 'I can be guaranteed to behave,' she assured him quietly, and felt her pulse quicken as he caught hold of her hand.

'Indeed.' The acknowledgement held a dry softness which was lethal, and an icy chill feathered across the surface of her skin.

'Charles,' Benedict greeted smoothly seconds later as Serg announced the first of their guests. 'Andrea.' His smile was warm, and he appeared relaxed and totally at ease. 'Come through to the lounge and let me get you a drink.'

Most of the remaining guests arrived within minutes, and Gabbi played her role as hostess to the hilt, circulating, smiling, all the time waiting for the moment Monique and Annaliese would precede her father into the lounge.

Monique believed in making an entrance, and her arrival was always carefully timed to provide maximum impact. While she was never unpardonably late, her timing nevertheless bordered on the edge of social acceptability.

Serg's announcement coincided with Gabbi's expectation and, excusing herself from conversation, she moved forward to greet her father.

'James.' She brushed his cheek with her lips and accepted the firm clasp on her shoulder in return before turning towards her stepmother to accept the salutatory air-kiss. 'Monique.' Her smile was without fault as she acknowledged the stunning young woman at Monique's side. 'Annaliese. How nice to see you.'

Benedict joined her, the light touch of his hand at the back of her waist a disturbing sensation that provided subtle reassurance and a hidden warning. That it also succeeded in sharpening her senses and made her incredibly aware of him was entirely a secondary consideration.

His greeting echoed her own, his voice assuming a subtle inflection that held genuine warmth with her father, utter charm with her stepmother, and an easy tolerance with Annaliese.

Monique's sweet smile in response was faultless. Annaliese, however, was pure feline and adept in the art of flirtation. A skill she seemed to delight in practising on any male past the age of twenty, with scant respect for his marital status.

'Benedict.' With just one word Annaliese managed to convey a wealth of meaning that set Gabbi's teeth on edge.

The pressure of Benedict's fingers increased, and Gabbi gave him a stunning smile, totally ignoring the warning flare in the depths of those dark eyes.

Dinner was a success. It would have been difficult for even the most discerning gourmand's palate to find fault with the serving of fine food beautifully cooked, superbly presented, and complemented by excellent wine.

Benedict was an exemplary host, and his inherent ability to absorb facts and figures combined with an almost photographic memory ensured conversation was varied and interesting. Men sought and valued his opinion on a business level, and envied him his appeal with women. Women, on the other hand, sought his attention and coveted Gabbi's position as his wife.

A MATCH MADE IN HEAVEN, the tabloids had announced at the time. THE WEDDING OF THE DECADE, a number of women's magazines had headlined, depicting a variety of photographs to endorse the projected image.

Only the romantically inclined accepted the media coverage as portrayed, while the city's—indeed, the entire country's—upper social echelons recognised the facts beneath the fairy floss.

The marriage of Benedict Nicols and Gabrielle Stanton had occurred as a direct result of the manipulative strategy by James Stanton to cement the Stanton-Nicols financial empire and forge it into another generation.

The reason for Benedict's participation was clear…he stood to gain total control of Stanton-Nicols. The bonus was a personable young woman eminently eligible to sire the necessary progeny.

Gabbi's compliance had been motivated in part by a desire to please her father and the realistic recognition that, given his enormous wealth, there would be very few men, if any, who would discount the financial and social advantage of being James Stanton's son-in-law.

'Shall we adjourn to the lounge for coffee?'

The smooth words caught Gabbi's attention, and she took Benedict's cue by summoning a gracious smile and rising to her feet. 'I'm sure Marie has it ready.'

'Treasure of a chef', 'wonderful meal', 'delightful evening'. Words echoed in polite praise, and she inclined her head in acknowledgement. 'Thank you. I'll pass on your compliments to Marie. She'll be pleased.' Which was true. Marie valued the high salary and separate live-in accommodation that formed part of the employment package, and her gratitude was reflected in her culinary efforts.

'You were rather quiet at dinner, darling.'

Gabbi heard Monique's softly toned voice, and turned towards her. 'Do you think so?'

'Annaliese is a little hurt, I think.' The reproach was accompanied by a wistful smile, and Gabbi allowed her eyes to widen slightly.

'Oh, dear,' she managed with credible regret. 'She gave such a convincing display of enjoying herself.'

Monique's eyes assumed a mistiness Gabbi knew to be contrived. *How did she do that?* Her stepmother had missed her vocation; as an actress she would have excelled.

'Annaliese has always regarded you as an elder sister.'

There was nothing *familial* about Annaliese's regard—for Gabbi. Benedict, however, fell into an entirely different category.

'I'm deeply flattered,' Gabbi acknowledged gently, and incurred Monique's sharp glance. They had lingered slightly behind the guests exiting the dining-room and were temporarily out of their earshot.

'She's very fond of you.'

Doubtful. Gabbi had always been regarded as a rival, and Annaliese was her mother's daughter. Perfectly groomed, beautifully dressed, perfumed...and on a mission. To tease and tantalise, and enjoy the challenge of the chase until she caught the right man.

Gabbi was saved from making a response as they

entered the lounge, and she accepted coffee from Marie, choosing to take it black, strong and sweet.

With a calm that was contrived she lifted her cup and took a sip of the strong, aromatic brew. 'If you'll excuse me? I really must have a word with James.'

It was almost midnight when the last guest departed, a time deemed neither too early nor too late for a mid-week dinner party to end.

Gabbi slid off her heeled sandals as she crossed the foyer to the lounge. Her head felt impossibly heavy, a knot of tension twisting a painful path from her right temple down to the edge of her nape.

Sophie had cleared the remaining coffee cups and liqueur glasses, and in the morning Marie would ensure the lounge was restored to its usual immaculate state.

'A successful evening, wouldn't you agree?'

Benedict's lazy drawl stirred the embers of resentment she'd kept carefully banked over the past few hours.

'How could it not be?' she countered as she turned to face him.

'You want to orchestrate a post-mortem?' he queried with deceptive mildness, and she glimpsed the tightly coiled strength beneath the indolent façade.

'Not particularly.'

He conducted a brief, encompassing appraisal of her features. 'Then I suggest you go upstairs to bed.'

Her chin tilted fractionally, and she met his dark gaze with equanimity. 'And prepare myself to accommodate you?'

There was a flicker of something dangerous in the

depths of his eyes, then it was gone, and his movements as he closed the distance between them held a smooth, panther-like grace.

'Accommodate?' he stressed silkily.

He was too close, his height and broad frame an intimidating entity that invaded her space. The clean, male smell of him combined with his exclusive brand of cologne weakened her defences and lodged an attack against the very core of her femininity.

He had no need to touch her, and it irked her unbearably that he knew it.

'Your sexual appetite is…' Gabbi paused, then added delicately, 'Consistent.' Her eyes flared slightly, the blue depths pure crystalline sapphire.

He lifted a hand and caught hold of her chin, lifting it so she had little option but to retain his gaze. 'It's a woman's prerogative to decline.'

She looked at him carefully, noting the fine lines fanning out from the corners of his eyes, the deep vertical crease slashing each cheek, and the firm, sensual lines of his mouth.

The tug of sexual awareness intensified at the thought of the havoc that mouth could wreak when it possessed her own, the pleasure as it explored the soft curves of her body.

'And a man's inclination to employ unfair persuasion,' Gabbi offered, damning the slight catch of her breath as the pad of his thumb traced an evocative pattern along the edge of her jaw, then slid down the pulsing cord to the hollow at the curve of her neck, cupping it while he loosened the pins holding her hair in place.

They fell to the carpet as his fingers combed the blonde length free, then his head lowered and she closed her eyes as his lips brushed her temple, then feathered a path to the edge of her mouth, teasing its outline as he tested the soft fullness and sensed the faint trembling as she tried for control.

She should stop him now, plead tiredness, the existence of a headache…say she didn't want to have to try to cope with the aftermath of his lovemaking. The futility of experiencing utter joy and knowing physical lust was an unsatisfactory substitute for love.

His body moved in close against her own, its hard length a potent force she fought hard to ignore. Without success, for she had little defence against the firm pressure of his lips as he angled her mouth and possessed it, gently at first, then with an increasing depth of passion which demanded her capitulation.

She didn't care when she felt his hands slide the length of her skirt up over her thighs, and she cared even less when he shaped her buttocks and lifted her up against him.

There was a sense of exultant pleasure as she curved her legs around his hips and tangled her arms together behind his neck, the movement of his body an exciting enticement as he ascended the stairs to their bedroom.

She was on fire, *aching* for the feel of his skin against her own, and her fingers feverishly freed his tie and attacked the buttons on his shirt, not satisfied until they found the silken whorls of hair covering his taut, muscled chest.

Her mouth slid down the firm column of his throat,

savoured the hollow at its base, then sought a tantalising path along one collarbone.

At some stage she became dimly aware she was standing, her clothes, and *his*, no longer a barrier, and she gave a soft cry as he pulled her down onto the bed.

Now, hard and fast. No preliminaries. And afterwards he could take all the time he wanted.

His deep, husky laugh brought faint colour to her cheeks. A colour that deepened at the comprehension that she'd inadvertently said the words out loud.

He sank into her, watching her expressive features as she accepted him, the fleeting changes as she stretched and the slight gasp as he buried his shaft deep inside her.

He stayed still for endlessly long seconds, and she felt him swell, then he began to withdraw, slowly, before plunging even more deeply, repeating the action and the tempo of his rhythm until she went up in flames.

The long, slow after-play, his expertise, the wicked treachery of skilful fingers, the erotic mouth, combined to bring her to the brink and hold her there until she begged for release—and she was unsure at the peak of ecstasy whether she loved or *hated* him for what he could do to her.

Good sex. Very good sex. That's all it was, she reflected sadly as she slid through the veils of sleep.

CHAPTER TWO

'VOGEL on line two.'

Gabbi's office was located high in an inner city architectural masterpiece and offered a panoramic view beyond the smoke-tinted glass exterior.

It was a beautiful summer morning, the sky a clear azure, with the sun's rays providing a dappled effect on the harbour. A Manly-bound ferry cleaved a smooth path several kilometres out from the city terminal and vied with small pleasure craft of varying sizes, all of which were eclipsed by a huge tanker heading slowly into port.

With a small degree of reluctance Gabbi turned back to her desk and picked up the receiver to deal with the call.

Five minutes later she replaced it, convinced no woman should have to cross verbal swords with an arrogant, *sexist* male whose sole purpose in life was to undermine a female contemporary.

Coffee, hot, sweet and strong, seemed like a good idea, and she rose to her feet, intent on fetching it herself rather than have her secretary do it for her. There were several files she needed to check, and she extracted the pertinent folders and laid them on her desk.

The private line beeped, and she reached for the receiver, expecting to hear James's or Benedict's voice. A lesser possibility was Marie and—even more remote—Monique.

'Gabbi.' The soft, feminine, breathy sound was unmistakable.

'Annaliese,' she acknowledged with a sinking feeling.

'Care to do lunch?'

Delaying the invitation would do no good at all, and she spared her appointment diary a quick glance. 'I can meet you at one.' She named an exclusive restaurant close by. 'Will you make the reservation, or shall I?'

'You do it, Gabbi,' Annaliese replied in a bored drawl. 'I have a meeting with my agent. I could be late.'

'I have to be back in my office at two-thirty,' Gabbi warned.

'In that case, give me ten minutes' grace, then go ahead and order.'

Gabbi replaced the receiver, had her secretary make the necessary reservation, fetched her coffee, then gave work her undivided attention until it was time to freshen up before leaving the building.

The powder-room mirror reflected an elegant image. Soft cream designer-label suit in a lightweight, uncrushable linen mix, and a silk camisole in matching tones. Her French pleat didn't need attention, and she added a touch of powder, a re-application of lipstick, then she was ready.

Ten minutes later Gabbi entered the restaurant foyer where she was greeted warmly by the maître d' and personally escorted to a table. She ordered mineral water and went through the motions of perusing the menu, opting for a Caesar salad with fresh fruit to follow.

Three-quarters of an hour after the appointed time Annaliese joined her in a waft of exclusive perfume. A slinky slither of red silk accentuated her model-slender curves. She was tall, with long slim legs, and her skilfully applied make-up enhanced her exotic features, emphasised by dark hair styled into a sleek bob.

No apology was offered, and Gabbi watched in silence as Annaliese ordered iced water, a garden salad and fresh fruit.

'When is your next assignment?'

A feline smile tilted the edges of her red mouth, and the dark eyes turned to liquid chocolate. 'So keen to see me gone?'

'A polite enquiry,' she responded with gentle mockery.

'Followed by an equally polite query regarding my career?'

Gabbi knew precisely how her stepsister's modelling career was progressing. Monique never failed to relay, in intricate detail, the events monitoring Annaliese's rise and rise on the world's catwalks.

'It was you who initiated lunch.' She picked up her glass and took a deliberate sip, then replaced it down on the table, her eyes remarkably level as she met those of her stepsister.

Annaliese's gaze narrowed with speculative contemplation. 'We've never been friends.'

In private, the younger girl had proven herself to

be a vindictive vixen. 'You worked hard to demolish any bond.'

One shoulder lifted with careless elegance. 'I wanted centre stage in our shared family, darling. *Numero uno.*' One long, red-lacquered nail tapped a careless tattoo against the stem of her glass.

Gabbi speared the last portion of cantaloupe on her plate. 'Suppose you cut to the chase and explain your purpose?'

Annaliese's eyes held a calculated gleam. 'Monique informed me James is becoming increasingly anxious for you to complete the deal.'

The fresh melon was succulent, but it had suddenly lost its taste. 'Which deal are we discussing?'

'The necessary Stanton-Nicols heir.'

Gabbi's gaze was carefully level as she rested the fork down onto her plate. 'You're way out of line, Annaliese.'

'Experiencing problems, darling?' The barb was intentional.

'Only with your intense interest in something that is none of your business.'

'It's *family* business,' Annaliese responded with deliberate emphasis.

Respect for the restaurant's fellow patrons prevented Gabbi from tipping a glass of iced water into her stepsister's lap.

'Really?' Confrontation was the favoured option. 'I have difficulty accepting my father would enrol you as messenger in such a personal matter.'

'You disbelieve me?'

'Yes.' The price of bravery might be high. Too high?

'Darling.' The word held a patronising intonation that implied the antithesis of affection. 'The only difference between daughter and stepdaughter is a legal adoption decree. Something,' she continued after a deliberate silence, 'Monique could easily persuade James to initiate.'

Oh, my. Now why didn't that devious plan surprise her? 'James's will is watertight. Monique inherits the principal residence, art and jewellery, plus a generous annuity. Shares in Stanton-Nicols come directly to me.'

One delicate brow arched high. 'You think I don't know that?' She lifted a fork and picked at her salad. 'You've missed the point.'

No, she hadn't. 'Benedict.'

Annaliese's eyes assumed an avaricious gleam. 'Clever of you, darling.'

'You want to be his mistress.'

Her soft, tinkling laugh held no humour. 'His wife.'

'You aim high.'

'The top, sweetheart.'

Iced water or hot coffee? Either was at her disposal, and she was sorely tempted to initiate an embarrassing incident. 'There's just one problem. He's already taken.'

'But so easily freed,' her stepsister purred.

'You sound very sure.' How was it possible to sound so calm, when inside she was a molten mass of fury?

'A wealthy man wants an exemplary hostess in the

lounge and a whore in his bedroom.' Annaliese examined her perfectly lacquered nails, then shot Gabbi a direct look. 'I can't imagine *passion* being your forte, or adventure your sexual preference.'

Gabbi didn't blink so much as an eyelash. 'I'm a quick study.'

'Really, darling? I wonder why I don't believe you?'

Gabbi summoned the waiter, requested the bill, and signed the credit slip. Then she rose to her feet and slid the strap of her bag over her shoulder.

'Shall we agree not to do this again?'

'Darling,' the young model almost purred. 'I'm between seasons, and where better to take in some rest and relaxation than one's home city?' Her eyes gleamed with satisfaction. 'As family, we're bound to see quite a lot of each other. The social scene is *so* interesting.'

'And you intend being included in every invitation,' Gabbi responded with soft mockery.

'Of course.'

There wasn't a single word she wanted to add. A contradiction—there were several…not one of which was in the least ladylike, and therefore unutterable in a public arena. It was easier to leave in dignified silence.

Three messages were waiting for her on her return. Two were business-oriented and she dealt with each, then logged the necessary notations into the computer before crossing to the private phone.

There was a strange curling sensation in the pit of her stomach as she waited for Benedict to answer.

'Nicols.'

His voice was deep and retained a slight American drawl that seemed more noticeable over the phone. The sound of it caused her pulse to accelerate to a faster beat.

'You rang while I was out.'

She had a mental image of him easing his lengthy frame in the high-backed leather chair. 'How was lunch?'

Her fingers gripped the receiver more tightly. 'Is there anything you don't know?'

'Annaliese requested your extension number.' He relayed the information with imperturbable calm.

Any excuse to have contact with Benedict; Gabbi silently derided her stepsister.

'You didn't answer my question.' His voice held a tinge of cynicism and prompted a terse response.

'Lunch was fine.' She drew a deep breath. 'Is that why you rang?'

'No. To let you know I won't be home for dinner. A Taiwanese associate wants to invest in property, and has requested I recommend a reputable agent. It would be impolite not to effect the introduction over dinner.'

'Very impolite,' she agreed solemnly. 'I won't wait up.'

'I'll take pleasure in waking you,' he mocked gently, ending the call.

A tiny shiver slithered the length of her spine as she recalled numerous occasions when the touch of his lips had woken her from the depths of sleep, and how she'd instinctively welcomed him, luxuriating in the agility of his hands as they traversed a tactile path over the slender curves of her body.

With concentrated effort she replaced the receiver down onto the handset, then focused her attention on work for what remained of the afternoon.

It was almost five-thirty when she left the building, and although traffic was heavy through the inner city it had begun to ease when she reached Rushcutter's Bay, resulting in a relatively clear run to Vaucluse.

The sun's rays were hot, the humidity level high. Too high, Gabbi reflected as she garaged the car and entered the house.

A long, cool drink, followed by a few lengths in the pool, would ease the strain of the day, she decided as she slipped off her jacket and made her way towards the kitchen.

Marie was putting the finishing touches to a cold platter, and her smile was warm as she watched Gabbi extract a glass and cross to the large refrigerator.

'Are you *sure* all you want is salad?'

Gabbi pushed the ice-maker lever, filled the glass with apple juice, then crossed to perch on one of four buffet stools lining the wide servery.

'Sure,' Gabbi confirmed as she leaned forward and filched a slice of fresh mango from the tastefully decorated bed of cos lettuce, avocado, nuts, and capsicum. 'Lovely,' she sighed blissfully.

Marie cast her an affectionate glance. 'There's fresh fruit and *gelato* to follow.'

Gabbi took a long swallow of iced juice, and felt the strain of the day begin to ebb. 'I think I'll change and have a swim.' The thought of a few laps in the pool followed by half an hour basking in the warm sunshine held definite appeal. 'Why don't you finish up here? There's no need for you to stay on just to rinse a few plates and stack them in the dishwasher.'

'Thanks.' The housekeeper's pleasure was evident, and Gabbi reciprocated with an impish grin.

It wasn't the first evening she'd spent alone, and was unlikely to be the last. 'Go,' she instructed. 'I'll see you at breakfast in the morning.'

Marie removed her apron and folded it neatly. 'Serg and I'll be in the flat, if you need us.'

'I know,' Gabbi said gently, grateful for the older woman's solicitous care.

Minutes later she drained the contents of her glass, then went upstairs to change, discarding her clothes in favour of a black bikini. Out of habit she removed her make-up, applied sunscreen cream, then she caught up a multi-patterned silk sarong and a towel and made her way down to the terraced pool.

Its free-form design was totally enclosed by non-reflective smoke-tinted glass, ensuring total privacy, and there were several loungers and cushioned chairs positioned on the tiled perimeters.

Gabbi dropped the sarong and towel onto a nearby chair, then performed a racing dive into the sparkling water. Seconds later she emerged to the surface, cleared excess moisture from her face, then began the first of several leisurely laps before slipping deftly onto her back to idle aimlessly for a while, enjoying the solitude and the quietness.

It was a wonderful way to relax, she mused, both mentally and physically. The cares of the day seemed to diminish to their correct perspective. Even lunch with Annaliese.

No, she amended with a faint grimace. That was taking things a bit too far. Calculating her stepsister's next move didn't require much effort, given the social scene of the city's sophisticated élite.

Stanton-Nicols supported a number of worthy charities, and Benedict generously continued in Diandra and Conrad Nicols' tradition—astutely aware that as much business was done out of the office as in it, Gabbi concluded wryly.

The thought of facing Annaliese at one function or another over the next few weeks didn't evoke much joy. Nor did the prospect of parrying Monique's subtle hints.

Damn. The relaxation cycle was well and truly broken. With a deft movement, Gabbi rolled onto her stomach and swam to the pool's edge, hauled her slim frame onto the tiled ledge, then reached for the towel and began blotting her body.

Faced with a choice of eating indoors or by the pool, she chose the latter and carried the salad and a glass of chilled water to a nearby table.

The view out over the harbour was spectacular, and she idly watched the seascape as numerous small craft cruised the waters in a bid to make the most of the daylight-saving time.

On finishing her meal, scorning television, Gabbi made herself some coffee, selected a few glossy magazines and returned to watch the sunset, the glorious streak of orange that changed and melded into a deep pink as the sun's orb sank slowly beneath the horizon providing a soft pale reflected glow before dusk turned into darkness.

A touch on the electronic modem activated the underwater light, turning the pool a brilliant aqua-blue. Another touch lit several electric flares, and she stretched out comfortably and flipped open a magazine, scanning the glossy pages for something that might capture her interest.

An article based on the behind-the-scenes life of a prominent fashion guru provided a riveting insight, and endorsed her own view on the artificiality of a society where one was never sure whether an acquaintance was friend or foe beneath the token façade.

The publishers had seen fit to include an in-depth account by a high-class madam, who, the article revealed, had procured escorts for some of the country's rich and famous, notably politicians and visiting rock stars, for a fee that was astronomical.

Somehow the article focusing on cellulite that followed it seemed extremely prosaic, and Gabbi flipped to the travel section.

Paris. What a city for ambience and *joie de vivre.* The language, the scents, the fashion. French women possessed a certain *élan* that was unmatched anywhere else in the world. And the food! *Très magnifique,* she accorded wistfully, recalling fond memories of the time she'd spent there. For a while she'd imagined herself in love with a dashing young student whose sensual expertise had almost persuaded her into his bed. Gabbi's mouth curved into a soft smile, and her eyes danced with hidden laughter in remembrance.

'An interesting article?'

Gabbi looked up at the sound of that deep, drawling voice and saw Benedict's tall frame outlined against the screened aperture leading into the large entertainment room.

His jacket was hooked over one shoulder, and he'd already removed his tie and loosened a few buttons on his blue cotton shirt.

Her eyes still held a hint of mischief as they met his. 'I didn't realise it was that late,' she managed lightly, watching as he closed the distance between them.

'It's just after ten.' He paused at her side, and scanned the open magazine. 'Pleasant memories?'

Gabbi met his gaze, and sensed the studied watchfulness beneath the surface. 'Yes,' she said with innate honesty, and saw his eyes narrow fractionally. 'It was a long time ago, and I was very young.'

'But old enough to be enchanted by a young man's attentions,' Benedict deduced with a degree of cynical amusement. 'What was his name?'

'Jacques,' she revealed without hesitation. 'He was a romantic, and he kissed divinely. We explored the art galleries together and drank coffee at numerous sidewalk cafés. On weekends I visited the family vineyard. It was fun,' she informed him simply, reflecting on the voluble and often gregarious meals she'd shared, the vivacity and sheer camaraderie of a large extended family.

'Define "fun".'

The temptation to tease and prevaricate was very strong, but there seemed little point. 'He had a very strict *maman*,' she revealed solemnly. 'Who was intent on matching him with the daughter of a neighbouring vintner. An *Anglaise* miss, albeit a very rich one, might persuade him to live on the other side of the world.'

Amusement lurked in the depths of his eyes. 'He married the vintner's daughter?'

'Yes. His devoted *maman* despatches a letter twice a year with family news.'

'Did you love him?' The query was soft, his voice silk-smooth.

Not the way I love you. 'We were very good friends,' she said with the utmost care.

His intense gaze sent a tiny flame flaring through her veins, warming her skin and heating the central core of her femininity.

'Who parted without regret or remorse when it was time for you to leave?' Benedict prompted gently.

A winsome smile curved the edges of her mouth. 'We promised never to forget each other. For a while we exchanged poetic prose.'

'Predictably the letters became shorter and few and far between?'

'You're a terrible cynic.'

'A realist,' he corrected her with subtle remonstrance.

Gabbi closed the magazine and placed it down on a nearby table. With an elegant economy of movement she rose to her feet, caught up the sarong and secured it at her waist. 'Would you like some coffee?'

'Please.'

He turned to follow her, and the hairs on the back

of her neck prickled in awareness. She subconsciously straightened her shoulders, and forced herself to walk at a leisurely pace.

In the kitchen she crossed to the servery, methodically filled the coffee-maker with water, spooned ground beans into the filter basket, then switched on the machine.

The large kitchen was a chef's delight, with every conceivable modern appliance. A central cooking island held several hobs, and there were twin ovens, two microwaves, and a capacious refrigerator and freezer.

With considerable ease Gabbi extracted two cups and saucers, then set out milk and sugar.

'How was dinner?'

'Genuine interest, or idle conversation, Gabbi?'

Was he aware of the effect he had on her? In bed, without doubt. But out of it? Probably not, she thought sadly. Men of Benedict's calibre were more concerned with creating a financial empire than examining a relationship.

It took considerable effort to meet his lightly mocking gaze. 'Genuine interest.'

'We ate Asian food in one of the city's finest restaurants,' Benedict informed her indolently. 'The business associate was suitably impressed, and the agent will probably earn a large commission.'

'Naturally you have offered them use of the private jet, which will earn you kudos with the Taiwanese associate, who in turn will recommend you to his contemporaries,' she concluded dryly, and his lips formed a twisted smile.

'It's called taking care of business.'

'And *business* is all-important.'

'Is that a statement or a complaint?'

Her eyes were remarkably steady as she held his gaze. 'It's a well-known fact that profits have soared beyond projected estimates in the past few years. Much of Stanton-Nicols' continuing success is directly attributed to your dedicated efforts.'

'You didn't answer the question.' The words held a dangerous softness that sent a tiny shiver down her spine, and her eyes clashed with his for a few immeasurable seconds before she summoned a credible smile.

'Why would I complain?' she queried evenly, supremely conscious of the quickening pulse at the base of her throat.

'Why, indeed?' he lightly mocked. 'You have a vested interest in the family firm.'

'In more ways than one.'

His eyes narrowed fractionally. 'Elaborate.'

Gabbi didn't hedge. 'The delay in providing James with a grandchild seems to be the subject of family conjecture.'

For a brief millisecond she caught a glimpse of something that resembled anger, then it was lost beneath an impenetrable mask. 'A fact which Annaliese felt compelled to bring to your attention?'

One finger came to rest against the corner of her mouth, while his thumb traced the heavy, pulsing cord at the side of her throat.

'Yes.'

His hand trailed lower to the firm swell of her

breast, teased a path along the edge of her bikini top, then brushed against the aroused peak before dropping back to his side.

'We agreed birth control should be your prerogative,' Benedict declared with unruffled ease, and she swallowed painfully, hating the way her body reacted to his touch.

'Your stepsister is too self-focused not to take any opportunity to initiate a verbal game of thrust and parry. Who won?'

'We each retired with superficial wounds,' Gabbi declared solemnly.

'Dare I ask when the game is to continue?'

'Who can tell?'

'And the weapon?'

She managed a smile. 'Why—Annaliese herself. With *you* as the prize. Her formal adoption by James would make her a *Stanton*. Our divorce is a mere formality in order to change Stanton to *Nicols*.'

He lifted a hand and brushed light fingers across her cheek. 'Am I to understand you are not impressed with that scenario?'

No. For a moment she thought she'd screamed the negative out loud, and she stood in mesmerised silence for several seconds, totally unaware that her expressive features were more explicit than any words.

'Do you believe,' Benedict began quietly, 'I deliberately chose you as my wife with the future of Stanton-Nicols foremost in mind?'

Straight for the jugular. Gabbi had expected no less. Her chin tilted slightly. 'Suitable marriages are manipulated among the wealthy for numerous reasons,' she said fearlessly. '*Love* isn't a necessary prerequisite.'

His expression didn't change, but she sensed a degree of anger and felt chilled by it.

'And what we share in bed? How would you define that?'

A lump rose in her throat, and she swallowed it. 'Skilled expertise.'

Something dark momentarily hardened the depths of his gaze, then it was gone. 'You'd relegate me to the position of *stud*?'

Oh, God. She closed her eyes, then opened them again. 'No. *No*,' she reiterated, stricken by his deliberate interpretation.

'I should be thankful for that small mercy.'

He was angry. Icily so. And it hurt, terribly.

Yet what had she expected? A heartfelt declaration that *she* was too important in his life for him to consider anyone taking her place?

Gabbi felt as if she couldn't breathe. Her eyes were trapped by his, her body transfixed as though in a state of suspended animation.

'The coffee has finished filtering.'

His voice held that familiar cynicism, and with an effort she focused her attention on pouring coffee into both cups, then added sugar.

Benedict picked up one. 'I'll take this through to the study.'

Her eyes settled on his broad back as he walked from the kitchen, her expression pensive.

Damn Annaliese, Gabbi cursed silently as she discarded her coffee down the sink. With automatic movements she rinsed the cup and stacked it in the dishwasher, then she switched off the coffee-maker and doused the lights before making her way upstairs.

Reaching the bedroom, she walked through to the *en suite*, stripped off her bikini, turned on the water and stepped into the shower.

It didn't take long to shampoo her hair, and fifteen minutes with the blow-drier restored it to its usual silky state.

In bed, she reached for a book and read a chapter before switching off the lamp.

She had no idea what time Benedict slid in beside her, nor did she sense him leave the bed in the early-morning hours, for when she woke she was alone and the only signs of his occupation were a dented pillow and the imprint of his body against the sheet.

CHAPTER THREE

GABBI glanced at the bedside clock and gave an inaudible groan. Seven-thirty. Time to rise and shine, hit the shower, breakfast, and join the queue of traffic heading into the city.

Thank heavens today was Friday and the weekend lay ahead.

Benedict had accepted an invitation to attend a tennis evening which Chris Evington, head partner in the accountancy firm Stanton-Nicols employed, had arranged at his home. Tomorrow evening they had tickets to the Australian première performance at the Sydney Entertainment Centre.

The possibility of Annaliese discovering their plans for tonight was remote, Gabbi decided as she slid in behind the wheel of her car. And it was doubtful even Monique would be able to arrange an extra seat for the première performance at such short notice.

It was a beautiful day, the sky clear of cloud, and at this early-morning hour free from pollution haze.

Gabbi was greeted by Security as she entered the car park, acknowledged at Reception *en route* to her office, and welcomed by her secretary who brought coffee in one hand and a notebook in the other.

As the morning progressed Gabbi fought against giving last night's scene too much thought, and failed.

During the afternoon she overlooked a miscalculation and lost valuable time in cross-checking. Consequently, it was a relief to slip behind the wheel of her car and head home.

Benedict's vehicle was already parked in the garage when she arrived, and she felt her stomach clench with unbidden nerves as she entered the house.

Gabbi checked with Marie, then went upstairs to change.

Benedict was in the process of discarding his tie when she reached the bedroom.

'You're home early.' As a greeting it lacked originality, but it was better than silence.

She met his dark gaze with equanimity, her eyes lingering on the hard planes of his face, and settling briefly on his mouth. Which was a mistake.

'Dinner will be ready at six.'

'So Marie informed me.' He began unbuttoning his shirt, and her eyes trailed the movement, paused, then returned to scan his features.

Nothing there to determine his mood. Damn. She hated friction. With Monique and Annaliese it was unavoidable—but Benedict was something else.

'I should apologise.' There, it wasn't hard at all. Did he know she'd summoned the courage, wrestled with the need to do so, for most of the day?

A faint smile tugged at the edges of his mouth, and the expression in his eyes was wholly cynical. 'Good manners, Gabbi?'

He shrugged off the business shirt, reached for a dark-coloured open-necked polo shirt and tugged it over his head.

Honesty was the only way to go. 'Genuine remorse.'

He removed his trousers and donned a casual cotton pair.

He looked up, and she caught the dark intensity of his gaze. 'Apology accepted.'

Her nervous tension dissolved, and the breath she'd unconsciously been holding slipped silently free. 'Thank you.'

Retreat seemed a viable option and she crossed to the capacious walk-in wardrobe, selected tennis gear, then extracted casual linen trousers and a blouse.

The buzz of the electric shaver sounded from the *en suite* bathroom, and he emerged as she finished changing.

Gabbi felt the familiar flood of warmth, and fought against it. 'What time do you want to leave?' It was amazing that her voice sounded so calm.

'Seven-fifteen.'

They descended the stairs together, and ate the delectable chicken salad Marie had prepared, washed it down with mineral water, then picked from a selection of fresh fruit. A light meal which would be supplemented by supper after the last game of tennis.

Conversation was confined to business and the proposed agenda at the next board meeting.

Chris and Leanne Evington resided at Woollahra in a large, rambling old home which had been lovingly restored. Neat lawns, beautiful gardens, precisely clipped hedges and shrubbed topiary lent an air of a past era. The immaculate grassed tennis court merely added to the impression.

A few cars lined the circular forecourt, and Gabbi slid from the Bentley as Benedict retrieved their sports bags from the boot.

Social tennis took on rules of its own, according to the host's inclination and the number of participating guests.

The best of seven games would ensure a relatively quick turn-around on the court, Chris and Leanne determined. Partners were selected by personal choice, and it was accepted that two rounds of mixed doubles would precede two rounds of women's doubles and conclude with two rounds of men's doubles.

Gabbi and Benedict were nominated first on the court, opposing a couple whom Gabbi hadn't previously met. All four were good players, although Benedict had the height, strength and skill to put the ball where he chose, and they emerged victorious at the end of the game with a five-two lead.

Chris and Leanne's son Todd had nominated himself umpire for the evening. A prominent athlete and law student, he had any number of pretty girls beating a path to his door. That there wasn't one in evidence this evening came as something of a surprise.

Until Annaliese arrived on the scene, looking sensational in designer tennis wear.

'Sorry I'm late.' Annaliese offered a winning smile.

'Mixed has just finished,' Leanne informed her. 'The girls are on next.'

Annaliese turned towards Gabbi. 'Will you be my partner? It'll be just like the old days.'

What old days? Gabbi queried silently. Surely

Annaliese wasn't referring to an occasional mismatch during school holidays?

Leanne allocated the pair to the second round, and Gabbi accepted a cool drink from a proffered tray.

The guests reassembled as Todd directed play from the umpire's seat. The men gravitated into two groups, and in no time at all Annaliese had managed to gain Gabbi's attention.

'I had a wonderful afternoon phoning friends and catching up on all their news.'

'One of whom just happened to mention the Evington tennis party?' Gabbi queried dryly.

'Why, *yes*.'

'Who better to know the guest list than Todd?'

'He's a sweet boy.'

'And easily flattered.'

Annaliese's smile was pure feline. 'Aren't most men?'

'Shall we join the others?'

It was thirty minutes before they took their position on the court, and evenly matched opponents ensured a tight score. Deuce was called three times in the final game before Annaliese took an advantage to winning point by serving an ace.

An elaborate seafood supper was provided at the close of the final game, followed by coffee and a selection of delicious petits fours.

Gabbi expected Annaliese to commandeer Benedict's attention. What she didn't anticipate was an elbow jolting her arm.

It happened so quickly that she was powerless to

do anything but watch in dismayed silence as coffee spilled onto the tiled floor.

'I'm fine,' Gabbi assured Benedict as he reached her side. She bore his swift appraisal with a determined smile.

Only a splash of hot liquid was splattered on her tennis shoes, and a cloth took care of the spillage.

'You could have been burnt,' Annaliese declared with apparent concern.

'Fortunately, I wasn't.'

'Are you sure you're OK, Gabbi?' Leanne queried. 'Can I get you some more coffee?' Her eyes took on a tinge of humour. 'Something stronger?'

She was tempted, but not for the reason her hostess imagined. A ready smile curved her mouth and she shook her head. 'Thanks all the same.'

It was almost midnight when she slid into the passenger seat of the Bentley. Benedict slipped in behind the wheel and activated the ignition.

'What happened in there?'

The car wheels crunched on the pebbled driveway, and Gabbi waited until they gained the road before responding.

'Could you be specific?'

He shot her a quick glance that lost much of its intensity in the darkness. 'You're not given to clumsiness.'

'Ah, *support*.'

'Annaliese?'

Tiredness settled like a mantle around her slim shoulders. Indecision forced a truthful answer. 'I don't know.'

'She was standing beside you.'

'I'd rather not discuss it.'

Gabbi was first indoors while Benedict garaged the car, and she went upstairs, stripped off her clothes and stepped into the shower-stall.

A few minutes later Benedict joined her, and she spared him a brief glance before continuing her actions with the soap. They each finished at the same time, emerged together and reached for individual towels.

Ignoring Benedict, especially a naked Benedict, was impossible, and there was nothing she could do to slow the quickened beat of her heart or prevent the warmth that crept through her body as she conducted her familiar nightly ritual.

A hand closed over her arm as she turned towards the door, and she didn't utter a word as he pulled her round to face him.

Eyes that were dark and impossibly slumberous held her own and she bore his scrutiny in silence, hating her inner fragility as she damned her inability to hide it.

More than anything she wanted the comfort of his arms, the satisfaction of his mouth on her own. Slowly she lifted a hand and traced the vertical indentation slashing his cheek, then pressed her fingers to the edge of his lips.

Her eyes flared as he took her fingers into his mouth, and heat unfurled deep inside her as he gently bit the tip of each finger in turn.

Unbidden, she reached for him, drawing him close, exulting in the feel of his body, his warm, musky scent, and she opened her mouth in generous acceptance of his in a deep, evocative kiss that hardened in irrefutable possession, wiping out any vestige of conscious thought.

Gabbi gave a husky purr of pleasure as he drew her into the bedroom and pulled her down onto the bed, lost in the sensual magic only he could evoke.

If business commitments didn't intrude, Benedict elected to spend Saturdays on the golf course, while Gabbi preferred to set the day aside to catch up on a variety of things a working week allowed little time for.

Occasionally she took in a matinée movie, or had lunch with friends.

Today she chose to add a few purchases to her wardrobe and keep an appointment with a beautician and her hairdresser.

Consequently it was almost six when she turned into their residential street and followed Benedict's four-wheel drive down the driveway.

He was waiting for her as she brought the car to a halt.

'Great day?' Gabbi asked teasingly as she emerged from behind the wheel.

'Indeed. And you?'

'I flashed plastic in a few too many boutiques,' she said ruefully, indicating several brightly assorted carrier bags on the rear seat.

He looked relaxed, his height and breadth accentuated by the casual open-necked shirt that fitted snugly over his well-honed muscles.

His potent masculinity ignited a familiar response deep within her as he reached past her and gathered the purchases together.

Maybe one day he wouldn't have quite this heightened effect on her equilibrium, she thought wryly as she followed him indoors. Then a silent laugh rose and died in her throat. Perhaps in another lifetime!

It was after seven when they left for the Entertainment Centre to witness the New Jersey-born son of a menswear storekeeper, who was known to mesmerise an audience with any one of the two hundred and fifty magic illusions in his repertoire.

Gabbi adored the show. Pure escapism that numbed the logical mind with wizardry and chilled the spine.

The fact that Annaliese was nowhere in sight added to her pleasure—a feeling that was compounded the next day when Gabbi and Benedict joined friends on a luxury cruiser.

Monday promised to be busier than most, Gabbi realised within minutes of arriving at the office and liaising with her secretary.

The morning hours sped by swiftly as she fed data into the computer. Concentration was required in order to maintain a high level of accuracy, and she didn't break at all when coffee was placed on her desk.

It was after midday when Gabbi sank back against the cushioned chair and flexed her shoulders as she surveyed the computer screen. The figures were keyed in, all she had to do was run a check on them after lunch.

A working lunch, she decided, fired with determination to meet a personal deadline. James had requested the information by one o'clock tomorrow. She intended that he would have it this afternoon.

Gabbi rose from her desk, extracted the chicken salad sandwich her secretary had placed in the concealed bar fridge an hour earlier, selected a bottle of apple juice and returned to her seat.

The bread was fresh, the chicken soft on a bed of crisp salad topped with a tangy mayonnaise dressing. Washed down with juice, it replenished her energy store.

The phone rang and she hurriedly plucked free a few tissues from the box on her desk, then reached for the receiver.

'Francesca Angeletti on line one.'

Surprise was quickly followed by pleasure. 'Put her through.' Two seconds ticked by. 'Francesca. Where are you?'

'Home. I flew in from Rome yesterday morning.'

'When are we going to get together?' There was no question that they wouldn't. They had shared the same boarding-school, the same classes, and each had a stepmother. It was a common bond that had drawn them together and fostered a friendship which had extended beyond school years.

Francesca's laugh sounded faintly husky. 'Tonight, if you and Benedict are attending Leon's exhibition.'

'Leon's soirées are high on our social calendar,' she acknowledged with an answering chuckle.

'James will be there with Monique?'

'And Annaliese,' Gabbi added dryly, and one eyebrow lifted at Francesca's forthright response. 'Nice girls don't swear,' she teased in admonition.

'This one does,' came the swift reply. 'How long has your dear stepsister been disturbing your home turf?'

'A week.'

'She is fond of playing the diva,' Francesca commented. 'I had the misfortune to share a few of the same catwalks with her in Italy.'

'Fun.'

'Not the kind that makes you laugh. Gabbi, I have to dash. We'll catch up tonight, OK?'

'I'll really look forward to it,' Gabbi assured her, and replaced the receiver.

For the space of a few minutes she allowed her mind to skim the years, highlighting the most vivid of shared memories: school holidays abroad together, guest of honour at each other's engagement party, bridesmaid at each other's wedding.

The automatic back-up flashed on the computer screen, and succeeded in returning her attention to the task at hand. With determination she drew her chair forward, reached for the sheaf of papers, and systematically began checking figure columns.

An hour later she printed out, collated, then had her secretary deliver copies to James and Benedict. She was well pleased with the result. The reduction of a percentage point gained by successful negotiations with the leasing firm for Stanton-Nicols' company car fleet could be used to boost the existing employee incentive package. At no extra cost to Stanton-Nicols, and no loss of tax advantage.

It was after five when she rode the lift down to the car park and almost six when she entered the house.

'Benedict just called,' Marie informed Gabbi when she appeared in the kitchen. 'He'll be another twenty minutes.'

Time for her to shower and wash and dry her hair. 'Smells delicious,' she complimented as she watched Marie deftly stir the contents of one saucepan, then tend to another.

'Asparagus in a hollandaise sauce, beef Wellington with vegetables and lemon tart for dessert.'

Gabbi grabbed a glass and crossed to the refrigerator for some iced water.

'A few invitations arrived in the mail. They're in the study.'

'Thanks,' she said, smiling.

A few minutes later she ran lightly up the stairs, and in the bedroom she quickly discarded her clothes then made for the shower.

Afterwards she donned fresh underwear, pulled on fitted jeans and a loose top, then twisted her damp hair into a knot on top of her head. A quick application of moisturiser, a light touch of colour to her lips and she was ready.

Benedict entered the bedroom as she emerged from the *en suite*, and she met his mocking smile with a deliberate slant of one eyebrow.

'A delayed meeting?'

'Two phone calls and a traffic snarl,' he elaborated as he shrugged off his jacket and loosened his tie.

She moved towards the door. 'Dinner will be ready in ten minutes.'

The gleam in those dark eyes was wholly sensual. 'I had hoped to share your shower.'

Something tugged at her deep inside, flared, then spread throughout her body. 'Too late,' she declared lightly as she drew level with him.

His smile widened, accentuating the vertical lines slashing each cheek. 'Shame.'

Her breath rose unsteadily in her throat as she attempted to still the rapid beat of her pulse. Did he take pleasure in deliberately teasing her?

'A cool shower might help.'

'So might this.' He reached for her, angling his mouth down over hers in a kiss that held the promise of passion and the control to keep it at bay.

Gabbi felt her composure waver, then splinter and fragment as he drew deeply, taking yet giving, until she surrendered herself to the evocative pleasure only he could provide.

A tiny moan sounded low in her throat as he slowly raised his head, and she swayed slightly, her eyes wide, luminous pools as she surveyed his features. Her breathing was rapid, her skin warm, and her mouth trembled as she drew back from his grasp.

'You don't play fair,' she accused him shakily, and stood still as he brushed the backs of his fingers across her cheek.

His lips curved, the corners lifting in a semblance of lazy humour. 'Go check with Marie,' he bade her gently. 'I'll be down soon.'

Dinner was superb, the asparagus tender, the beef succulent and the lemon tart an excellent finale.

'Coffee?' Marie asked as she packed dishes onto a trolley.

Gabbi spared her watch a quick glance. It would take thirty minutes to dress, apply make-up and style her hair. 'Not for me.'

'Thanks, Marie. Black,' Benedict requested as Gabbi rose from the table.

CHAPTER FOUR

Gabbi chose red silk evening trousers, matching camisole and beaded jacket. It was a striking outfit, complete with matching evening sandals and clutch-purse. The colour enhanced her delicate honey-coloured skin, and provided an attractive contrast for her blonde hair.

With extreme care she put the finishing touches to her make-up, donned the trousers and camisole, then brushed her hair. Loose, she decided, after sweeping it high and discarding the customary French pleat.

Her mirrored image revealed a confident young woman whose clothes and jewellery bore the exclusivity of wealth. There was a coolness to her composure, a serenity she was far from feeling.

Which proved just how deceptive one's appearance could be, she decided wryly as she slid her feet into the elegant sandals.

'Is the colour choice deliberate?'

'Why do you ask?' Gabbi countered as she met Benedict's indolent gaze.

'I get the impression you're bent on making a statement,' he drawled, and she directed a deceptively sweet smile at him.

'How perceptive of you.'

He looked the epitome of male sophistication, the

dark evening suit a stark contrast to the white cotton shirt and black bow tie.

It was almost a sin, she reflected, for any one man to exude such a degree of sexual chemistry. The strong angles and planes of his facial features bore the stamp of his character. The unwavering eyes were hard and inflexible in the boardroom, yet they filled with brooding passion in the bedroom. And the promise of his mouth was to die for, she concluded, all too aware of the havoc it could cause.

He possessed the aura of a predator, arresting and potentially dangerous. Compelling, she added silently.

A tiny thrill of excitement quivered deep inside her at the thought of the pleasure it would give her to pull his tie free and help discard his clothes. And have him remove her own.

'Why the faint smile?'

The desire to shock deepened the smile and lent her eyes a tantalising sparkle. 'Anticipation,' she enlightened him wickedly.

'Of Leon's exhibition?'

She doubted he was fooled in the slightest, for he seemed to find her achingly transparent. 'Naturally.'

'We could always arrive late,' Benedict suggested in dry, mocking tones, and the edges of her mouth formed a delicious curve.

'Leon would be disappointed.' Not to mention Annaliese, she added silently, mentally weighing up which might be the worst offence.

'I could always placate him by making an exorbitant purchase.'

She gave it consideration, then shook her head with apparent reluctance.

'Teasing incurs a penalty,' Benedict declared with soft emphasis.

'I am suitably chastened.'

'That compounds with every hour,' he completed silkily, and saw the momentary flicker of uncertainty cloud those beautiful eyes. It made him want to reach out and touch his hand to her cheek, see the uncertainty fade as he bent his head to claim her mouth. He succumbed to the first but passed on the latter.

Gabbi collected her clutch-purse and preceded him from the room, and, seated inside the Jaguar, she remained silent, aware that the latent power of the sports car equalled that of the man seated behind the wheel.

To attempt to play a game with him, even an innocuous one, was foolish, she perceived as the car purred along the suburban streets. For even when she won she really lost. It didn't seem quite fair that he held such an enormous advantage. Yet the likelihood of tipping the scales in her favour seemed incredibly remote.

'How did James react to your proposal?' Business was always a safe subject.

Benedict turned his head slightly and directed a brief glance at her before focusing his attention on the road. 'Small talk, Gabbi?'

'I can ask James,' she responded steadily.

'I fly to Melbourne in a couple of weeks.'

I, not *we*, she thought dully. 'How long will you be away?'

'Three, maybe four days.'

She should have been used to his frequent trips interstate and overseas. Yet she felt each absence more keenly than the last, intensely aware of her own vulnerability, *and*, dammit, incredibly insecure emotionally.

Gabbi wanted to say she'd miss him, but that would be tantamount to an admission she wasn't prepared to make. Instead, she focused her attention on the scene beyond the windscreen, noting the soft haze that had settled over the city, the azure, pink-fringed sky as the sun sank beyond the horizon. Summer daylight-time delayed the onset of dusk, but soon numerous street-lamps would provide a fairy tracery of light, and the city would be lit with flashing neon.

The views were magnificent: numerous coves and inlets, the grandeur of the Opera House against the backdrop of Harbour Bridge. It was a vista she took for granted every day as she drove to work, and now she examined it carefully, aware that the plaudits acclaiming it one of the most attractive harbours in the world were well deserved.

Traffic at this hour was relatively minimal, and they reached Double Bay without delay. There was private parking adjacent to the gallery, and Benedict brought the Jaguar to a smooth halt in an empty bay.

Gabbi released the door-latch and slid out of the passenger seat, resisting the urge to smooth suddenly nervous fingers over the length of her hair. It was merely another evening in which she was required to smile and converse and pretend that everything was as it appeared to be.

She'd had a lot of practice, she assured herself silently as she walked at Benedict's side to the entrance.

The gallery held an interesting mix of patrons, Gabbi could see as she preceded Benedict into the elegant foyer.

Their presence elicited an ebullient greeting from the gallery owner, whose flamboyant dress style and extravagant jewellery were as much an act as was his effusive manner. A decade devoted to creating an image and fostering clientele had paid off, for his *'invitation only'* soirées were considered *de rigueur* by the city's social élite.

'Darlings, how are we, *ça va*?'

Gabbi accepted the salutatory kiss on each cheek and smiled at the shrewd pair of eyes regarding her with affection.

'Leon,' she responded quietly, aware that the Italian-born Leo had acknowledged his French roots after discovering his ancestors had fled France during the French Revolution. 'Well, *merci*.'

'That is good.' He caught hold of Benedict's hand and pumped it enthusiastically. 'There are some *wonderful* pieces. At least one I'm sure will be of immense interest. I shall show it to you personally. But first some champagne, *oui*?' He beckoned a hovering waiter and plucked two flutes from the tray, then commanded a uniformed waitress to bring forth a selection of hors d'oeuvres. 'Beluga, smoked salmon, anchovy.'

Gabbi selected a thin wafer artfully decorated with smoked salmon topped with a cream cheese and caper dressing. 'Delicious,' she complimented. 'Franz has excelled himself.'

'Thank you, darling,' Leon said gently. 'Now, do mingle. You already know almost everyone. I'll be back with you later.'

She moved forward, conscious of the interest their presence aroused. It was definitely smile-time, and she greeted one fellow guest after another with innate charm, pausing to indulge in idle chatter before moving on.

How long would it be before James made an entrance with Monique on one arm and Annaliese on the other? Ten, fifteen minutes?

Twenty, Gabbi acknowledged when she caught sight of her father, caught his smile and returned it as he threaded his way through the throng of guests.

'Hello, darling.' He squeezed her hand, then turned to greet his son-in-law. 'Benedict.'

'Monique.' Gabbi went through with the air-kiss routine. 'Annaliese.'

Her stepsister's perfume was subtle. Her dress, however, was not. Black, it fitted Annaliese's slender curves like a glove, the hemline revealing an almost obscene length of long, smooth thigh and highlighting the absence of a bra.

There wasn't a red-blooded man in the room whose eyes didn't momentarily gleam with appreciation. Nor was there a woman in doubt of her man who didn't fail to still the slither of alarm at the sight of this feline female on the prowl.

Gabbi could have assured each and every one of

them that their fears were unfounded. Benedict was the target, *she* the victim.

'Have you seen anything you like?'

To anyone overhearing the enquiry, it sounded remarkably genuine. Gabbi, infinitely more sensitive, recognised the innuendo in Annaliese's voice and searched for it in Benedict's reply.

'Yes. One or two pieces have caught my interest.'

'Are you going to buy?' asked Monique, intrigued, yet able to portray dispassionate detachment.

Gabbi doubted if James was aware of his stepdaughter's machinations, or her collusion with his wife.

'Possibly,' Benedict enlightened her smoothly.

'You must point them out to me,' Annaliese purred in a voice filled with seductive promise.

Gabbi wanted to hit her. For a wild second she envisaged the scene and drew satisfaction from a mental victory.

'Numbers five and thirty-seven,' Benedict was informing Annaliese.

'Gabbi, why don't you take Monique and Annaliese on a tour of the exhibits?' James suggested. 'I have something I'd like to discuss with Benedict.'

Oh, my. Did her father realise he'd just thrown her to the lions?

'The girls can go,' Monique said sweetly. 'I'll have a word with Bertrice Osterman.'

How opportune for one of the society doyennes to be within close proximity. Gabbi offered Annaliese a faint smile. 'Shall we begin?'

It took two minutes and something like twenty

paces to reach Benedict's first choice. 'It leans towards the avant garde,' Gabbi declared. 'But it will brighten up one of the office walls.'

'Cut the spiel, Gabbi,' Annaliese said in bored tones. 'These art exhibitions are the pits.'

'But socially stimulating, wouldn't you agree?'

'Monique came along to be seen, and—'

'So did you,' Gabbi interceded quietly.

'By Benedict.'

She felt the breath catch in her throat, and willed her expression not to change.

'Surely you didn't doubt it, darling?'

'I expected nothing less,' she managed civilly.

'Then we understand each other.'

Gabbi extended a hand towards a row of paintings. 'Shall we pretend to look at the other exhibits?' She even managed a credible smile. 'It will provide you with a topic of conversation.'

Annaliese was, Gabbi conceded, a consummate actress. No one in the room would guess there was no love lost between the two stepsisters. And Gabbi hated participating in the façade.

For fifteen minutes they wandered, paused and examined, before rejoining James and Benedict. Monique was nowhere in sight.

'Wonderful choice, Benedict,' Annaliese said in a deliberately throaty tone. 'There's a sculpture that would look incredible in the corner of your office. You must come and see it.' She turned towards Gabbi. 'It is quite spectacular, isn't it, darling?'

'Spectacular,' Gabbi conceded, taking a fresh flute of champagne from the tray proffered by a waiter. She lifted the glass to her lips and took a pensive sip, then dared to raise her eyes to meet those of her husband. They were dark and faintly brooding, with just a tinge of latent humour. He was amused, damn him!

'Then I shall have to take a look.'

'Talk to James, darling, while I drag Benedict away.'

It was a beautiful manoeuvre, Gabbi applauded silently as Annaliese drew Benedict across the room.

'She's grown into a very attractive girl,' James said quietly, and Gabbi inclined her head.

'Very attractive,' she agreed solemnly.

'Incredibly successful, too.'

'Yes.' She took a careful sip of champagne and steeled herself not to glance towards where Annaliese held Benedict's attention.

'I looked at those figures you submitted. They're excellent.'

'Thank you,' she accepted, pleased at his praise.

'You possess your mother's integrity, her sense of style,' he said gently. 'I'm very proud of you, Gabbi. And of what you've achieved.'

She brushed a quick kiss over his cheek. 'I love you too.'

'James.'

Gabbi turned at the sound of an unfamiliar voice, smiled, and stood quietly as her father completed an introduction. A business associate who seemed intent on discussing the effects of an upcoming state election. With a murmured excuse, she left the two men to converse and began threading her way towards the opposite side of the room.

There were quite a few people present whom she knew, and she paused to exchange greetings.

A painting had caught her eye shortly after they'd arrived, and she wanted to take another look at it.

'Gabbi.'

'Francesca!' Her smile was genuinely warm as she embraced the tall, svelte auburn-haired model. 'It seems ages since I last saw you.'

'Too long,' Francesca agreed. 'The catwalks were exhausting, and—' she paused fractionally '—the family daunting.'

'Do we get to talk about this over lunch?'

Francesca's smile was infectious. 'Tomorrow?'

'Love to,' Gabbi agreed, and named a fashionable restaurant a short distance from the office. 'Twelve-thirty?'

'Done.' Francesca took hold of her arm. 'Do you particularly *want* to watch Annaliese's attempt to snare Benedict?'

'No.'

'Then let's do the unexpected and examine the art exhibits for any hidden talent!' An eyebrow arched in a sardonic gesture as she cast a glance at a nearby sculpture. 'There has to be *some*, surely?'

'It's a case of beauty being in the eye of the beholder,' Gabbi vouchsafed solemnly as they moved from one painting to another.

'The prices are scandalous,' Francesca opined in a quiet aside. 'Does anyone actually make a purchase?'

'You'd be surprised.'

'Utterly.'

'Some of the city's rich and famous are known to

buy on a whim, then years later make a killing when the artist becomes well-known.'

'And if the artist doesn't?'

Gabbi smiled. 'They place it in the foyer of their office and pretend its obscure origin makes it a curiosity piece. The added advantage being the item then becomes a legitimate tax deduction.'

'Oh, my,' Francesca breathed. 'When did you become so cynical?'

'I grew up.' It shouldn't hurt so much. But it did.

'And Benedict?'

She hesitated a moment too long. 'We understand each other.'

'That's a loaded statement, darling. I rather imagined he was your knight in shining armour.'

'That myth belongs in a story book.'

'Not always,' Francesca disagreed gently. 'I experienced a brief taste of it.'

Too brief. Francesca's marriage to a world-famous Italian racing-car driver had lasted six months. A freak accident three years ago on a tight turn had claimed his life and that of another driver, the horrific scene captured for ever on news-film.

Gabbi had flown to Monaco to attend the funeral, and hadn't been able to express adequate words then, any more than she could now.

'It's OK,' Francesca said quietly, almost as if she knew. 'I'm learning to deal with it.'

Gabbi had witnessed the magic, *seen* for herself the rare depth of their shared love, and wondered if it was possible to cope with such a loss.

'Mario was—'

'One of a kind,' Francesca interrupted gently. 'For a while he was mine. At least I have that.' She pointed out a glaring canvas whose colours shrieked with vivid, bold strokes. 'Was that a kindergarten tot let loose with brush and palette, do you suppose? Or is there some mysterious but meaningful symmetry that momentarily escapes the scope of my imagination?'

'It's an abstract,' an amused male voice revealed. 'And you're looking at the kindergarten tot who took an afternoon to slash the canvas with paint in the hope someone might pay for the privilege of putting bread on my table.'

'Expensive bread,' Francesca remarked without missing a beat. 'The artist favours hand-stitched shoes, a Hermes tie and wears a Rolex.'

'They could be fake,' he declared.

'No,' Francesca asserted with the certainty of one who *knew* designer apparel.

Gabbi watched the interplay between her friend and the tall, broad-framed man whose dark eyes held a piercing brilliance.

'Next you'll tell me where I live and what car I drive.'

'Not what people would expect of an artist,' Francesca considered with scarcely a thought. 'Northern suburbs, overlooking water, trees in the garden, a detached studio and a BMW in the garage.'

Gabbi sensed Benedict's presence an instant before she felt the touch of firm fingers at the edge of her waist, and she summoned a dazzling smile as she turned slightly towards him.

The eyes that lanced hers were dark and impossible to fathom so she didn't even try.

'Benedict,' Francesca greeted him warmly. 'It's been a while.'

'Indeed,' he agreed urbanely. 'You've met Dominic?'

'We haven't been formally introduced.' Francesca's smile was deliberately warm as she turned her head towards the man at her side.

'Dominic Andrea. Entrepreneur and part-time artist,' Benedict informed her. 'Francesca Angeletti.'

'How opportune. The designer luggage won't require a change of initials.'

Gabbi registered Dominic's words and heard Francesca's almost inaudible gasp one second ahead of Benedict's husky chuckle.

'You must come to dinner,' Dominic insisted. 'Bring Francesca.'

'Gabbi?' Benedict deferred, and she caught her breath that the decision should be hers.

'Thank you, we'd love to.'

'No,' the glamorous widow declined.

'I have yet to nominate a night,' Dominic said in mild remonstrance. 'And with Benedict and Gabbi present you'll be quite safe.' His smile was dangerously soft and filled with latent charm. 'Aren't you in the least curious to see if you're right?'

Gabbi watched Francesca's eyes narrow and heard her voice chill to ice. 'Where you live doesn't interest me.'

'Tomorrow,' he insisted gently. 'Six-thirty.' He

turned and threaded his way to the opposite side of the gallery.

'What a preposterous man,' Francesca hissed disdainfully the moment he was out of earshot.

'A very rich and successful one,' Benedict added mildly. 'Who dabbles in art and donates his work to worthwhile charities.'

'He's a friend of yours?'

'We occasionally do business together. He spends a lot of time overseas. New York, Athens, Rome,' Benedict enlightened her.

'Champagne, caviare and camaraderie aren't my style,' Francesca dismissed.

'You share something in common,' Benedict informed her with a degree of cynical amusement.

'Then why the dinner invitation?'

'He admires your charming wit,' Benedict responded wryly, and his mouth curved to form an amused smile.

'An attempt to charm wasn't my intention,' Francesca declared with an expressive lift of one eyebrow.

'Perhaps he is sufficiently intrigued to want to discover why not?' Benedict ventured in a dry undertone.

'I presume women rarely refuse him.'

A low chuckle escaped Benedict's throat. 'Rarely.'

Gabbi witnessed the faint sparkle evident in her friend's eyes, and was unable to repress a winsome smile. 'So you'll accept?'

'It's a long time since I've been offered such an

interesting evening,' Francesca conceded. 'I'll let you know at lunch tomorrow.'

Benedict drew their attention to an intricate steel sculpture that was garnering a great deal of notice, and after a few minutes Francesca indicated her intention to leave.

'Do you want to stay for Leon's party?' Benedict queried minutes later, and Gabbi cast him a studied glance.

'I imagine you've already presented him with a sizeable cheque, sufficient to appease any regret he might express at our absence?' The words were lightly voiced and brought a faint smile to his lips.

'Exhibits five and thirty-seven, plus the sculpture Annaliese admired.'

A knife twisted inside her stomach.

'A gift for James,' he added with gentle mockery.

She held his gaze with difficulty, unsure what interpretation to place on his words, or if there was *any* hidden innuendo in them. 'I'm sure he'll be most appreciative,' she said after a measurable silence.

'You didn't answer my question,' Benedict reminded her gently.

'James, Monique and Annaliese have yet to leave.' It was amazing that her voice sounded so calm, equally surprising that she was able to project an outward serenity. But then she'd had plenty of practice at conveying both.

Humour tugged at the edges of his mouth. 'I was unaware that their presence, or absence, dictated our own,' he countered with deceptive mildness.

It didn't, but she hadn't quite forgiven him for being so easily led away by Annaliese or for being caught so long in conversation.

She effected a slight shrug he could interpret any way he chose. 'If you want to leave—'

'You're not going?' Monique intervened, her voice tinged with mild reproach, and Gabbi wondered if lip-reading was one of her stepmother's acquired skills. 'Leon will be most upset if you miss his party.'

'A headache,' Benedict invented smoothly.

Monique spared Gabbi a penetrating look. 'Oh darling, really?' Her eyes sharpened suspiciously.

Annaliese's mouth formed a pretty pout. 'What a shame to end the evening so early.' She turned sultry eyes towards Benedict. 'Perhaps Gabbi won't mind if you drop her home and come back for the party?'

Benedict's smile didn't quite reach his eyes. 'I'm the one who is suffering,' he informed her, subjecting Gabbi to a deliberate appraisal that left no one in any doubt that his suffering was of a sexual nature.

Monique's expression didn't change and James's features remained deliberately bland, although Gabbi thought she glimpsed a fleeting humorous twinkle in his eyes. Annaliese, however, shot her a brief, malevolent glare before masking it with a faint smile.

'Have fun,' Annaliese murmured, pressing her scarlet-tipped fingers to Benedict's arm in a light caress.

Gabbi prayed that the soft flood of warmth to her cheeks wasn't accompanied by a telling tide of pink as Benedict smoothly uttered the few necessary words in farewell, and her fingers clenched against his in silent retaliation as he caught hold of her hand and began threading his way across the room to where Leon was holding court with a captive audience.

'Oh, darlings, you're leaving?'

'You don't mind?'

'I'm so pleased you were able to attend.' Leon's smile was beatific, courtesy of Benedict's cheque in his wallet.

Gabbi waited until Benedict had steered the Jaguar clear of the car park before launching into a verbal attack.

'That was unforgivable!'

'What, precisely, did you find unforgivable?' Benedict drawled in amusement as he joined the traffic travelling eastward along the New South Head road.

She wanted to rage at him, physically *hit* him. Instead she chose to remain silent for the time it took him to reach Vaucluse, garage the car and enter the house.

'Coffee?' Benedict enquired as he turned from resetting the alarm system.

'No,' she refused tightly, raising stormy eyes to meet his as he closed the distance between them.

He made no attempt to touch her, and she stood firmly resolute, hating him for a variety of reasons that were too numerous to mention.

'So much anger,' he observed indolently.

'What did you expect?'

'A little gratitude, perhaps, for initiating a premature escape?'

Words warred with each other in her mind as she fought for control. More than anything she wanted to lash out and hit him, and only the silent warning apparent in those dark features stopped her.

'You take exception to the fact I want to make love with you?' he queried silkily. Lifting a hand, he slid it beneath the curtain of her hair.

'I didn't expect a clichéd announcement of your intention,' she threw at him angrily, gasping as he cupped her nape and angled his head down to hers. *'Don't.'*

The plea went unheeded as his mouth closed over hers, and she strained against the strength of his arm as it curved down her back and held her to him.

Slowly, insidiously, warmth coursed through her veins until her whole body was one aching mass, craving his touch, and she opened her mouth to accept the possession of his own.

Passion replaced anger, and a tiny part of her brain registered the transition and wondered at the traitorous dictates of her own heart.

It wasn't fair that he should have quite this effect on her, or that she should have so little control. Sex motivated by lust wasn't undesired, but *love* was the ultimate prize.

She wanted to protest when he swept an arm beneath her knees and lifted her against his chest. She knew she should as he climbed the stairs to the upper floor. And when he entered their bedroom and let her slip down to her feet she stood, quiescent, as he gently removed her beaded jacket and tossed it over a nearby chair.

The soft light from twin lamps reflected against the mirror and she caught a momentary glimpse of two figures—one tall and dark, the other slender in red, then she became lost in the heat of Benedict's impassioned gaze, her fingers as dexterous as his in their quest to remove each layer of clothing.

Yet there was care apparent, almost a teasing quality as they each dealt with buttons and zip-fastenings, the slide of his hands on her exposed flesh increasing the steady spiral of excitement.

He wasn't unmoved by her ministrations either, and she exulted in the feel of tightening sinews as she caressed his muscled chest, the taut waist and the thrust of his powerful thighs.

His heartbeat quickened in tempo with her own as he pulled her down onto the bed and she rose up above him, every nerve, every *cell* alive with anticipation. She sought to give as much pleasure as she knew she'd receive, taking the path to climactic nirvana with deliberate slowness, enjoying and enhancing each step of the emotional journey until there was no sense of the individual, only the merging of two souls so in tune with each other that they became one.

And afterwards they lay, arms and legs entwined, exchanging the soft caress of fingers against warm flesh, the light, lingering brush of lips, in an afterplay that held great tenderness and care, until sleep claimed them both.

CHAPTER FIVE

THE sun's rays were hot after the controlled coolness of the building's air-conditioning, and Gabbi felt the heat come up from the pavement combined with the jostle of midday city staff anxious to make the most of their lunch hour, elderly matrons *en route* from one shopping mall to another and mothers with young children in tow.

Sydney was a vibrant city alive with people from different cultures, and Gabbi witnessed a vivid kaleidoscope of couture and grunge as she walked the block and a half to meet Francesca.

The restaurant was filled with patrons, but she'd rung ahead for a reservation, and the maître d' offered an effusive greeting and ushered her to a table.

There was barely time to order iced water before Francesca slid into the opposite seat in a soft cloud of Hermes Calèche perfume.

'The traffic was every bit as bad as I expected,' Francesca commented as she ordered the same drink as Gabbi. 'And securing a parking space was worse.'

Gabbi smiled in commiseration. 'City commuting is the pits.' She picked up the menu. 'Shall we order?'

'Good idea. I'm starving,' Francesca admitted with relish, selecting the *soupe du jour* followed by a Greek salad and fresh fruit.

Gabbi also selected her friend's choice, but opted for linguini instead of soup as a starter.

'How long will you be Sydney-based?' Her smile was warm, her interest genuine.

Ice-cubes chinked as Francesca picked up her glass. 'Not long. A few weeks, then I'll head back to Europe.'

True friendship was rare, and with it came the benefit of dispensing with the niceties of idle conversation. 'So, tell me about Rome.'

Francesca's expression became pensive. 'Mario's mother was diagnosed with inoperable cancer.'

Gabbi's heart constricted with pain, and she reached out and covered her friend's hand with her own. 'Francesca, I'm so sorry.'

'We had a few short weeks together before she was hospitalised, and after that it was only a matter of days.' Francesca's eyes darkened with repressed emotion. 'She bequeathed me everything.'

'Mario was her only child,' Gabbi reminded her gently.

'Nevertheless, it was—' she paused fractionally '—unexpected.'

The waiter's appearance with their starters provided an interruption.

'What's new with the family?' Francesca asked as soon as he was out of earshot.

'Not a thing.'

'Benedict is to die for, Monique superficially gracious, Annaliese a bitch and James remains oblivious?'

The assessment was so accurate, Gabbi didn't

know whether to laugh or cry. 'Selectively oblivious,' she qualified.

'A clever man, your father.'

'And yours, Francesca?'

'Consumed with business in order to keep my dear stepmama in the incredible style she insists is important.' She managed a tight smile. 'While Mother continues to flit from one man to the next with time out in between for the requisite nip and tuck.'

They finished the starters and began on the salads.

'Dominic Andrea,' Francesca ventured speculatively. 'Greek?'

'Second generation. His mother is Australian.'

'Irritating man.'

Dominic was many things, but irritating wasn't one of them. 'Do you think so?'

'And arrogant.'

Perhaps. Although Gabbi would have substituted self-assured. 'You want to opt out of dinner tonight?'

Francesca forked the last mouthful of salad, took her time with it, then replaced the utensil onto her plate. 'No,' she said thoughtfully, her gaze startlingly direct. 'Why deny myself an interesting evening?'

Gabbi's mouth curved with humour. 'A clash between two Titans?'

Francesca's eyes assumed a speculative gleam. 'It will be an intriguing challenge to beat the man at his own game.'

Indeed, Gabbi accorded silently. Although she wasn't sure that Francesca would win.

The waiter brought a fruit platter and they ordered coffee.

'Shall I give you Dominic's address?' Gabbi queried as she picked up the bill, quelling Francesca's protest. 'Or will we collect you?'

'I'll meet you there.' She extracted a pen and paper from her handbag and took down the address. 'Six-thirty?'

'Yes,' Gabbi confirmed as they emerged out onto the pavement. She accepted Francesca's light kiss on each cheek, and touched her hand as they parted. 'It's been great to catch up. Take care.'

'Always,' Francesca promised. 'See you tonight.'

There were several messages on Gabbi's desk when she returned, and she dealt with each, dictated several letters and worked on streamlining overheads in a subsidiary company. Systematic checking was required to discover alternative suppliers who, she was convinced, could provide an equal service for a more competitive price. She made a list of relevant numbers to call.

The intercom buzzed, and Gabbi depressed the button. 'Yes, Halle?'

'There's a parcel in Reception for you. Shall I bring it down?'

She eased her shoulders and pushed a stray tendril of hair behind one ear. 'Please.'

A minute later her secretary appeared carrying a flat rectangular parcel wrapped in brown paper. 'There's an envelope. Want me to open it?'

It couldn't be...could it? Gabbi rose to her feet and crossed round to the front of her desk. 'No, I'll take care of it. Thanks, Halle.'

She placed the attached envelope on her desk, then

undid the wrapping, pleasure lighting up her features as she revealed the painting she'd admired at Leon's gallery.

It was perfect for the southern wall of her office.

The card held a simple message: 'For you.' It was signed 'Benedict.'

Gabbi reached for the private phone and punched in Benedict's coded number.

He answered on the second ring. 'Nicols.'

'You noticed my interest in the painting,' she said with evident warmth. 'I love it. Thanks.'

'Why don't you take a walk to my office and thank me in person?' The lazy drawl held mild amusement, and a soft laugh emerged from her throat.

'A momentary diversion?'

'Very momentary,' Benedict agreed with light humour. 'An associate is waiting in my private lounge.'

'In that case, you shouldn't delay seeing him,' she chastised him sweetly, and heard his husky chuckle in response.

'Tonight, Gabbi.'

She heard the faint click as he replaced the receiver.

The rest of the afternoon went quickly, and at five she shut down the computer, signed the completed letters then collected her briefcase and took the lift down to the car park.

Benedict's four-wheel drive was in the garage when she arrived home, and as they were to dine out she bypassed the kitchen and made for the stairs.

It would be nice to strip off and relax in the Jacuzzi, she thought longingly as she entered the master suite, but there wasn't time. Twenty-five minutes in which to shower, dress, apply make-up and style her hair didn't allow for a leisurely approach.

The sound of an electric razor in action could be heard from the bathroom and she quickly shed her clothes, pulled on a silk robe and pushed open the door.

Benedict was standing in front of the wide mirror dispensing with a day's growth of beard, a towel hitched at his waist. It was evident from his damp hair that he hadn't long emerged from the shower.

'Hi.' It irked her that her voice sounded vaguely breathless. Maybe in another twenty years she would be able to view his partly naked form and not feel so completely *consumed* by the sight of him.

If, that far down the track, she was still part of his life. The thought that she might not be brought a stab of unbearable pain.

He looked up from his task and met her eyes in the mirror. 'Hi, yourself.'

His appraisal was warm and lingered a little too long on the soft curve of her mouth. With determined effort she reached into the shower-stall, turned on the water, slipped off her robe and stepped beneath the warm jet-spray. When she emerged it was to find she had sole occupancy of the bathroom.

Ten minutes later her hair was swept into a sleek pleat, her make-up complete. In the bedroom she crossed to the walk-in closet and selected silk evening trousers in delicate ivory, added a beaded camisole and slid her arms into a matching silk jacket. Gold jewellery and elegant evening sandals completed the outfit, and she took time to dab her favourite perfume to a few exposed pulse-points before catching up an evening purse.

'Ready?'

With a few minutes to spare. She directed a cool glance at him. 'Yes. Shall we leave?'

Dominic's home was a brilliant example of architectural design in suburban Beauty Point overlooking the middle harbour.

Dominic greeted them at the door and drew them into the lounge.

High ceilings and floor-to-ceiling glass lent the room spaciousness and light, with folding white-painted wooden shutters and deep-cushioned furniture providing a hint of the Caribbean.

There was no sign of Francesca, and Gabbi wondered if she was deliberately planning her arrival to be a fashionable, but excusable, five minutes late.

Ten, Gabbi noted, as the bell-chimes pealed when she was partway through a delicious fruit cocktail. Dominic allowed his housekeeper to answer the door.

It would seem that if Francesca had a strategy Dominic had elected to choose one of his own.

Stunning was an apt description of Francesca's appearance, Gabbi silently applauded as she greeted her friend. Francesca's expression was carefully bland, but there was a wicked twinkle apparent in those dark eyes for one infinitesimal second before she turned towards her host.

'Please accept my apologies.'

'Accepted,' drawled Dominic. 'You'll join us in a drink?'

'Chilled water,' Francesca requested with a singularly sweet smile. 'With ice.'

'Bottled? Sparkling or still?'

'Still, if you have it.'

Gabbi hid a faint smile and took another sip of her cocktail.

Francesca had dressed to kill in black, designed perhaps to emphasise her widowed state? She looked every inch the successful international model. The length of her auburn hair was swept into a careless knot, with a few wispy tendrils allowed to escape to frame her face. The make-up was perfection, although Gabbi doubted it had taken Fran more than ten minutes to apply. The perfume was her preferred Hermes Calèche, and there was little doubt that the gown was an Italian designer original bought or bargained for at an outrageously discounted price.

Gabbi wondered how long it would take Dominic to dig beneath Francesca's protective shell and reveal her true nature. Or if Francesca would permit him to try.

Dinner was a convivial meal, the courses varied and many, and while exquisitely presented on the finest bone china they were the antithesis of designer food. There was, however, an artistically displayed platter of salads adorned with avocado, mango and sprinkled with pine nuts. A subtle concession to what Dominic suspected was a model's necessity to diet? Gabbi wondered.

Francesca, Gabbi knew, ate wisely and well, with

little need to watch her intake of food. Tonight, however, she forked dainty portions from each course, declined dessert and opted for herbal tea instead of the ruinously strong black coffee she preferred.

'Northern suburbs, overlooking water and trees in the garden,' Francesca mocked lightly as she met Dominic's level gaze over the rim of her delicate teacup.

'Three out of five,' he conceded in a voice that was tinged with humour. 'Are you sufficiently curious to discover if you're right about the remaining two?'

Her eyes were cool. 'The detached studio and a BMW in the garage?'

'Yes.'

One eyebrow lifted. 'A subtle invitation to admire your etchings?'

'I paint in the studio and confine lovemaking to the bedroom.'

Gabbi had to admire Francesca's panache, for there was no artifice in the long, considering look she cast him.

'How—prosaic.'

Give it up, Francesca, Gabbi beseeched silently. You're playing with dynamite. Besides, the 'BMW' is a Lexus and although the studio is detached it's above the treble garage and linked to the house via a glass-enclosed walkway.

'More tea?' Dominic enquired with urbanity.

'Thank you, no.'

Benedict rose to his feet in one smooth movement, his eyes enigmatic as they met those of his wife. 'If you'll excuse us, Dominic?' His smile was warm, and tinged with humour. 'Dinner was superb. Do give our compliments to Louise.'

'It's been a lovely evening,' Gabbi said gently, collecting her purse. She spared Francesca a brief, enquiring glance and could determine little from her friend's expression. Their imminent departure provided an excellent excuse for Francesca to leave, and Gabbi's interest intensified when her friend failed to express that intention.

Perhaps, Gabbi speculated, Francesca was determined not to cut and run at the flimsiest excuse to avoid being alone with Dominic.

'Francesca is quite able to handle herself,' Benedict assured her as he eased the car through the electronically controlled gates and turned onto the street.

'So is Dominic,' Gabbi reminded him as she spared him a frowning glance.

'That worries you?'

'Yes,' she answered starkly. 'I wouldn't like to see Francesca hurt.'

'I failed to see any hint of coercion on Dominic's part,' Benedict returned tolerantly. 'And she chose not to take the opportunity to leave when we did.' He brought the car to a halt at a traffic-controlled intersection.

'Next you'll predict we'll dance at their wedding,' Gabbi declared with a degree of acerbity, and heard his subdued splutter of laughter.

'It wouldn't surprise me.'

'Mario—'

'Is dead,' Benedict stated gently. 'And Francesca

is a beautiful young woman who deserves to be happy.'

The lights changed and the car picked up speed. Gabbi turned her attention to the tracery of electric lights on the opposite side of the harbour. It was a picture-postcard scene, and one she'd admired on many occasions in the past. Tonight, however, it failed to hold any attraction.

'You don't think she could fall in love again?'

Gabbi was silent for several long seconds. 'Not the way she loved Mario,' she decided at last.

'Affection, stability and security can be a satisfactory substitute.'

She felt something clench deep inside her, and she caught her breath at the sudden pain. Was that what he thought about *their* marriage? The fire and the passion...were they solely *hers*?

The car traversed the Harbour Bridge, then turned left towards the eastern suburbs. Soon they would be home. And, like the nights that had preceded this one, she would go to sleep in his arms. After the loving.

To deny him was to deny herself. Yet tonight she wanted to, for the sake of sheer perversity.

Gabbi made for the stairs as soon as they entered the house. 'I'll go change.' And slip into the Jacuzzi, she decided as she gained the upper floor. The pulsating jets would ease the tension in her body and help relax her mind.

It didn't, at least not to any satisfactory degree. The doubts that were ever-present in her subconscious rose to the surface with damning ease.

One by one she examined them. Benedict wanted

her in his bed, but did he *need* her? *Only* her? Probably not, she admitted sadly, all too aware that there were a hundred women who would rush to take her place. With or without marriage.

One couldn't deny the security factor…for each of them. In her, Benedict had a wife who one day would inherit a share of a billion-dollar corporation, thereby doubling *his* share. Yet, conversely, she also stood to gain.

And stability would be cemented with the addition of children. Why, then, did she continue to take precautions to avoid conception?

Gabbi closed her eyes as images swirled in her mind. The shared joy of early pregnancy, her body swollen with Benedict's child, and afterwards the newborn suckling at her breast.

But it was more than that. Much more. The newborn would develop and grow into a child who became aware of its surroundings, its parents. Financial security would not be an issue. But emotional security?

Divorce had a traumatic effect, and having to accept a stepparent in the place of a loved one was infinitely worse.

Fiercely protective, she wanted desperately for her child to grow up in a happy home with two emotionally committed parents. A marriage based on a business merger lacked the one ingredient essential for a mutually successful long-term relationship: love.

A one-sided love wasn't nearly enough.

Damn. Introspection didn't help at all.

'Sleeping in a Jacuzzi isn't a good idea.'

Gabbi didn't open her eyes. 'I wasn't sleeping.'

'I'm relieved to hear it. Do you intend staying there long?'

'A while.'

He didn't comment, and she sensed rather than heard him leave. Perhaps he'd go downstairs and peruse the latest financial bulletin faxed through from London, New York and Tokyo.

Somehow she doubted he'd simply undress and slide between the sheets, for he was a man who could maintain maximum energy on six hours' sleep in any given twenty-four.

The warm, pulsating water had a soporific effect, and she allowed her thoughts to drift. To her childhood, early treasured memories of her mother, and James. After James followed Monique, and—

Gabbi's eyes flew open as a foot brushed her own. Her startled gaze met a pair of dark brown, almost black eyes heavy with slumberous, vaguely mocking humour.

'What are you doing here?' Why did she sound so—shocked? It was hardly the first time they'd shared the Jacuzzi.

'Is my presence such an unwelcome intrusion?'

'Yes.' Except that wasn't strictly true. 'No,' she amended, unable to tear her eyes away from the strong features within touching distance of her own. Broad cheekbones, a well-defined jaw and the sensual curve of his mouth.

The mouth tilted slightly, and she caught sight of strong white teeth. 'You sound unsure.'

Her gaze didn't waver. 'Perhaps because I am.'

Sinews moved beneath the smooth skin sheathing the powerful breadth of his chest as he extended a hand to trail a gentle pattern across her cheek.

The faint aroma of his cologne had a tantalising effect on her equilibrium, and her pupils dilated as one finger traced the outline of her lower lip.

Please, she begged silently. Don't do this to me.

Slowly, with infinite patience, he began to erode her defences, breaking them down one by one with the brush of his fingers against the pulse at the base of her throat where it beat in an increasingly visible tattoo.

Those same fingers trailed the contours of each breast, cupped and weighed them in his palm, then teased each tender nub.

Her lips parted and her eyelids drooped low.

No one person should have this much emotional control over another, she thought. There should be some in-built mechanism in one's psyche to prevent such an invasion.

Possession, she substituted as her bones began to liquefy.

Strong hands settled at her waist, and with no effort at all he turned her round to sit in front of him. She felt caged by the strength of his shoulders, the muscled arms that curved beneath her own.

There was warmth, a heat that had nothing to do with the temperature of the water, and when his lips grazed the delicate hollow at the edge of her neck Gabbi sighed in unspoken acceptance.

He had the touch, she mused dreamily, and the knowledge to arouse a woman to the brink of madness. And the control to hold her on the edge until she almost wept for release.

It was a sensual journey that traversed many paths, along which Gabbi had no desire to travel with anyone but him. She knew she'd give up her fortune, her *life*, *everything*...if only he felt the same.

His hands slid to her shoulders, shifting her so that she faced him, and his mouth took possession of her own.

Her arms lifted to encircle his neck, her fingers burying themselves in the thickness of his hair as she held him close.

There was passion as he tasted and took his fill, and she met his raw energy with matching ardour, then let her mouth soften beneath the teasing influence of his, savouring the lingering sweetness, all too aware of the leashed power as he traced the full curve with the tip of his tongue.

She wanted to tease him, test the level of his control. And see if she could break it.

Gabbi let her arms drift down, trailing her fingers over the muscled cord of his neck, taking time to explore the hard ridges, the strong sinews stretching down to each shoulder.

Dark, springy hair covered his chest, and she played with the short curls, twisting them round her fingers, pulling gently, only to release them as she moved to capture a few more.

She lowered her head and touched her lips to his shoulder, then gently trailed a path inch by inch to his ear, using the tip of her tongue with wicked delight on the hollow beneath the lobe before nuzzling and nipping at the sensitive flesh.

With extreme care she caressed the length of his jaw, traced a path across his cheek, then moved to brush each eyelid closed before trailing the slope of his nose.

The sensual mouth was a temptation she couldn't resist, and she touched her lips to its edge, nibbling and tasting as she explored the lower fullness before traversing the upper curve, withdrawing as she felt it firm in preparation to take control.

Gabbi shook her head in silent remonstrance, then slid to her feet and stepped out of the Jacuzzi, grabbed a towel and wrapped it round her slender form, reaching for another as she turned and extended a beckoning hand.

Benedict held her gaze for a few heart-stopping seconds, and she saw his eyes darken with smouldering passion as he reared to his feet.

He loomed large, his frame a testament to male magnificence, muscled sinew moving with easy fluidity, darkened whorls of hair glistening on his water-drenched skin.

His movements were deliberate as he stepped onto the marble-tiled floor, his pace slow as he shortened the distance between them, and his eyes never left hers for a second.

He held out his hand for the towel, and she shook her head, bunching it in her hand as she reached forward to blot the moisture from his skin.

Gabbi began with one shoulder, then the other, and moved to his chest, taking time and care as she slowly traversed his ribcage, his waist, the lean hips, then the muscled length of his powerful thighs. With deliberate casualness she stepped behind him and tended to the width of his back, watching the play of muscles as they flexed and tensed at her touch.

'Nice butt,' she teased gently as she trailed the towel down the back of each thigh.

'You're playing a dangerous game,' Benedict warned with ominous softness as she moved round to stand in front of him.

'Really?' Her lips tilted slightly as she feigned a lack of guile. 'I haven't finished yet.'

'And I haven't even begun.'

Each word possessed the smoothness of silk, and a slight tremor slithered across the surface of her skin.

Was she mad? In setting out to smash his control, was she inviting something she couldn't handle?

Yet she couldn't, *wouldn't* throw in the towel. Literally, she established with a choked laugh as she brushed the thick cotton pile over the matt of dark, curling hair at the apex of his thighs.

A man's arousal was a potent erotic testimony to his sex, his power and his strength. And instrument of a woman's pleasure. With knowledge and expertise, it could drive a woman wild.

Gabbi looked at it with fascination. Unbidden, she trailed the length, gently traced the tip, and brushed a light finger down the shaft.

She wanted to taste him, to use her tongue and her mouth as if she were savouring an exotic confection.

'Do you know what you're inviting?'

Did he read minds? And was it her imagination, or did his voice sound husky and vaguely strained?

She lifted her head and met the burning intensity of his darkened gaze. 'Yes.'

A thrill of anticipatory excitement arrowed through her body at the thought of what demands he might make when caught in the throes of passion. With it came a sense of fear of his strength if it was ever unleashed without restraint.

She swallowed, the only visible sign of her nervousness, and his eyes registered the movement then flicked back to trap her own.

'Then what are you waiting for?' he queried softly. The silent challenge was evident in the depth of his eyes and apparent in the sensual slant of his mouth.

She'd begun this; now she needed to finish it.

Without a word she held out her hand, and felt the enclosing warmth as he clasped it in his own.

In silence Gabbi led him into the bedroom. When she reached the bed she leant forward and dragged the covers free. She turned towards him and placed both hands against his chest, then gently pushed until he lay sprawled against the pale percale sheets.

This was for his pleasure, and she slid down onto her knees beside him.

Slowly she set about exploring every inch of his hair-roughened skin, tangling the tip of her tongue in the whorls and soft curls, the smooth texture that was neither soft nor hard, but wholly male and musky to the taste.

She felt a thrill of satisfaction as muscles tensed and contracted, as she heard the faint catch of his breath, the slight hiss as it was expelled, the soft groan as her hands sought the turgid length of his arousal. With the utmost delicacy she explored the sensitive head, traced the shaft and flicked it gently. Then she lowered her mouth and began a similar exploration with a feather-light touch, allowing sheer instinct to guide her.

Not content, she trailed a path to his hip, traversed the taut stomach, and traced a series of soft kisses to his inner thigh.

With deliberately slow movements she raised her head and looked at him, then she loosened the pins from her hair and shook its length free.

A tiny smile curved her lips as she bent her head and trailed her hair in a teasing path down his chest, past his waist, forming a curtain for the delights her lips offered to the most vulnerable, sensitive part of his anatomy.

Control. He had it. Yet she could only wonder for how long as she lifted her head and lightly traced his moistened shaft with the tips of her fingers.

Her eyes never left his as she brought her fingers up to her mouth, and his eyes flared as she sucked each tip, one by one. Then she rose to her knees and straddled his hips with a graceful movement.

He didn't touch her, but his eyes were dark, so dark they were almost black, and his skin bore the faint flush of restrained passion.

She wanted to kiss him, but didn't dare. This was her game, but there was no doubt who was in charge of the score.

The element of surprise was her only weapon, and

she used it shamelessly as she shifted slightly and teased his length with the moist, sensitive heart of her femininity. Then she arched against him, savouring the anticipation of complete possession for a few heart-stopping seconds before she accepted him in a long, slow descent.

Totally enclosed, she felt him swell even further, and gasped at the sensation. Then she began to move, enjoying the feeling of partial loss followed by complete enclosure in a slow, circling dance that tore at the level of her own control.

Her fingers tightened their grip on his shoulders as she fought against the insidious demands of desire, and she cried out when his hands caught hold of her hips and held them, steadying her as he thrust deep inside her, then repeated the action again and again until she became lost to the rhythm, mindless, in a vortex of emotion.

When she was spent he slid a hand behind her nape and brought her head down to rest against him.

Gabbi lay still, her breathing gradually slowing in tune with his. There was a sense of power, of satisfaction that had little to do with sexual climax in her post-orgasmic state. His skin was warm and damp and tasted vaguely of salt. She savoured it, and felt the spasm of hard-muscled flesh within her own.

Did a man experience this sensation of glory after taking a woman? That the sexual symphony he'd orchestrated and conducted had climaxed with such a wondrous crescendo?

And when it was over, did he want an encore?

Gabbi lifted her head and stared down at the slumberous warmth in Benedict's dark eyes, glimpsed the latent humour in their depths and caught the soft slant of his mouth.

'Thank you,' he murmured gently as he angled her mouth down to meet his in a possession that was a simulation of what they'd just shared.

His hand slid down her spine, and she gasped as he rolled with her until she felt the mattress beneath her back.

It was a long while before she lay curled in the circle of his arms. As an encore, it had surpassed all that had gone before. And, she reflected a trifle sadly, it was she who had lost control, she who had cried out in the throes of passion.

On the edge of sleep, she told herself she didn't care. If pleasure was the prize, it was possible to win even when you lost.

CHAPTER SIX

WHY was it that some days were destined to be more eventful than others? Gabbi wondered silently as she entered the house and made her way through to the kitchen.

She'd been very calm at the board meeting when Maxwell Fremont had verbally challenged her to explain in minute detail why it would be beneficial to re-finance a subsidiary arm to maximise the company's tax advantage. The initial margin was narrow, given the re-financing costs involved, but the long-term prospect was considerably more favourable than the existing financial structure. Her research had been thorough, the figure projections carefully checked, and there had been a degree of satisfaction when the proposal had gained acceptance.

The afternoon had concluded with a misplaced file and a computer glitch, and on the way home a careless motorist hadn't braked in time and her car had suffered a few scratches and a broken tail-light. Which was a nuisance, for insurance red tape meant that the Mercedes would be out of action while the damage was assessed, and again when it went into the workshop for repair.

A few laps of the swimming pool, followed by an alfresco meal on the terrace, held more appeal than dressing up and attending a formal fund-raising ball.

However, the ball was a prominent annual event for which Benedict had tickets and a vague disinclination to attend was not sufficient reason to initiate a protest. Although the thought of crossing verbal swords with Annaliese over pâté, roast beef and chocolate mousse wasn't Gabbi's idea of a fun evening.

And any minute now Benedict would drive into the garage, see a smashed tail-light and demand an explanation.

She crossed to the refrigerator, filled a glass with fresh orange juice and took a long, appreciative swallow.

'Care to tell me what happened?'

Right on cue. She looked at him and rolled her eyes. 'Heavy traffic, a driver more intent on his mobile phone conversation than the road, the lights changed, I stopped, he didn't.' That about encapsulated it. 'We exchanged names and insurance details,' she concluded.

He crossed to where she stood and his fingers probed the back of her neck. 'Headache? Any symptoms of whiplash?'

'No.' His concern was gratifying, but his standing this close didn't do much to stabilise her equilibrium. 'Traffic was crawling at the time.'

'Want to cancel out on tonight?'

She looked at him carefully. 'What if I said yes?'

'I'd make a phone call and we'd stay at home.'

'Just like that?' One eyebrow rose. 'I didn't realise I held such power. Aren't you worried I might misuse it?'

His hand slid forward and captured her chin, tilting

it slightly so that he could examine her expression. 'Not your style, Gabbi.'

At this precise moment she felt disinclined to pursue an in-depth evaluation. 'What time do you want to leave?'

He released her and crossed to the refrigerator. 'Seven.'

She had an hour, part of which she intended to spend indulging in a leisurely shower.

In the bedroom she stripped down to her underwear then crossed to the bathroom and activated the water.

Bliss, she acknowledged several minutes later as she rinsed off shampoo and allowed the water to stream down her back. Scented soap freshened her skin with a delicate fragrance, and she lifted her hands to slick back her hair.

The glass door slid open and Benedict stepped into the stall. His naked body ignited a familiar fire deep inside her, and she attempted to dampen it down. 'I've almost finished.' How could her voice sound so calm, so matter-of-fact, when inside she was slowly going up in flames? she wondered.

Would he…? No, there wasn't time. Unless they were to arrive late…

Gabbi subconsciously held her breath as he moved behind her, then released it as his hands settled on her shoulders. Firm fingers began a soothing massage that felt good. So good that she murmured her appreciation.

She let her head fall forward as he worked the tense muscles and she relaxed, unwilling to move.

'Fremont gave you a hard time at the board meeting this morning.'

'Anticipating his queries kept me on my toes.'

'You came well prepared.'

'Being *family* isn't regarded by some as an advantage,' she responded dryly.

'Should it be?'

'You obviously didn't think so.'

Benedict's fingers didn't still. 'My father was a very powerful man. I chose not to compete on his turf.'

'Yet you're where he wanted you to be.'

'There was never any question I wouldn't eventually take his place.'

No, just a matter of when, Gabbi added silently, and wondered whether destiny had played a part. For if Conrad hadn't died Benedict would still be living in America. And the marriage between Benedict Nicols and Gabbi Stanton would not have taken place. It was a sobering thought.

She lifted her head and moved away from him. 'I must get ready.' He made no attempt to stop her as she stepped out of the stall.

It took fifteen minutes to dry and style her hair, a further fifteen to complete her make-up. The gown she'd chosen to wear was dramatic black in a figure-hugging design with shoestring shoulder-straps. Long black gloves added glamour, as did jewellery, black hosiery and stiletto-heeled evening shoes. A few dabs of her favourite perfume completed the image.

Benedict's frame, height and looks were guaranteed to weaken a woman's knees no matter what he wore…or didn't wear. In a tailored black evening suit and white cotton shirt he was positively awesome.

Gabbi cast him a studied glance, and felt the familiar trip of her pulse as it leapt to a quickened beat. The heat flared inside her stomach and slowly spread, licking each nerve-ending into vibrant life.

Less than an hour ago she'd stood naked with him in the shower, yet she felt more acutely vulnerable *now*, fully clothed, than she had then.

To dispel the feeling she spread her arms, completed a full turn and summoned a mischievous smile. 'What do you think?'

His eyes were dark, and his mouth tugged wide over gleaming teeth as he deliberated.

Perhaps she should have worn her hair down, instead of caught into a carelessly contrived knot? Was black too dramatic, too stark?

'Stunning,' Benedict complimented, and saw relief beneath her carefully guarded expression.

'Flattery is an excellent way to begin the evening,' Gabbi said lightly as she turned away to collect her evening bag.

Thirty minutes later a parking valet swept the Bentley down into the vast concrete cavern beneath the hotel as she walked at Benedict's side through the main entrance.

Smile-time, show-time. She knew she shouldn't be such a cynic at twenty-five. Yet *years* spent taking an active part in the social scene had taught her she was expected to play a part. And she'd learned to do it well—the radiant smile, the light-hearted greeting, the spontaneous small talk.

The Grand Ballroom looked resplendent with its decorative theme, the DJ had unobtrusive mood-music playing, and impeccably uniformed waiters and waitresses hovered dutifully, taking and delivering drink orders.

A sell-out, one of the committee members delighted in informing Benedict as she directed him to their appointed table.

Gabbi entertained the slight hope that Annaliese might bring a partner, and she brightened visibly for all of two seconds before recognising the man on her stepsister's arm as none other than Dominic Andrea. More of a mismatch was difficult to imagine, and hot on the heels of that thought was...*what about Francesca*?

'A migraine,' Dominic said for her ears only as he seated Annaliese on his right and then slid into the seat beside Gabbi. 'Annaliese's date will be late.'

A smile curved her mouth. 'You read minds?'

'I anticipated your reaction.'

'Am I that transparent?'

His smile was slow and his eyes sparkled with devilish humour.

'Subtlety isn't my strong point.'

No, but determination was. She thought of Francesca and smiled. If Dominic was intent on pursuit, Francesca didn't have much of a chance.

'She intrigues me.'

Gabbi's smile widened. 'I had noticed.'

'Wish me luck?'

'All you need.'

James arrived with Monique and they took the seats

opposite, exchanged greetings, and placed orders with the drinks waiter.

Monique looked radiant in a royal blue gown and a matching evening jacket. Sapphire and diamond jewellery graced her neck and her wrist, and a large sapphire and diamond dress ring on her right hand almost eclipsed the magnificent diamond above her wedding band.

Annaliese had chosen deep emerald silk that hugged her curves like a second skin, with a side-split that bordered on the indecent.

The two remaining couples at their table slid into their seats as the DJ changed CDs and played an introductory number that was followed by the charity chairman's welcoming speech.

A prawn cocktail starter was served. Soft music filtered unobtrusively while the guests ate, providing a pleasant background.

The main course followed, comprising grilled chicken breast served with mango sauce and vegetables.

Delicious, Gabbi complimented silently as she forked delicate portions. A sandwich eaten at her desk around midday seemed inadequate sustenance by comparison.

A few sips of excellent Chardonnay proved relaxing, and she listened with interest as the host extolled the virtues of the charity, cited the money raised at this evening's event and thanked various sponsors for their generous donations.

A tall male figure slid into the empty seat beside

Annaliese and, when the speech was concluded, Annaliese performed the necessary introductions.

Not that one was needed. Aaron Jacob was equally well-known as an eminently successful male model as he was as a star in a long-running television series.

A heartthrob and a hunk, Gabbi acknowledged in feminine appreciation of a near-perfect male specimen. Pity he had an inflated ego and a reputation for changing his dates as often as his socks!

As a couple, Annaliese and Aaron were guaranteed to have their photo prominently displayed on the society page in tomorrow's newspaper. Perhaps that was the purpose of their date? *Be nice,* Gabbi silently chided in self-admonishment as she sipped her wine.

Soon the DJ would increase the volume of the music and invite guests to take to the dance floor. It would be a signal for everyone to mix and mingle, dance and provide an opportunity for the society doyennes to flaunt their latest designer gowns.

'More wine?'

Gabbi turned slightly and met Benedict's warm gaze. 'No, thanks. I'd prefer water.'

One eyebrow lifted in silent enquiry, and she offered him a brilliant smile. 'I thought you might like me to drive home.'

'Considerate of you.' His quiet drawl held a degree of musing cynicism, aware as she was that he rarely took more than one glass of wine with an evening meal and that therefore the offer was unnecessary.

'Yes, isn't it?'

'Benedict.'

Monique's intrusion commanded his attention.

'I've managed to get a few tickets to *Phantom of the Opera*, Wednesday evening. You and Gabrielle will join us, won't you?'

Was it coincidence that Monique had tickets for the same night that Gabbi and Benedict had invited Francesca and Dominic to make up a foursome?

'Thank you, Monique. I already have tickets.'

'Perhaps we could arrange to meet afterwards for supper?'

Familial togetherness was a fine thing, Gabbi acknowledged. But Monique's stage-managing was becoming a little overt.

'Unfortunately we've made other arrangements.'

'Annaliese and Gabrielle are so close, and see so little of each other.' Monique injected just the right amount of regret into her voice then moved in for the figurative kill. 'It seems such a shame not to take advantage of every opportunity to get together while Annaliese is home.'

Oh, my, her stepmother was good. Gabbi almost held her breath, waiting for Benedict's response.

'Another time, Monique.'

'You must come to dinner. Just family. Monday, Tuesday? Either evening is free.'

Persistence, thy name is Monique!

'Gabbi?'

That's right, she thought wryly; pass the buck. Avoiding the dinner was impossible, therefore decisiveness was the only way to go. 'Monday. We'll look forward to it.' Were polite lies considered *real* lies? If so, she'd be damned in hell. Yet she felt justified in telling them for her father's sake.

'Shall we dance?'

Now there was a question. Dancing with Benedict inevitably became a dangerous pleasure. 'Thank you, darling.' She rose to her feet and allowed him to lead her onto the dance floor.

The Celine Dion number was perfect, the lyrics revealing a certain poignancy that echoed most women's hopes and dreams.

Gabbi's body fitted the contours of his with easy familiarity, and she had the crazy desire to discard her conventional hold and wind her arms round his neck.

Did he sense how she felt? He was the very air that she breathed. Everything she wanted, all she would ever need. In a way it was frightening. What if she ever lost him?

'Cold?'

She lifted her head and looked at him for a few seconds without comprehension.

'You shivered,' Benedict enlightened her gently.

Get a grip, Gabbi, she chided herself. She summoned a smile and dismissed it lightly. 'Old ghosts.'

'Want to go back to the table?'

'You think I need to conserve my strength?' she queried solemnly as he led her to the edge of the dance floor.

'Tomorrow's Saturday.'

She shot him a sparkling smile. 'An hour of morning decadence before enjoying a late breakfast on the terrace?'

'*Early*-morning decadence, breakfast on the terrace, followed by a drive to the airport.'

'We're *escaping*?' Gabbi looked at him with due reverence. 'Alone? *Where?* No, don't tell me. Someone might overhear.'

'Witch,' he murmured close to her ear.

Dessert was served as they resumed their seats, followed by coffee and after-dinner mints.

Annaliese drifted onto the dance floor with Aaron, then paused and posed for a vigilant photographer.

'May I?'

Gabbi glanced at Dominic and rose to her feet. Benedict broke his conversation with James and cast her a quick smile.

'Benedict is selective with men who want to partner his wife.'

Gabbi cast Dominic a startled glance as he led her towards the dance floor and pulled her gently into his arms.

'Don't you believe me?'

How did she respond to that? Her light, amused laugh seemed relatively noncommittal.

They circled the floor, twice, then Dominic stepped to one side as Aaron and Annaliese suggested an exchange in partners.

Gabbi smiled as she moved into Aaron's clasp, then winced as he pulled her close. Too close.

'Watch my show?' The query was smooth, and she felt reluctant to enter the game he expected every female to play.

'No, I don't.' She tried to sound vaguely regretful, but it didn't quite come off.

'You don't watch television?'

The temptation to take him down was difficult to resist. 'Of course. Mainly news and documentaries.'

'You're a brain.'

Gabbi wasn't sure it was a compliment. 'We all have one.'

'In my business you have to look after the body. It's the visual thing, you know? Nutrition, gym, beauty therapist, manicurist, hair stylist. Waxing's the worst.'

'Painful,' she agreed.

'Oh, yeah,' he conceded with a realistic shudder. 'I'm jetting out to LA next week. Been offered a part in a film. Could be the big break.'

She attempted enthusiasm. 'Good luck.'

'Thanks.'

'Mind if I cut in?'

Gabbi heard the quiet, drawling tone and detected the faint edge to her husband's voice.

'Sure.' Aaron relinquished her without argument.

'You interrupted an interesting conversation,' she said mildly as Benedict drew her close.

'Define interesting.'

'Waxing body hair. His.'

'Up front and personal, hmm?'

She stifled a bubble of laughter. 'Oh, yeah,' she agreed in wicked imitation.

As they circled the floor she wondered how he would react if she said she hungered to feel his skin next to her own, his mouth in possession of hers in the slow dance towards sexual fulfilment.

'Darling Gabrielle. Isn't it about time I danced with my brother-in-law?'

No. And he isn't. At least, not technically. However, the words stayed locked in her throat as she graciously acknowledged Annaliese and moved into Dominic's arms.

'I was outfoxed,' Dominic murmured, and Gabbi offered a philosophical smile. 'Want me to complete a round of the floor, intervene and switch partners?'

'No, but thanks anyway.'

A few minutes later there was a break in the music and they returned to the table.

Gabbi collected her evening bag and with a murmured excuse she moved towards the foyer with the intention of freshening her make-up in an adjacent powder room.

There was a queue, and it was some time before she was able to find free space at the mirror to effect repairs.

A number of people had escaped the ballroom to smoke in the adjoining foyer, and Gabbi exchanged a greeting with one guest, then another, before turning to re-enter the ballroom.

'Ah, there you are, darling.' Annaliese projected a high-voltage smile. 'I was sent on a rescue mission.'

'By whom?'

Annaliese's eyes widened in artful surprise. 'Why, Benedict. Who else?'

'An absence of ten minutes hardly constitutes the need for a search party,' Gabbi said evenly.

Annaliese examined the perfection of her manicured nails.

'Benedict likes to guard his possessions.'

Attack was the best form of defence, yet Gabbi opted for a tactical sidestep. 'Yes.'

'Doesn't it bother you?'

'What, precisely?'

'Being regarded as an expensive ornament in a wealthy man's collection.'

This could get nasty without any effort at all. 'A trophy wife?' Gabbi arched one eyebrow and proffered a winsome smile. 'Did it ever occur to you to examine the reverse situation? In Benedict I have an attentive husband who indulges my slightest whim.' She ticked off the advantages one by one. 'He's attractive, socially eminent and he's good in bed.' She allowed the smile to widen. 'I consider I made the perfect choice.'

A flash of fury was clearly evident before Annaliese managed to conquer it. 'You seem a little peaky, darling. Pre-menstrual tension?'

'Sibling aggravation,' Gabbi corrected her, resisting the temptation to add more fuel to her stepsister's fire. 'Shall we return to the ballroom?'

'I intend to use the powder room.'

'In that case…' She paused, and effected a faint lift of her shoulder. 'See you back at the table.'

The minor victory was sweet, but she entertained no doubt that the war was far from over. However, a weekend away would provide a welcome break from the battlefield. The thought was enough to lighten her expression and bring a smile to her lips.

Benedict was deep in conversation with Dominic, Aaron and Monique were conducting animated small talk and James seemed content being an observer. Gabbi took the vacant seat beside her father.

'Would you like some more coffee?'

She shook her head. 'You could ask me to dance.'

A smile slanted his mouth. 'Dear, sweet Gabbi. I'm honoured.' He rose to his feet and held out his hand. 'Shall we?'

'Enjoying yourself?'

Gabbi considered his question as they circled the dance floor, and opted to counter it. 'Are you?'

'Monique assures me such occasions are a social advantage.'

'I suspect she considers you need a welcome break from wheeling and dealing,' she teased lightly, and incurred his soft laughter.

'More likely a woman's ploy to justify spending a small fortune on a new gown and half the day being pampered by a beautician and hairdresser.'

'Which men are content to allow, in the knowledge that said social occasions provide equal opportunity for proposing or cementing a business deal.'

He spared her a thoughtful glance. 'Do I detect a note of cynicism?'

'Perhaps.'

'Benedict adores you.'

She could accept respect and affection, but wasn't *adore* a little over the top? Fortunately with James there was no need to perpetuate the myth. 'He's very good to me.'

'I would never have sanctioned the marriage if I hadn't been convinced that he would take care of you.'

The music wound down for a break between numbers, and Gabbi preceded her father to their table.

Annaliese had taken an empty seat next to Benedict, Monique was conversing with Dominic and Aaron was nowhere in sight. Musical chairs, Gabbi decided with a touch of black humour as she slid into a vacant one.

Guests were slowly beginning to dissipate. In half an hour the bar would close and the DJ would shut down for the night. Any time soon they could begin drifting towards the foyer, take the lift to the main entrance and have the doorman summon their car.

Benedict lifted his head at that moment and cast her a searching glance, raised one eyebrow a fraction, then smoothly extricated himself from Annaliese's clutches. Literally, as the scarlet-tipped fingers of one hand trailed a persuasive path down the fabric sheathing his forearm, followed by a coy smile and an upward sweep of mascaraed eyelashes in a deliberate attempt at flirtation.

Gabbi tried to assure herself that it didn't matter. But it did.

She smiled graciously all the way to the main entrance, completed the air-kiss routine with Monique and Annaliese, brushed lips over her father's cheek, bade Dominic and Aaron goodnight, then slipped into the passenger seat of the Bentley.

Benedict eased the car towards the busy main street, paused until he gained clear passage into the flow of traffic then quickly increased speed.

Gabbi leaned her head back and focused her attention on the view of the city. Bright flashing neon signs and illuminated shop windows soon gave way to inner-city suburban streets and shuttered windows, some dark, others showing a glimmer of muted electricity. And, as they began to ascend the New South Head road, they gained a view of the harbour, its waters darkened by night and tipped with ribbons of reflected light.

'You're very quiet.'

She turned her head and examined Benedict's shadowed profile. 'I was enjoying the peaceful silence after several hours of music and noisy chatter.' It was true, but she doubted he was fooled by her explanation. 'If there's something you want to discuss…' She trailed off, and gave a slight shrug.

'Annaliese.'

No doubt about it, he aimed straight for the main target. But two could play at that game.

The Bentley turned into their street, slowed as they reached the electronically controlled gates guarding their property, swept along the curved driveway and came to a halt inside the garage.

Gabbi released the seat belt, unfastened the door-clasp and slid out of the car, aware that Benedict was mirroring her actions. He attended to the house alarm and followed her indoors, keyed in the re-set code then drew her into the lounge.

'Would you like a drink?'

She looked at him carefully, and chose a light-hearted response. 'Champagne.'

He crossed to the bar, removed a bottle from the fridge, opened it, filled two flutes then retraced his steps.

Gabbi took one flute and raised it in a silent salute, then sipped the contents. 'What particular aspect of my stepsister's character do you want to discuss?'

She could read nothing in his expression, and she had no idea whether he intended to damn her with faint praise or offer a compliment on her remarkable restraint.

'Annaliese's determination to cause trouble.'

Gabbi allowed her eyes to widen measurably, and she placed a hand over her heart. 'Oh, my goodness. I hadn't noticed.'

'Don't be facetious.'

'It's *obvious*?'

'Stop it, Gabbi,' Benedict warned.

'Why? I'm on a roll.'

'Quit while you're ahead.'

'OK. Pick a scenario. Annaliese wants you, you want her. Annaliese wants you, you don't want her.'

'The latter.'

She hadn't realised she'd been holding her breath, and she released it slowly. 'Well, now, that's a relief. I can kiss goodbye visions of throwing out monogrammed towels, ruining your hand-stitched shoes and cutting up every one of your suits.' She gave him a hard smile that didn't quite match the vulnerability apparent in her eyes. 'I had intentions of being quite vicious if you decided on divorce.'

Humour gleamed in those dark eyes, and a deep chuckle emerged from his throat.

'It's not funny.'

'No.'

'Then don't laugh. I was serious.'

Benedict took a long swallow of champagne and placed his flute down on a nearby pedestal. 'Why in hell would I consider divorcing a sassy young woman who delights in challenging me on every level in favour of someone like Annaliese?' He removed her champagne flute and lowered it to join his own. Then he pulled her into his arms.

Gabbi didn't have a chance to answer before his mouth closed over hers, and she drank in the taste of him mingled with the sweet tang of vintage French champagne, generously giving everything he asked, more than he demanded, until mutual need spiralled to the edge of their control.

'I could take you here, now,' Benedict groaned huskily as his lips grazed a path down her throat, and she arched her head to allow him easy access to the sensitive hollow at its base, the swell of her breasts as he trailed lower.

A soft laugh choked in her throat as he freed one tender globe and took a liberty with its peak. Then she cried out as he lifted her over one shoulder and began striding from the room.

'Caveman tactics,' she accused as he ascended the stairs.

He gained the upper floor, then headed for the main suite. When he reached it, he released her to stand within the circle of his arms.

'Want to undress me?'

Her eyes sparkled with wicked humour. 'Might be quicker if you did it yourself.'

'That bad, huh?'

'Yes,' she said with honest simplicity, her own fingers as busy as his as clothes layered the carpet.

Their loving was all heat and hunger the first time round, followed by a long, sweet after-play that led to the slow slaking of mutual need.

Afterwards she lay with her head pillowed against his chest, the sound of his heartbeat beneath her cheek.

'I don't think I could bear to lose you,' Gabbi said, on the edge of sleep, and wasn't sure whether she heard or dreamed his response.

'What makes you think you will?'

CHAPTER SEVEN

QUEENSLAND'S Gold Coast lay little more than an hour's flight north of Sydney, and the Stanton-Nicols' Lear jet ensured private airport access, luxurious cabin space and personalised service.

Cleared for take-off, the streamlined jet cruised the runway and achieved a rapid ascent before levelling out.

'No laptop?' Gabbi quizzed as she loosened her seat belt. 'No papers in your briefcase?'

Benedict sank back in his chair and regarded her with indolent amusement. 'Each within easy access.'

'Are you going to work during the flight?'

'Would you prefer me to?'

'No.' Her eyes assumed a mischievous gleam. 'It's not often I get one hour of your undivided attention.' She saw one eyebrow slant, and quickly qualified this. 'Alone. Out of the bedroom,' she added, then spread her hands in helpless acceptance at having stepped into a verbal quagmire. 'I'll give up while I'm ahead.'

'Wise.'

'Coffee, Mr Nicols? Juice, Mrs Nicols?'

'Thanks, Melanie.'

The cabin stewardess's intrusion was timely. Her smile was professional as she unloaded the tray, then poured coffee and juice. 'I'll be in the cockpit. Buzz me if you need anything.'

Gabbi leaned forward, picked up the glass of fresh orange juice and took an appreciative sip. 'Tell me about the deal you and James are involved in with Gibson Electronics.'

He proceeded to do so, answering her queries as she debated various points.

'It's tight, but fair,' she conceded after a lengthy discussion. 'Think we'll pull it off?'

'Gibson needs Stanton-Nicols' proven reputation with the Asian market.'

'And in return we gain a slice of Gibson Electronics.'

Business. The common factor that forged the link between them. Without it, she doubted she'd be Benedict Nicols' wife. A chilling thought, and one she chose not to dwell on.

The 'fasten seat belt' sign flashed on as the jet began its descent towards Coolangatta airport.

A car was waiting for them, and it took only a few minutes to transfer the minimal luggage into the boot. Benedict signalled to the pilot and had a brief word with the driver while Gabbi took the passenger seat, then he strode round and slid in behind the wheel.

The Gold Coast was Australia's major tourist mecca. Long, sweeping beaches, surf, golden sands, towering high-rise buildings, modern shopping complexes and a subtropical climate all combined to make it a highly sought-after holiday destination. Theme parks, a casino, hotels, cruise boats, canal developments and luxurious prestige housing estates promoted a lifestyle that belonged in part to the rich and famous.

Gabbi loved the casual atmosphere, the spacious residential sprawl. A city with few disadvantages, she mused as Benedict joined the north-bound traffic.

High-rise apartment buildings lined the foreshore, their names varying from the prosaic to the exotic. Warm temperatures, sunshine, azure-blue sky, palm fronds swaying beneath a gentle breeze.

A smile curved her generous mouth, and her eyes filled with latent laughter. Paradise. And Benedict. They were hers for two days.

Conrad and Diandra Nicols had purchased a beach-front block of land and built a three-level vacation home in the days before prestigious real estate lining Mermaid Beach's Hedges Avenue had gained multi-million-dollar price-tags.

Benedict had chosen to retain it as an investment, persuaded from time to time to lease it short-term to visiting dignitaries who desired the privacy of a personal residence instead of a hotel suite or apartment block. Gabbi loved its location, its direct access onto the beach and the open-plan design.

A sigh of pure pleasure left her lips as Benedict drew the car to a halt before the electronically controlled gates, depressed the modem that released them and keyed in a code to operate the garage doors.

The three-car garage was backed by a games-room that led out to a terraced swimming pool. The first level comprised an office, lounge, kitchen and dining-room, with a master suite, three guest bedrooms and two bathrooms on the upper floor.

Each level was connected by a wide curved staircase leading onto a semi-circular, balustraded landing, providing a circular central space highlighted by a magnificent chandelier suspended from the top-level ceiling and reaching down to almost touching distance from the ground-level entertainment room. Lit up at night, it was a spectacular sight.

'You sound like a student let out of school,' Benedict commented as they ascended the stairs to the uppermost floor.

'I love it here,' she said simply as she swung round to face him.

'What do you suggest we do with the day?'

'Oh, my, what a responsibility.' Her eyes danced with impish humour, and she pretended to deliberate. 'I could drag you off to visit a theme park. We could hire a boat and cruise the broadwater. Do a bit of sun-worshipping by the pool. Or take in a movie at the cinema.' Her mouth curved into a winsome smile. 'On the other hand, I could be an understanding wife and tell you to go set up a game of golf...something you'd enjoy.'

Benedict reached out a hand and brushed light fingers across her cheek. 'And in return?'

'I get to choose where we have dinner.'

'Done.' He bent down and gave her a brief, hard kiss. 'We'll go on to a show or the movies.'

'You ring the golf course while I unpack.' She had a plan, and she put it into action. 'Do you want to take the four-wheel drive or the sedan?'

'The four-wheel drive.'

Half an hour later she backed the sedan out of the garage and headed for the nearest major shopping complex. It was fun to browse the boutiques, sip a cappuccino, before getting down to the serious business of shopping.

She had a list, and she entered the food hall, selected a trolley and began.

It was almost midday when she re-entered the house with no less than five carrier bags, the contents of which were systematically stored in the refrigerator and pantry.

The menu was basic. The accompanying sauces would be anything but. Wine, French breadsticks. A delicious tiramisu for dessert. Liqueur coffee. And she had hired a video.

At five she set the table with fine linen and lace, silver cutlery and china. Then she checked the kitchen and went upstairs to shower. After selecting fresh underwear, she donned elegant blue silk evening trousers and a matching top, then groomed her hair into a smooth knot on top of her head. She then tended to her make-up, which was understated, with just a hint of blusher, soft eyeshadow and a touch of clear rose-pink lip-gloss.

It was after six when the security system beeped, alerting her to the fact that the gates were being released, followed by the garage doors. She heard a refined clunk as the vehicle door closed, then Benedict came into view.

Gabbi stilled the nervous fluttering inside her stomach as she moved out onto the landing to greet him.

He looked magnificent. Dark hair teased by a faint breeze. Broad shoulders and superb musculature emphasised by a navy open-necked polo shirt. Strong facial features, tanned a deeper shade by several hours spent in the sun.

'Hi. How was the game?'

He looked intensely male, emanating a slight air of aggressive goodwill that spoke of achievement and satisfaction at having pitted his skill against a rival and won.

He reached the landing and moved towards her, pausing to bestow a brief, evocative kiss. 'I'll hit the shower.'

'Don't bother dressing.'

One eyebrow lifted and his lips twisted to form a humorous smile. 'My dear Gabbi. You want me to be arrested?'

'We're eating in.' Now that she'd taken the decision upon herself, she was unsure of his reaction. 'I've made dinner.'

He looked at her carefully, noting the slight uncertainty, the faint nervousness apparent, and her effort to camouflage it. 'Give me ten minutes.'

He rejoined her in nine. Freshly shaven, showered, and dressed in casual trousers and a short-sleeved shirt.

'Would you like a drink?'

Gabbi shook her head. 'You have one. I'll wait until we eat.'

He followed her into the kitchen, caught sight of numerous saucepans washed and stacked to drain. 'Looks professional. Smells delicious. Hidden talents, Gabbi?'

She wrinkled her nose at him, then swatted his hand as he reached forward to sample the sauce. 'No advance tasting, no peeking. Open the wine. It needs to breathe.'

She served the starter. Delicate stuffed mushrooms that melted in the mouth. French bread heated to crunchy perfection.

The main course was an exquisite *filet mignon* so tender that the flesh parted at the slightest pressure of the knife. With it they had asparagus with hollandaise sauce, baby potatoes in their jackets split and anointed with garlic butter and glazed baby carrots.

When they'd finished, Benedict touched his glass to hers in a silent salute. 'I haven't tasted better in any restaurant.'

'To the French, food is a passion. The meals I shared with Jacques's family were gastronomical feasts, visual works of art.' Her eyes sparkled with remembered pleasure. 'I made a deal with his mother,' she said solemnly.

'You kept your hands off her son, and she taught you to cook?'

Gabbi began to laugh. 'Close.'

'One look at you and any mother would fear for her son's emotional sanity,' Benedict drawled.

She met his gaze and held it. What about *his* emotional sanity? Was it so controlled that no woman could disturb it?

'I'll get dessert.' She rose to her feet and stacked his plate and cutlery with her own, then took them through to the kitchen.

Two wide individual crystal bowls held the creamy ambrosia of liqueur-soaked sponge, cream and shaved chocolate that was tiramisu.

It was good; she'd even have said delicious.

Benedict sat back in his chair and discarded his napkin. 'Superb, Gabbi.'

She lifted one shoulder in a negligible shrug. 'We dine out so often, I thought it would make a change to stay home.'

'I'll help with the dishes.'

'All done,' she assured lightly. 'I'll make coffee. There's a video in the VCR.'

When the coffee had filtered, she poured it, added liqueur and topped it with cream, then took both stemmed glasses through to the lounge.

Benedict had chosen one of three double-seater leather settees, and he indicated the empty space beside him.

The movie was a comedy, loosely adapted from the original *La cage aux folies*. It was amusing, well acted and entertaining.

Gabbi sipped her coffee slowly, then, when she had finished, Benedict took the glass and placed it together with his on a side table.

She relaxed and leaned her head back against the cushioned rest. Being here like this was magical. No guests, no intrusions.

An arm curved round her shoulders and drew her close. She felt his breath stir her hair. And she made no protest as he used a modem to switch off the lights.

The only illumination came from the television screen, and the electric candles reflected from the chandelier. Which he dimmed.

Awareness flared as his fingers brushed against her breast and stayed. His lips lingered at her temple.

She let her hand rest on his thigh, and didn't explore.

Occasionally his fingers would move in an absent pattern that quickened her pulse and triggered the heat deep inside her.

It was a delightful, leisurely prelude to a rhapsody that would gather momentum and crest in a passionate climax.

Gabbi wasn't disappointed. Just when she thought there were no more paths she could travel, Benedict took her along another, gently coaxing, pacing his pleasure to match her own before tipping her over the edge.

Close to sleep, she whispered, *Je t'aime, mon amour,* to the measured heartbeat beneath her lips. And wondered if he heard, if he knew.

They rose early and took a leisurely walk along the beach, then stripped down to swimwear and ventured into the ocean.

The water was cool and calm, the waves tame, and afterwards they sprinted back to the house and rinsed the sea from their skin and hair, donned casual clothes and ate a hearty breakfast out on the terrace.

'How do you feel about a drive to the mountains?'

Gabbi took a sip of coffee, then rested the cup between both hands. Visions of a picnic lunch and panoramic views were enticing. 'What of the call you're expecting?'

Benedict subjected her to a measured appraisal, then moved his shoulders in an indolent gesture. 'Divert the house phone to my mobile, sling the briefcase and laptop onto the rear seat.'

It wasn't often he took an entire weekend off. All too frequently his time was spent in the study in front of the computer, surfing various global financial sites on the Internet. Leisure was relegated to social occasions, and even then business was inevitably an ongoing topic of discussion.

Hesitation wasn't an option. 'Let's do it.' She replaced her cup on the table and rose to her feet. 'I'll make sandwiches.'

He put a restraining hand on her arm. 'We'll pick up something along the way.'

The phone rang, and Gabbi froze as Benedict crossed into the house to take the call. The day's pleasure disappeared as she heard the curt tone of his voice, saw him make notes on paper then fold the sheet into his shirt pocket.

Nice plans, she thought with wistful regret as she cleared their breakfast dishes onto a tray and carried them through to the kitchen. Pity they had to be abandoned.

She was determined not to show her disappointment. 'Shall I take more coffee through to the study?'

He shot her a sharp look. 'I need an hour, maybe less. Then we'll leave.'

'Can I help?'

He gave a brief nod of assent, and she followed him to the study.

The fax machine held paper, and Benedict collected it *en route* to the desk. Within seconds the laptop was up and running.

They worked together side by side and, when the document was done and checked, it was consigned to the printer then faxed through to the States.

'OK. Let's get out of here.'

Five minutes later Benedict reversed the four-wheel drive from the garage and, once clear of suburbia, he headed west, taking the mountain road to Mount Tamborine.

'Thanks.'

'Whatever for?'

The terrain was lush green after seasonal subtropical rain. Grassed paddocks, bush-clad hills, homes on acreage, working farms.

They were gaining height as the bitumen road curved round the foothills and began its snaking ascent towards the peak.

'The weekend,' Gabbi elaborated. 'Today.' For the simple pleasures that cost only his time and therefore were infinitely more precious to her than anything money could buy.

'It's not over yet.'

No. The sun suddenly appeared much brighter, the sky a magical azure.

As the road wound higher there was a spectacular view of the hinterland, and in the distance lay the ocean, a sapphire jewel.

They reached the uppermost peak and travelled the road that traversed its crest, past houses of various ages and designs, an old-English-style hotel, and a quaint café.

The village was a mixture of shops with broad verandahs clumped together, and they stopped to purchase a large bottle of chilled mineral water, some delicious ham and salad rolls and fruit. Then they walked back to the four-wheel drive and drove to a grassed reserve with magnificent views over the valley.

It was isolated, picturesque, and Gabbi felt as if they were perched on top of the world, removed from everything and everyone. It was a heady feeling, more intoxicating than wine, breathtaking.

Benedict unfolded a rug and spread it over the grass beneath the shade of a nearby tree. They ate until they were replete then sprawled comfortably, at ease with the vista and the silence.

A true picnic, it reminded Gabbi of the many she'd shared with Jacques in the days when laughter had risen readily to her lips and the only cares she had had were studying and excelling in her exams.

'Penny for them.'

Gabbi turned at the sound of Benedict's drawling voice, and gave him a slow smile. 'We should do this more often.'

'That's it?'

He sounded mildly amused, but she could play the faintly teasing game as well as he. 'You want my innermost thoughts?'

'It would be a start.'

'I love you' was so easy to say, so difficult to retract. Whispered in the deep night hours was one thing—voiced in the early afternoon on a mountaintop was something else.

'I was thinking this is a little piece of heaven,' she

said lightly. 'Far away from the city, business pressures, people.'

'The place, or the fact we're sharing it?'

She offered him a wide smile that reached her eyes and lit them as vividly as the blue of the ocean in the distance. 'Why, *both*, of course. It wouldn't be nearly as much fun on my own.'

He curled a hand beneath her nape and brought his mouth down over hers in an evocative kiss that teased, tantalised and stopped just short of total possession.

'Witch,' he murmured a few moments later against her temple. 'Do you want to stay here, or explore the mountain further?'

She pressed a kiss to the hollow at the base of his throat and savoured the faint taste that was his alone—male heat mingled with cleanliness and exclusive cologne.

'We're close to a public road, it's a public park, and we wouldn't want to shock anyone passing by,' she teased, using the edge of her teeth to nip his skin. 'Besides, there's a plane waiting to take us back to the rat race.'

'Tomorrow morning. Dawn.'

They had the night. 'We shouldn't waste a moment,' Gabbi said with mock reverence, and gave his chest a gentle push. 'When we reach the coast we'll get some prawns and Moreton Bay bugs which you can cook on the barbecue while I get a salad together. We'll open a bottle of wine, eat, and watch the sun go down.'

He let her go, watched as she rose lithely to her

feet, then took her outstretched hand and levered himself upright in one fluid movement.

It was after five when they entered the house, and by tacit agreement they took a long walk over the damp, packed sand of an outgoing tide, then reluctantly turned and retraced their steps.

Her hand was held lightly clasped in his, and a faint breeze tugged her blouse and teased loose tendrils free from the careless knot of her hair. Her skin glowed from its exposure to the fresh sea air, and her eyes held a mystic depth that owed much to the pleasure of the day, and the anticipation of the night.

After preparing the meal there was time to change into swimwear and swim several lengths of the pool before emerging to dry the excess water from their skin.

The aroma of barbecued seafood heightened their appetite, and, seated out on the terrace, Gabbi reached for a prawn with her fingers, declared it ambrosia, then reached for another as she dug her fork into a delectable portion of salad.

'You've got prawn juice on your chin,' Benedict said lazily, and she directed a dazzling smile at him.

'Terribly inelegant.' She tore flesh from the shell of a perfectly cooked bug and ate it in slow, delicate bites. Monique would have been appalled. There wasn't a lemon-scented fingerbowl in sight. And paper napkins weren't an accepted substitute for fine Irish linen.

The sun began to sink, and the light dimmed, streaking the sky to the west with reflected pink that slowly changed to orange, a brilliant flare of colour that slowly faded, then disappeared, leaving behind a dusky glow.

Timed lights sprang up around the pool, lit the terrace, and cast a reflection that was almost ethereal until darkness fell and obliterated everything beyond their immediate line of vision.

Gabbi heard the phone, and watched as Benedict rose from his chair to answer it. She gathered the seafood debris together, stacked plates onto the tray, took it indoors to the electronic food trolley, then pressed the button that lifted it up to the kitchen. Then she closed the doors onto the terrace and activated the security system.

Dishes and cutlery were dispensed into the dishwasher, the kitchen soon restored to order. Her hair had long since dried, but needed to be rinsed of chlorine from the pool, and she made her way upstairs to the shower.

Afterwards she donned briefs, pulled on long white trousers in a soft cheesecloth, then added a matching sleeveless button-through blouse. Several minutes with the hair-drier removed the excess moisture from her hair, and she left it loose, added a touch of lipgloss, then ran lightly down to the kitchen.

Coffee. Hot, strong and black, with a dash of liqueur.

The coffee had just finished filtering into the glass carafe when Benedict joined her, and she cast him a searching look.

'Problems?'

'Nothing I can't handle.'

She didn't doubt it. She poured the brew into a cup and handed it to him. 'Need me?'

His eyes flared. 'Yes.' His implication was unmistakable, and her heart skipped a beat, quickened, then slowly settled. 'But right now I have to make a series of phone calls.' He lowered his head and took her mouth in a soft kiss that made her ache for more. Then he turned and made his way across the landing to the study.

Gabbi took her coffee into the lounge, settled in a comfortable settee and switched on the television set. Cable TV ensured instant entertainment to satisfy every whim, and she flicked through the channels until she found a sitcom that promised lightness and mirth.

One programme ran into another, and she fought against an increasing drowsiness, succumbing without conscious effort.

There was a vague feeling of being held in strong arms, the sensation of being divested of her outer clothes, then the softness of a pillow beneath her cheek, and a warm body moulded against her back.

CHAPTER EIGHT

THE Lear jet turned off the runway and cruised slowly into a private parking bay at Sydney's domestic airport.

Serg was waiting with the Bentley, and after transferring overnight bags into the boot he slipped behind the wheel and headed the car towards the eastern suburbs.

Gabbi sank back against the leather cushioning and viewed the scene beyond the windscreen. Traffic was already building up, clogging the main arterial roads as commuters drove to their places of work.

In an hour she'd join them. She looked at her casual cotton shirt, trousers and trainers. Soon she'd exchange them for a suit, tights and high heels.

Even now she could sense Benedict withdrawing, his mind already preoccupied with business and the day ahead.

Marie served breakfast within minutes of their arrival home, and shortly after eight Gabbi slid behind the wheel of her car and trailed Benedict's Bentley down the drive.

The day was uneventful, although busy, and lunch was something she sent out for and ate at her desk. Waiting for a faxed confirmation and acting on it provided an unwanted delay, and consequently it was almost six when she garaged the car.

While Monique took liberties with time as a guest, as a hostess she insisted on punctuality. Six-thirty for seven meant exactly that. Which left Gabbi twenty minutes in which to shower, dress, apply make-up and tend to her hair.

She began unbuttoning her suit jacket as she raced up the stairs, hopping from one foot to the other as she paused to remove her heeled pumps. By the time she reached the bedroom she'd released the zip-fastener of her skirt and her fingers were busy with the buttons on her blouse.

Benedict looked up from applying the electric razor to a day's growth of beard and raised an enquiring eyebrow as she entered the *en suite* bathroom.

'Don't ask,' Gabbi flung at him as she slid open the shower door and turned on the water.

Black silk evening trousers, a matching singlet top and a black beaded jacket. High-heeled black pumps. Gold jewellery. Hair swept on top of her head, light make-up with emphasis on the eyes.

Gabbi didn't even think, she just went with it, relying on speed and dexterity for a finished result which, she accepted with a cursory glance in the cheval-glass, would pass muster.

She reached for her evening bag, pushed its long gold chain over one shoulder and turned to see Benedict regarding her with a degree of lazy amusement.

'No one would guess you achieved that result in so short a time,' he commented as they descended the staircase and made their way to the garage.

'I'll take three deep breaths in the car and think pleasant thoughts.'

She did. Not that it helped much. With every passing kilometre the nerves inside her stomach intensified, which was foolish, for Annaliese was unlikely to misbehave in Monique and James's presence.

'Darlings.' Annaliese greeted them individually with a kiss to both cheeks. 'Two of my favourite people.' Her smile was stunning as she moved between Gabbi and Benedict and linked an arm through each of theirs. 'Come through to the lounge.'

One eyebrow slanted as she ruefully glanced from Gabbi's black evening suit to her own figure-moulding black cocktail gown. 'Great minds, darling?' The light tinkling laugh held humour that failed to reach her eyes. 'We always did have an extraordinarily similar taste in clothes.'

Except I paid for my own, while you racked up Alaia and Calvin Klein on James's credit card, Gabbi added silently. *Stop it,* she chided herself.

Her father's home was beautiful, tastefully if expensively decorated, and a superb show-case for a man of James's wealth and social position. Why, then, did she feel uncomfortable every time she stepped inside the door? Was it because Monique had carefully redecorated, systematically replacing drapes, subtly altering colour schemes, until almost every memory of Gabbi's mother had been removed?

Yet why shouldn't Monique impose her own taste? James had obviously been willing to indulge her. And the past, no matter how idyllic a memory, had little place in today's reality.

'Gabbi. Benedict.' Monique moved towards them with both hands outstretched. 'I was afraid you were going to be late.'

James gave his daughter a hug and laid a hand on Benedict's arm. 'Come and sit down. I'll get you both a drink.'

Innocuous social small talk. They were each adept at the art—the smiles, the laughter. To an outsider they resembled a happy, united family, Gabbi reflected as she took a seat next to Benedict at the dining table.

Monique's cook had prepared exquisitely presented courses that tantalised the taste buds. Tonight she excelled with *vichyssoise verte* as a starter.

'We arranged an impromptu tennis evening last night,' Monique revealed as they finished the soup. 'I put a call through, hoping you might be able to join us, but Marie informed me that you were away for the weekend.'

Monique possessed the ability to phrase a statement so that it resembled a question, and Gabbi fingered the stem of her water-glass, then chose to lift it to her lips.

'We flew to the coast,' Benedict drawled in response.

'Really?' Annaliese directed a brilliant smile at Gabbi. 'I'm surprised you were able to drag Benedict away from Sydney.' She switched her attention to Benedict and the smile became coquettish. 'I thought it was a requisite of the corporate wife to be able to entertain herself.'

Gabbi replaced her glass carefully. 'Surely not to

the exclusion of spending quality time with her husband?'

The cook served a superb *poulet français*, with accompanying vegetables.

'Of course not, darling.' Annaliese proffered a condescending smile. 'It was very thoughtful of Benedict to indulge you.'

Gabbi picked up her cutlery and speared her portion of chicken, then she sliced a bite-size piece with delicate precision. 'Yes, wasn't it?' She forked the morsel into her mouth, savoured it, then offered a compliment that the chef deserved. 'This is delicious, Monique.'

'Thank you, Gabrielle.'

Gabbi completed a mental count to three. Any second now Monique would instigate a subtle third degree.

'I trust you had an enjoyable time?'

'It was very relaxing.'

'Did you take in a show at the Casino?'

'No,' Benedict intervened. 'Gabbi cooked dinner and we stayed home.' He turned towards Gabbi with a warm intimate smile which melted her bones.

Great, Gabbi sighed silently. You've taken control of Monique's game, and provided Annaliese with the ammunition to fire another round.

'You never cooked at home, darling.' The tinkling laugh was without humour.

'There was no need. We always had a chef to prepare meals.' Besides, Monique hadn't wanted her in the kitchen, even on the chef's night off.

'It could have been arranged, Gabbi.'

She looked at James and smiled. 'It was never that important.'

'You should give us the opportunity to sample your culinary efforts, Gabrielle.'

After all these years, Monique? 'I wouldn't think of hurting Marie's feelings by suggesting I usurp her position in the kitchen.'

'Marie *does* have a night off, darling,' Annaliese remonstrated in faintly bored tones.

'Yes,' she responded evenly. 'On the evenings Benedict and I eat out.'

Her stepsister examined the perfection of her lacquered nails, then spared Gabbi a teasing smile. 'You're hedging at extending an invitation.'

Venom, packaged in velvet and presented with pseudo-sincerity. Gabbi handled it with the ease of long practice. 'Not at all. Which evening would suit?'

It was a polite battle, but a battle nonetheless.

'Monique? James?' Annaliese was gracious in her deferral.

'Can I check my diary, darling, and get back to you?'

Gabbi was equally gracious. 'Of course.'

'I'm intrigued to learn what you will serve,' Annaliese purred.

'Marie can always be guaranteed to present an excellent meal,' Gabbi supplied, determined not to be backed into a corner.

Monique's eyes narrowed, as did her daughter's, and each man picked up on the tension, electing to defuse it by initiating a discussion totally unrelated to social niceties.

Bombe au chocolat was served for dessert. Afterwards they retired to the lounge for coffee.

'I thought we might play cards,' Monique suggested. 'Poker?'

'As long as it's not strip poker,' Annaliese teased with a provocative smile. 'I'll lose every stitch I'm wearing.'

And love every minute of it, Gabbi thought hatefully.

'We close the table at eleven-thirty. Winning hand takes the pool.' James deferred to Benedict. 'Agreed?'

'Agreed.'

The game wasn't about skill or luck, winning or losing. The stakes were minuscule, the ensuing two hours merely entertainment.

Annaliese seemed to delight in leaning forward at every opportunity in a deliberate attempt to display the delicate curve of her breasts and the fact that she wore nothing to support them.

Add a tantalising smile and sparkling witchery every time she looked at Benedict and Gabbi was feeling positively feral by the time the evening drew to a close.

'No comment?' Benedict ventured as he drove through the gates and turned onto the road.

Gabbi drew a deep breath then released it slowly. 'Where would you like me to begin?'

He spared her a quizzical glance, then concentrated on merging with the traffic. 'Anywhere will do, as long as you release some of that fine rage.'

'You noticed.'

'I was probably the only one who did.'

'It's such a relief to know that.' Dammit, she wanted to *hit* something.

'Don't,' Benedict cautioned with dangerous softness, and she turned on him at once.

'Don't—*what*?'

'Slam a fist against the dashboard. You'll only hurt yourself.'

'Perhaps I should hit you instead.'

'Want me to pull over, or can it wait until we get home?'

'Don't try to humour me, Benedict.' She focused her attention on the scene beyond the windscreen: the bright headlights of oncoming traffic, fluorescent street-lamps and the elongated shadows they cast in the darkness.

Gabbi hurried indoors as soon as Benedict released the alarm system, not even pausing as he reset it. She made for the foyer and had almost reached the staircase when a hand clamped on her arm.

Any words she might have uttered were stilled as he swung her round and caught her close. There was nothing she could do to halt the descent of his mouth, or deny its possession of her own.

Hard, hungry, almost punishing. It defused her anger, as he meant it to do. And when her body softened and leant in against his he altered the nature of the kiss, deepening it until she clung to him.

A husky groan emerged from her throat as he swung an arm beneath her knees and lifted her into his arms. There wasn't a word she could think of uttering as he carried her up the stairs to their room. Or an action she wanted to take to stop him removing her clothes and his, before he drew her down onto the bed.

A long, slow exploration of the pleasure spots, the touch of his lips against the curve of her calf, the sensitive crease behind her knee, then the evocative path along her inner thigh… Gabbi felt her body begin to melt like wax beneath the onslaught of flame, until she was totally malleable, *his*, to do with as he chose.

Shared intimacy. Mutual sexual gratification. Was that all it was to Benedict?

Love. While her heart craved the words, her head ruled that she should be content without them.

Premium seating tickets for *Phantom of the Opera* were sold out weeks in advance. Benedict had undoubtedly wielded some influence to gain four tickets at such short notice, Gabbi mused as she took her seat beside him.

'Wonderful position,' Francesca murmured as the orchestra began an introductory number prior to the opening of the first act.

'Yes, isn't it?'

'You look stunning in that colour.'

The compliment was genuine, and Gabbi accepted it with a smile. 'Thanks.' Peacock-blue silk shot with green, it highlighted the texture of her skin and emphasised her blonde hair. 'So do you,' she returned warmly.

Deep ruby-red velvet did wonders for Francesca's colouring, and moulded her slim curves to perfection.

The music swelled, the curtain rose, and Act One began.

Gabbi adored the visual dimension of live performance—the presence of the actors, the costumes, the faint smell of greasepaint and make-up, the sounds. It was a totally different experience to film.

The interval between each act allowed sufficient time for patrons to emerge into the foyer for a drink, or a cigarette for those who smoked.

Gabbi expected to see James, Monique and Annaliese in the crowd. What she didn't expect was for Annaliese to readily abandon Monique and James and spend the interval conversing with Francesca, Dominic and Benedict. Apart from a perfunctory greeting, Gabbi was barely acknowledged.

The buzzer sounded its warning for patrons to resume their seats. As soon as the lights dimmed Benedict reached for her hand and held it firmly within his own. At the close of the next act he didn't release it when they stood and moved towards the foyer.

'The powder-room?' Francesca queried, and Gabbi inclined her head in agreement a split second before she caught sight of Annaliese weaving a determined path towards them.

'Fabulous evening,' her stepsister enthused with a dazzling smile.

'Yes, isn't it?' Gabbi agreed as she slipped her hand free. 'If you'll excuse Fran and me for a few minutes?'

'Of course.' Annaliese's delight was almost evident. 'I'll keep Benedict and Dominic amused in your absence.'

And relish every second, Gabbi observed uncharitably.

'Doesn't give up, does she?' Francesca said quietly as she followed Gabbi through the crowd. 'Have you told her to get lost?'

'Yes.' They entered the powder-room and joined the queue.

'The polite version?' Francesca asked. 'Or the no-holds-barred cat-fight rendition?'

'Would you accept icily civil?' Gabbi countered with a smile.

'A little bit of fire wouldn't go amiss. Italians are very good at it.' A wicked gleam lit her eyes. 'We yell, we throw things.'

'I've never seen you in action,' Gabbi said with genuine amusement.

'That's because I've never been mad at you.'

'Heaven forbid.' They moved forward a few paces. 'Dare I ask how things are going between you and Dominic?'

'I shall probably throw something at him soon.'

A bubble of laughter rose in Gabbi's throat. 'Should I warn him, do you think?'

'Let it be a surprise.'

Dominic was a man of Benedict's calibre. Dynamic, compelling, *electrifying*. And mercilessly indomitable in his pursuit of the seemingly unattainable. Gabbi was unsure how much longer Dominic would allow Francesca to maintain an upper hand.

The outcome, she decided with a secret smile, would be interesting.

The buzzer for the commencement of the following act sounded as they freshened their make-up, and they resumed their seats as the lights began to dim.

It was a faultless performance, the singers in excellent voice. As the curtain fell on the final act there was a burst of applause from the audience that succeeded in a further curtain call.

Emerging from the crush of the dispersing crowd took some time.

'Shall we go on somewhere for a light supper?' Dominic asked as they reached the car park.

'Love to,' Gabbi accepted. 'Where do you have in mind?'

'Benedict?'

'Your choice, Dom,' he drawled.

'There's an excellent place at Double Bay.' He named it. 'We'll meet you there.'

'Relax,' Benedict bade Gabbi as the Bentley bypassed the Botanical Gardens. 'I doubt Annaliese will embark on a club crawl in an effort to determine our whereabouts.'

'How astute,' Gabbi congratulated with a degree of mockery. 'Her enthusiasm hasn't escaped you.'

'And you, Gabbi,' he continued, 'are fully aware I provide Annaliese with no encouragement whatsoever.'

'*Darling* Benedict, are you aware that you don't need to?'

'You sound like a jealous wife.'

'Well, of course.'

He slanted her a dark glance and chided softly, 'Don't be facetious.'

Her lips curved to form a wicked smile. 'One has to develop a sense of humour.'

'I could, and probably should, spank you.'

'Do that, and I'll seek my own revenge.'

He gave a husky laugh. 'It might almost be worth it.'

'I think,' Gabbi said judiciously, 'you should give the road your full attention.'

The restaurant was situated above a block of shops on the main Double Bay thoroughfare. The ambience was authentically Greek, and it soon became apparent that Dominic was not only a favoured patron but also a personal friend of the owner.

Gabbi declined strong coffee in favour of tea, and nibbled from a platter filled with a variety of sweet and savory pastries.

Dominic was a skilled raconteur, possessed of a dry sense of humour which frequently brought laughter to Gabbi's lips and, unless she was mistaken, penetrated a chink in Francesca's façade.

It was after midnight when they bade each other goodnight and slid into separate cars, almost one when Gabbi slid between the sheets and Benedict snapped off the bedside lamp.

CHAPTER NINE

STANTON-NICOLS supported a few select charities, and tonight's event was in the form of a prestigious annual dinner held in the banquet room of a prominent city hotel.

Noted as an important occasion among the social élite, it achieved attendance in the region of a thousand patrons.

Haute couture was clearly evident as society doyennes strove to outdo each other, and Gabbi suppressed the wry observation that their jewellery, collectively, would probably fund a starving nation with food.

Men fared much better than women in the fashion stakes. They simply chose a black evening suit, white shirt and black bow-tie, albeit the suit might be Armani or Zegna, the shoes hand-stitched and the shirt expensive pure cotton.

Gabbi had chosen a full-length slimline strapless gown of multicoloured silk organza featuring the muted colours of spring. Cut low at the back, it was complemented by an attached panel and completed by a long, trailing neck-scarf in matching silk organza.

Tonight she'd elected to leave her hair loose, and the carefree windswept style enhanced her attractive features.

Six-thirty for seven allowed time for those who chose to arrive early to mix and mingle over drinks in the large foyer. The banquet-room doors were opened at seven, and dinner was served thirty minutes later.

'A glass of champagne?'

'Orange juice,' Gabbi decided as a waiter hovered with a tray of partly filled flutes. She removed the appropriate flute and caught the glimmer of amusement apparent in Benedict's dark eyes.

'The need for a clear head?'

Her mouth curved to form a winsome smile. 'You read me well.' James, Monique and Annaliese would be seated at the same table, together with five fellow guests.

'Every time, *querida*,' he mocked softly, and saw the faint dilation of her pupils at his use of the Spanish endearment. Did he know the occasional use of his late mother's native language had the power to stir her emotions?

Her momentary disconcertion was quickly masked as Benedict greeted a colleague, and with skilled ease she engaged in small talk with the colleague's wife for the few minutes until Benedict indicated the necessity to locate their designated table.

Stanton-Nicols was one of several sponsors contributing to the event, and already seated at their table was the charity chairman and his wife and a visiting titled dignitary together with his wife and son.

The five minutes remaining before dinner was served were crucial for those who chose to make an entrance. James, Monique and Annaliese slid into their seats with barely one minute to spare, with the obligatory air-kiss, the smiles and the faint touch of a hand. Perfect, Gabbi noted silently. Monique had done it again, ensuring they were the last to arrive, and their passage, weaving through countless tables, observed by almost everyone in the room.

As the waiters distributed the first of three courses, the compère welcomed the guests, outlined the evening's programme, and thanked everyone for their patronage.

Light background music filtered unobtrusively from numerous speakers as Gabbi lifted her fork and started on an appetising prawn and avocado cocktail.

Someone—Monique, as a dedicated committee member? Gabbi pondered—had seen fit to seat Annaliese on Benedict's left and the visiting titled dignitary's son on Gabbi's right.

The seemingly careless placing of Annaliese's hand on Benedict's thigh during the starter could have been coincidental, although Gabbi doubted it.

'Pleasant evening,' the dignitary's son observed. 'Good turn-out.'

Hardly scintillating conversation, but it provided a necessary distraction, and Gabbi offered a polite rejoinder.

'An interesting mix,' he continued. 'A professional singer and a fashion parade.'

'Plus the obligatory speeches.'

His smile was disarming. 'You've been here before.'

Gabbi's mouth slanted to form a generous curve. 'Numerous times.'

'May I say you look enchanting?'

Her eyes held mild amusement as she took in his kindly features. 'Thank you.'

Their plates were removed, and she offered Benedict a wide smile as he filled her water glass. His eyes were dark, enigmatic, and she pressed a hand on his right thigh. 'Thank you, darling.'

'My pleasure.'

A *double entendre* if ever there was one, and she deliberately held his gaze, silently challenging him.

An announcement by the compère that they were to be entertained with two songs by the guest singer was a timely diversion, and Gabbi listened with polite attention.

The main course was served: chicken Kiev, baby potatoes and an assortment of vegetables.

'Wonderful food,' the dignitary's son declared as he demolished his serving with enthusiasm, and Gabbi tried not to notice Annaliese's scarlet-tipped fingers settling on Benedict's forearm.

The singer performed another medley, which was followed by dessert, then the charity chairman took the podium.

At that point Annaliese slid to her feet and discreetly disappeared to one side of the stage.

Coffee was served as the compère announced the fashion parade, and with professional panache three male and three female models appeared on the catwalk, displaying creations from prominent Sydney designers in a variety of styles ranging from resort, city and career, to designer day, cocktail and formal evening wear.

'Stunning, isn't she?'

Gabbi turned towards the titled dignitary's son and saw his attention was focused on Annaliese's progress down the catwalk. 'Yes.' It was nothing less than the truth. Her stepsister exuded self-confidence and had the height, the body, the face…all the qualities essential for success in the modelling arena.

Most men took one look and were entranced by the visual package; most women recognised the artificiality beneath the flawless figure and exquisite features.

Annaliese participated in each section, her smile practised and serene. Although as the parade progressed it became increasingly obvious that she singled out one table for special attention…one man as the recipient of an incredibly sexy smile.

Gabbi's tension mounted with each successive procession down the catwalk, and it irked her unbearably that she was powerless to do anything about it. Except smile.

Benedict, damn him, took an interest in each model and every item displayed. Resort wear included swimwear. The bikini, the high-cut maillot. Annaliese looked superb in a minuscule bikini…and was well aware of her effect.

Gabbi felt the urge to kill and controlled it. The slightest hint of her displeasure at Annaliese's provocative behaviour would be seen as a victory, and she refused to give her stepsister that satisfaction.

Evening wear provided Annaliese with another opportunity to stun when she appeared in a backless, strapless creation that moulded her curves like a second skin.

The finale brought all the participating models on stage for one last turn on the catwalk.

'Is there anything that catches your eye?' Benedict enquired.

'The tall blond male model,' Gabbi responded with a deliberate smile, and glimpsed the amusement that lightened his features.

'Naturally you refer to the clothes he's wearing.'

She allowed her eyes to widen, and they held a glint of wicked humour. 'Naturally. Although the whole package is very attractive. He was magnificently *impressive* in swimwear.'

'Payback time?'

'Why, Benedict. Whatever do you mean?'

His expression held a degree of lazy tolerance. 'It'll keep.'

'You think so?'

A gleam lit his dark eyes. 'We could always leave and continue this conversation in private.'

'And commit a social *faux pas*?'

With indolent ease he reached for her left hand and raised it to his lips. 'I'm fortunate. I get to take you home.'

He kissed each finger in turn, then enfolded her hand in his on the table. Sensation flared and travelled like flame through her veins, but there was no visible change in his expression except for the crooked smile twitching the edges of his mouth as his thumb traced an idle pattern back and forth across the throbbing pulse at her wrist.

His eyes speared hers, faintly mocking beneath slightly hooded lids, and the breath caught in her throat.

'Some consolation,' she managed in an attempt at humour.

'The prize.'

She wanted quite desperately for it to be the truth, but she was all too aware it was part of the game. 'Ah,' she said with soft cynicism. 'You say the sweetest things.'

'Gracias.'

The waiters served another round of coffee as guests moved from one table to another, pausing to chat with friends as they made a slow progression towards the foyer.

'I've enjoyed your company.'

Gabbi heard the words and turned towards the dignitary's son. 'Thank you.' She included his parents. 'It's been a pleasant evening.'

'Most pleasant,' James agreed as he moved to his daughter's side and brushed a light kiss over her cheek. 'You look wonderful.'

'Thanks,' she murmured, and endeavoured to keep a smile in place as Annaliese rejoined them.

'A few of us are going on to a nightclub.' Her eyes focused on Benedict as she touched a hand to his shoulder. 'Why don't you join us?'

Gabbi wasn't aware that she held her breath as she waited for his reply.

'Another time perhaps.'

'We must do lunch, Gabrielle,' Monique insisted as she bade them goodnight. 'I'll ring.'

Gabbi felt a sense of remorse at wanting to refuse. It wasn't very often that her stepmother suggested a *tête-à-tête*. 'Please do.'

It was half an hour before they reached the car park and a further thirty minutes before Benedict brought the Bentley to a halt inside the garage.

'A record attendance,' he commented as they entered the house. 'The committee will be pleased.'

'Yes.'

'You sound less than enthused.'

'I'm disappointed.'

'Explain,' Benedict commanded as he reset the security alarm.

'I was just *dying* to go on to the nightclub.'

He turned and closed the distance between them, and her eyes took on a defiant gleam as he pushed a hand beneath her hair and captured her nape.

'Were you, indeed?'

He was much too close. His cologne teased her nostrils and melded with the musky male fragrance that was his alone.

'Yes. It would have been such *fun* watching Annaliese trying to seduce you.' She lifted a hand and trailed her fingers down the lapel of his suit.

'Your claws are showing.'

'And I thought I was being so subtle.'

'Do you want to debate Annaliese's behaviour?'

Her eyes glittered with inner anger, their depths darkening to deep sapphire. 'I don't think "debate" quite covers it.'

One eyebrow slanted in quizzical humour. 'It's a little late for a punishing set of tennis. Besides, I'd probably win.' His warm breath teased the tendrils of hair drifting close to one ear. 'And that,' he persisted quietly, 'wouldn't be the object of the exercise, would it?'

She wanted to generate a reaction that would allow her to vent her own indignation. 'At least I'd get some satisfaction from thrashing the ball with a racquet.'

His eyes were dark, fathomless. 'I can think of a far more productive way to expend all that pent-up energy.'

A thumb traced the edge of her jaw, then trailed lightly down the pulsing cord of her neck.

Gabbi could feel the insidious warmth spread through her veins, her skin begin to tingle as fine body hair rose in anticipation of his touch. 'You're not playing fair.'

He lowered his head and brushed his lips against her temple. 'I'm not *playing* at anything.'

Gabbi closed her eyes and absorbed the intoxicating feel of him as he angled his mouth over her own. His fingers tangled in her hair as he steadily deepened the kiss, intensifying the slow, burning heat of her arousal until it threatened to rage out of control.

Her body strained against his, pulsing, needing so much more, and she was hardly conscious of the small, encouraging sounds low in her throat as she urged him on.

Slowly, gently, he eased back and broke the contact, then swept an arm beneath her knees and crossed the foyer to the stairs.

'The bedroom is so civilised,' Gabbi breathed

softly as she traced the lobe of his ear with her tongue and gently bit its centre.

When they reached their suite the door closed behind them with a satisfying clunk. 'You want *uncivilised*, Gabbi?' he demanded as he let her slide down to her feet.

The words conjured up a mental image so evocatively erotic that she had to fight to control the jolt of feeling that surged through her body.

'This is a very expensive gown,' she announced in a dismal attempt at flippancy. 'One I'd like to wear again.'

Something leapt in his eyes and remained there. A dark, primitive glitter that momentarily arrested the thudding beat of her heart before it kicked in at a wildly accelerated pace.

The breath caught in her throat as he reached for the zip-fastening and freed it so that the gown slid down to the carpet. With mesmerised fascination she stepped aside and watched as he carelessly tossed it over a nearby chair.

His eyes never left hers as he traced the swell of her breasts, teased each sensitive peak, then slowly slipped his fingers beneath the band of her briefs and slid them to her feet.

Her evening sandals came next, and she watched as he removed his jacket and tossed it across the valet-frame.

The bow-tie followed, and his shirt. Shoes and socks were abandoned, and his trousers landed on top of his jacket.

Then he captured her face in his hands and lowered

his mouth to hers, initiating a kiss that took possession and demanded complete capitulation.

This was no seduction. It was claim-staking. Ruthless hunger and treacherous devastation.

She didn't fight it. Didn't want to. She rode the crest of his passion, and exulted in the ravishment of unleashed emotions.

It became a ravaging of body and mind—hers—as she gave herself up to him, her surrender complete as he tasted and suckled, tormenting her to the point of madness.

She had no control over her shuddering body, or the way it convulsed in the storm of her own passion. And she was completely unaware of the emotional sobs tearing free from her throat as she begged him not to stop.

A beautiful way to die, Gabbi decided with dizzying certainty as he dragged her down onto the bed. Then she was conscious only of unspeakable pleasure as he drove himself into her, again and again, deeper and deeper as she arched up to him in a dark, rhythmic beat that flung them both over the edge.

Afterwards she lay in a tangle of sheets, her limbs entwined with his, disinclined to move.

She didn't have the energy to lift a hand, and her eyes remained closed, for to open them required too much effort.

'Did I hurt you?'

She ached. Dear God, *how* she ached. But it was with acute pleasure, not pain. 'No.' A soft smile curved her lips. 'Although I don't think I'm ready for an encore just yet.'

He leaned forward and pressed a lingering kiss to the sensitive hollow at the base of her throat, then trailed a path to the edge of her mouth. 'Relax, *querida*. It's not an act I could follow too soon.'

'Some act.'

She felt him move, and the sheet settled down onto soft, highly sensitised skin. She sighed and let her head settle into the curve of his shoulder. Heaven didn't get any better than this.

Gabbi woke to the touch of lips brushing against her cheek, and she stretched, arching the slim bow of her body like a contented feline beneath the stroke of its master.

A smile teased her mouth and she let her eyes drift open.

'Is it late?'

'Late enough, *querida*.'

He was dressed, shaven and, unless she was mistaken, ready to leave.

Regret tinged her expression. 'I was going to drive with you to the airport.'

'Instead you can relax in the Jacuzzi, enjoy a leisurely breakfast and scan the newspaper before going in to the office.'

'You should have woken me,' she protested, and saw the gleam of humour evident in the dark eyes above her own.

'I just have.' He indicated a tray on the bedside pedestal. 'And brought orange juice and coffee.'

She eased herself into a sitting position and hugged

her knees. A mischievous twinkle lightened her eyes. 'In that case, you're forgiven.'

'You can reach me on my mobile phone.'

He had assumed the mantle of business executive along with the three-piece suit. His mind, she knew, was already on the first of several meetings scheduled over the next few days in Melbourne.

She reached for the orange juice and took a long swallow, grateful for the refreshing, cool taste of freshly squeezed juice.

She'd wanted to wake early, share a slow loving, join him in the Jacuzzi and linger over breakfast. Now she had to settle for a swift kiss and watch him walk out the door.

The kiss was more than she'd hoped for, but less than she needed, and her eyes were wistful as he disappeared from the room.

Four days, three nights. Hardly any time at all. He'd been gone for much longer in the past. Why now did she place such emphasis on his absence?

She finished the orange juice, slid from the bed and made for the bathroom. Half an hour later she ran lightly down the stairs and made her way to the kitchen.

'Morning, Marie.'

The housekeeper's smile held genuine warmth. 'Good morning. Do you want to eat inside, or on the terrace?'

'The terrace,' Gabbi answered promptly.

'Cereal and fruit, toast, coffee? Or would you prefer a cooked breakfast?'

'Cereal, thanks. I'll get it.' She plucked a bowl

from the cupboard, retrieved the appropriate cereal container, added a banana, extracted milk from the refrigerator then moved through the wide sliding glass doors that led out onto the terrace.

The sun was warm on her skin, despite the early-morning hour. It would be all too easy to banish work from the day, stay home and spend several lazy hours reading a book beneath the shade of an umbrella…

CHAPTER TEN

'SERG asked me to remind you to take the Bentley this morning.'

Gabbi looked up from scanning the daily newspaper and placed her cup down onto its saucer. She offered Marie a teasing smile. 'Not the XJ220?'

'We won't give him a heart attack,' Marie responded dryly, and Gabbi laughed.

'No, let's not.' The powerful sports car might be Benedict's possession, but it was Serg's pride and joy. Together with the Bentley and Mercedes, he ensured it was immaculately maintained. If the engine of any one of them didn't purr to his satisfaction, he organised a mechanical check-up. For the next few days the Mercedes would be in the panel shop having a new tail-light fitted and the scratches painted over.

The telephone rang, and Marie crossed to answer it. 'Nicols residence.' A few seconds later she covered the mouthpiece and held out the receiver. 'It's for you. Mrs Stanton.'

Gabbi rolled her eyes and rose to her feet to take the call. 'Monique. How are you?'

'Fine, Gabrielle. I thought we might do lunch today. Is that suitable?'

Exchanging social chit-chat with her stepmother over iced water and a lettuce leaf didn't rank high on her list of favoured pastimes. There had to be a reason for the invitation, and doubtless she'd find out what it was soon enough.

'Of course,' she responded politely. 'What time, and where shall I meet you?'

Monique named an exclusive establishment not too far from Stanton-Nicols Towers. 'Twelve-thirty, darling?'

'I'll look forward to it.' Oh, my, how you lie, an inner voice taunted. No, that wasn't strictly fair. Life was full of interesting experiences. Her relationship with Monique just happened to be one of them.

The traffic was heavy, drivers seemed more impatient than usual, and an accident at an intersection banked up a line of cars for several kilometres.

Consequently Gabbi was late, there was a message to say her secretary had reported in sick and the courier bag failed to contain promised documentation. Not an auspicious start to the day, she decided as she made the first of several phone calls.

By mid-morning she'd elicited a promise that the missing documentation would arrive in the afternoon courier delivery. It meant the loss of several hours, and if she was to assemble the figures, check and collate them for the board meeting tomorrow she'd need to work late, take work home or come in early in the morning.

Lunch with Monique loomed close, and with a resigned sigh she closed down the computer and retreated to the powder-room to repair her make-up.

Ten minutes later she emerged from the building and set out at a brisk pace, reaching the restaurant with less than a minute to spare.

Gabbi followed the maître d' to Monique's table and slid into the seat he held out.

'Gabrielle.'

'Monique.'

Superficial warmth, artificial affection. Ten years down the track, Gabbi was resigned to it never being any different.

As always, Monique was perfectly groomed, with co-ordinated accessories. Chanel bag, Magli shoes, and a few pieces of expensive jewellery. Tasteful, but not ostentatious.

'Annaliese will join us. I hope you don't mind?'

Wonderful. 'Of course not,' she responded politely, and ordered mineral water from the hovering drinks waiter.

'Annaliese felt you might appreciate some family support while Benedict is away.'

Gabbi doubted it very much. The only person Annaliese considered was herself. 'How thoughtful.'

'The banquet dinner was very enjoyable.'

As a conversational gambit, it was entirely neutral. 'A well-presented menu,' she agreed. 'And the fashion parade was excellent.'

'Shall we order a starter? Annaliese might be late.'

Annaliese rarely arrived on time, so why should today be any different? Gabbi settled on avocado with diced mango served on lettuce, then took a sip of mineral water.

'I've managed to persuade James to take a holiday,' Monique began as they waited for their starters.

'What a good idea. When?'

'Next month. A cruise. The *QEII*. We'll pick it up in New York.'

The cruise would be relaxing for James, and sufficiently social to please Monique. 'How long do you plan on being away?'

'Almost three weeks, including flights and stopovers.'

'It'll be a nice break for you both.' And well deserved for her father, whose devotion to Stanton-Nicols' continued success extended way beyond the nine-to-five, five-day-a-week routine.

Their starters arrived, and they were awaiting the main course when Annaliese sauntered up to the table in a cloud of perfume.

'The showing went way over time,' she offered as she sank into the chair opposite her mother. Two waiters hovered solicitously while she made a selection, then each received a haughty dismissal. As soon as they were out of earshot she turned towards Gabbi.

'How are you managing without Benedict?'

The temptation to elaborate was irresistible. 'With great difficulty.'

Annaliese's eyes narrowed fractionally. 'If you were so—' She paused, then went on to add with deliberate emphasis, 'So desperate, you could have accompanied him.'

Gabbi determined to even the score. 'It's not always easy to co-ordinate time away together.'

Annaliese picked up her water-glass and took a delicate sip. 'Really, darling? Why?' She replaced the glass down on the table. 'Everyone knows you hold a token job and take a sizeable salary from a company which regards your services as superfluous.'

Two down. This wasn't looking good. And she was hampered from entering into a verbal cat-fight by Monique's presence.

'My qualifications earned me the token job and standard salary from in excess of twenty applicants,' she declared coolly, knowing she didn't need to justify anything. However, the barb had struck a vulnerable target. 'At the time, James made it very clear his final choice was based entirely on proven results and performance.'

'You expect me to believe he didn't wield any influence?'

It was time to end this, and end it cleanly. 'The directorial board would never sanction wasting company funds on a manufactured position.' Her gaze was level, with only a hint of carefully banked anger apparent.

She wanted to get up and leave, but a degree of courtesy and innate good manners ensured she stayed for the main course and coffee. The food was superb, but her appetite had disappeared, and there was a heaviness at her temple that signalled the onset of a headache.

As soon as she finished her coffee she extracted a credit card from her bag.

'Put that away, Gabrielle,' Monique instructed. 'You're my guest.'

'Thank you. Would you excuse me? I have a two o'clock appointment.'

Annaliese lifted one eyebrow in silent derision, then opined, 'Such dedication.'

'Consideration,' Gabbi corrected her quietly as she rose to her feet. 'To a client-company representative's known punctuality.'

As an exit note it served her reasonably well.

A pity Monique had been present, Gabbi mused as she walked back to the office. On a one-to-one with Annaliese she would have fared much better.

On her return, she found a single red rose in an elegant crystal vase on her desk, along with a white embossed envelope.

Gabbi tore it open and removed the card: 'Missing you. Benedict.'

Not as much as I miss you, she vowed silently as she bent to smell the sweet fragrance from the tight bud.

Tomorrow he would be home. She'd consult with Marie and arrange a special dinner *à deux*. Candles, fine wine, soft music. And afterwards…

The buzz of the intercom brought her back to the present, and she leaned across the desk and depressed the button.

'Michelle Bouchet is waiting in Reception.'

'Thanks, Halle. Have Katherine bring her down.'

Gabbi replaced the receiver and lifted a hand to ease the faint throbbing at her temple. A soft curse left her lips as she caught sight of the time.

It would take at least an hour before she finished reviewing the files on her desk, and a further thirty minutes to log them into the computer.

There were two options. She could take the files and the computer disk home and complete the work there, or she could stay on.

Let's face it, what did she have to rush home for? Besides, Annaliese's deliberate barbs had found their mark.

The decision made, she placed a call through to Marie and let her know she'd be late. Then she sent out for coffee, took two headache tablets and set to work.

It was almost seven when Gabbi exited the program and shut down the computer. Freshly printed pages were collated ready for presentation, and there was satisfaction in knowing the board would be pleased with her analysis.

She collected her bag and vacated the office, bade the attending floor-security officer a polite goodnight, then when the lift arrived she stepped into the cubicle and programmed it for the underground car park.

A swim in the pool, she decided as the lift descended in electronic silence. Followed by a long hot shower. Then she'd settle for a plate of chicken salad, watch television and retire to bed with a book.

The lift came to a halt, and she stepped out as soon as the doors slid open. The car park was well lit, and there were still a number of cars remaining in reserved bays. Executives tying up the day's business, appointments running over time. Dedication to their employer, a determination to earn the mighty dollar? Most likely the latter, Gabbi mused as she walked towards the Bentley.

Deactivating the alarm system, she released the locking mechanism and depressed the door-handle.

'Quietly, miss.' The voice was male, the command ominously soft.

She felt something hard press against her ribs in the same instant that a hand closed over her arm.

'Don't scream, don't struggle and you won't get hurt.'

'Take my bag.' Her voice was cool, calm, although her heart was hammering inside her ribs. 'Take the car.'

The rear door was wrenched open. 'Get in.'

He was going to *kidnap* her? Images flashed through her brain, none of which were reassuring. Dammit, she wasn't going *meekly*. 'No.'

'Listen, sweetheart,' the voice whispered coldly against her ear. 'We don't want anything except a few photos.'

'We'. So there was more than one. It narrowed her chances considerably.

'Now, you can co-operate and make it easy on yourself, or you can fight and get hurt.'

Hands pushed her unceremoniously onto the rear seat, and she gasped out loud as he came down on top of her.

'Get off me!'

Hands found her blouse and ripped it open. Gabbi fought like a wildcat, only to cry out in pain as first one wrist was caught, then the other, and they were held together in a merciless grip. She felt a savage tug as her bra was dragged down, and she twisted her head in a desperate bid to escape his mouth.

Her strength didn't match his, and an outraged growl sounded low in her throat as he ground his teeth against her lips.

Lights flashed as she twisted against him, and when he freed her hands she reached for his head, raking her nails against his scalp and down the side of his neck.

'You bitch!'

He lowered his mouth to her breast and bit hard.

It hurt like hell. Sheer rage and divine assistance allowed her to succeed in manoeuvring her knee between his legs. The tight, upward jerk brought forth an anguished howl and a stream of incomprehensible epithets.

Then Gabbi heard the opposite door open, and two hands dragged her assailant out of the car.

'Come on, man. Let's get the hell out of here. I've got what I need.'

'Bloody little wildcat. I'm going to get her!'

'You were told to rough her up a little. Nothing else. *Remember*?' The door shut with a refined clunk, and Gabbi pulled the door closest to her closed and hit the central locking mechanism.

Then she wriggled over the centre console and slid into the driver's seat. The keys. Where were the keys? Oh, God, they were probably still in the lock.

The two men were walking quickly, one not quite as steadily as the other, and she watched them get into a van, heard the engine roar into life, then speed towards the exit ramp.

Only when the van was out of sight did she lower the car window and retrieve the keys.

Her blouse still gaped open, and she secured it as best she could. She was shaking so badly it took two attempts to insert the ignition key, then she fired the engine and eased the Bentley onto ground level.

Gabbi focused on the traffic, glad for once that there was so much of it. Cars, buses, trucks. Noise. People. They made her feel safe.

Home. She had never felt more grateful to reach the security of Benedict's palatial Vaucluse mansion.

Marie and Serg would be in their flat, and she had no intention of alarming them. Once indoors, she went straight upstairs to the bedroom and removed her clothes. Skirt, torn blouse, underwear. She bundled them together ready for disposal into the rubbish bin. She never wanted to see them again.

Then Gabbi went into the *en suite* bathroom and ran the shower. How long she stayed beneath the stream of water she wasn't sure. She only knew she scrubbed every inch of skin twice over, shampooed her hair not once, but three times. Then she stood still and let the water cascade over her gleaming skin.

Who? *Why?* The questions repeated themselves over and over in her brain as she replayed the scene again and again. Photos. *Blackmail?* The idea seemed ludicrous. Who would want to threaten her? What would they have to gain?

Then other words intruded…and she stood still, examining each one slowly with a sense of growing disbelief.

'You were told to rough her up a little. Nothing else. *Remember?*'

Who would want to frighten but not hurt her?

Dared not harm her, to give such explicit instructions?

Gabbi shook her head as if to clear it. Photos. Damning shots taken with a specific purpose in mind.

Annaliese. Even her stepsister wouldn't go to such lengths… Would she?

Slowly Gabbi reached out and turned off the water. Then she froze. Someone was in the bedroom.

'Gabbi?'

Benedict.

She swayed, and put out a hand to steady herself. He couldn't be home. He wasn't due back until tomorrow. In a gesture born of desperation she reached for a towel and secured it above her breasts as he entered the *en suite* bathroom.

Her eyes skidded over his tall frame, registered his smile, and glimpsed the faint narrowing of his dark gaze as it swept over her features.

'You're back early.' Dear God. She had to get a grip on herself.

She was too pale, her eyes too dark, dilated and wide, and it was almost impossible to still the faint trembling of her mouth. Without benefit of make-up and a few essential seconds in which to adopt a nonchalant air, she didn't stand a chance.

His silence was ominous, filling the room until she felt like screaming for him to break it.

When he did, she almost wished he hadn't, for his voice was so quiet it turned the blood in her veins to ice.

'What happened?' No preamble, just a chilling demand that brooked no evasion.

Was she so transparent that he had only to take one look? she wondered. She fingered the towel, and fixed her attention on the knot of his impeccable silk tie. 'How was the flight?'

'It doesn't matter a damn in hell about the flight,' he dismissed with lethal softness. *'Tell me.'*

She heard the tension in his voice and was aware there was no easy way to say the words. 'I stayed back at the office to work on some figures.'

His eyes never left hers. 'Why did you do that, when you could easily have brought the disk home?'

Good question. Why *had* she? She swallowed, and saw his eyes follow the movement at her throat.

'Someone slipped through car park security.'

'Are you hurt?' The words held a deadly softness, and a tremor shook her body as his eyes raked every visible inch of her slender frame.

She lifted a hand, then let it fall. 'A few bruises.' He'd see evidence of them soon enough.

'Slowly, Gabbi,' Benedict bit out softly. He reached out a hand and soothed her cheek with his palm. 'From the beginning. And don't omit a single detail.'

His anger was palpable, and she felt afraid. Not for herself. But fearful of what might happen should that anger slip free.

'I unlocked the car door,' she revealed steadily. 'Then someone grabbed me from behind and pushed me onto the rear seat.'

'Don't stop there.' His voice sounded like the swish of a whip, and she flinched as if its tip had flayed her skin.

'He climbed in after me.'

A muscle tensed at the edge of his jaw. 'Did he touch you?'

She shivered at the memory of those brutal fingers manacling her wrists while he ripped open her blouse.

'Not the way you mean.'

Benedict's eyes hardened. 'You called the police?'

She shook her head. 'Nothing was stolen. The car wasn't damaged. I wasn't assaulted.'

His hands settled on her shoulders and slid gently down her arms. 'Assault is a multi-faceted term.' His fingers were incredibly gentle and thorough. Her breath caught when he touched her wrists, and she flinched as he carefully examined first one then the other before raising them to his lips.

His hands reached for the towel, and she froze, all too aware of several deep pink smudges darkening the paleness of her breasts.

Naked fury darkened his features, and his hands clenched until the knuckles showed white.

Gabbi registered dimly that she had wanted to test his control and break it. But never like this.

'I scratched him rather badly,' she offered in explanation. 'And he retaliated.'

There was something primitive in his expression, a stark ruthlessness that frightened her. She needed to diminish it to something approaching civilised restraint. 'His purpose wasn't to harm me. He had an accomplice with a camera.'

Dark, nearly black eyes assumed an almost predatory alertness.

The shrill sound of the telephone made her jump,

and she stared in mesmerised fascination at the bathroom extension.

'Pick it up when I lift the bedroom connection.'

Each word was a harsh directive she didn't think to ignore, and she watched, wide-eyed, as Benedict quickly crossed to the bedside pedestal. Her movements synchronised with his, she reached out and lifted the receiver.

'Gabbi Nicols.'

'Gabrielle.' Her name was a distinctive purr on the line, and Gabbi's fingers tightened measurably.

'Annaliese,' she greeted cautiously.

'I have in my possession photos which show you in a state of remarkable *déshabillé*, *mon enfant*.' It was almost possible to *see* Annaliese's cruel smile. 'Copies of them will be despatched to Benedict by courier an hour after his return tomorrow. Together with a file on Tony detailing his career as a professional escort.' She paused, then added with delicate emphasis, 'And listing other services he's only too willing to provide for a price.'

Gabbi felt sick at the thought of being a victim of so much hatred.

'Lost for words, darling?'

'Speechless.'

A tinkle of brittle laughter sounded down the line. 'If you had taken me seriously, it wouldn't have been necessary to go this far.'

Gabbi tightened her grip on the receiver. 'Don't be surprised if Tony hits you up for danger money. He received a knee in the groin and a few deep scratches.'

'The photographs are worth it. Show a little wisdom and start packing,' Annaliese suggested with saccharine sweetness.

'Benedict—'

'Will be shocked at the evidence.'

'Yes.'

There was a momentary silence.

'You can present me with the photos and the file personally, Annaliese,' Benedict directed in a voice so silk-smooth it sent shivers scudding down the length of Gabbi's spine. 'If you're wise, you'll be waiting at your front door with them in your hand ten minutes from now. After which you'll explain to Monique and James that you've received an urgent call from your agent demanding your presence elsewhere. So urgent,' he continued with deadly softness, 'that you need to board a plane tomorrow. I'll arrange the airline ticket.

'If you should be sufficiently foolish to set foot in Sydney again I'll lay charges against you for assault and extortion. And don't,' he advised icily, 'put a warning call through to the infamous Tony. There isn't a place he can go that I won't eventually find him. Do we understand each other?'

Benedict replaced the receiver with such care, Gabbi felt afraid. With numbed fingers she replaced the bathroom receiver onto the wall handset.

Her eyes were impossibly large as he crossed the room, and she was powerless to utter so much as a word when he lowered his head down to hers and took reverent possession of her mouth.

'I'll be back.'

Then he was gone, with a swiftness that made her shiver. Within minutes she heard an engine start up, and the refined purr as the car headed towards the gates. Then silence.

Gabbi discarded the towel and selected a pair of ivory satin pyjamas. She crossed to the large bed and turned back the covering. Then she sank down onto the stool in front of the mirrored dressing table and picked up her hairbrush.

It was twenty-five minutes later when Benedict re-entered the bedroom, and her arm slowed to a faltering halt as he moved to her side.

Her mouth trembled when he removed the brush from her hand.

'Where are they?' Was that her voice? It sounded so hushed it was almost indistinct.

'I destroyed them,' Benedict said gently.

She had to ask. 'Did you look at them?'

His hands curved over her shoulders. 'Yes.'

Her eyes filled, and she barely kept the tears at bay. 'I imagine they were—'

'Damning.'

A muscle contracted in one cheek. 'Would you have believed—?'

'No.' He touched a finger to her cheek, then trailed its tip to the corner of her mouth. 'They were intended to be held against you as blackmail.' He traced the fullness of her lower lip. 'What was the price, Gabbi?'

'Me,' she enlightened him with stark honesty. 'Out of your life.'

His hand slid to her throat and caressed the soft hollows at its base.

'You imagined I would let you go?'

'Annaliese was counting on it.'

His fingers slid to the top button of her pyjama shirt and dealt with it, before slipping down to the next one. The second button slid free, as did the third and last. Gently, he pulled the satin shirt free from her arms.

Gabbi watched his eyes darken as they rested on the pink smudges marking each pale globe.

'It's to be hoped the infamous Tony was well paid. Expert medical care can be expensive.'

Her mouth opened, then closed again as he brushed it with his own.

She shivered at the extent of his power. At how quickly he could exert it, and how far it could reach.

'You came home early,' Gabbi whispered. 'Why?'

His lips curved. 'Because I didn't want to spend another night away from you.'

Unbidden, the tears welled up and spilled, trickling down each cheek in twin rivulets. Gentle fingers tilted her chin, and she felt the touch of his mouth as it trailed one cheek, then the other, before he kissed each eyelid in turn.

'Don't,' Benedict bade her quietly.

She wanted to say she loved him. The words hovered near the edge of her lips, but remained unspoken.

'Tomorrow morning we're flying out to Hawaii.'

A protest rose to her lips. 'The office—'

'Can get by without us,' Benedict assured her as he scooped her into his arms.

'The Gibson deal—'

'James will handle it.'

'Benedict—'

'Shut up,' he ordered softly as he sank down onto the bed with her cradled on his lap.

Her pulse leapt then accelerated to a faster beat as his mouth brushed her temple then slid to the sensitive hollow beneath her ear.

She felt secure. And protected. For now, it was enough.

Gabbi's fingers worked the knot on his tie, then slid to the buttons on his shirt. 'I need to feel your skin next to mine.'

Benedict placed her carefully against the nest of pillows, then straightened to his feet. He didn't hurry, and she watched every movement as he divested himself of one garment after the other.

Then he came down onto the bed and pulled her to lie beside him. He propped himself up on an elbow and examined the soft mouth, the blue eyes looking at him with unblinking solemnity.

'Do you want to talk?'

Gabbi considered the question, then slowly shook her head. Tomorrow, maybe. Tonight she wanted the reassurance of his arms around her, his body intimately joined to hers.

Lifting a hand, she trailed his cheek with tentative fingers, and her eyes widened fractionally as he caught and carried them to his lips.

With infinite care he kissed them, one by one, before traversing to the bones at her wrist. Then he released her hand and bent his head to her breast, caressing each bruise with his mouth.

'Benedict.'

He lifted his head and met her gaze in silent query.

'I *need* you,' she said quietly, and saw desire flare in the dark eyes close to her own.

Her hands lifted to encircle his neck, and her mouth trembled beneath the soft touch of his before the pressure increased.

His tongue was an invasive entity as it explored the soft tissues, and she felt him tense as he found the abrasions where Tony had briefly ground his mouth against her own, heard the low growl of his anger, and sought to soothe it.

The slow reverence of his lovemaking made her want to cry, and afterwards she slept in his arms, her head pillowed against his chest.

CHAPTER ELEVEN

WAIKIKI BEACH was a glorious sight. Deep blue ocean, white sand, with multi-level high-rise hotels and apartment buildings lining the foreshore.

There were beaches to equal and surpass it in Australia, and many believed Queensland's Gold Coast to be comparable to Honolulu.

The climate was similar, the designer boutiques many and varied, but it was the cosmopolitan population and the friendly Hawaiian people which fascinated Gabbi.

It wasn't her first visit nor, she hoped, would it be her last.

Benedict had chosen the Royal Hawaiian hotel, known as the 'pink palace' due to its pink-washed exterior. Originally home to Hawaiian royalty, it held an aura of tradition and timelessness, and was unique in comparison to the many modern hotels bordering the foreshore. Crystal chandeliers featured in the foyer, and there was an abundance of luxurious Oriental rose-pink carpets.

Gracious was a word that sprang to mind, Gabbi decided as she sank into a chair and ordered a virgin piña colada from the hovering drinks waiter.

Five days of blissful relaxation had done wonders to repair her peace of mind, she mused as she gazed idly out to sea. Careful sunbathing had coloured her skin to a warm honey-gold.

By tacit agreement, they'd avoided the tourist attractions, choosing instead to commission a limousine with driver for a day to drive round the main island.

Shopping wasn't a priority, although she had explored some of the boutiques and made a few purchases.

'Feel like sharing?'

Gabbi pushed her sunglasses up on top of her head as she turned towards Benedict.

'My piña colada?' she countered with a teasing smile.

'You've been deep in thought for the past five minutes,' he drawled.

Gabbi allowed her gaze to wander towards a young woman whose slender, model-proportioned curves were unadorned except for a black thong-bikini brief. Tall, gorgeous and tanned, she seemed intent on spending equal time anointing her firm body with oil and worshipping the sun.

'I was just surveying the scene,' she said easily. 'And wondering where you're taking me to dinner.'

'Hungry?'

For you. Only you. Was it such a sin to want to be with one man so badly? To laugh, pleasure, *love him* so much that he became the very air that she breathed?

'Yes.' She wrinkled her nose at him. 'I think it must be all the fresh sea air and sunshine.'

A smile lifted the edges of his mouth. 'You get to choose.'

'Somewhere exotic, I think.'

'Define "exotic".'

'Soft lights, dreamy music, exquisitely presented food and—' she paused, her eyes filling with wicked warmth '—black-suited waiters who look as if they're just waiting to be discovered by some international film-studio executive.'

His eyelids drooped fractionally, and his expression was deceptively indolent. 'You have a particular restaurant in mind?'

A soft bubble of laughter emerged from her throat. 'Yes. It will be interesting to discover if one particular waiter still works there. He displayed such flair, such panache.' Her eyes gleamed with irrepressible humour. 'Definitely *sigh* material.'

'And did he sigh over you?'

'No more than that attractive, scantily clad brunette is sighing at the sight of you.' She hadn't missed the veiled interest or the subtle preening as the slim-curved beauty displayed her perfect body.

Benedict's gaze skimmed to the girl in question, assessed and dismissed her, and returned to Gabbi.

'Pleasant to look at.'

'Is that all you have to say?'

His eyes were dark, slumberous. 'She's not *you*.'

A flippant response rose to her lips, and died before it could be voiced. 'Words are easy,' she managed after a long silence.

'There's an axiom about actions speaking louder than words,' he offered, and she held his gaze, suddenly brave.

'Maybe I need both.'

He leaned forward in his chair and surveyed her expressive features. 'A verbal attestation of love?'

Gabbi tried for nonchalance and failed. 'Only if you mean it.' She tore her eyes away from his and looked beyond the pink and white striped canopies fronting the terrace to the distant horizon.

It seemed as if she'd waited ages for this precise moment. But now that it had come she wasn't sure she was ready. The breath seemed locked in her throat, suspending her breathing, and she was oblivious to the people around them, the dull chatter of voices, the soft background music.

'Look at me.'

It was a softly voiced command she chose not to ignore.

His features appeared sculpted, the gleam of artificial and fading natural light accentuating the strong planes and angles, toning his skin a deeper shade and highlighting the darkness of his hair.

For one brief second she was reminded of boardroom meetings where a glance from those deep dark eyes could lance a colleague's façade and reduce him to a quivering, inarticulate fool.

'*Love,* Gabbi?' A slow, warm smile lightened his features, and she caught a glimpse of the passion, the desire. And the need. 'I don't want to spend a day, a night without you by my side. You're sunshine and laughter.' He took hold of her hand and brought her palm to his lips and bestowed an evocative, open-mouthed kiss on its centre. 'Warmth and love. Everything.'

Heat coursed through her veins, sensitising nerve

cells until her whole body was an aching entity demanding his touch.

The words that had lain imprisoned in her heart for so long seemed hesitant to emerge. She swallowed, and saw that his eyes followed the movement.

A faint smile tugged at the corners of his mouth. 'Is it so difficult to reciprocate?' he queried gently.

Gabbi looked at him carefully. She hadn't expected to find vulnerability in any form. Yet it was there, in his eyes. A waiting, watchful quality that allowed her a glimpse of his inner soul.

There was a sense of wonder in the knowledge that she was probably the only one who would ever be permitted to witness it.

'The first day you entered the boardroom,' she began quietly, 'it was the embodiment of every cliché.' An impish smile curved her mouth. '*Electric*. I don't remember a word I said. Yet your words stayed engraved in my mind. Every gesture, every smile.' She reached up and touched the palm of her hand to his jaw. 'When James invited you to dinner, I think I knew, even then, the idea formulating in his mind. It should have mattered. But it didn't,' she said simply.

Benedict watched the play of emotions in her expressive eyes. They held few secrets from him. Soon they would hold none.

'I fell in love with *you*. Not Conrad Nicols' son and heir. If I hadn't felt like that, I would never have agreed to marriage.'

'Yet you chose to establish a façade,' he pursued, and her eyes remained steady.

'Monique congratulated me after the wedding.' The

words were almost painful as she forced them past the lump in her throat. 'On winning an eminently successful husband. I hadn't realised marrying you was a competition, or that Annaliese had been a contender.'

The leap of anger was clearly evident in the depths of his eyes. 'You believed her?'

'It all seemed to fit.' Too well, Gabbi reflected. 'Monique is James's wife. I would never say or do anything to destroy his happiness.'

'I don't share your generosity.'

'I can afford to be generous,' she said gently. And it was true.

The light was fading to dusk. Already the candles were being lit outside on the terrace tables, and electric lamps provided a welcome glow.

A faint smile tilted the edges of Gabbi's mouth. 'Are you going to feed me?'

His features softened. 'We could always order Room Service.'

The smile deepened. 'The food is superb at the Sheraton Waikiki's restaurant.' Set on a high floor, the restaurant offered panoramic views from every window. She cast him a teasing glance. 'We could dance a little, linger over coffee.'

'If that's what you want.'

She laughed, a light, bubbly sound that echoed her happiness and deepened the teasing gleam in her eyes. 'It'll suffice, for a few hours.'

'And afterwards?'

'We have the night.'

A low chuckle escaped from his throat. 'Sounds interesting.'

Gabbi fought the temptation to lean forward and kiss him. 'You can count on it.'

She made no protest as he stood and pulled her to her feet. Then together they walked down to the main entrance and crossed the path to the Sheraton Waikiki hotel.

It was early, and there was a choice of several empty tables. Gabbi chose one by the window, and Benedict ordered champagne—Cristal.

The food was presented with imaginative flair, and each course was a superb attestation to the chef's culinary skill.

'Magical,' Gabbi declared as she glanced at the fairy tracery of lit high-rise buildings lining the darkening foreshore as it curved towards Diamond Head.

'Yes.'

Except Benedict wasn't looking at the view. A delicate blush coloured her cheeks at the degree of warmth evident as his gaze lingered on her features.

'Shall we dance?'

When they reached the dance floor he gathered her close, and she melted against him, unselfconsciously lifting her arms to link her hands together at his nape.

The music was slow and dreamy, the lights low, and she rested against him as they drifted together. Her body stirred, warming with the promise of passion.

It was quite remarkable, she mused, how she could almost feel the blood coursing through her veins, the heavy, faster beat of her heart. And the kindling fire deep within her that slowly invaded every nerve, every cell, until she was aware of nothing else but a deep, physical need for more than his touch.

Yet there was a certain pleasure in delaying the moment when they would leave and wander back to their suite. It heightened the senses, deepened the desire, and slowly drove her wild.

His breath whispered against her ear. 'Let's get out of here.'

She lifted her face and brushed his lips with her own. 'Soon.'

As soon as they reached their table a waiter appeared.

'Would you care for coffee? A liqueur?'

Benedict deferred the decision to Gabbi, and his eyes assumed a musing gleam when she agreed with the waiter that a liqueur coffee would be an excellent choice with which to end the meal.

It was late when they entered their suite, and Gabbi slid off her heeled sandals, then reached to loosen the pins confining her hair.

His hands closed over her shoulders and pulled her close, then he lowered his head and took possession of her mouth.

Heat suffused her body, bringing it achingly alive. A tiny groan emerged from her throat as his lips slid down the sensitive cord of her neck, teased the hollows, then trailed the edge of her gown.

Layer by layer they slowly dispensed with their clothes, and Gabbi stifled a moan as Benedict began a slow tasting of each breast before tracing a path down to savour the most intimate crevice of all.

She felt the initial wave of sensation and gloried in it, and caught the next, exulting in each successive contraction as she rode higher and higher before soaring over the precipice to sensual nirvana.

It was so intensely erotic that her whole body shook with emotional involvement, and afterwards she lay still, enjoying the gentle drift of his fingers over her skin.

With one sinuous movement she rose up and placed her lips against his, initiating a long, evocative kiss. Now it was his turn, and she took her time, treasuring each indrawn breath, every tensed muscle, the faint sound deep in his throat as she teased and tantalised.

So much power, harnessed, yet almost totally beneath her control. It was a heady sensation to take him to the brink, and see how long she could hold him there before he tumbled her down beside him.

His possession was swift, and she gasped at the level of his penetration, arching again and again as she rose to meet each deep thrust.

Afterwards he rolled onto his back, carrying her with him, and he cradled her close, his lips brushing across her temple as he trailed his fingers lazily up and down her spine.

'I love you.' She felt fulfilled and at peace. Gone were the agonising afterthoughts, the wishful longing for something more.

Benedict slid a hand beneath her chin and sought her mouth with his own in a slow, sweet kiss.

Afterwards she settled her head down onto his chest.

'Comfortable?'

'Mmm,' she murmured sleepily. 'Want me to move?'

Gentle fingers stroked through her hair. 'No.'

Gabbi smiled and pressed her lips into the hollow at the base of his throat. This was as close to heaven as it was possible to get.

'How do you feel about babies?'

'In general?'

'Ours.'

The fingers stilled. 'Are you trying to tell me something?'

Her lips teased a path along his collarbone. 'It should be a mutual decision, don't you think?'

'Gabbi.' Her name emerged as a soft growl, and she smiled.

'Is that a yes, or a no?'

'Of course—*yes*. The thought of you enceinte is enough to—'

A husky laugh escaped from her throat. 'Mmm,' she murmured appreciatively as she felt his length harden and extend deep within her. 'Such a positive reaction.'

Benedict's possession of her mouth was an evocative experience, and she sighed as she trailed a butterfly caress along the edge of his jaw.

'I'd like to continue my role with Stanton-Nicols. Flexibility, an office at home when I'm pregnant and afterwards…' She deliberated, her expressive eyes becoming pensive. 'Once the children are in school I'd like to return to the city. Part-time,' she added, knowing she'd want to be home to greet them, to be involved in their extra-curricular activities.

She indulged herself in a fleeting image of a small, dark-haired boy, a petite, pale-haired girl. Ball practice, swimming lessons, ballet, music, gymnastics. Homework. Walks in the park, picnics at the beach. Laughter. *Family.* And Benedict. Dear God, always Benedict at her side.

'I love you,' Gabbi reiterated quietly.

Benedict kissed her deeply, then slowly rolled until she lay beneath him. 'You're my life,' he assured her simply, and kissed her again.

She gave a satisfied sigh as he began to move, and she linked her hands together behind his neck.

Magic, she concluded a long time later as she lay curved close against his side. Sheer magic. The merging of two bodies, two souls, in a mutual exploration of pleasure. And love. *Always* love.

Margaret Way takes great pleasure in her work and works hard at her pleasure. She enjoys tearing off to the beach with her family on weekends, loves haunting galleries and auctions and is completely given over to French champagne "for every possible joyous occasion." Her home, perched high on a hill overlooking Brisbane, Australia, is her haven. She started writing when her son was a baby, and now she finds there is no better way to spend her time.

Look out for
OUTBACK FIRE by Margaret Way
In Tender Romance™, December 2001

GEORGIA AND THE TYCOON

by
Margaret Way

CHAPTER ONE

''EXCUSE me,'' Georgia said sweetly, grabbing for the rear door handle of the taxi and holding on for dear life.

''*My* cab, I think.'' He regarded her very coolly, his vibrant voice abrasive, conveying a fine disregard for long-stemmed blondes who demanded equal rights on the one hand and all the old female perks on the other.

''How do you fathom that?'' It came out with just the right note of wide-eyed astonishment.

''Try, I was here *first*.''

Georgia looked at him in some consternation, discovering he was in his early thirties, very tall, strongly built, impeccably tailored. So close to, she could see the fine grain of his tawny gold skin, the sheen of his black hair and the way his thick black eyelashes curved away from remarkable light eyes. He was certainly very handsome but of a type she had always disliked. The corporate dynamo. The decision maker. The power broker. Someone, in fact, like her father.

''As far as I'm concerned our race was a dead heat,'' she pointed out fairly. ''Maybe your hand touched down first, but that's only because you have a much longer arm.'' Long used to male indulgence, the last thing Georgia had expected was coming up against a brick wall.

"Why don't you just admit it. You expected me to back off."

Sparks flew around them, but still Georgia tried one of her melting smiles. They usually worked. "Look," she confided, "I'm running late and I have a *plane* to catch."

"Of course you do." His tone was crisp. "It so happens, so do I."

Damn! No sign of a breakthrough. He wasn't getting into the spirit of things at all.

"What's it to be, folks?" the taxi driver called. "There are a lot of hysterical people right behind you on the pavement."

"Sharing's fine." Georgia made the bright suggestion.

"Why don't you get in then." He looked down his arrogant straight nose at her. One saw them on Roman statues.

Georgia made a point of smiling sweetly. "Thank you *so* much," she said with exaggerated politeness. She ducked her blonde head, half wanting to tell the taxi driver to take off. At least the wretched man didn't try to sit beside her. He swung into the front seat beside the driver, very lithe and coordinated.

"Domestic, international?" he asked, giving her a brief searing backward glance. Or was that the eyes? They were grey. But shatteringly bright. Some might even call them silver. Not *pure* silver, of course. But close enough.

"Domestic, thank you," Georgia replied coolly, smoothing her long gleaming hair and looking out the window. "The Ansett terminal."

"Ansett for me, too," he told the driver as though further irritated by the fact they shared a destination.

Georgia moved closer to the window feigning interest in the swirling noonday crowds. What an objectionable man. He made her feel like a no-account social butterfly flitting madly all over town when she was a career woman with her own successful business.

She worked hard. Harder than any of her staff. *Too* hard, according to her doctor. Only a few weeks before, her immune system had temporarily gone on the blink when she came down with a severe case of winter flu. She hadn't recovered with her usual speed or vitality. On top of that she had broken up with Gavin. Gavin was a trial lawyer, a good one. But he'd brought his courtroom tactics to bear on her once too often. Most of the time he was just plain jealous. As there hadn't been any kind of basis for his histrionics, she'd thought it time to call it off. Not that it was really *working*. Gavin kept showing up with all kinds of displays of his affection. She was tired of sending back the flowers.

Up front the dynamo and the taxi driver were having an in-depth discussion about the China crisis. Deng Xiaoping. Who would fill the power vacuum. Both of them seemed to know a lot about it. When they got around to Hong Kong Georgia thought she might have something to offer but didn't feel like risking another one of those mind-bending stares. The minutes were ticking away, and she felt in danger of missing her plane. Not that it would be a catastrophe. She could simply fax Uncle Robert to say she'd been delayed.

Robert Mowbray was her mother's only brother and Georgia's godfather. It was he who had suggested she recuperate on Sunset, the tropical resort he owned and ran on that glorious Great Barrier Reef island. Just to think of Sunset was to have an instant vision of peacock blue skies, palm-fringed white beaches and a sparkling turquoise sea of incredible translucence. A few weeks of sea and sunshine, delicious food and exploring the breathtaking coral gardens should restore her in mind and body. She would be company for Uncle Robert, too, since he lost Dee, his adored wife and partner of thirty years. The whole family found it hard to believe Dee had gone. She had been such a bright, energetic person and wonderfully competent. Uncle Robert would be missing her dreadfully not only as his dearest friend and life's companion but as his partner in the business. There had been plans to build a nine-hole golf course on Sunset but without Dee it hadn't happened. Dee had always been full of life. Full of plans.

When she came out of her poignant thoughts Georgia saw to her relief they were clear of the city and into the suburbs. The two up front were now discussing big game fishing. Why didn't they stick to the really important things in life? To the extent she was trapped and had no place else to look she was struck by the attractiveness of the back of the dynamo's head. Not every man had such a shapely head or that smooth golden nape. She glanced away quickly. The sooner they were at the airport the better. She had more important things to do than study a man's nape with fevered attention.

Fifteen minutes later they arrived, splitting the fare.

Exactly. Right down the middle. Not a cent more or a cent less. At over six feet *he* had to fend for himself, but a porter charged to Georgia's assistance. She smiled as he loaded her two pieces of luggage. By the time they made it to the counter, the dynamo was there before her. A tall, indeed dominating figure in the queue. Their shared destination was a leading tourist town in North Queensland and a point of departure for several of the Barrier Reef resorts. A detail that annoyed her.

With any luck at all he would be going to Hayman, an international five-star. Sunset, though physically very beautiful with an extensive fringing reef and good accommodation, was considerably down-market from Royal Hayman.

In the boarding lounge Georgia sat as far away from the dynamo as she could. Something about him endangered her psyche. That striking appearance and vibrant voice didn't fool her. Men like that were rather more trouble than they were worth. Her father, a top businessman, though indulgent in his fashion, had never taken her mother seriously since the day they were married. There had been no sign he was going to take Georgia seriously, either, until the day she'd left home. So much for controlling males. Males for whom *the job* came first.

Georgia took a seat, crossing her legs. There were people everywhere. The flight had been fully booked. While the southern states of Australia still shivered, Queensland was paradise, especially north of Capricorn. Most of the passengers wore colourful resort clothes, obviously heading for the islands. To her right several young women were chattering excitedly about all the attractive guys they were going to meet. It didn't necessarily have to happen, Georgia thought, but she wished them well. One of the girls confessed in a very forthright, open way she had invested her last dollar on a fabulous wardrobe in the hope of catching a rich husband. Georgia was startled. It didn't sound in the least *romantic*. Besides, were there any millionaires left on the market? Surely most had been snatched up. For the third or fourth time, Georgia reflected she had met a tall, dark and handsome stranger in the past *hour*. From the way he looked and dressed he had money, as well, but all *she* had felt was hostility. It wasn't just that his type reminded her of her father. It was *personal*. A man-woman thing. Merely thinking about it made her direct a quick glance towards the far end of the room. At that moment the dynamo looked up from the open pages of the *Financial Review* to smile at a passing air hostess, a young woman he apparently knew. It was a smile of heart-stopping charm, quirky, sexy, white teeth against a tanned skin. It even had a real warmth in it. Georgia almost clicked her tongue in amazement. Obviously he wasn't as grim as she'd thought.

She turned back, realising in the next second this was going to be her day for incidents. A plump toddler with a fuzz of fiery curls, his face and hands covered in chocolate, made a staggering beeline for her, knowing, in the way children did, Georgia loved kids. Ordinarily she would have handled the situation easily, perhaps got into conversation, but she was dressed from head to toe in pristine summer white, a designer shirt and matching linen trousers.

Georgia stood up hurriedly, but despite her evasive

action there was no sign of parental intervention until the very last moment, when the child's father seized the boy up with a loud, "Ha, Josh! Mustn't put chocky on the lovely lady."

Josh roared his protest but was carried away nonetheless. There were plenty of witnesses to the little incident, including the dynamo, who gave Georgia another one of his high-intensity glances, this time spiked with undeniable black humour. It was obvious he had written her off as one of those vain creatures who lived in constant fear of having her outfits ruined. Georgia flicked her long hair away from her nape and resumed her seat, feeling a tingle of heat in her face. She realised she was taking this man a lot more seriously than he deserved. But then he appeared to be keeping a rather sharp eye on *her*. Maybe her father had sent him. It wasn't impossible. Though her father was fairly careful to keep his inquiries discreet, he had never stopped keeping tabs on her. The worst time had been when he hid himself in the back of her car.

All for nothing. She'd had absolutely no intention of going away with Gavin for the weekend. Her father had neither liked nor approved of Gavin, which may have been part of his attraction. That, and he closely resembled the American actor James Spader.

Georgia was busy writing a little note for herself when a male voice called, "Georgia, darling!"

It was an open display of affection in a public place. At least fifty people looked up, including the girls, who collectively sat forward.

"Gavin." Georgia felt a lurch of dismay.

"Darling." He flopped into the seat beside her,

puffing slightly because he'd needed to run. "Trish told me only an hour ago you were off to Sunset. I just jumped in the car and drove straight here. Risked a fine, as well. Something I don't need."

"Trish will be hearing from me," Georgia murmured, feeling betrayed.

"If you don't ask, you'll never know," Gavin told her with a grin. "Actually poor old Trish told me before she even realised what she'd said. I don't know why you keep her on. She's as thick as a brick."

"She doesn't have much to do with trial lawyers," Georgia said tartly. "Anyway, no one, absolutely *no one* makes better curtains, cushions, bedspreads, things like that."

"Hell, I didn't come here to talk about Trish," Gavin said, looking around at his captive audience much as he did in court. He reached out and touched Georgia's long hair, running a caressing hand down its long, shining length. "So, why all the secrecy, princess?"

Georgia raised her delicate brows. "Since you ask, it's no longer any of your business. We split up, remember?" Gently but firmly she pulled away.

Gavin looked into her eyes soulfully. "We didn't split up, my darling. you simply *panicked*. You've been ill, though you're starting to look your old gorgeous self. You're overworked. God knows *why*, when your father would give you everything you want on a silver platter. The job got on top of you. It *can* happen. We're still best friends, aren't we?"

"Sorry, no. But I suppose we could be friendly again one of these days." Georgia sighed. "I need space."

Gavin laughed. ''You're lying to me, doll. So tell me, how long do you intend to stay?''

''At least a couple of years.''

''I could do with a break myself,'' Gavin said slowly, thoughtfully.

''Sunset is absolutely full up.'' Georgia shook her head. ''I have it from Uncle Robert they're camping out on the balconies.''

''I don't think so, Georgia,'' Gavin said with an unblinking look. ''Word is Sunset's not getting the bookings these days.''

''A temporary thing.'' Georgia felt sad. ''Uncle Robert is missing Dee frightfully.''

''It can't be easy,'' Gavin said. ''What he really ought to do is sell.''

''That's out of the question. Sunset is Uncle Robert's life.''

Gavin stared at her for a moment, his good-looking face expressionless. ''That's rather a dumb thing to say, Georgie, and you're far from dumb.''

''Have you heard something I haven't?'' she challenged.

''I like to get a line on all your family, princess. Your Uncle Robert's in a few financial straits. Surely you know that?''

''Nothing he can't get out of,'' Georgia said heatedly. ''Why don't you mind your own business, Gavin, instead of running around like a private detective.''

''I don't have to run around, hon,'' he said casually. ''I simply have to pick up the phone. Investigating is part of my job. Anyway, look what I've got you.'' He reached into his breast pocket and withdrew a small velvet box.

''No!'' Georgia began to shake her head, realising what was coming.

''You haven't seen it yet.'' Gavin smiled complacently, opening it up and turning it towards her. ''Three months' salary. A full carat. For my one and only girl.'' He leaned forward and kissed her hungrily on the mouth.

''You expect us to become *engaged*?'' Georgia said when she was able, desperately trying to keep her tone quiet.

''Sure, sweetie. I'm counting on it.''

''I wouldn't have thought even *you* could be so thick-skinned.'' Anger was quickly overcoming Georgia's distaste for a public row.

''Georgie, I *know* you.'' Gavin's voice was pure courtroom. ''You like to cover up your feelings. But you *love* me. I know you better than you know yourself.'' Before she could stop him Gavin pushed his ring on her finger as though the very action settled the matter.

''What a bully you are.'' Despite herself Georgia flapped the ring back and forth. It was a very nice ring, but she pulled it off her finger and tossed it lightly in the air. ''I hope you kept your sales docket, because this is going back.''

It was too much for the group to the right. ''Isn't that *awful*!'' one of the girls cried.

''Just awful! The poor guy.''

''I'd never knock an engagement ring back myself,'' said a third.

Georgia began to wonder if they weren't going to make a chorus.

''You don't *mean* this, Georgie,'' Gavin protested, neatly pocketing the ring. ''You're just into being your own woman for a while.''

''Tell me about it.'' Georgia stood up determinedly as over the public address system the passengers were advised their flight was now boarding. ''I have to go, Gavin,'' she said. ''Forgive me if I've hurt you but you had no right to pull a stunt like that.''

Gavin's super confidence faded slightly, but characteristically he was unwilling to give up. ''We've had our troubles, Georgie, but you love me. That's the point.''

Georgia picked up her hand luggage. Gavin moved with her. ''How could you do this to me, Gavin?'' She felt she could hardly stand it.

''If I've upset you I'm sorry.'' The thing was he made it sound like an outright lie.

''You *know* we've split up yet you turn up here and propose. You got an audience, too, which is what you really love.''

The passengers were all converging on the door and Georgia tensed as she realised the dynamo was regarding them with a considerable degree of irony in his sparkling eyes. Perhaps he had seen her toss Gavin's ring away. The little ceremony had scarcely been private.

''I'll say goodbye now, darling,'' Gavin said, beginning to draw her into his arms. ''You'll be seeing me soon.''

Georgia pulled away, hardening her voice. ''I

won't lie to you, Gavin. That would be a big mistake."

"You'll feel better after a week or two." He gave her a look of endless patience, but Georgia shook her head dismissively and turned away. With nothing left to say, Gavin shot a quick glance at the tall dynamic guy he knew from somewhere or other. He even gave an uncertain, "Hi!" searching his mind for details. The guy nodded but didn't speak.

A few moments later Georgia was walking across the tarmac trying to control her feelings of upset and frustration. Men were such strange creatures. Most of them viewed women as *property*. Under her cool she was perturbed about what Gavin might do. Take his stunt today. She had made it perfectly plain their affair was over no matter *what* he did. Persistence was one thing, but this was harassment, wasn't it? At least in her eyes. She had never told Gavin she loved him. She had never slept with him, although she couldn't count the times he had begged her to. What *had* she seen in him? He could be funny, good company. He was good-looking, clever, if overly opinionated. There wasn't the slightest doubt he loved having her on his arm, but he'd shown no interest whatsoever in her career. As far as he was concerned, it fell into the none-too-serious bracket.

There was a fairly brisk cross wind blowing. Georgia put a restraining hand to her streaming hair, only to be pulled up short. The ends were caught in something. What? She turned quickly, feeling another tiny tug of pain.

"Hang on a moment." The dynamo was looking

at her with a hint of impatience. ''A strand of your hair is caught in my sunglasses.''

''Good heavens!'' Her tone suggested he had engineered it.

''One of the hazards of having a long mane, I should think.''

He was disturbingly close, his long, elegant fingers extracting a few shining strands from the section of raised gold on an arm of his expensive sunglasses. He must have been in the act of slipping them on or holding them up in the air.

''Caught like a nymph in a Greek legend,'' he said mockingly, then with another little tug freed her. ''Maybe a few split ends.''

''I won't worry about that.''

''And here *I* thought you wouldn't settle for less than perfection.''

''Looking good is part of my job,'' Georgia said crisply. ''Thanks anyway.''

He continued to keep pace with her. ''I seem to know your boyfriend. Would you mind telling me his name?''

''I don't pass out that sort of information to complete strangers.''

''Come on,'' he said with a scoffing inflection. ''I'm perfectly respectable.''

''I've lost track of the number of tricksters who fit into that category.''

''That's true.'' He sounded amused. ''One can't be too careful. It's all right anyway. I've just remembered. Gavin Underwood, the barrister?''

''Yes, and you know what *that* means.''

''No. Tell me.''

''You wouldn't want to tangle with him.''

''Really?'' This time he laughed. ''You don't seem to want to, either. You threw something. I couldn't quite figure out if it was a ring.''

''A fake, if you're interested.''

''It looked like a diamond ten rows away.''

''Maybe he got it cheaply in Hong Kong. Anyway, why all the questions?''

''Just idle chatter. Besides, we seem to be seeing rather a lot of each other.''

''Which is odd. I must have imagined your anti-social behaviour.''

''I've no idea what you're getting at.'' He looked at her.

''I think you do. It crossed my mind at one point I'd have to fight you for the cab.''

He gave a brief laugh. ''My feelings of outrage have undergone a change. Strictly speaking it's not *your* fault. I expect you've been indulged since the days your brown eyes peeped out of a shawl.''

''I have to admit to getting my fair share of notice,'' Georgia replied almost recklessly, ''but I don't think it spoiled me.''

''So I can't cite this afternoon?''

''No. I don't ordinarily fight over cabs, but I told you it was an emergency.''

''Well, we got here.'' He shrugged lazily. ''Don't worry about it.''

''I'm trying hard not to.'' Georgia felt genuinely rattled. ''Anyway, I think we're about to part company.''

''I wouldn't be too sure of it,'' he commented

lightly. "We're both forward. It's even possible we might sit together."

"I'm going first class." She knew in a split second so was he.

"I knew that the moment I laid eyes on you."

"Well, enjoy the trip." Georgia was surprised by her own turn of speed. This man was having an incredible effect on her. It wasn't often she lost her cool confidence, and she wasn't enjoying it.

A few minutes later, when she was comfortably settled on the plane, the air hostess paused beside her, as though she couldn't believe Georgia's luck.

"Yours is the window seat, Mr. Robards." She smiled brilliantly at the tall man just behind her.

"Thank you." The silvery eyes positively glittered. "You'd prefer the window seat, wouldn't you?" He addressed Georgia directly.

"I couldn't think of depriving you of it." Despite herself a powerful thrill spread through her.

"I insist."

"Very well." She wasn't about to press it. Robards. She knew that name.

"Please let me know if there's anything you want." The air hostess was still murmuring to him. Obviously she knew who he was. From his dark golden tan, he was probably a frequent commuter.

While he was settling himself Georgia glanced out the window, glad she had thought to bring a book, one of the courtroom genre she'd become addicted to. She even went so far as to take it out of her bag and settle it in the seat pocket in front of her. The last thing she needed was nearly three hours of highly charged conversation with the man beside her. It struck her she could fly to New Zealand in the time it took her to get from one end of Queensland to the other, and that left out the entire wilderness area of Cape York.

''Do you enjoy flying?'' he asked, as they gathered speed for the takeoff.

''I can think of things I like better.''

''Oh, Lord!''

The sarcasm again. ''I have no intention of bothering *you*,'' she said coolly. ''I'll call the hostess if a wing drops off.''

''If you think she can help. Actually I spotted the hostility between us an hour or so back.''

''And no improvement so far.''

''Obviously you believe in giving it to a guy straight.''

''I do, too.'' Georgia broke off to take a toffee the air hostess passed.

Moments later they were airborne, and the faint popping in her ears quickly stopped.

''There, that wasn't so bad.'' He gave her a brief sidelong smile.

''Landing is more dangerous,'' she pointed out. ''Look, you don't *have* to talk to me. I have a book to read.''

''You should have asked about it before you picked it up. I'd give it a four out of ten.''

''Then there's a distinct possibility I'll enjoy it.''

''I expect you like all that lawyer stuff because of Underwood?''

''Not at all,'' Georgia corrected him gently. ''*Despite* him, I'd say. And you? Don't you have work to do? Where's your laptop?''

''I left it at home. I'm on holiday,'' he said lazily.

''Royal Hayman?''

''Not this time. I'm off to Sunset.''

''Really?'' she finally managed to say.

''So help me out. Where are *you* going? Not Sunset by any chance?''

''Actually, yes.'' She didn't tell him of the connection.

''Why so glum? I do hope it doesn't have anything to do with me.''

''Don't be absurd!'' She eased forward and withdrew the thick paperback from the seat pocket.

''I think this is a simple case of starting off badly.''

''I won't argue.'' Pointedly Georgia turned to page one.

''I'm sure you'll guess who dunnit right off,'' he said, a sardonic sparkle in his crystal-clear eyes.

''Believe me, if *you* did, I will, too.''

He laughed, the most attractive sound she'd heard in a long while.

It was a full fifteen minutes before he spoke to her again, during which time the same air hostess wandered up for a little husky chat. Georgia, who was supposed to be reading her book, understood he was a regular commuter, unmarried by the sound of it, and clearly regarded by the airline as a VIP. They were almost at the end of their conversation before it suddenly hit her.

Robards.

Why hadn't she thought of it before? Anyone in the hotel business would know the name. Sam Robards was an enormously successful hotel magnate. Not that there had to be any connection. Sam Robards would have to be in his sixties. The dynamo was thirty-one or thirty-two at the outside. Anyway, the Robards chain was confined to the major capital cities and several provincial towns. She had never heard any mention they had interests in the north.

A short time later another attendant arrived with lunch, which they both declined, settling for coffee.

''Watching the calories?'' Georgia asked, as if she'd never seen anyone in worse shape.

''If I don't feel like it I don't eat.'' The silver-grey eyes mocked her. ''You look like someone with a passion for diet and the gym yourself.''

''I try to stick to a very healthy regime. I work out but I don't have time to get down to the gym. Generally I run.''

''I did notice your turn of speed,'' he said dryly. ''May I ask what you *do*?''

She shook her head, then changed her mind. ''I run a successful interior design business. What's your story?''

''What about names first?'' he suggested. ''I'm Link Robards.''

''Georgia Bennett. How do you do?''

He leaned back indolently in the seat, studying her profile. ''So you're a career woman?''

''Do you have a problem with that?'' She flashed him a cool look.

''Hardly. Why so toey?''

''I expect it's because I've spent years leaping to my own defence.''

''I wouldn't worry about it,'' he said in a sardonic voice. ''It must have helped. You obviously thrive on a challenge.''

"And I've decided *you're* a corporate dynamo."

"So who told you?" He lifted a mocking eyebrow.

"I've lived with one for most of my life."

"I take it you mean your father?"

Georgia nodded. "Much as I love him, he tried to thwart my ambitions at every turn."

"That must have been a frustrating experience," he said. "Your father's not Dawson Bennett, by any chance?"

"I was hoping you'd fill me in on *your* father," Georgia countered. "He's not Sam Robards, the hotel magnate?"

"I believe he has achieved that status."

"And you work for him, of course?"

"I'm right up there at the top," he said smoothly. "I have two sisters also in the family business, along with their husbands, a couple of uncles and several of my cousins. No one could accuse Dad of not being family-minded."

"And you never wanted to strike out on your own?" She knew her tone was too challenging, but he affected her that way.

He glanced at her in recognition, eyes narrowing. "There *was* a time." He paused, shrugging philosophically. "A few years out of university. An architect full of plans, but it all fell flat when my father had his first heart attack. He's had a triple bypass since, but it took quite a while before he was ready to raise hell again. His one request was for me to *be* there, to be ready to take over. In due course I will."

"But surely in your business you'd be able to use your skills as an architect?"

"To an extent," he agreed. "I have a lot of say. I

do my own thing. I respect my father enormously, but we don't always agree."

"So why are you dropping in on Sunset?" Georgia asked, starting to feel uneasy.

"I'm not allowed to?" His eyes were as hard as diamonds.

"I thought being in the business you'd go for the top of the range."

"Not at all. Besides, I've seen Sunset. It may need a major overhaul, but the island is very beautiful and so's the fringing reef. How come *you* picked it?"

Georgia gripped her book. "I've been there several times, and I always want to go back. I'm wondering, though, if *you* have some ulterior motive?"

"You think you're entitled to know?" He gave her another sharp look.

"It hardly matters, at this point. You know what they say. Strangers tend to confide in one another."

Her words made him laugh. "Mostly I don't tell anyone a *thing*! It has to be the flower eyes, soft and guileless as pansies. They should be at odds with your blonde hair but they're not. Don't tell me if you touch it up. I'd be terribly disappointed."

"Not with anything more drastic than shampoo and conditioner," Georgia said. "Hair and eye colour are my own."

"So *are* you Dawson Bennett's daughter? You don't sound too sure."

"For heaven's sake, of course I am." Georgia tossed her blonde hair. Something about him made her unbearably self-conscious. Aware of herself as a woman. "He was certainly there when I was born," she said. ''He raised me. We've been arguing for years. I am, in fact, his only child.''

''It looks like he took extremely good care of you.''

Georgia nodded. ''But he has very archaic ideas about a woman's place.''

''You mean, find a comfortable easy job until you're married?''

''In my case not even as adventurous as that. According to Dad it's *his* job to take care of my mother and me. I didn't actually *need* a job. My mother spends all her time visiting art galleries and antique shops, having lunches, going shopping, playing bridge. Filling in the time.''

''I'm not too sure what to say to that,'' he remarked, understanding in his voice. ''My mother does pretty much the same thing. Plenty of women in jobs might like to change places with them.''

''Well, I'm a little more ambitious than that,'' Georgia said, a sparkle in her eyes. ''I like to use what talents I have.''

''Did you train before you became an interior designer?''

''Are you patronising me?'' Georgia demanded, responding to the faint slash in his tone.

''Well, *yes*.'' His smile flashed like a bright light. ''At least until you get rid of that chip on your shoulder.''

''Lord, I *know*! But I've had some funny things happen to me. I doubt they would have happened to a male colleague. To answer your question, I did a Fine Arts course at university and later I worked for

Bobby St. George for a couple of years. You've heard of him, haven't you?''

''I have.'' His handsome mouth compressed. ''As an architect I have to tell you I dislike his interiors. Over the top, if you like.''

''I don't love them, either,'' Georgia admitted, ''but Bobby's an enthralling character. A professional through and through. He deserves to be at the top of the profession even if one doesn't go for knock-em-dead glamour.''

''I know a lot of better people than that,'' he said flatly.

''Well, you're going to be amazed to hear I won Young Designer of the Year when I was still with Bobby. The judges were very impressed with my use of colour, scale and detailing. They said I had a light, elegant hand.''

''Thank God for that!'' he said in a crisp voice.

''I can even go one better. I won Best Residential Interior last year. It was featured in at least two design and decorating magazines. Even my father sent out for copies.''

''If you tell me the issue I'll have my staff search it out.''

''I'm going back to my book,'' Georgia said disgustedly.

''Don't be like that. We're actually getting along rather well.''

''Aside from the little gibes.''

She was trying to find her page when the aircraft seemed to shudder then drop. Never the best of travellers, Georgia gave an involuntary little cry that abruptly cut out. She flailed in the air for something to hold onto, eventually settling on a strong supporting hand. She had never come to terms with hitting air pockets. Probably never would.

It was moments more before the aircraft levelled out, and Georgia started to wonder what the fuss was all about. "I just hate it when that happens," she remarked apologetically to the man beside her.

"I knew it would have to take a crisis before you'd grab my hand."

"Oh, I'm sorry." Her look was mortified. Her left arm was fully extended towards him, her hand locked in his. "Actually I had no idea I did that."

"If it makes you feel any better we could hold hands for the rest of the trip," he suggested.

"Forget it. My momentary panic is over," she confided though a thousand tingles prickled her skin.

He looked at her pale, slender hand for a moment before releasing it. "So there's nothing definite between you and Underwood?"

"I've asked absolutely nothing about *your* love life." Georgia gave him a severe look.

"What can I tell you? I'm not married."

"You're waiting for the right woman?"

"I've had to grapple with the possibility there mightn't *be* one."

"Well, you could present a formidable prospect to some. Not every woman can deal with corporate dynamos," she pointed out.

"It's pretty clear to *me* where your antagonisms spring from."

"It's a mistake to confide."

"And you do it so charmingly. Do you live alone?"

"I'm not in any relationship, if that's what you mean."

"I wondered about Underwood, that's all."

"You're *very* curious," Georgia returned.

"Not normally. But I haven't met anyone like you before."

"You must have." Her voice was laced with astonishment, a certain alarm.

"I'm sure I'd recall. Aside from all that, we're going to the same place. We're bound to run into each other."

Georgia didn't even try to keep the asperity out of her voice. "I admit it's a problem, but I'm there to relax, not for the social activities."

"My plans exactly." He settled his raven head and shut his eyes.

Georgia returned to her book, turning the pages for a full twenty minutes without taking in a word. Link Robards wasn't going to Sunset for nothing. His trip wasn't as simple or as innocent as that. There were a few possibilities. One was the Robardses were out to collect yet another hotel.

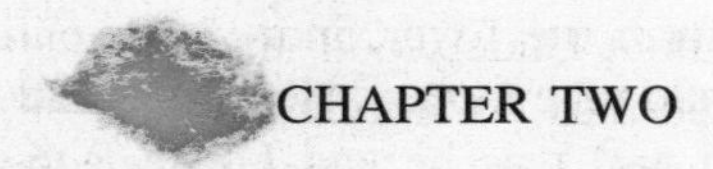

CHAPTER TWO

STANDING on her balustraded balcony, Georgia looked out over the dazzling tropical gardens to the fabulous crystal purity of the deep blue lagoon. Sunset was a glorious world. A world of seascapes and tropical flowers and plants. Towering coconut palms stood like sentinels in the grounds, at their feet beds of hibiscus of every known colour, with flowers of incredible size. There were countless other tropical plants, as well, flowers, shrubs, climbing vines all thriving prolifically in the year-round warm conditions. Everywhere Georgia looked she saw oleanders, frangipani, white ginger blossom, banks of gardenias, showy orchids and colourful bromeliads. In the shade of the water gardens grew wonderful ferns and aquatic plants. Dee had been acknowledged a great gardener. The grounds of Sunset were her living memorial.

Georgia hadn't spoken to her uncle as yet. He'd been busy when she'd arrived. They'd only exchanged a brief wave, but she expected he would pop in on her when he had an available minute. Though the grounds were as spectacular as ever, Georgia couldn't help noticing the hotel foyer badly needed refurbishing. There was a faintly scuffed look about the place. Even the furnishings in her room had seen better days. She would have to find out the full extent of her uncle's apparent plight. Perhaps she could help in some way. Georgia Bennett Interiors had been doing rather well of late. She knew perfectly well how she could transform the foyer, indeed the entire entrance, but it would take money. Her father had plenty of that. The sad part was he and Uncle Robert had never really got on, and Dee had been a great one for taking the mickey out of Dawson Bennett.

Georgia took another deep breath of perfumed air then turned to her room. There was a magnificent basket of tropical fruits on the sideboard and another of white orchids like a flight of butterflies on the coffee table. The warm temperature and the sea breezes were just perfect. She felt better already, full of energy. She hoped as a matter of pride her uncle had alloted Link Robards one of the best rooms. Possibly he had taken one of the six self-contained villas that gave directly onto the beach via the gardens and white coral paths. Her uncle had offered her one, but as she was coming as his guest she didn't feel happy about commandeering the hotel's best accommodation. A room in the main building would do her fine.

Georgia was hanging up her chic resort clothes when there was a knock on her door.

She flew to it, her face wreathed in smiles. "Uncle Robert. How lovely to see you."

"Georgie girl!" He, too, was smiling broadly, using his and Dee's pet name for her. "There's no one, but *no one* like you. You look absolutely enchanting."

"I promise you I was quite ill." She smiled.

"It doesn't show, dear. I'm sorry I couldn't be there to greet you. I wanted to but I had a VIP arriving."

''It wouldn't be someone called Link Robards?''

''Now how did you discover that?'' He swivelled in her direction.

''Simple. I met him on the plane. In fact we struck up some kind of rapport when we were both rushing for the taxi.''

''I see,'' he said with a slight head shake. ''I think he's looking the place over. In fact, I'm sure of it.''

''That was my guess, too. But it's not on the market is it, Uncle Robert?''

For answer her uncle sighed deeply, then went to one of the floral upholstered rattan chairs and slumped into it, his handsome, weathered face tired and worn. ''I'd be lying if I told you it's been easy going, Georgie. Sunset used to be my life, but it all means nothing without Dee.''

''I know.'' Georgia sat on the matching lounge near him. ''I feel for you, Uncle Robert, with all my heart. Dee was a wonderful woman. I know how much you meant to each other. It's only natural her loss has left an unfillable gap in your life. My life, too.''

''And no children.'' Robert Mowbray whipped out a handkerchief and polished his glasses. ''There *was* a time we were going to adopt. But then we bought the island, and the hotel became our child. It's sad, really. Only family matters. The great blessing was we had you, Georgie. Our godchild. How is my poor sister?'' He slipped his glasses on his nose.

''It's hard to know with Mum. She always says she's fine.''

''She could have had a much better life if she hadn't married Dawson,'' Robert murmured with some anguish. "She was such a *lovely* girl. Bright, too. None of us ever understood how she fell in love with such a domineering, difficult man. It's to your great credit, Georgie, you've shown him your mettle. You can stand on your own two feet. How's that barrister fellow, Underwood?"

She gave him a wry smile. "Fear no more. We've split up."

"I can't say I'm not pleased. So full of himself for a young man, and that courtroom voice. I always felt I had to explain myself. There's something I'd like you to do for me tonight if you wouldn't mind."

Robert Mowbray regarded his niece with a loving, grateful expression. "I've invited Link to have dinner with us. Myself and my niece. I thought it would be a nice gesture. I've met Link on a number of occasions. Conventions and the like. He's a very impressive young man. A brilliant architect, with all of his father's business acumen and drive. Sam had a major heart attack some years back. Someone told me he'd actually died, but there were paramedics on hand to resuscitate him. Big, handsome bloke, too. A bit of a rough diamond in the old days. He married Katherine Lincoln, a beautiful creature. To the manor born. Link got all the mother's class. Anyway you'd know that already. Would you help me out?"

"No problem," Georgia said, though her heart did a flip. "It might be a bit tricky. I didn't mention our connection."

"Any particular reason why not?" Her uncle peered at her.

"I wanted to remain incognito for a while. It struck

me although he said he was here on holiday it could be business, as well.''

''It would be unusual for them to want to do up an old hotel,'' Robert Mowbray said.

''Sunset is very beautiful, Uncle Robert. And it does have an extensive fringing reef. The coral gardens are marvellous.''

''There's that,'' he agreed. ''They haven't moved into the north, as yet. On the other hand it could be just as Link said. He wants privacy. A quiet time with no one to bother him. He looks a very athletic chap. I expect he wants to sail, go scuba diving and the like. He's not married, either, in case you're interested.''

''Now don't you start matchmaking,'' Georgia said. ''You know better than anyone I don't go for the corporate dynamo type.''

Her uncle looked at her for a few searching moments. ''You sound like you're confusing him with someone like your father.''

''The power brokers *do* have special qualities,'' Georgia pointed out with a wry smile.

''You must be looking at him differently. I find him charming. Courteous, too, which isn't always the case with the young lions. Anyway, I seem to remember he has some involvement with that Harper girl.''

''Tania Harper?'' Georgia experienced a rush of upset.

''She's the one who gets into all the social pages? Public relations director with one of Sam's hotels? Very glamorous creature with lots of dark hair.''

''I swear she's had it bonded like Diana Ross. He never mentioned a girlfriend.''

Her uncle shrugged. ''Then it can't be a big deal. A young man like that would have women swooning in a queue.''

''I'm afraid so,'' Georgia responded a little tartly, ''but he's definitely not *my* type.''

''That's what Dee said about *me*. But we were blissfully happy for over thirty years.'' Robert Mowbray stood up, very tall and spare with thinning fair hair. ''Now I must away, Georgie. I've got a number of things left to do. I want you to enjoy yourself while you're here. I don't want you paying for anything. You're here as my guest. Please remember that.''

''That's very generous of you, Uncle Robert,'' Georgia said gently. ''But there must be something I can do for you in return. Some area where my professional expertise might come in handy.''

Her uncle hesitated for a moment. ''The place *could* do with refurbishing. With guests moving in and out so frequently, things can become dilapidated very quickly. Dee used to attend to all that, as you know. I have to go now, but we'll speak of this again. Don't think I'm not proud of my clever niece. We may be able to work something out together.''

''What time this evening?'' Georgia asked.

Her uncle turned. ''Would around seven suit you? We could have a pre-dinner drink in the lounge, then dinner in the Hibiscus Room. It's our best restaurant. Mario's promised to come up with something really special. It might make it easier if I simply introduced you as strangers.''

''That's okay. I don't want him to think we've discussed him, anyway.''

''Until this evening then.''

"I'm looking forward to it," Georgia said with an unusual mix of excitement and trepidation. Some people, she realised, had the power to change lives. Link Robards was one of them. Of that she was totally sure.

She couldn't resist a late afternoon swim in the lagoon. She gloried in the crystal water and its fresh, exhilarating effect. For more than an hour she gave herself up to the sea's seduction. The collage of colours was marvellous. Beyond the exposed pinnacles of the reef, the sea was cobalt, the lagoon a lambent turquoise fading into a lovely aquamarine then apple green before it ran up onto the pure white beach that girdled the small crescent-shaped emerald island.

The Great Barrier Reef was a wonderland, but as breathtaking as were the seascapes Georgia couldn't wait to explore the coral gardens, a fantastic kaleidoscope of colours and intricate designs and home to brilliantly patterned fish and aquatic creatures of astounding variety and numbers. The waters of the reef teemed with life. She supposed the dynamo would organise some big game fishing for himself while he was here. She wanted to see the Outer Reef if she possibly could. The Outer Reef bore the full brunt of the mighty Pacific's waves, the seaward side pitching steeply into the dark depths of the ocean. The only thing was it was difficult to see. Conditions had to be just right.

She, Uncle Robert and Dee had walked it once when she was around twelve. She had never forgotten the incredible experience or the fear that the tides would suddenly overtake them and they would be stranded in the middle of the ocean. One could walk for miles along the exposed reef, but very few people were foolhardy enough to wander too far. She remembered how the French navigator Bougainville had been so perturbed by the sight of the thundering, foaming breakers crashing against the mighty submerged rampart he had sailed away from the unknown continent to the islands of the South Pacific. It was Captain James Cook flying the British flag who had finally managed to navigate the perilous waters of the Great Barrier Reef. Once inside he must have thought he was this side of Paradise. It was an incredibly beautiful part of the world.

When Georgia finally came out of the water, the sun was sinking in a ball of fiery rose gold. Sunset was a magical time, the sky a glory, the last golden rays caught in the great feathery crowns of the palms. Lightly she towelled her body, already drying in the soft, warm breezes. She would have to wash the salt water out of her hair, but that was no problem. For now she caught it into a Grecian knot, then as she walked up the sandy slope she broke off a beautiful deep pink hibiscus and stuck it into her coil of hair. It was almost the deep fuchsia pink of her clinging one-piece swimsuit. She had a few bikinis, as well, but she always liked the classic one-piece for real swimming. Her skin all over was the colour of cream, but in a day or two it would turn the palest gold. She never sunbathed in full sun, but she always managed to pick up a perfect light tan.

Through the thick screen of flowering shrubs and golden canes she could see the South Sea style villas. It occurred to her she would like to reinvent them in a way that created much more of a sense of mystery and magic. So many ideas were already formulating in her head. She was very good with colour. That was one of her great strengths. An established Sydney firm had handled the last lot of renovations some years before. Even as a student Georgia had found the treatment much too safe for such a glorious environment, where nature's colours glowed like jewels. It had to be said, though, they had to please Dee, who had leaned more towards the practical than creating brilliant and imaginative effects. But it was an island, after all. The colours could be as dazzling as the colours of the world around them. She had the perfect suggestion for the foyer, a giant cupola to flood the interior with light, perhaps a beautiful fountain and a water garden beneath, but it would put her uncle to too much expense.

Transforming environments from drab to successful always made Georgia happy. Even a different palette of colours would make an enormous difference. *Solid* colours, not the almost washed out patterns that really hadn't survived the test of time. What she saw were all the brilliant colours of sea and sky, the whole spectrum of blues, greens, violets, the hot pinks of the bougainvillea and lots of white to reflect the purity of the white sands.

The prints on the walls needed changing, as well. She knew a wonderful young Queensland artist, one of her favourites, who specialised in painting the brilliant flora and bird life of tropical North Queensland, enchanting work, a blend of realism with fantasy. Now was the time to commission him before his work became too pricey. Georgia was so engrossed in her thoughts she didn't see the tall, broad-shouldered, lean-hipped athlete loping down the coral path towards her until it was too late.

"So what is someone supposed to do around here?" Link Robards asked in that spiked yet so intimate voice. "Shout ahoy?"

She had been acutely aware of him on the mainland, but on the island his effect on her was nothing short of explosive.

"Surely you were walking into *me*?" Georgia pulled away almost violently, her sun-flushed body filled with a hot, peppery excitement. Even her skin felt singed where he'd touched her.

"As a matter of fact I did know you were on the beach," he admitted, silvery eyes cool as crystal. "I've been watching you sporting like a mermaid for the best part of an hour. Tell me, is it true you can breathe underwater?"

"Absolutely. For several seconds at a time." Considering how he was looking at her, Georgia was surprised how calm she sounded.

"From my vantage point it looked more like whole minutes." He towered over her, darkly, vividly handsome in white cotton trousers and a red and white striped casual shirt. "You look incredibly sensuous in that get-up."

"Tormentor." Her velvet soft eyes flashed. Sparks were flying wildly. In a moment she'd catch fire.

"I couldn't be more serious," he assured her. "I expect you know the hibiscus is the same colour as your swimsuit?"

"Actually it's a shade lighter." Georgia touched a hand to the large, brilliant flower, still in place.

"A tiny point, Miss Georgia. Dare I invite you to

have dinner with me one evening? Tonight's on my mind, but I'm afraid I'm tied up."

"Really? And you've only just arrived. How did you manage that?"

"Duty, if you like. A courtesy. I know the owner. He's a very nice man and a bit of a matchmaker, I suspect. He wants me to meet his niece."

"She could be gorgeous!" Georgia offered sweetly, determined to look just that.

"Or she could be ever so *ordinary*. Either way I don't have the time for romance."

"How so?" Georgia moved out of a slanting ray of sunlight into the exquisite green cool. "Surely you're often mentioned with Tania Harper? Not that that's much to go on."

His sparkling eyes narrowed. "You surprise me, mermaid. You really do. You denied any knowledge of me."

"Quite true. It's only subsequently I've put two and two together."

"They still don't make five," he answered bluntly. "I was totally uncommitted up to a day ago."

"So, has someone new come into your life?"

"She appears to be working on it," he said in a challenging voice.

Every line of Georgia's fine, slender body registered confusion. "I beg your pardon?"

"How do you know I meant *you*?"

He laughed. She could see he was laughing at her. "It can't be *me*," she protested. "I can't *stand* men like you. Now if you don't mind, Mr. Robards, I'd like to get past."

He moved instantly, sunlight gilding his tawny

skin. "The path *is* rather narrow. Romantic, too, if one cares for that sort of thing. Mercifully we don't. I only planned a stroll before dinner. Not an assignation. The sunset is quite glorious in this part of the world."

Georgia nodded, shouldering into her matching cover-up. *Too late*. "Can I ask you something?" She turned and looked at him. Odd little ripples were moving down her spine. And no denying them, either.

"Go right ahead." There was a trace of mild sarcasm.

"Why are you *really* here?"

His mouth firmed, and he raised his handsome head. "I take it you don't believe a *holiday*?"

"As a matter of fact, I don't."

He reached out abruptly and plucked the hibiscus out of her hair. "So what has it got to do with you?" The silver eyes were studying her very intently, brilliant against dark hair and skin.

"Nothing, really. I'm only using my intuition on this. You might as well tell me."

"I'm sorry, Georgia," he drawled. "I don't know you nearly so well."

He smiled just like a tiger, she thought.

"Well, it was worth a try." She gave him a little mocking finger wave. "Enjoy your stroll."

"May I call you?"

Georgia walked a few paces up the sandy slope before she turned. "I don't know yet. What would you want to say to me?"

"Hello, Georgia. That sort of thing."

"Then I guess that isn't a problem. I'm like you. The last thing I have on my mind is romance."

''Because of the big affair with Underwood?'' He tilted an eyebrow.

''That could have something to do with it. And it wasn't any big affair, either,'' she added hotly. ''So you don't have to sound so nasty.''

''Nasty! My dear Miss Bennett, how extraordinarily touchy you are. On the whole you *do* need a holiday. It might make sense if we stuck together. Mutual protection and so forth. I couldn't help overhearing Underwood mention he'd see you soon.''

''I'll figure out a way to stop him.'' Georgia tilted her chin. ''Anyway, you may change your mind about sticking together when you meet the owner's niece.''

The silvery eyes flicked over her. ''I don't think so, Georgia,'' he said in a voice that made every bone in her body melt. ''Ciao for now.'' He moved off, whistling melodiously that hit song of the Seekers from so many years before. It followed Georgia all the way from the beach.

She spent more time than usual dressing for dinner, in the end choosing a silk georgette toga-style dress that was like a caress on the body. The moulded ankle-length skirt split to show her legs. With it she wore gold sandals that laced up the leg on a classic Roman design. The colour of the dress was especially beautiful, neither blue nor violet but somewhere in between. She experimented with several hairstyles, looking to continue the theme, but finally decided on her usual straight shining fall.

She was going to a lot of trouble to make an impression on a man she knew could only endanger her, but there it was. Memories of those minutes on the coral path flooded her, the golden heat, the air full of sparks, the powerful effect he had on her. She had to face up to the fact she attracted him much as he made an ironic joke of it. These things did happen. The great thing was to be aware of it and take the appropriate defensive measures. Or so she told herself, applying a touch of heavenly fragrance.

As she entered the lounge every male head in the place shot up except the head of Link Robards, who had his back to her. Georgia threaded her way gracefully between the chairs, smiling at her uncle, who sprang to his feet, his face alight with love and pride.

"Georgia!" he called.

If he hadn't guessed beforehand, he certainly knew now. Georgia watched Link Robards rise to his impressive six three, turning courteously at her approach. For a spit second he let his true feelings show, then his dynamic face resumed its cool, practised charm.

"Georgia, darling!" Robert Mowbray kissed the smooth, flawless cheek Georgia presented. "You look lovelier than ever. May I present a young man who's behind the very best the hotel industry can offer. Link Robards. My niece, Georgia Bennett, Link. She runs her own interior design firm."

"How very clever and enterprising of you, Miss Bennett." Suavely Link Robards took Georgia's hand, applying just a little more pressure than was warranted.

So that was how he was going to play it. "I don't think I could possibly match *you*, Mr. Robards." Georgia gave him an admiring smile that didn't fool him one bit.

"Link, please," he insisted. "My name is actually

James, but my mother called me Link right from the beginning. She was Katherine Lincoln.''

''Why, thank you for sharing that with us, Link.'' Georgia sat in the chair her uncle held for her. ''And what do you actually *do* in the hotel industry?''

For an instant her uncle looked perplexed. Both Georgia and Link Robards were smiling, but there was a trace of something like smoke in the air. ''Link is right-hand man to his father, Sam Robards, Georgie,'' he explained, trying to catch her eye. ''I don't need to tell you who Sam Robards is, I'm sure.''

''Oh, *sorry*!'' Georgia touched Link's cream-jacketed arm impulsively. ''The hotel tycoon, of course. I think that's marvellous.''

He glanced at her with a don't-play-dumb-with-me expression. ''It is as a matter of fact.''

''Georgie, what would you like to drink?'' her uncle intervened hastily, unsure just exactly what was going on.

''A glass of champagne would do nicely.''

''You have something to celebrate?'' Link Robards asked as his host turned away to attract the attention of the waiter.

''Catching *you* on the wrong foot. If only for a moment.''

''I shouldn't be surprised.'' He sounded like it was obvious she had emotional problems.

''But you *were*?''

''I might do the same to you some time,'' he said with soft menace.

''We're getting a steady flow of guests into the lounge,'' Robert Mowbray remarked with satisfaction, turning to them. ''Things were a little slow last month.''

''You should put your niece's photograph on all your brochures,'' Link Robards suggested.

''She'd be perfect,'' Robert Mowbray agreed happily. ''And she's so passionate about water sports.'' He immediately launched into a story about Georgia's brilliant sporting career since pre-kindergarten days. ''Why, she could swim when she was barely two.''

''Neptune's daughter. She's even wearing her goddess dress.''

''You like it?'' Georgia met the glittering diamond-hard eyes.

''Miss Bennett, your beauty takes my breath away.''

A fraught fifteen minutes later they went in to dinner. Robert Mowbray was called away temporarily almost as soon as they'd ordered.

''You're annoyed with me, I suppose?'' Georgia flashed a look at the striking dark profile. Already he'd picked up extra colour.

''Come on,'' he said crisply, ''why wouldn't I be?''

''It was a harmless enough—''

''Deception?'' he cut her off.

''I was going to say *charade*.''

''To get me to talk?''

''About what?''

''Don't play the pansy-eyed innocent. I'm not impressed.''

''Then that's a shame. I could have mentioned the connection, but the moment passed.''

''At least you were right about the *gorgeous*,'' he

taunted her. "Tell me, did you get yourself up tonight with me in mind?"

"Whatever do you mean?" She gave him a regal stare.

"That dress doesn't leave any possible doubt what shape you're in." He studied her dryly. "If it's at all possible, it's a damned sight more seductive than the swimsuit."

"I'm always trying to look my best," Georgia said calmly.

"So I've got lots more to look forward to?"

"You're not worried, are you?"

"I'm enjoying it, as a matter of fact. As long as we can keep our relationship fairly casual."

"*What* relationship?" Despite herself her voice rose.

"Well, fate has rather shoved us together. Tell me, were you trying to get some information out of me to pass on to your uncle?"

"Mr. Robards, in this business, it's each man for himself."

His mouth twisted in a sardonic smile. "Really? You didn't seem so hard-headed to me."

"While you're the corporate dynamo," she retaliated. "That's largely why I'm so hostile towards you."

"There, now," he said maddeningly. "Your father must have given you a rough time."

"In many ways, I regret to say yes."

"But you've survived."

"Not only that, I've made my way. All on my own."

"Do I detect yet another challenge?"

She glanced quickly at him then away again. That blazing dark vitality. It made her feel almost giddy. "A simple statement of fact."

"Are you sure?" His voice had that abrasive quality again. "You've been dashing yourself against me ever since we met."

"So we've agreed I have a problem." Her heart seemed to be thudding. "I wonder what's keeping Uncle Robert?" She sounded almost plaintive.

"I realise you're nervous."

"I am not!"

"Then what are those tiny little tremors in your fingers?"

Of course he was aware of her tension. "I think it has something to do with the way you're looking at me."

"Georgia, you're a woman men look at," he explained patiently. "Long blonde hair. Big brown eyes. Flawless skin. You'd stop conversations even without the beautiful feminine body."

"Be that as it may, no one else makes me want to turn and run."

"So what was it I witnessed at the airport?"

"I *told* you, Gavin and I are no longer an item," she said with a touch of heat.

"That's good, because you're better off without him," he said bluntly.

"You think so? And you've only seen him once."

"On the contrary. I was in court when he got that con man Jack Ullman off. I was a prosecution witness."

"When was this?" Georgia turned a perturbed face to him.

"I take it you don't know about it?"

"I vaguely remember the case. Gavin was thrilled about the outcome."

"He must have half the Mob calling on him." Contempt crossed his face.

Georgia paled a little. "Are you telling me it was a wrong decision?"

"It all came down to how the evidence was gathered. Ullman was as guilty as hell. He got off on a technicality. All his victims knew that. A few days later one of them committed suicide. Ullman took his money and sent him to the wall."

"I'm so sorry." Georgia swallowed, somewhat daunted by his demeanour. "But Gavin was only doing his job."

"He used the law to get a guilty man off."

"We all know it happens from time to time. I can't do much about it. It's an imperfect world. Gavin's a defence lawyer. I wouldn't care to defend someone I thought guilty myself, but someone has to do it."

"I realise that, but I wouldn't have found a verdict like that something to rejoice over."

"I suppose not." Georgia dropped her eyes. "Anyway, I've learned a few truths of my own about Gavin. He's in the past."

"I don't think he intends to stay there." His look was both level and deep.

"If he wants to hold on to his career, he will. I don't intend to be harassed."

"Good for you." The words were terse, holding a remembered anger.

A few moments later Robert Mowbray returned, apologising for his absence. "One of our more difficult guests,'' he explained. ''The little boy was missing.''

''Missing?'' Georgia was dismayed. ''You found him, didn't you?''

''Don't worry so, Georgie.'' Gently her uncle patted her hand. ''The little scamp was hiding, that's all. I think myself as a way of gaining attention. The father is a very serious sort of chap. Very self-engrossed. He's quite well known in the musical world, I believe. A pianist and composer.''

''Not Adam Caswell?'' Link asked quietly.

Robert Mowbray blinked behind his glasses. ''I suppose I should keep it confidential, but seeing it's *you*, Link, yes. No sign of a wife. Father and son are here by themselves.''

''How old's the little boy?'' Georgia searched her uncle's face.

''Around six or seven. A problematic little fellow, I would think.''

''Probably he has reason to be,'' Link Robards remarked. ''It's no secret the marriage isn't working. A child would take that very hard.''

''Poor little boy.'' Georgia's voice was sad. ''It's funny—'' she began then abruptly stopped.

''What's funny?'' Link Robards followed it up, his look long and thoughtful.

''Oh, nothing. Better leave it.''

''It sounded as though it might be important.''

''How would you know that?'' She was really starting to feel he knew her too well.

''I've been studying you very carefully.''

''What, exactly? The emotional content of my conversation?''

"Among other things." He smiled.

Its effect on her was like being on a roller-coaster, and she hadn't been on one for years. Even the arrival of the first course came as a very necessary breathing space. Georgia had decided on the wonderful reef oysters steamed with ginger, shallot and chilli, and both men chose entrees of roasted reef fish with a Thai sauce. Georgia saw to her satisfaction the food was beautifully presented and tasted even better. Whatever else needed changing, it wasn't the chef, she thought thankfully.

All in all, it was a remarkably pleasant evening. They all settled on various seafood dishes for the main course. In such a part of the world it was impossible to go past the marvellous bounty of the sea. Mindful of her figure, Georgia delicately waved away any notion of dessert, but like most men her uncle and Link Robards had a sweet tooth, and made their selections from the delectable pastries on the trolley. Not that either of them carried a superfluous ounce for it, she thought with a twinge of envy.

The conversation ranged over a number of subjects, interesting and pleasant, nothing too profound. At no time was the possible fate of the hotel mentioned. Nor did Link Robards elaborate on his reasons for being there. Afterwards Robert Mowbray excused himself, and Georgia and Link were left together in the foyer.

"It's early yet," he said. "Would you like to go on to the nightclub?"

"Why not?" How easily rash decisions were made.

Inside the Hideaway a slightly passé chanteuse was singing the blues, an old Peggy Lee number. Her voice was very deep and throaty, and she was almost swallowing the mike.

"What do you make of that?" Georgia asked, sliding into an empty banquette.

"Marginally better than the bagpipes?"

"That's a little unkind." She looked at him, brown eyes reproachful.

"You started it. Now, what are you having to drink?"

"Mineral water with a twist of lemon."

"You certainly do things in style."

"I had two glasses of wine with dinner. That's all I allow myself."

"What a boon you are to society."

"*I* think so. There ought to be more like me."

"Modesty, Miss Bennett."

"I'm that, too."

"And so young to be so successful."

"I'm doing well, but I've a long way to go."

"*Bobby* can't speak highly enough of you," he said like a provocateur.

"Have you been checking up on me?" Georgia demanded.

"I do it all the time."

"You actually spoke to Bobby St. George?" Her eyes were huge in her creamy face.

"I didn't go so far as that. My mother looked you up."

"What?" Georgia felt like pounding the table.

"There's no need to look so perturbed. It was all very flattering."

"And what exactly was it in aid of?" She searched his face angrily.

"It crossed my mind you might try talking your uncle into refurbishing the hotel. Georgia Bennett Interiors hoping to get the commission, of course."

"Uncle Robert wouldn't be doing me any real favours. I really do know what I'm about. What's it to you, anyway?"

"I really like your uncle. I can see what a depressed state he's in. I haven't the slightest doubt you're as talented as you're beautiful, but your uncle might be taking a big risk allowing a virtual unknown with little corporate experience to take on a big and complex commission."

"So it's all altruism, is it?"

"Quite a degree of it."

"With the Robards's interests hidden behind a smokescreen?"

"I told you, I came here for a holiday. It's my nature to look around."

"I do recall your saying the place needed a major overhaul."

"Do you disagree?"

She looked at him resentfully. "Oh, darn, you know I don't. You're quite right about Uncle Robert's depression. He and my late aunt were a devoted couple. When one is heartbroken it's difficult to take note of the surroundings. Dee always took care of the day-to-day maintenance. Uncle Robert managed the financial side of things."

"Then you know the hotel's losing money?"

"One doesn't have to be a corporate dynamo to realise that," she said tartly. "Uncle Robert has lost heart."

"And I understand entirely. I care about *my* father.

His heart attack was a major trauma. I can imagine how shocking sudden death can be.''

Georgia bent her head, and her hair fell around her face in a shimmering blonde curtain. ''Frankly I don't know how he's standing up to his loss at all. He and Dee did *everything* together. They had no children.''

''They had the next best thing. They had you.''

''The three of us were very close.''

''I can see the love you have for each other.'' He reached out and tucked her long hair behind her ear. ''*Hello*, Georgia.''

''Hello, James.''

''Don't you dare.'' His voice was faintly rough and incredibly sexy.

''James is a nice name. It's a bit too tame for you, though.''

''Well, Georgia's just right for you. When we get to know each other better I hope you allow me to call you Georgie.''

''I'm sure you'd only turn it into a joke.''

''What wrong with a joke now and then?''

The singer finished her bracket of songs, and they both clapped politely. ''Where the heck's the waiter?'' Link asked.

''Maybe he got restless and went out for a swim.''

''Well, if the mountain won't come to Mohammed I guess I'd better go to the bar.'' He stood up and looked at her, the vivid, mettlesome, stunning male. ''Still with the mineral water?'' he asked dryly.

''Absolutely. What does Tania do? Toss off a few rums?''

''As I recall she goes for concoctions. Things with little purple umbrellas and great chunks of fruit.''

''How do you stand it?'' Georgia cast her eyes heavenward.

''Tania Harper, I have to tell you, is hotly pursued.''

''How come she hasn't landed you?''

''I've been a contented bachelor for years,'' he said, a diamond dazzle in his eyes.

''All that has to *change*, James. The years are going by, and the dynasty must be secured.''

''Would you like me to consider you?'' he asked brazenly.

She shook her head. ''The *very* last thing in the world I need is a high-powered husband. But I would like that cold drink.''

He flashed her another one of those heart-stopping smiles. ''Comin' up, ma'am.''

CHAPTER THREE

GEORGIA awoke to a wonderful sense of well-being, a tingling anticipation of what the day might bring. It was just after seven but already the light was dazzling, illuminating a huge, blue glazed pot of yellow marguerite daisies on her balcony. There were hundreds of radiant heads, and Georgia found the sight enchanting. Bird calls sounded all over the island, a carolling counterpoint to the eternal song of the sea. The birds' colours were exquisite amid all the green.

She turned on her back, luxuriating in the knowledge she was on Sunset and didn't have to fly out of bed for an early morning appointment somewhere across town. Felicity and Martyn, her two assistants, would hold the fort for her. She deserved this break even if she could only manage ten days. In some ways she realised she was a workaholic like her father, but she knew she would never possess his stop-at-nothing ruthlessness to achieve his ends. The shocking truth was Georgia both loved and loathed her father. Her biggest sense of outrage, of powerlessness was reserved for her mother. Her parents had stayed together all these years, but Georgia was of the strong opinion her mother should have packed up and left long ago. She had won her own independence at a price. Her mother was still a prisoner in a gilded cage, an ornament to take out and display on all the right social occasions, but forgotten for most of the time. It wasn't as though Dawson Bennett had been faithful, either. Georgia and her mother both knew of his many transitory affairs. But her father wanted no part of divorce. He was married to a beautiful, refined, wealthy wife who long ago had elected to sublimate her will to his. The only thing her mother *had* been adamant about was Georgia's right to love and be loved by her grandparents and uncle.

Even that hadn't been easy, because Dawson Bennett bitterly resented any attention being directed away from him. *He* was to be the centre of his family's world. But Georgia had always loved her uncle Robert. Dee had occasionally put their close relationship at risk by openly questioning Dawson Bennett's opinions and judgments, delivered as they were from a position of pre-eminence. Dawson Bennett hadn't liked it, always referring to Dee as a woman who had "too much to say for herself." As a consequence Georgia had been refused permission to see them for months at a time. At these times Dawson Bennett praised his wife, who had "known her place" from the very beginning of their marriage.

In her early teens, when Georgia began to truly grasp her beautiful mother's entrenched sense of worthlessness, she began to press her to take action to resist her father's very real domination. But her mother could see no solution to her problems. She had married for better or worse, she told Georgia. Privately, Georgia considered her mother's spirit had been broken.

As always when Georgia began to think of her parent's marriage her mood became depressed. She couldn't allow that to happen at the very start of her holiday. Her mother had chosen her path in life. Georgia was determined the same thing wasn't going to happen to her. She leapt out of bed, deciding on an early morning run before breakfast. Her body was much admired, but it hadn't been achieved without discipline—watching what she ate and a daily exercise program. She was by no means a fitness freak, but she really did miss her daily run if she didn't go for some reason. Uncle Robert hadn't been exaggerating when he'd told Link Robards about her sporting prowess. As a schoolgirl she had dominated pool and track at her excellent fitness-oriented girls' school. In fact her friends had nicknamed her Atlanta after the fleet-of-foot goddess and the fact her Christian name was Georgia.

Dressed in a pink tank top and matching shorts, pink and white joggers on her feet, her thick blonde hair braided, Georgia studied herself in the mirror. She looked pretty good. Ready, in fact, for a three-mile run. The last thing Link Robards had said to her was, "I'll call you in the morning." She wasn't about to sit around waiting. The terrible irony was she was tempted. Attraction was like a monster. It gobbled up all one's natural caution.

For an hour Georgia ran, the sea breeze at her heels. She took the trail that encircled the island, meeting up with several other joggers, passing them with a wave, all the while looking out at the sparkling blue sea and the dreaming coral cays. One day she intended to have a picnic on Tryon, an unhabited coral cay she had been visiting since age ten, when Uncle Robert and Dee had taken over Sunset. Tryon was located on the windward side of Sunset, but was in easy striking distance when the tides were right. Tryon carried a light covering of trees and palms in addition to succulents and grasses, so there was plenty of shelter, but no water. It had been the Treasure Island of her childhood, mainly because Uncle Robert and Dee had always planted some little surprise for her to find. Usually she had come to Sunset alone. Her father had visited only once or twice, making non-stop criticisms as though Uncle Robert and Dee were his employees. Her mother only had to mention she might accompany Georgia on a visit for Dawson Bennett to find some pressing reason she shouldn't. Her place was by his side, not gallivanting up north.

On her return run, when she was nearing the hotel, Georgia veered off towards the beach. She unlaced her joggers and ran down to the lagoon. She dearly would have liked to walk straight into the water, but as she wasn't wearing a swimsuit, she settled for splashing herself generously with salt water. She had worked up a healthy sweat, so the blood ran clearly beneath her translucent skin, causing it to glow. The effect of the cold water was wonderfully bracing, and she continued to splash it over her face and throat so it ran down the upper slopes of her breasts and into the cleft. Her light sports bra and tank top were getting soaked. Had it been Tryon, with only the seagulls and noddy terns for company, she could have stripped off her clothes, but as it was her swim would have to wait. With a single quick motion she freed her braid, and her hair was caught by the wind and sprayed out all around her in long skeins of silk.

''Neptune's daughter!'' someone called.

She recognized the voice. Smooth, assured, damn near hypnotic.

Link Robards.

Georgia turned, her heart kicking in like a motor. This man was something else! He was moving lithely over the sand, a tall and powerful figure in a swimsuit of dark tartan. Irresistibly he evoked a piece of sculpture, something heroic cast in bronze, broad-shouldered, deep-chested, tapering to the long, clean, narrow lines of the athlete. Everything about him turned her inside out.

"I'd thought of catching up to you on your run," he said as he drew closer, "but I didn't want to break your concentration." His sparkling glance held her in place while he studied her face, then the near drenched shirt that outlined so clearly the curves of her breasts. It was as if he knew how her flesh felt, its smoothness and texture. She needed to spin veils to protect herself.

"As a matter of fact I think you'd find it difficult to keep up with me," she retorted. "How did you know I went for a run, anyway?"

"I was up fairly early myself. Had a swim, did a bit of exploring and there you were! Running like a gazelle up the trail. Why didn't you wear a swimsuit?"

And have you send what's left of my composure up in flames? Ah, no!

Georgia turned her gaze to the lagoon and managed to sound casual. "I was thinking that myself."

"So what have you planned for us today?"

He hadn't moved an inch, yet she felt she had lost

her own body space. The two of them might just as well have been enclosed in a giant bubble.

"I haven't planned anything." She shrugged, momentarily nonplussed.

"I thought we agreed it would be best to stick together."

"I said nothing of the kind."

"You can't talk your way out of it, Georgia," he teased. "Besides, there are endless possibilities. What about scuba diving off the reef?"

"Do you usually get what you want?"

His brief laugh held the suggestion of irony. "Like you, I've been spoiled."

"I don't know that *I've* been spoiled," she said, thinking of her dysfunctional childhood.

"I'm ready to listen." Very gently he reached out and pushed a long strand of hair behind her ear. In the process his hand brushed her cheek.

"Actually I don't need anyone to straighten me out." She swallowed against the sudden rush of sensations.

"Talking about it might help. It's odd how we keep the most important things about ourselves secret."

She turned her head away. "Link, I don't know you. I don't know that I trust you, either."

"When I'm more trustworthy than most. Your friend Gavin, for one," he said bluntly.

"Let's leave Gavin out of it." Her voice picked up heat.

"I don't think he's going to give you the chance. That's only *my* opinion, of course. You know him so much better."

"I find it extraordinary you should be concerned."

"Actually it's taken *me* by surprise, as well. I think it has something to do with the fawn's eyes. Behind the softness there's *hurt*."

"You see that, do you?"

"Very clearly." Something in his smile wrung her heart. Lord, did she show it so badly? Her emotional deprivation?

"So are we going diving or not?"

She could have drawn back. There was time. Instead she found herself saying, "Why not? It'll give me an opportunity to show off."

Back in her room Georgia took a quick shower to cool down. Link Robards was having an incredible effect on her, a mixture of caution and excitement. She felt charged. Full of energy and passion, even when all the warning bells were going off.

On her way to breakfast her progress was arrested by a curious sight. The contents of a laundry basket standing outside one of the empty rooms were stirring and bunching as though they had come alive. Georgia had one panicky moment thinking of snakes, but of course there weren't any on the island. She stepped out valiantly, wondering if it could possibly be a pet that belonged to one of the staff. If so, it had no place playing near the guestrooms, much less hiding in a laundry basket.

She peered into the empty room, expecting to see a maid going about her business, but there was no one around. She turned back and picked up a long-handled duster standing against the wall. A few exploratory pokes should do it.

The cry that resulted took her by surprise. No bark, but a loud little-boy squeal. Georgia threw back the laundry, her astonished eyes meeting those of a child around six or seven. Beautiful sapphire blue eyes stared up at her from beneath a thick, dark, shining fringe sitting flush with his eyebrows. The classic ''puddin' basin'' cut.

''Well, really!'' she said. ''You nearly gave me a heart attack.''

''I'm sorry.'' He grinned at her as though sharing a good joke.

''That's all right. All's forgiven. Do you need a hand getting out of there?''

''No way!'' He sent the basket crashing to the floor, then rolled out.

''What were you doing, anyway?'' Georgia helped him up.

''Just having a bit of fun. Dad's asleep and I'm bored.''

''Well, you can't play in the laundry baskets.''

''I won't anymore. I just got the idea when the cleaning lady moved off.''

He was a very thin little fellow but undeniably cute, with a look of high intelligence that sat oddly on his narrow shoulders. He wasn't dressed for the beach, either. More like he was about to give a violin recital, right down to an incredible bow tie.

''So what's your name?'' Georgia asked, curious and intrigued.

''Leon.'' He gave her a smile like a magic wand.

''How do you do, Leon, I'm Georgia.'' Georgia held out her hand, and the little boy shook it with considerable aplomb. ''Leon's an unusual name. I like it.''

"Mummy's idea. I was born in August. You know, Leo the lion?"

"I sure do." Georgia smiled. "I'm another one. Isn't that nice?"

"Yes. It makes us friends."

"Good, so we can talk. What room are you in, Leon? Are you with your parents?"

The little boy unexpectedly dropped his head. "Mummy doesn't live with us anymore."

"Oh, I'm sorry." Georgia's tender heart smote her. She patted the little boy gently on the shoulder.

"They're not getting divorced or anything," Leon told her hastily, his heart in his blue eyes. "It's a separation."

"I'm sure it will work out, Leon," Georgia said.

"Oh, so am I." He sighed deeply. "Mummy couldn't listen to Daddy playing the piano all the time."

Of course. Adam Caswell, Georgia thought. This must be his little boy.

"Sometimes he plays it *all night*." Leon gestured with upturned hands. "I never hear him, but Mummy says it drives her batty."

"Perhaps Daddy should think of a soundproof room," Georgia suggested.

"It's a really *big* house," Leon said with great loyalty. "Mummy doesn't love music like Daddy and I do."

"I see." Georgia shook her head a little helplessly. "So have you had your breakfast?" she asked more brightly by way of diversion.

"Nope, and I'm hungry."

"I'm not surprised." Georgia glanced at her watch.

''It's past eight-thirty. I'm sure Daddy's up by now. I'll take you to your room.'' Georgia took his hand, and he didn't resist. Rather her presence seemed to offer comfort. Obviously he was badly missing his mother. ''Which is it?''

Leon pointed. ''Twenty-four A. I'm B. Daddy is composing something now. It's all about the sea. That's why we're here. Daddy's very clever. Grandpa says it's Mummy who has the little problem.''

They were almost at the room when a tall, very thin man emerged, looking anxiously up and down the corridor. He was somewhere in his late thirties, good-looking in a nerve ridden way, with long dark hair drawn back into a ponytail and soulful dark eyes.

''Leon!'' he called, relief mixed up with exasperation.

''It's okay, Dad,'' Leon answered cheerfully. ''This is Georgia. We met in the hallway.''

''Hello, there, Mr. Caswell, Georgia Bennett,'' Georgia introduced herself as they met up. ''I hope you weren't worried?''

''Not really. Leon's very good at taking care of himself.'' He gave her his son's illuminating smile, a smile that wiped the intensely retrospective look from his face. ''I do hope the little monkey wasn't bothering you.''

''Not at all,'' she disclaimed. ''We've had a pleasant conversation, but now Leon's hungry.''

''Of course!'' Adam Caswell struck a hand to his forehead. ''I'm afraid I slept in. I was working into the early hours. Poor Leon. He doesn't have much of a father.''

Immediately Leon went to his father and hugged

him around the knees. ''That's all right, Dad. I told Georgia you were composing something special.''

''It's a great honour to have you on the island, Mr. Caswell.'' Georgia smiled.

''Please, it's Adam.'' All the time he was talking, Adam Caswell was studying Georgia intently, rather as one might study an inspirational figure. It was slightly disconcerting.

''You're very beautiful,'' he said at last.

''Thank you.'' Georgia accepted the compliment gracefully. ''I can't take any credit. I have a beautiful mother. By the way it's my uncle who owns and runs this hotel, Robert Mowbray. Perhaps you didn't know, but we have an excellent child minding facility for when parents need a little time to themselves or the children want company of their own age. They're supervised at all times.''

''That's handy to know.''

''Well, I must be on my way.'' Georgia looked at Leon and smiled. ''I'm sure we'll meet again.''

''Can I come down to breakfast with you, Georgia?'' Leon pleaded. ''Dad will take ages.''

''Leon, *please*. We can't impose on Miss Bennett any longer,'' his father hastily intervened.

Georgia considered briefly. She didn't really mind taking Leon to breakfast. ''No imposition at all.''

Adam Caswell's smile grew. ''In that case, behave yourself, young man. It's very kind of you, Miss Bennett. Breakfast is not a meal I'm much interested in.''

''And they say it's the most important meal of the day,'' she said lightly.

''That's what *Mummy* says, too,'' Leon piped up.

"She says Dad would be all the better if he ate properly."

Adam Caswell smiled helplessly.

"Can we go out onto the terrace, Georgia?" Leon asked excitedly when they arrived in the dining room.

"Of course, but we'll get breakfast first. It's buffet style."

"Great!" Leon looked elated. "We've had meals in our room ever since we arrived."

"Then this morning we'll make up for it." Georgia led the child to the buffet, where a dozen or more guests were making the most of a wealth of dishes. "Would you like me to help or do you want to serve yourself? There's no need to pile the plate. We can keep coming back if you want a little more."

"You do it, Georgia. No cereal. I hate it."

"What about some fruit instead? The sliced mango looks nice."

"Oh, I don't mind mango." Leon sounded much relieved. "Then I want—"

"Sausages, bacon and hash browns."

He smiled, blue eyes alight. "And maybe an egg if you turn it upside down."

A short time later they were seated at their table on the sun-drenched terrace with its foaming balustrade of Thai pink bougainvillea. Georgia sipped at her grapefruit juice. Leon speared succulent slices of mango and popped them into his mouth.

"This is *much* better than muesli," he paused to say. "Why doesn't Mummy know about it?"

"I'm quite sure she does. Maybe you could alternate the fruit with the cereal. There are all kinds of cereals. The one with the Iron Man on the box is quite nice. Good for you, too. All the champion swimmers and Iron Men eat their cereal.''

Leon nodded and took a sip of orange juice. ''I don't really have to bother, Georgie, I'm going to be a musician like Dad.''

''Really? You've made up your mind so early?'' Georgia was impressed.

''I'm a prodigy, Georgie, didn't you know?'' Somehow Georgia had turned into Georgie.

''I should have guessed.'' Georgia smiled. ''You have that air about you. What instrument do you play?''

''The piano like Dad. Not his Steinway. He has a big concert grand. I have to make do with an upright until I'm older.''

''So what does Mummy think about having a prodigy for a son?''

''Oh, she doesn't mind me,'' Leon said artlessly. ''She's proud of *me*. So what do *you* do, Georgie?'' he asked in his surprisingly adult fashion, smiling his thanks as Georgia removed his fruit bowl and set his cooked breakfast before him.

''I'm an interior designer. Do you know what that is?''

''Sure!'' Leon hooted. ''Mummy had an interior decorator do up the farmhouse where we lived. She said it was spooky the way it was. All the gloomy rooms! Dad and I *liked* it, but Mummy said being in the country was ruining her life.''

Georgia was beginning to think Mummy and Daddy were like chalk and cheese. ''It's not a working farm, Leon?'' she asked, quite unable to see Adam Caswell on a tractor.

"Dad's the only one who works," Leon said. "Sometimes he even falls asleep at the piano. Grandpa said he should take a holiday before he has a breakdown. He and Mummy squabble all the time. I *hate* it when they're like that." He shook his head gloomily.

"I'm sorry, Leon." Georgia gripped a small hand for a moment, then deliberately changed the subject. "I'm looking forward to hearing you play. I learned the piano myself. In fact, I sat all my exams and gained two diplomas while I was still at school."

"Did you go on to the conservatorium?" Leon asked and opened his mouth for more sausage.

"No, I went on to university. I'm not all that good, Leon. Certainly not a prodigy. But I love music."

"What would you like me to play for you?" Leon asked, buttering a slice of toast.

"I don't know your repertoire. It took a few years before anyone wanted to listen to me."

"Do you know Mozart's Sonata in C?" Leon asked.

"You can't play *that*! Surely?"

"I can, too."

"Then you're indeed a prodigy, Leon. I do envy you."

From music they moved on to sports, but Georgia was surprised to hear Leon couldn't swim when all the children she knew of Leon's age could. "We'll have to do something about that while you're here. That's if Daddy says yes."

"I'm sure it'll be O.K." Leon set down his knife and fork. "As long as Dad doesn't have to come.

He's not the least bit interested in sports. Not even *cricket*.'' This with amazement.

''I could arrange a lesson this morning,'' Georgia said, after a brief consideration.

''With *you*, Georgie?'' Leon asked hopefully.

''No. We have a professional coach. Bill Draper. He's great with kids. For that matter there are quite a few children on the island. Would you like to meet them?''

''Dad mightn't want me to get involved,'' Leon said uncertainly. ''He's a very quiet person.''

''But you have to have young companionship, Leon. Why don't you let me speak to him?''

''Gee, thanks, Georgie.'' The little boy brightened. ''Why don't we ask him as soon as we're finished? I think I could just fit in that little Danish pastry.''

''You've got a good appetite.'' Georgia smiled and passed the basket.

It took quite some time to get Leon settled, but Georgia didn't regret the demands on her limited time. Sunset was family-oriented, and children were well catered for. Leon would join the other children for his swimming lesson, and he seemed quite agreeable about joining the games that had been organized for the day. It hadn't taken her more than five minutes to gain Adam Caswell's approval, though Georgia couldn't remember a time when she'd met such a self-absorbed man. It was apparent he loved his son, indeed was very proud of him, but he lived for his music. Georgia wondered how he would survive without his beloved Steinway. There were pianos on the island and a baby grand in the Hideaway, which he was welcome to play if he cared to, but it seemed he had no need of any instrument to work out his compositions on manuscript. Had he been a more outgoing man she might have asked him something about the opus he was working on, but she didn't want to get too close. From the way he stared at her she had the feeling she might be landed with the role of muse.

Having offered to collect Leon after his swimming lesson, Georgia was surprised when Adam Caswell found his way to the pool, stopping to chat with her for several minutes before taking Leon off to dress. It was as she was walking to the main building that Georgia encountered Link, who was drinking coffee under one of the fringed umbrellas.

"Care to join me?" he asked, standing up and pulling out a chair. "I was looking for you, as a matter of fact, but your uncle told me you were busy organizing the Caswell boy's day."

"Someone had to do it," Georgia said, meeting those brilliant all-seeing eyes. "An iced coffee would be nice."

"Anything with it?" He signalled the waiter and gave the order.

"Good lord, no. I have to work off breakfast."

"Which you had with young Leon." He sat down again. "Didn't his father care to join you?"

"He wasn't asked."

"I did tell you the marriage is said to be on the rocks."

"Just a minute, now," Georgia warned.

"Let me finish. Then again it could be saved. Should be, for the boy's sake."

"You want to warn me about something?"

''Georgia, I couldn't help noticing the way Caswell was staring into your face.''

''With all due modesty, I have to tell you I'm used to being stared at.''

''Indeed, yes,'' he drawled. ''After all, I've stared at you myself, but there was too much intensity about it, that's the trouble. He looked like a man who's been on some inspirational journey then found the answer right under his nose. Surely you got that feeling, as well?''

''Link, what are you talking about?'' She sighed.

''It's not all that complicated. In fact, you *know*.''

''It's the little boy who appeals to me. Not the father.''

''Then I suggest you make that perfectly plain, Georgia, otherwise you might land yourself in an unwanted situation.''

''Thanks for the advice,'' Georgia answered.

''I'm a kindly soul.''

''Really? You sound more like you're on a crusade. Anyway, I thought we were going to use one another for mutual protection.''

''It does hold the key to a trouble-free vacation, don't you think?'' he asked tauntingly. ''Ah, here's your iced coffee. What time would you like to head off this afternoon?''

''With the tide. We'll need to organise the gear. Fill the tanks.''

''I've already seen to everything.'' He gave her that charming, mocking smile. ''Tell me, just for the fun of it, how would you go about refurbishing the hotel if you had a chance?''

''What, little me, the virtual unknown?'' Georgia

raised her delicate eyebrows, reminding him of his words.

"Don't take it so much to heart. After all, you're only twenty-four or so."

"Would you care to check my teeth?"

"Dear me," he tutted. "I didn't call for a copy of your birth certificate. Your uncle happened to mention your age in passing. How much you've achieved in such a short time. Words to that effect."

"I see." She relaxed slightly. "Well, I have to tell you, Link Robards, I'm not going to allow you to pick my brains."

"So what do you charge for a consultation?"

"I have to *like* the client first."

"Which is why I asked. You *do* like me, Georgia. In fact, you want to have dinner with me tonight."

"I didn't come to Sunset to pick up strange men." she said coolly. "So what would *you* do to the hotel, you brilliant architect?"

"How about start again?" he answered bluntly.

"You mean *demolish* the place?" Georgia's dark eyes widened.

"It's a hypothetical case, of course. We're two professionals. We can discuss it objectively."

"Hypothetical? Is that so?" Georgia gave a brittle laugh. "If your name weren't Robards. If you and your father weren't perhaps thinking of investing in North Queensland. It's the top tourist destination in the country, after all. The Great Barrier Reef is one of the wonders of the world."

"Interestingly enough, I was sold on it long ago, Miss Bennett. In fact I might know this part of the world rather better than you."

''Well, you've got a good ten years' start,'' Georgia retaliated in a tart voice.

''For your information, Miss Bennett. I'm thirty-one,'' he countered.

''Which is regarded as almost middle-aged by many.'' She smiled sweetly.

''You mean like young Leon?''

Georgia's smile broadened at his perceptiveness. ''He tells me he's a child prodigy.''

He laughed. ''Well, he certainly knows a beautiful woman when he sees one. And how to start up a friendship. What instrument does he play?''

''The piano.''

''Then you'll have to arrange a little concert if he's agreeable. He looks a nice kid. Pity about the haircut.''

''Lord, yes!'' Georgia sighed. ''His fringe is falling right into his eyes. I think I might ask permission to have his hair cut at the salon. And he needs some casual clothes.''

''I thought you came for a holiday, not to play nanny.'' His tone had an odd inflection in it.

''But Leon's here, and he needs help.''

His glance whipped over her and lingered on her full, soft mouth. ''Bless your tender heart, Georgia, but why don't you leave it to his father? I don't think he's quite a clueless as he looks.''

''Nerve-ridden,'' Georgia corrected. ''I thought he looked nerve-ridden.''

''Just the sort of people I've learned to avoid.''

''Of course. You're the corporate dynamo, while he's a musician from a totally different world.''

''What have you got against corporate dynamos

when you're a dedicated career woman yourself?'' he asked.

''Maybe I've got a few skeletons locked away in the cupboard.''

''The answer to that is to open up the cupboard.''

''I've considered that, but I don't think it would work.'' Briskly Georgia changed the subject. ''So you'd pull down the hotel, would you?''

''Shh, Georgia.'' He put an elegant, tanned finger to his shapely mouth.

''You're very devious, Link Robards.'' Devious. Dangerous. Devastating, she thought, feeling as though her body was made of melting wax.

''It's not a mortal sin, is it? Anyway, I look seriously at all aspects of the hotel industry. Your uncle established this resort some fifteen years ago. He did a good job. But that was *then*. I think the whole concept should be changed.''

''And which way would *you* go?'' Georgia asked in a satiric voice, trying to steel herself against him.

''One central complex and individual bungalows all around the island,'' he said, enthusiasm in his voice. ''Many of the other islands cater for families. They're bigger, less fragile. I see Sunset as a private retreat for adults only. People who care deeply about these small, very special sanctuaries.''

''So you'd shut out the kids?'' For a minute Georgia overreacted on principle.

''Listen,'' he said reasonably. ''You know as well as anyone the damage inflicted on reefs by increasing numbers of tourists. Sunset has a very beautiful fringing reef. Your uncle told me himself he's become worried by the amount of damage inflicted on it of recent times. It can't be allowed to become substantial. Not everyone teaches their child to become environmentally sensitive. Coral boulders get overturned and delicate corals smashed in the hunt for all the shells. Children are the worst offenders when it comes to overcollecting. You've been coming here since you were a child. You must know some of the most beautiful specimens are no longer common. Even the walking track around the island is being overused. I would definitely cut numbers. No more than fifty guests at any one time. Change the concept, as I said.''

''And what about Uncle Robert? I'm sure you're aware he doesn't have that kind of money.''

''No.''

''So you're here to report to your father?''

''You sound as though you'd like to send me to prison,'' he observed rather tersely. ''I think you could describe this trip as a mixture of pleasure and business. I needed a short, quiet break and I wanted to see how one of the smaller resorts operates. There was no plan, Georgia. Only a looksee with a bit of paradise thrown in.''

''A very *keen* looksee,'' she commented, meeting the light piercing eyes.

''I'm sure you realise one has to be very keen to survive.''

She shrugged a shoulder. ''If it means anything at all, I agree with you about reducing numbers. I don't want to see the reef damaged any more than you, but we could keep the central complex as guest accommodation and build some more bungalows over a period of time.''

''The central complex already needs a great deal of money spent on it. The foyer is too dark.''

''I've been thinking about that. I'd go for a giant cupola. A beautiful big dome to let in the light. I'd put a fountain beneath it and a lush water garden.''

''Would you, indeed?''

''Don't patronise me, Link Robards.''

''Come on, was I doing that?''

''It's all in your regard. But to continue, I'd change the colour scheme, as well. Dee had a very practical bent, and one can understand why, but I'd mirror all the brilliant jewel colours of the island.''

''And you're looking to your uncle to offer you the job?''

It was said smoothly, but Georgia stood up, hot colour glowing beneath her luminous skin. ''I wasn't aware we had to get the okay off you.''

''Don't be like that, Georgia. I only asked a question.'' He caught hold of her hand. Held it, while her heart fluttered like beating wings.

''Really? I thought you were spending a lot of time prying into our affairs.''

''You were throwing a few smokescreens yourself. Now, we didn't actually set a time for our dive, did we?''

''I was waiting for you to *tell* me,'' she said shortly. ''You're the dominant type.''

''And here I was thinking I was just an ordinary guy.''

A few people on the terrace were beginning to look their way, so Georgia swooped down close to him and murmured into his ear. ''You're abrasive and you're jarring and I don't trust you at all. Two o'clock will do just fine."

"Splendid!" He gave her that quirky, mocking smile and released her hand. "Shall we say the jetty?"

"The jetty it is." She nodded to him briskly, though her flesh was all a-tingle. "I hope you know how all your gear works. I just might leave you out there."

CHAPTER FOUR

THOUSANDS of glorious little fish came to stare at them, mouths agape at these alien creatures in their exquisite realm. The water was so transparent Georgia could see from the hull of their fifteen-foot dinghy almost to the sea floor. The enormous clarity of her vision was further illuminated by the dazzling beams of sunlight that broke through the gaps in the reef and rayed deep into this silent green-lit world.

From time to time myriads of small silvery-blue fish covered with draperies like floating chiffon swum over her in shoals, dimming the light with their sheer numbers before darting into the multicoloured branching corals as delicate as fern gardens. The beautiful little butterfly fish were quite friendly, fluttering slowly and gracefully around her like the exotic butterflies in the rain forests of the mainland. Several feet away from her in the marvellous staghorn corals the Morish idols hovered, easily identifiable with their yellow, white and black stripes, playful companions to the harlequin fish with their bright bands of red. Georgia had learned long ago why so many of the coral reef fishes were so brilliantly marked and coloured. There were so many species of fish on the reef, characteristic colour patterns had evolved for inter- and intra-specific recognition. Males could be distinguished from females, and the fantastic range of colours in the corals provided very effective camouflage from predators.

The little seahorses Georgia loved floated in and out of the waving seagrasses, the axis of their bodies held vertically while they propelled themselves along with their small dorsal fins. Georgia found it extraordinary that many coral reef fish like the butterfly, damsel and angelfish adhered strictly to their own patch, selecting a specific coral clump and rarely straying from it for their life span. The larger fish moved farther afield in schools, but even they adhered to a particular reef.

A short distance from her Link was reaching out a hand to a curious butterfly fish, deep violet in colour with a multitude of trailing winglike fins. It was quite extraordinary how quickly the undersea creatures came to accept you if you didn't do anything to frighten them. As experienced divers she and Link were staying close together for mutual protection. They'd also agreed on exploring only one particular section of the reef for that day and then only for an agreed length of time. Both of them knew it was as easy to lose oneself in the coral jungles as it was to become disoriented in the mainland rain forests. The reef was the greatest known storehouse of corals, some three hundred species compared with the Caribbean's eighty.

In such an environment scuba diving was very popular, but one had to take sensible precautions. With waters of such crystal clarity it was difficult to correctly estimate water depth and as a consequence it was easy to dive too deeply. Then, too, the marine environment was so full of exquisite sights it was all too easy to lose track of time. Neither of them was getting too near the coral pinnacles. It was easy enough to get the scuba gear hooked.

Above them their dinghy was flying the international diver's flag, and they had taken care to gauge the strength of the currents before swimming away from it. Link wasn't wearing a wetsuit. Neither was she. They'd both agreed wetsuits became uncomfortably hot in the tropics. She wore a Lycra swim shirt over her bikini. Link wore an old shirt and shorts. At least it was some protection from coral lacerations should they be washed into it, but the currents were calm.

For Georgia and Link it was an enthralling experience exploring the deep water, a fantasy filled with the most beautiful aquatic wonders where giant flowers of all shapes and colours grew. Every kind of coral known to man was represented. Every conceivable colour. Pink, orange, scarlet, mauve, bright purple and vivid green. There were huge colonies of indigo blue mushroom corals fringed by circular fans of amethyst, carpets of soft yellow corals tipped with blue and green buds, ruby and almond-green organ pipe corals that were so aptly named. It was such an incredible world Georgia had the feeling it wasn't of this planet but the dream world of science fiction.

On the under surfaces of the coral boulders, in the crevices and caverns, a fantastic array of sponges occurred, not ordinary sponges like the ones used in the bath but all shapes and colours. The armoured crustaceans, too, showed an amazing variety of form and colour, some glowing like opals as they scurried into the dense petrified forest. One of the features of the

Great Barrier Reef was its tremendous species richness. Georgia knew this was because of its precise location in the tropics, lying as it did near the centre of the vast Indo-West Pacific region where marine life was the most prolific.

Time simply flies when you're one with the fishes, Georgia thought. She and Link were drifting together as a pair, rather in the manner of the glorious little butterfly fish who swam mostly in twos. It was less than a minute after Link pointed to his underwater watch, the signal that their time was up, that they had their only encounter with danger, though both knew from experience the sea could be as violent as it was beautiful. During their dive they had seen sea snakes, eels, stringrays, manrays, huge fish of all kinds. Now they were confronted by a twenty-foot tiger shark.

It materialized from behind a towering coral pinnacle, swimming directly towards them, an awesome sight because of its bulk and fearsome reputation. While it was true most sharks took no notice of divers intruding into their silent green domain, it was a heart-stopping moment. In a split second Georgia recalled tiger sharks had been involved in fatalities in Queensland waters but rarely in the Great Barrier Reef waters where there was an enormous abundance of natural prey. When the shark came within a couple of metres of them both clapped their hands, not an easy thing to do underwater, but the startled shark caught the sound. It turned a half circle in dazzling time, fleeing in the opposite direction but leaving the crystal waters churned up with white bubbles.

They made it to the boat in record time, heaving themselves over the side and disposing of their cumbersome scuba gear in a silence that was broken only by the sound of the gulls and their harsh breathing.

"You've a hell of a nerve," Link grunted finally, leaning over to help her remove her flippers and protective leg knife.

Now the danger was over she could afford to be flippant. "You didn't think I was just going to *freeze*?"

He looked at her hard, his manner unfathomable. Was he angry with her? Pleased with her? What? "I know you're an experienced diver," he said tersely, "but, lady, a tiger shark is one frightening sight."

"Trust me, I know." She smiled sweetly, squeezing sea water out of her thick golden plait. "Anyway, you know as well as I do sharks don't attack as a matter of course. They get more than enough to eat on the reef."

"This isn't funny!" he snapped.

"Hey, what's wrong?" She stared at him in perplexity. He looked too damned tall. Powerful. Magnetic. *Male*. His splendid body was a dark silhouette against the blazing blue sky.

He shrugged abruptly, obviously trying to lighten up. "I'm searching myself for the answer. I have to tell you I was infinitely more worried about you than me."

"But I didn't let you down, did I?"

"No." His eyes swept her. "In fact, congratulations are more in order." He lowered himself onto the bench beside her.

"So what do you have in mind?" She hadn't meant to be provocative. Not at all, only his eyes flared with intense brilliance.

"Only this." He caught her chin, turned her face to him, staring for a moment at her wet, parted mouth, with its slick, cushiony surface. "You really are Neptune's daughter," he murmured.

She felt so strangely weakened she couldn't move. His fingers slipped down her throat while his mouth came down over hers in one long, hard kiss that left all her senses flooded. She knew she was supposed to take the kiss as it was meant. A celebration of life. Recognition of a shared danger. But it told her more powerfully than anything else could have done that this man had the potential to change her life.

There was a message from her uncle when Georgia returned to her room, suggesting they might make a quick inspection of the hotel in the late afternoon. It sounded as though he was serious about carrying out refurbishments, Georgia thought, a decision he made clear when she found her way to his office.

"I've been in such a daze, Georgie," he confided, removing his glasses and rubbing his eyes. "I've let things slide. It's taken you and Link to shock me out of it." He put his glasses on.

"What has Link said?" Georgia looked startled.

"Nothing, but he has that all-seeing regard. I expect he finds the place pretty shabby after what he's used to."

"He understands your situation, Uncle Robert. I'll say that for him. His father's heart attack then bypass operation obviously caused him great concern. They must be close."

"So I've heard. Sam Robards has the reputation for being a mighty tough man. Came from nothing, married well. But I told you that. How did the diving go?''

''Wonderful!'' she said casually, though it cost her an effort. ''Even had an encounter with a tiger shark.''

''Georgie!'' Robert Mowbray looked dismayed and astonished.

''It wasn't a real problem, just a bit of a scare. The shark was more frightened of us than we were of it.''

''It's as well our waters are teeming with fish. I couldn't bear to see our one-hundred-per-cent safety record broken. What do you think of Link?'' Robert Mowbray looked at his niece over his glasses.

''To tell the truth—'' Georgia picked up a paper-weight and set it down again ''—I'm attracted to him. Don't know that it's bright, but it's the way it is.''

''And he's as attracted to you?''

''Perhaps. But it could never work out.''

''Why not?''

''I know what it's like living with high-powered men.''

Robert Mowbray sighed. ''I blame your attitude on your father. He might be high-powered but he's also without humour and so domineering. I don't want to hurt you, Georgie, I know you want to love him, but he's ruined my sister's life. She doesn't even *have* one. You can't call running around art galleries living. Why, she's never crossed him. She won't even come up here for a visit if he says no.''

''There's not much we can do about it,'' Georgia said. ''Mum made her own bed, now she's got to lie in it. Not *my* words, hers. I have to admit I've suffered, as well. Dad always gave me everything I wanted. In the material sense. The only thing he tried to deny me was my independence.''

''But you got it anyway.''

''Not without many upsets and a lot of harsh words,'' Georgia said, struggling to keep her tone calm. ''The thing that really upset me was Mum never took my part.''

''She had problems. She was married too young,'' Robert Mowbray said flatly. ''Dawson moulded her into just the sort of woman he wanted. Unswervingly loyal but with no mind of her own.''

''Don't let's talk about it,'' Georgia begged. ''It raises my blood pressure just as much as yours. So why don't we start on our rounds?'' She stood up.

''I'd like to begin with the foyer,'' her uncle said. ''It seems to me it needs lightening up.''

By the end of their tour it was decided Georgia Bennett Interiors would be given the brief for the refurbishment of the hotel. Robert Mowbray called for a bottle of champagne and they drank a celebratory glass in his office.

''I can't thank you enough, Uncle Robert,'' Georgia said, her face alight with enthusiasm. ''I'll work very hard to make it a great success.''

''I have faith in you, Georgie. You're a very clever young woman. You even have a touch of your father in you when it comes to drive.''

''I've thought that myself.'' Georgia looked into the bubbles in her glass. ''I can get started on the proposals almost immediately, if you like. We'll need to have a budget.''

''Of course.'' Robert Mowbray nodded matter-of-factly. ''It will involve a loan, but I don't foresee a problem. We can't get carried away, though.''

''I won't. What I have in mind is imaginative yet practical. Above all, cost-effective. Let me submit a proposal first. I can make estimates along the way. Structural changes cost the most. They have to be done first, and they can be very disruptive.''

''Structural changes, Georgie?'' Robert Mowbray looked a little alarmed. ''What did you have in mind?''

''Well, I didn't say, but a cupola, a giant dome, would transform the lobby.''

''I daresay it would, but it might seriously eat into the budget.''

''We'd cost it first and then decide. We'd need to consult a structural engineer and an architect.''

''We've got one right on the premises,'' Robert Mowbray reminded her.

''You mean Link?''

Her uncle nodded. ''I have it on the best authority he's brilliant. He designed the Lincoln in Perth.''

''Gracious!'' Georgia fell back in her chair in astonishment. ''I didn't even know it was a Robards hotel.''

''Lincoln was his mother's maiden name, remember?''

''I know *now*. I didn't then. I haven't been to Perth for years, but someone told me the new hotel is terrific. Strange Link never mentioned it.''

''I don't think he's into singing his own praises. By the same token he's wonderfully assured. Secure in the knowledge he's very gifted.''

''And doesn't he look it? But what's he doing

here? *Really*. I know he *says* he wants peace and quiet. Naturally he'd be observant of his surroundings, but he's taking too great an interest in the layout of the hotel. He's even asked me how I'd go about refurbishing it if I had the chance.''

''Did he?'' Robert Mowbray nibbled his lower lip. ''It could be you're a professional, like him. Did you tell him?''

''I told him more than I intended to,'' Georgia admitted in a rueful voice. ''He has that effect on me. He has his own ideas, as well.''

''I would think so. I'd be interested to hear them.''

''I wonder.'' Georgia hesitated then plunged on. ''Link sees Sunset as an adults-only resort. One central complex servicing beach-front villas. No more than fifty guests at any time.''

''Well, it would manage the human impact,'' Robert Mowbray pointed out fairly. ''Not that Dee and I ever let the lure of the dollar override our commitment to the environment. But tourism has grown so fast.''

Georgia nodded. ''I can see what he's getting at. The island *is* small. It has a beautiful fringing reef to be protected. It's a new concept entirely.''

''And one *I* couldn't afford. I don't have the Robards megabucks. I'm not a young man any more, either. I've lost Dee.''

''You're not still considering selling, Uncle Robert,'' Georgia prompted.

Robert Mowbray shook his head. ''The hotel is all I know.''

''Link hasn't approached you directly?''

''Georgie, I'd *tell* you.''

"I'm sorry. Of course you would. But my instinct, like yours, tells me he'd like to acquire it for the chain."

"The price would have to be right," her uncle maintained a little grimly, betraying his fluctuating thoughts. "And that means *high*! The hotel may have become run-down of recent times, but the gardens are Dee's living memorial. They're glorious in a part of the world where dazzling flora is everywhere. Then there's our reef. It's our great draw card."

"I'm positively certain he's taken that into account." Georgia looked at her uncle's worn face, feeling a sharp tug of concern.

"But I'm *not* selling, Georgie. That's the thing. We're refurbishing." Unashamed tears came into his eyes. "Besides, *Dee's* here. She's everywhere on the island. I can *feel* her. Sometimes in the early morning I can even see her moving about the gardens." He blinked hard, then spoke in a more businesslike voice. "We might cut back on the number, though. Sunset has always been family oriented, but there are much bigger islands to cater for their special needs. I'll have to give some serious thought to this. I have to admit to a few concerns of my own."

"What you decide will directly affect our refurbishments," Georgia reminded him gently.

"I know. Bookings are in for the holiday period. After that we could close down for a few months."

"We'd need to," Georgia agreed, "but it would be wonderfully worthwhile."

"I'm sure of it, dear." Rather sadly Robert Mowbray removed his glasses and began to polish them. "You're such a comfort to me, Georgie girl. Dee loved you like her own daughter. She loved your spirit.''

''I loved her, too, Uncle Robert.'' Georgia got up to hug him and drop a soft kiss on his cheek. ''I promise you, we'll do her proud.''

Georgia was putting the finishing touches to her appearance when there were several very loud raps on the door. For a moment she was at a total loss. Link had asked her to join him for dinner, but it surely couldn't be he. He had considerably more finesse than that. Besides, they had agreed to meet in the foyer. It wouldn't be her uncle, and she definitely hadn't requested room service. She went to the door and peered through the peephole.

No one. Or a very short person. Possibly her little pal.

Georgia threw open the door, looking downwards.

''Leon, whatever is the matter?'' She bent to him, noting the pinched cheeks and the overbright eyes.

''It's Daddy. I can't wake him up.''

Georgia's heart lurched violently. ''He's asleep, pet?''

''He must be. He's snoring.''

''Thank the lord!'' Immediately Georgia's fears abated. Adam Caswell really wasn't the best person to be in charge of a small child. ''What's that you've got in your hand?'' she asked.

''One of Dad's dumbbells.'' Leon suddenly gave his impish grin. ''He does exercises for his hands and arms.''

''And that's what you used on my door?''

"I'm sorry." He looked chastened. "I got a bit excited."

"That's okay." Georgia checked to see if any paint had come off the woodwork. It had. "Let's see." She closed her door and took the little boy's hand. "The first thing to do is check on Daddy. See he's all right."

"Why does he sleep so hard?" Leon's valiant little chin quivered.

"I expect its because he's working through all the night hours."

"Yes, on his symphonic poem," Leon confirmed.

"Have you had something to eat?"

"Nothin'!" Leon shook his head.

"Dear, dear." Georgia clicked her tongue. "Next time you could ring room service."

"Could I? That would be great, Georgie!" Leon bucked up, his mind obviously filled with visions of hamburgers and chips.

Adam Caswell came to the door at the third urgent knock, the living, breathing embodiment of a lost-in-a-fog slightly dotty composer. "Good grief!" he said blearily. "Miss Bennett to the rescue again. You're so good. And so patient. I had such a head I had to take a couple of strong painkillers. I'm afraid they knocked me out."

"Leon was really worried about you, Adam." Georgia held tightly to the child's trembling hand.

"I couldn't wake you, Dad."

Adam Caswell sighed deeply. "God, I'm a lousy father."

"Grandpa says Dad is heading for a breakdown," Leon told Georgia, his glossy head cocked to the side.

"Ssh! Grandpa talks too much," Adam Caswell said in a wry voice. "I'm a little run-down, that's all. I expect you know, Miss Bennett, my wife and I are separated."

"Yes. I'm so sorry. Please call me Georgia. It can't be easy for you or Leon. I hope I'm not being presumptuous, but mightn't it be better if you simply forgot your work for a while and enjoyed all the island has to offer? It must be very easy for a creative person like yourself to suffer burnout."

To both Georgia's and Leon's surprise, Adam swooped suddenly and gave Georgia a grateful kiss on the cheek. "To tell the truth I'm an obsessive personality. Nothing much I can do about it, either. God knows I did try to turn myself into a nine-to-five man for a time. But it didn't work. I'm a night creature. Not for the fun of it. It's the way my brain is."

"Well, I do know something about it." Georgia smiled. "I work a lot at night myself. I'm very committed, as well."

"An interior designer!" Adam exclaimed as though it was splendid. "Leon told me. You *would* work with beautiful things. In fact, and I hope you'll take this the right way, I find your golden beauty inspirational. I'm working on a symphonic impression for piano and orchestra."

"How lovely!" Georgia was becoming more concerned about Leon and his growling tummy. "Sunset should provide you with all the wonderful sights and sounds you need. *Under* the sea is another world. I went scuba diving just this afternoon. It was a wonderful experience. Beautiful beyond belief."

Adam Caswell's soulful eyes filled with tiny lights.

''Under the sea. Of course. Under the sea. A watery kingdom ruled by a beautiful sea goddess. Strictly speaking, your eyes should be green.''

''There are always contact lenses,'' Georgia joked. ''Now, young man, what about your dinner?'' She glanced at Leon, pressing his hand in encouragement.

''Can I come with *you*, Georgie?'' he asked.

''Perhaps we could all go together?'' Adam Caswell suggested.

Georgia shook her head gently. ''That would be nice, but I'm having dinner with a friend tonight.''

''Perhaps another time,'' Adam Caswell murmured, a slight flush on his cheeks.

''There's Mr. Robards,'' Leon cried suddenly, looking towards the stairs.

It was, indeed.

Leon continued to wave, signalling Link to join them. Not that it was necessary. Link was coming on as though he definitely sought an introduction.

''Leon, isn't it?'' He smiled at the small boy as he drew close, holding out his hand.

''Leon Caswell, Mr. Robards,'' Leon said, shaking hands delightedly. ''This is my father, Adam Caswell, the pianist and composer. You know Georgie.''

''Of course. Good evening, *Georgie*.'' Link gave her a searing silver glance. ''I got a little worried when you were running late.''

''My son's fault, I'm afraid,'' Adam Caswell apologized. ''Nice to meet you, Robards.''

The two men shook hands. ''I'm familiar with your works,'' Link said pleasantly. ''In fact I saw your lyrical drama in Sydney recently. I was highly impressed.''

''That's very kind of you.'' Adam Caswell looked pleased. ''It took a great deal out of me.''

''Daddy's writing something about the sea,'' Leon said proudly. ''He's going to dedicate it to Georgie.''

Georgia caught a startled exclamation in the nick of time, but Link's black eyebrows rose. ''Is that so?''

''The things you come up with, Leon,'' his father protested, looking more like a schoolboy caught out than a heralded composer.

''Then what did you actually *say*, Dad?'' Leon flashed him an uncertain look.

''I believe I *said* Miss Bennett is very beautiful.''

''Like a goddess of the sea,'' Leon confirmed owlishly.

''My thoughts exactly.'' Link was suave. ''Now we really *must* go.'' He turned to the speechless Georgia, taking her arm.

''A pleasure to meet you, Caswell. You, too, Leon.''

''Night, Georgie. See you in the morning,'' Leon called. ''I'm going to ring room service.''

''He's a bright little kid but he could turn out to be a nuisance,'' Link murmured when they were well out of earshot.

''He's lonely,'' Georgia said. ''And neglected.''

''There are other kids on the island. He'll have to join up with them.''

''Of course he will, but he's used to adult company. And he's missing his mother.''

''But you're not his mother, Georgia, so don't get carried away.''

''It's difficult not to become a little involved. Adam is an intensely self-oriented man. He loves his son, but he tends to forget about him. As far as I can make out, he falls into deep sleeps and Leon can't wake him.''

''Maybe he's on drugs,'' Link said a little harshly.

''Oh, I hope not.'' Georgia shuddered. ''I don't really think so. His eyes looked perfectly all right.''

''Look into them, did you?''

''He has a very soulful gaze.''

''Well, he's certainly taken with you.''

''Except for my eyes.''

''What is that supposed to mean?'' Link glanced at her, ultra feminine in a full-skirted, strapless white dress embroidered with daisies.

''They should be green.''

''Ah!'' Link released a sharp sigh. ''The sea goddess, of course. Neptune's daughter.''

''It appears he sees me that way.''

Link steered her into the lounge and towards an empty table. ''Someone should tell his wife what's going on,'' he murmured into her ear as he seated her.

''What's going on?'' Georgia responded with such fire three couples turned. ''Whatever do you mean?'' she demanded more quietly when he was seated opposite her.

His silver eyes glittered. ''Georgia, could you deny he's found a new muse?''

Despite herself she flushed. ''Don't blame me. I haven't given him the slightest encouragement.''

''Look, you don't *have* to. Every time you walk into a room all heads swivel.''

''Oh, Link, for heaven's sake!'' she said with real annoyance.

He shrugged. ''I don't want you to stumble into a complicated situation, that's all. As I recall he dedicated the lyrical drama to his wife.''

''You mean you really saw it?'' she asked acidly.

''I don't tell lies.''

''I bet you do!''

''No more than you. Actually, he's very gifted. But the whole thing was a bit beyond my musical range. I go for people like Beethoven and Brahms. I'm looking for an actual melody.''

''I practically insist on it,'' Georgia said.

He lifted a hand to signal the waiter.

''Now what are you going to have, and don't tell me a Perrier water.''

''One very dry Spanish sherry. Chilled. I like to keep a clear head.'' And yet it was hard not to be seduced by his smooth charm, which had a tantalizing bite to it.

They talked of many things, books, films, travel, world politics, a smattering of gossip. Georgia asked after his work, referring to the hotel she had found out he'd designed. In turn he listened with evident interest to her stories of interiors and the various solutions she had come up with. Yet another thing that distinguished him from Gavin, who'd found interior design downright boring. Even his congratulations when she'd won prizes had been fairly grudging. Link Robards, on the other hand, was very much into not only architectural design but interior treatments.

''How would you perk up the restaurant?'' he asked, looking around the Hibiscus Room, which had been papered, not so surprisingly, in a bold hibiscus print.

''Let me tell you my news first.'' Georgia took a last bite of her delicious coconut and lime marinated coral trout, then set down her knife and fork. ''Uncle Robert has commissioned me to refurbish the hotel.''

''What a very uncle-like thing to do,'' he said dryly. ''It would take a lot of work. I wonder if you know precisely what that entails?''

''So I've never done a hotel before,'' Georgia fired. ''That doesn't mean I don't know how to go about it.''

''This is definite, is it?'' His face in the golden wash of light was all hard planes and angles. Of a sudden tough enough to remind her forcibly of her father.

''You're darned right. I might even invite you back when we get it all together. Anyhow, thanks for the congratulations.''

''Georgia, it's not as though there's very little that needs changing.'' He looked wryly across the candle-lit table. ''Before you start to think in terms of colours, fabrics, whatever, you would have to consider a few structural changes. Your idea about the cupola was good, but your uncle wouldn't want to involve himself in a lot of expense. He would have to stick to a fairly tight budget.''

''You've figured that out?'' There was a certain urgent challenge in Georgia's voice. A need to assert herself.

''I don't have to. I'm in the business. I know which tourist projects are working and which are running into trouble. I intended to have a word with your uncle myself.''

''Ah, now we get to it,'' she said with deep irony.

''I was going to suggest how he could update the hotel with the minimal outlay and mess,'' he returned tersely.

''And you think I'd make a mess?'' Georgia's voice rose fractionally.

''Really, is there any need to get emotional? You're a professional. I'm sure you've got lots of ability to have achieved what you have, but you need to listen to hard common sense.''

''I've got that along with the rest, so don't put me down. I've had a lifetime of that. I know how to stick to a budget. I know how to create atmosphere where there isn't any. It might interest you to know Lennox Larson did the last lot of refurbishments, and they're a big firm.''

''They might be—'' he shrugged ''—but they're essentially conservative. There's no drama in anything they do. They like to play it safe, and many times it works. The only thing I can't see is how they picked that wallpaper.'' He looked at the wall.

''Dee might have had something to do with it,'' Georgia confessed. ''The hibiscus was *her* flower.''

''And they work brilliantly in the garden. Not so well on the walls. The hibiscus motif could have been used in other ways.''

''The room should have been painted a pale yellow.'' Georgia said. ''Fabric could have mirrored the garden.''

''I agree.'' He watched her face intently. ''It seems to me, Georgia, the way to go is scale the place down.''

''So you've said.'' She drew a little pattern on the tablecloth with a pearly nail.

"Surely you can see my point?"

"Of course I can see it." Georgia lifted her head. "My uncle can see it, but he doesn't have the kind of money to develop a new concept."

"There are partners," Link suggested, as if she should have thought of it.

"Uncle Robert doesn't *want* a partner. This is family."

"Your father is a very rich man."

Her dark eyes froze. "My father's as hard as nails. A bit like *you*," she tacked on, weighed down by her ambiguous feelings.

"You can't stand constructive criticism?" His voice was tinged with recognition.

"Most of the time, but it seems to me you have an agenda of your own. Whatever it is."

"I'm not about to make your uncle an offer, if that's what you mean. I'm having a holiday and I'm checking out the territory. I don't know whether you're aware of it, but there was quite a bit of talk at one stage that Sunset was going on the market. Only your uncle would have given out that information. It wasn't a rumour that was put about."

Georgia took a quick sip of wine. Her mouth had gone dry. "That would have been after Dee died. Uncle Robert admitted he had thought of selling during a period of deep grief."

"One could scarcely blame him. So many memories crowding in on him day and night."

"He thinks Dee's still here," Georgia said in a husky voice.

"I'm sure her bright spirit still hovers about the

place. The gardens she created are breathtakingly beautiful.''

''You wouldn't change them then? *If* you had the chance?''

''I'm an architect, remember? I pay homage to beauty wherever I find it. *You're* very beautiful, Georgia.''

''And you're a devilish man.''

''No-one's perfect.'' He took her hand, and Georgia's pulse picked up dramatically. ''What do you say to a walk on the beach after dinner?''

She turned her face away, unwilling for him to see her eyes. ''What exactly have you in mind?'' Seduction by moonlight? A sea breeze blowing, a billion stars reflected in the lagoon, the two of them alone in a world of indigo and silver?

''If you must know I'd very much like to continue our kiss.''

Excitement washed her, but she managed to keep her tone light. ''Wouldn't that compromise our agreement?''

He laughed, a deep vibrant sound. ''I don't think so. I'm not asking for a commitment. Just a civilised kiss.''

A cloud of doubt showed itself on her face. Both of them were throwing out banter like bright ribbons, but underneath ran a swift, silent current. One false move and it would whirl her away.

''Georgia?'' he prompted. ''I'll settle for only one of your thoughts.''

She took another sip of her wine. ''Wouldn't it be risking your relationship with Tania Harper, as well?''

He studied her with brilliant, faintly hooded eyes. "The fact is I'm committed to no one. You could even say I've never really *connected*."

"As in mind and spirit?" Despite herself her voice turned brittle. He was a stunning man. He was into his thirties. He must have had several relationships. Some serious, surely?

"Exactly. You don't believe me?"

"I'm entitled to have my doubts."

"You think I'm into casual affairs?" His eyes held her. Mesmerized her.

"I can only assure you *I'm* not."

"I'm not, either. Apart from the fact I'm not so inclined, I don't have the time. What's really troubling you, Georgia? You feel safe with me, don't you? You've been relaxed all evening."

She looked at the hand that still held hers lightly. It was strong, lean, clever looking, the nails so clean and beautifully trimmed.

"On one level I have to confess I'm a little wary of you," she said truthfully.

"Surely that needs explaining?"

"Maybe if we were close friends."

"Well, we're off to a good start. I think you know me well enough to confide."

"You wouldn't understand." Georgia withdrew her hand, brushing her fingertips across her forehead.

"Try me. Obviously it's got something to do with your father," he said shrewdly. "I'd say you grew up in a patriarchal environment. Perhaps under a strict domination. You have hang-ups about your mother. I learned that the first day."

"I love my mother." Georgia felt her body go

rigid. "I love my father, too but I don't actually *like* him. He's something of a benevolent dictator. Or at least he's benevolent until he's crossed."

Link leaned back in his chair, searching her face. "You surely can't be telling me I seem like *that* to you?"

"It's overreaction, I guess, but you're a dominant man, clever and high mettled. Hard when you have to be. I'm inordinately wary of that."

"When you seem so self-assured yourself? Your own woman?"

"You don't understand. I had to *work* at it. Fight all the time." She shook her head. "One gets a little torn about in the process."

"Have you spoken to someone about this?" He looked at her from under his strongly marked brows.

"As in psychiatrist?" she joked.

"Psychiatrists are trained to help people with their special problems," he said reasonably.

"I have nothing against them. In fact, I'm all for people going after help. It so happens I can handle my own levels of rage."

"Underwood didn't make you wary?" Link asked crisply.

"Not at all. Our friendship was good up to a point. He was good company, very much into enjoying life."

"Demanding?"

"No more than any other man," Georgia said with some asperity, "but he always did what he was told."

"So there was nothing to worry about."

"Until he started getting jealous."

"There were other men in your life?" Link queried, his expression suave.

"About the same as you," Georgia retorted. "Gavin was miffed I didn't want a *permanent* relationship."

"Hence the ring. If you threw it at me like you threw it at him I wouldn't let you back into my life."

"Really?" She gave a short laugh. "You think I treat men badly?"

"I think you could be the ice goddess. Just how frosted were you with Gavin?"

"We weren't lovers, if that's what you mean," Georgia answered coolly, "not that it's any of your business."

"That's quite true, Georgia." He inclined his head in mock apology. "It's only that I'm trying to get to know you better."

"I'm not exactly sure I know why."

"Let me think." The silvery glance moved slowly over her. "I like *looking* at you. I like *talking* to you. I like the way you're so athletic. I missed that in a lot of women."

"Tania wasn't into three-mile runs, I gather?"

His glance was sharp with amusement. "I know for a fact she always uses the hotel's gym. She's in exceptionally good shape."

"She'd have to be, wouldn't she, in a business where looking good is important."

"I expect so." He consulted the menu. "Do you think we should risk a dessert?"

"Coffee will do me."

"I think you could chance a sliver of orange tart

with ginger cream.'' He glanced up. ''After all, a brisk stroll should walk it off.''

Far from being a brisk stroll, it turned out to be a slow, enchanting experience, a tropical night's idyll.

The moon illuminated the white beach fringed by towering coconut palms and stands of pandanus that were deeply etched against a sky densely populated with stars. In one of the villas someone was playing a guitar, a haunting, romantic melody, Spanish in origin. It was as much a part of the night as the sound of the breeze that played in and out of thousands of leaves.

The lagoon they walked along was a magical sight. Its surface glowed with a silvery blue luminescence, a marvellous effect of all the sea creatures that gave off a wondrous phosphorescence. The air was laden with perfumes, sweet and bracing, the lovely scents of gardenias, oleander and white ginger blossom, the incomparable tang of the wind off the sea.

It tugged at her hair again, launching it into a flying silk pennant. She put up a hand, but Link beat her to it, catching up one side and tucking it behind her ear. ''This has been lovely, Georgia,'' he murmured, ''but I can only resist you for so long.''

For a moment her head reeled at the note in his voice. His hands were locked at her waist, holding her lightly but firmly. She discovered she was trembling.

''Georgia?'' he prompted in a low voice.

Such a shock of desire ran through her she broke away as though burned.

''You'll have to catch me first!'' she called in a kind of defiance over her shoulder.

"Done."

She had a few yards' start and was very fleet of foot, fast over short distances but not the stayer he undoubtedly would be. Except her heart was pumping violently. She was running as though from an explosive situation. Running as though scared of her own sensuality. And in her twenty-four years only he had unlocked it.

When he caught her she was not only pinned but swung into his arms. "You seem a bit out of training," he taunted her in triumph, not even out of breath.

Her sense of humour reasserted itself. "I never did figure out how to run on sand."

"I think your own panic let you down."

"Panic about a kiss? I've been kissed a thousand times."

"Then you know precious few are truly memorable."

"Perhaps." Her voice registered a faint tremor. "Trust my intuition on this, Link. I don't think it's a good idea."

"That brief kiss on the boat was a revelation to me. Of course it could have been a fluke. Aren't you the least bit curious to know?"

"Let me down first." She spoke as calmly as she could. Not easy.

"You might cheat and run away again."

"I'll pay up." *Go on.* Pretend she was playing a game when she wanted him to devour her!

"Splendid! It couldn't be as bad as you think, anyway."

He lowered her to the sand, and when she turned her face to say something moved into kissing her.

It was a moment of molten gold. A brief glimpse into bliss. And it was over almost as soon as it had begun.

She knew she swayed, clutched the lapel of his jacket with her hand, perhaps even moaned. Lord, why not?

''There, that's our little bet discharged.'' On the other hand, Link spoke in a perfectly calm voice.

''It might be smart not to repeat it.'' Georgia drew a steadying breath and looked out over the blue-glowing lagoon.

He turned her face to him, cupping her chin. ''When it was so memorable, shouldn't we try again?''

In the moonlight his eyes glittered, lending his face a satiric expression.

''You're a dreadful tease,'' she snapped.

''I'm not teasing at all. I'm trying to persuade you.''

''Maybe I prefer things as they are,'' Georgia said over her wild, knocking heart.

''And maybe you don't. Change *is* inevitable.'' He drew her into his arms again, lowering his head until his mouth brushed her bare shoulder. ''Neptune's daughter. A sea goddess. I can understand how Caswell found his inspiration.''

''Don't make me furious, Link,'' Georgia warned.

''Heaven forbid! You're just a little high-strung. And you taste delicious!'' His mouth ascending, trailing little nibbly kisses along the line of her throat, her cheek, moving sideways towards her mouth.

There was not the slightest hint of force, yet Georgia felt powerless. She who had arranged her life so she had herself in sole control. Now her head was swimming with excitement.

"This isn't the seduction scene, is it?" she asked with forced lightness, which was her way of keeping the high sensations down.

"Certainly not," he mocked her, but very gently his mouth covered hers, rendering it sweet and open to his slow exploration.

It was a kiss that had such depth Georgia imagined it touched her soul. It continued for some time, steadily gathering such fire Georgia felt a deep warning start up inside her. It was easy to start something like this, very difficult to stop it. She drew back immediately, tossing her head, but he arched her body still further, kissing the centre of the wildly beating soft hollow at the base of her throat.

"Link?" He let her up, and she leaned against his shoulder, her voice a shaky undertone.

"So this is what it's like to kiss a goddess," he murmured, his glance on her silver-sheened hair. "I'll be damned if it's not the only kiss I've ever known."

Was there the faintest male hostility in his vibrant voice? Woman the eternal temptress. She knew it well. His expression was in shadow while the moon was shining directly on her. "I think we should go back."

"Hey, no argument!" He released her, his tone faintly edgy, yet amused. "A man would do well to fear such pleasure."

"You're not going to blame *me* surely?" she asked.

''For opening the doorway to another world? Why not?''

''Kissing wasn't my idea, remember? Sometimes it can quite destroy a friendship.'' Georgia charged up the slope, and he came after her with long easy strides. ''If you looked into my eyes right now—'' she began, whirling to face him.

''I'd *love* to!'' He gave a sardonic laugh. ''My place?''

''No way!'' A kind of rage was on her. She launched herself more determinedly towards firm ground. A minute more and she stumbled across the prop root of one of the pandanus half hidden in the sand. ''Damn, damn, damn!'' She all but fell flat. He caught her up with cool mastery. ''Don't you dare laugh at me.'' She swung at him, hair flying, like a smiting angel.

''Georgia, I'm *not*! I was only joking. Don't be mad at me. Did you stub your poor toe?''

Inside she was fighting a desperate war. It was quite fabulous to be so enfolded. For a moment she thought it was like being home. She didn't want to pull away. But she absolutely *had* to. ''Probably I've broken it.'' She bit her lip, her breath rising and falling in genuine agitation.

Immediately his amusement turned to utter concern. ''You're not serious?''

''I could find myself hospitalized.'' There was an odd pleasure in exaggerating.

''What if I take a look at it,'' he suggested quietly. ''My villa's over there. I'm good with injuries.''

That set her off again. ''I think it's improving.''

She turned to begin the final ascent, favouring her left foot, which had indeed taken a small jolt.

''Here, lean on me.''

''Okay.'' She looked down and flexed her foot. ''Maybe I should have worn boots.''

He laughed, the sound attractive and deep in his throat. ''I'm driven to say you'd look wonderful in them.''

I'm out of control, Georgia thought. *Endlessly, helplessly falling in love.*

There were no words to describe what an utter idiot she was.

He was exquisitely considerate all the way to her room, even carrying her gold sandals dangling from one hand.

''I suppose this puts paid to your early morning run?'' There was a teasing look on his face.

She shook her head. ''I don't think so. It's not much.''

''Then you won't mind if I join you?''

She looked at him and smiled. ''If you think you can keep up. It's hard track, not sand.''

''I'll call on my mortal reservoir of energies,'' he assured her. ''Didn't your uncle say they called you Atlanta at school?''

She nodded. ''I was very popular when I won a lot of ribbons for us at the school sports.''

''You must have looked electrifying heading towards the tape. Did you always have long hair?''

She met his astonishing eyes. Felt trapped by them. ''Always.'' Such excitement was dangerous, yet she had never felt so alive in her life.

''Now, you're sure you're all right?'' he asked, almost as though he could catch the rapture trembling out of her.

"I'm fine. Thank you, Link, for a lovely evening." Her need was so great she felt like pulling him into her room, but of course she didn't.

"My sentiments exactly." He bent his dynamic head and kissed her briefly on the cheek. "Sleep well. I'll see you in the morning. What time?"

"Why don't we say seven, before it gets too hot? I'll come down past your villa."

He turned, saluted her. "Perfect! Wear a swimsuit so we can take a dip later."

CHAPTER FIVE

IT WAS the start of a week so idyllic Georgia knew in her heart it had to come to an end. The closer she got to Link the more emotional radiation she sustained. His personality was so vivid, so vital, she felt enormously energised just to be with him. They continued their running, swimming, diving, even fishing, getting in so much exercise it was possible to enjoy the wonderful food so lavishly on offer. Australian waters yielded luscious seafood, and the Great Barrier Reef waters, the best. Often they took Leon with them on strolls and reef walks when the tides were right. The little boy seemed to live for these outings, and she quickly realised Link Robards was as fond of children as she was. In fact he told her he adored his two little nieces from his sister Patrice's marriage. His younger sister, Kimberley, was newly married and longed to start a family. His mother had been urging him towards matrimony for some considerable time. It all came out in the course of the days.

Leon, although vastly entertaining, didn't show a lot of promise as a swimmer. His main problem was he disliked ducking his head underwater. But with help from both of them he was making progress. His piano playing, on the other hand, was marvellous for one so young. Enough for Georgia to organise an afternoon concert for any of the guests who wished to come along. First she had to get Adam's permission, but he seemed more amused than actively interested. All his talk was of his budding symphonic work. Georgia had already made sure both he and Leon had daytime access to the baby grand in the Hideaway, the venue for Leon's concert, but there wasn't the slightest indication from Adam he would attend, let alone offer an item or join his son in a duet. He had more serious things on his mind. It was Georgia who thought out a piece for four hands. She had intended to take the more difficult part, but it soon became obvious Leon was more than capable of handling it. It was his concert, after all.

On that particular Friday afternoon Georgia was delighted to see the island nightclub not only well filled, but packed. Even her uncle had made time to attend, but after handing Leon over to her, Adam had returned to his musical labyrinths, a fact that made Link stare at her in disbelief.

''What kind of a father is he?'' he demanded.

''He *cares* about him, Link.''

''He doesn't care *enough*. I'm getting tired of the way he lies in wait for you, too. Isn't he able to visualize his own sea goddess without fixating on you?''

''It's artistic stimulation, that's all,'' Georgia pointed out soothingly. ''Don't worry about it.''

His black brows knotted. ''I'm worried he mightn't just be satisfied with *looking*. You don't need that kind of hassle.''

Indeed she didn't. What she was trying to do was help Leon, but even that mightn't work out. Leon was now looking on her and Link as honorary aunt and uncle. She didn't mind, but the little boy's life appeared to be so limited he could well miss them when it was time to go home. She badly wanted to talk to Leon's mother. Why was she so neglecting her son? She more than anyone would know just how self-absorbed her husband was. Adam seemed incapable of giving himself, let alone his son, a holiday. He might as well have been on the moon as a beautiful tropical island for all the notice he took of it. Yet paradoxically he was composing a symphonic impression of the sea. An underwater kingdom ruled by a goddess, peopled with fantastic creatures in a glorious environment. All suggesting to Georgia he might have liked to do a little research. But no. He had come to Sunset to prop himself up against a piano while kind-hearted people baby-sat his son.

For a seven-year-old Leon had superb stage presence. He walked to the piano, bowed, settled himself comfortably on the seat to a smiling round of encouragement, but Georgia was certain not a one in the audience with the exception of her and Link had the slightest idea just how gifted Leon was. As concert organiser and fellow performer Georgia sat in the front row flanked by her uncle and Link. Once seated, Leon looked towards her with his beautiful blue eyes and grinned engagingly. She nodded, feeling the nervousness of a parent.

She needn't have. For almost a half hour Leon showed the full range of his powers, present and potential. He had remarkable manual dexterity, surprising strength coming from his bony wrists, but more importantly an amazing musicality and singing tone. He played his party piece, then several pieces composed especially for him by his father.

Their duet at the finish brought the house down. To Georgia's delighted surprise both she and Leon were presented with a beautiful sheaf of flowers gathered with a satin bow. Something she found later Link had organised.

''Excellent, man,'' another boy, all of eight, wandered up to congratulate Leon. ''I never thought much of playing the piano, but that was really cool.''

''Someday I'm going to do this for a living,'' Leon said, grinning.

Afterwards Georgia and Link took him to afternoon tea, where he swooped on chocolate brownies, little cupcakes and mango ice-cream.

''Terrific,'' he told them, his top lip decorated with sauce.

Link handed him a crisp white napkin. ''We're glad you enjoyed it, Leon. But there's not the slightest doubt you'll be sick if you have any more.''

''This is simply my best holiday ever!'' Leon jumped up and hugged Georgia first, then Link, who held the little boy as though he really cared. For a second Georgia's velvety brown eyes dewed over with tears. It hadn't taken long, but Leon was tugging at their heartstrings. And no one had heard anything from the mother.

They were almost ready to leave when Adam Caswell approached their table, violet shadows under his eyes, a broody expression on his face.

''Well, how did it go?'' He slumped into a chair, clearly expecting to be welcomed.

''They *loved* me, Dad.'' Leon rose to hug him.

''That's splendid, Leon!'' Adam's smile had so

much warmth, Georgia felt a little more kindly towards him.

''Georgia and I brought the house down with our duet.''

''Georgia? Duet?'' He looked amazed. ''You played one?''

''I *did* tell you, Adam,'' Georgia said.

''Good lord, I mustn't have been listening. I'd have come down had I known.''

''You mean to see Georgia?'' Link laughed shortly.

Adam squinted. ''I didn't even know Georgia played the piano.''

''You do now!'' Wickedly Link kissed his fingers.

''You have to tell Dad a couple of times, Georgie,'' Leon explained earnestly. ''When he's working he's really deaf.''

''I'm wide awake now, thank you, Leon,'' Adam said briefly, tossing his ponytail aside.

''And how's the new opus going?'' Link asked suavely.

''Oh, fine! Georgia has been a revelation.''

''What's a revelation?'' Leon stared at Link.

''It's sort of a brainwave,'' he explained, his expression saturnine. ''Divine inspiration. I've been told you've dedicated most of your works to your wife.''

Adam turned and waved at a waitress. ''I have. But that was in better times,'' he said sadly. ''You're going to join me, aren't you?''

Link looked towards Georgia, his expression sharp. ''I think I'll pass.''

''You'll keep me company, Georgia, won't you?'' Adam begged.

''For a few minutes.'' Georgia had no wish to be rude.

Link rose to his imposing height and helped Leon from his chair. ''Come on, young fella. We'll kick a ball along the beach until Georgia joins us.''

''Excellent!'' Leon cried, looking as though he was in heaven. ''Are you going to join us, Dad?''

''No, son. That's not my scene. It's *awfully* good of you, Link, to befriend my son. Thank you,'' Adam said.

''Actually he should be learning how to kick a ball with his *father*.''

''Well...I'm a real dolt at that sort of thing,'' Adam said with a rueful smile. ''Believe me.''

''He is, too,'' Leon seconded cheerfully.

Georgia tried successfully to catch Link's eye. ''Have a good time, you two. I won't be long.''

''Fine.'' Link gave them both a brisk salute and strolled away.

''I don't think Link much approves of me,'' Adam said, as Link disappeared after Leon.

''I can't really say,'' Georgia lied.

''He's just the kind of man I've always admired but can never be. He displays all those male qualities both men and women seem to love. I feel a wimp beside him.''

''Why should you say that?'' Georgia murmured kindly when she was in entire agreement.

''He's very *physical*, isn't he? Very much the athlete and sportsman.''

''He's a brilliant architect, as well,'' Georgia replied a shade dryly.

"Really? I thought he was just in the hotel business."

"He is. He's his father's right-hand man and heir, but he also designs hotels. He designed the new Lincoln in Perth."

Adam stared at her with something like wonder. "How extraordinary! He's never once mentioned it."

"I suppose he's trying to forget business. He's on holiday."

"Are you quite sure of that?" Adam looked at her for a long moment.

"What do you mean?"

"Isn't there a rumour going around Sunset is on the market?"

"You actually *heard* it?"

"Yes, as a matter of fact."

"The hotel is *not* for sale, Adam. My uncle plans on refurbishing it after the season is over."

"That's interesting. You should come into your own there."

"I'd like to think I could help."

"You've been of enormous help to me," Adam said without hesitation. "Not only with Leon but for projecting an image of my central character. It may seem odd to you but I don't have to actually experience these underwater explorations to create an atmosphere in music. I *see* the water. I *hear* the music of the tides. I'm aware of the abundant birdsong, the harmonies of the wind. I can sight brilliantly coloured fish without ever laying my eyes on them. For that matter I can see *you* in the floating draperies of my sea goddess. I have an inner vision."

"Of course you have. Your success as a composer

is proof of that. I only wish you'd been present at Leon's concert. He was quite extraordinary.''

''Yes, I know.'' Adam Caswell nodded matter-of-factly. ''I was a child prodigy myself.''

''Leon's mother must be proud of him.'' She gave him an encouraging smile.

''She is, indeed. But Liz isn't musical.''

''Is that a source of grief between you?''

''Sometimes insurmountable. It didn't seem to matter so much in the old days. But Liz has become increasingly intolerant of my work.''

''Perhaps she thinks your music excludes her,'' Georgia said, taking Liz's part. ''Composing must be very demanding.''

''Very much so. I often feel drained. Then again I'm a difficult person to live with. I'm not interested in the social scene. Liz is. I'm not terribly into food but Liz adores dining out. I like living out of town. She doesn't. Small wonder she dumped me. She thinks I should take more responsibility for Leon, as well.''

By the time Georgia made it down to the beach she felt limp. For a quiet man, Adam's confidences had been vastly outgoing. He was missing his wife more than he liked to let on. In fact, as far as Georgia could see he needed his wife to survive.

Leon, the little victim, was splashing happily in the shallows while Link lay a short distance away keeping an eye on him. Link sat up at Georgia's approach, his eyes moving over her matchless young body in another of her sleek, high-cut swimsuits, this one in a multicoloured design. Her long slender limbs had turned from cream to pale gold. She was wearing a large straw hat and carrying her wrap and towel.

"So you finally made it!" he commented in a dry, laconic tone.

"I couldn't be rude. For Leon's sake."

"Indeed, no." Link stood up, a tawny gold sun god. "He's a damned sight too high-intensity for me. Here, sit down. I'll spread your towel."

"Hi, Georgie!" Leon called from the water.

"Hi, Leon. Don't move any farther out now."

"I won't." The little boy turned back to splashing.

"And what's with that blessed ponytail?" Link asked in a wry voice. "All that hair. I can't figure it out."

"I think it's called a statement. He hasn't noticed I've had Leon's fringe trimmed. Or bought him a few T-shirts. One gets so involved with children."

Link nodded. "Send him the bill. I'd say he was in good shape dollar wise. Leon's a great kid, but what's going to happen when he goes home? He's become so fond of you."

"He'll forget all about me," Georgia said. "I don't figure in the scheme of things."

"I don't know about that! It seems to me you're landing yourself in one hell of a situation. Caswell needs a muse. His wife appears to have run out of steam. Now it's your turn."

"Don't be absurd," Georgia said a shade uneasily, removing her hat and shaking out her long hair.

"Is it, though? These seemingly weak guys have phenomenal strength when it comes to attaching themselves to hapless females."

"Hapless females!" Georgia's indignant eyes flew to his. "There's nothing hapless about me."

"Don't you think your sense of compassion makes you vulnerable?"

"You've been very kind to Leon yourself."

"But Georgia—" Link flashed her a taut smile "—I'm definitely not Caswell's type."

"Actually he quite admires you. The doer opposed to the dreamer. As for me, I have to say he's becoming a mite importunate."

"So give it to him straight."

"Good lord, what would you suggest? Get lost?"

"A touch crude. You could tell him you're thinking of marrying me."

For an instant the whole world tilted dangerously. "I'm not into telling lies." She had to breathe deeply to control her confusion, a flare of excitement that couldn't be denied.

"Not lies, Georgia. Protection. I think I might do as a likely candidate. Temporarily speaking, of course. We take our careers much too seriously to tie ourselves down to marriage."

"Absolutely!" She just managed to regain her aplomb. "Anyway, I'm only passing inspiration for Adam. It happens all the time, this business of muses. Lagerfeld has Claudia Schiffer. Saint Laurent has someone or other."

"And to top it all off you're a *musician*!" Link continued, scarcely listening.

"I couldn't hold a candle to Leon at his age."

"No need to be *too* modest," he said dryly. "You play extremely well. You love music. You're very knowledgeable about it even if you aren't familiar with Caswell's work."

"Well, he *is* the new wave," Georgia remarked, feeling suddenly tired of Adam Caswell. "And, speaking of waves, I'm going for a swim." She rose to her feet in one fluid movement, long legs gleaming, feet planted firmly in the sand.

"Only for ten minutes," Link warned, glancing up at her. A cool sparkling look with the heat of fire. "I'll give Leon another swimming lesson, then it's *your* turn to baby-sit."

Georgia, busy knotting her long hair, bent to drop a swift, grateful kiss on the top of his head. "You've been terribly good, Link. Don't think I don't appreciate it. When the right woman catches up with you you're going to make a wonderful father."

Unexpectedly he caught her hand, causing a thousand tingles to run up her arm. "Not to mention husband. And *lover*."

"I thought we weren't going to mention husbands," Georgia said softly, holding his glance.

"The right woman can work miracles." His eyes were so bright Georgia felt dizzy. "And who can predict when that miracle is going to happen?"

Who, indeed!

Morning brought a fresh wave of guests. Georgia saw Gavin before she saw anyone else. He was standing at reception, a dashing figure in sand-coloured trousers and a great-looking shirt, chatting up Marianne, the senior receptionist. Marianne was laughing and preening, cheeks flushed, touching her raven-tinted beehive.

Why raven, Georgia wondered. Raven was such a very difficult colour outside Asia. Gavin was a very attractive man, but Georgia had the violent desire to run. She started to backtrack, but as luck would have it he turned and glanced in her direction.

"Darling!"

Every head in the vicinity whipped around. Even Georgia almost held up her palms in surrender.

Gavin broke away from a deflated-looking Marianne to surge towards her, arms outstretched.

Being a barrister had only increased his sense of drama, Georgia thought. The whole thing was too depressing to contemplate. Gavin had come to Sunset to spoil her holiday.

"Darling, how's it going? How are you surviving without me?" He gave her his super confident smile.

How did I start up with you in the first place? Georgia thought, just managing to wipe a grimace from her face.

"What are you doing here, Gavin?" she asked.

He did a theatrical double take. "Honey baby, is that any way to act? How about a kiss first?"

"If I were you, I'd settle for a smile," she said smartly.

"Let's give it a go anyway." Completely self-assured, he wrapped his arms around her, playing out a screen kiss that drew a sprinkling of applause.

What Georgia wanted most of all was to kick him in the shins, but she got the impression everyone, with the possible exception of Marianne, was thrilled for her.

"If you do that again, so help me..."

"Darling, can we go somewhere private where we

can talk?'' Gavin asked as though she hadn't made one word of protest. He drew her alongside a billowy golden cane, staring warmly into her eyes.

''No,'' Georgia said as firmly as she could.

''When I've come all this way just to be with you? Hell of a trip, too, but I'm not complaining.'' He glanced briefly around the lobby, pulled a face. ''The place has slipped a bit, hasn't it? Unk ought to let you work on it.''

That hurt. ''Gavin, you're such a jerk,'' she said angrily.

He tut-tutted. ''That's not very kind of you, darling.''

''I have it from a reliable source.''

He ignored that, as well, glancing towards reception. ''Listen, I haven't finished checking in. I've got myself one of those beach-front villas. We're going to love it.''

Georgia sighed aloud in frustration. ''I'm sure *you* will. Leave *me* out of it.''

He picked up her hand, kissed the palm. ''I love it when you play hard to get. By the way, you look fabulous. You've lost that look of stress. I'm fascinated by the golden tan. It does wonders for your hair and eyes.''

''I know,'' she said flatly.

''But of course! Golden girl. How about a swim as soon as I check in?''

''Sorry.'' She shook her head. ''I just don't feel like it.''

''Not you, the mermaid?''

''It's *over*, Gavin.''

Something hard came into his blue eyes, giving his

face an entirely different look. "That's what *you* say, sweetie. I don't agree."

"Then you'll find out."

"Why, have you replaced me?"

"All too swiftly."

"Really?" He stopped laughing abruptly. "What's his name?"

"None of your business, Gavin."

He gave her a glassy stare. "That's what *you* think. If you've met another guy you can bet your life I'm more determined. I've never doubted for a minute you and I were going to make a go of it. I've even come around to marriage, if that's what you want. You're a good, old-fashioned girl. I like that."

Georgia's heart sank. "I'm not a girl, Gavin. I'm a *woman*. What's more, I know my own mind. Enjoy your holiday, by all means. Just don't call on me." She turned on her heel and swept away, only to confront Adam and Leon, wearing identical expressions.

"Who's *that*, Georgie?" Leon's eyes were like saucers.

She shrugged, trying to keep her tone light. "An over-excitable ex-friend."

"Then why did he kiss you like that?" Leon asked, obviously trying to puzzle it out.

"He loves an audience, Leon. I'm sure you can understand that."

"Would you like me to have a word with him, Georgia?" Adam offered astonishingly, like his son troubled by what he had seen.

"Good lord, no. I can handle it."

"Don't like the look of him at all," Adam muttered

as though Gavin had been bullying her. ''Too flashy.''

This from a man who wore his hair well beyond shoulder length. ''Honestly, Adam, it's no problem at all,'' she said, trying to smile brightly.

''If you say so.'' Adam looked unconvinced. ''We thought you looked a bit upset.''

She shook her head. ''Nothing at all to worry about.''

''Right,'' Adam replied gruffly. ''Leon and I were waiting to ask you if you'd lunch with us. We'd like to repay your many kindnesses to both of us. It's been marvellous having the use of the piano in the Hideaway.''

''That was nothing at all, Adam. A pleasure.'' Georgia reached out and ruffled Leon's hair, watching the anxious expression recede from his beautiful wide eyes. ''Lunch would be lovely.''

Adam, too, bucked up, but he was still keeping watch on Gavin at reception. ''Shall we say one o'clock on the terrace?''

''One o'clock it is,'' Georgia said with a smile. ''I'll look forward to it.''

Georgia had barely reached the first floor gallery before Gavin caught her up again. ''Listen, Georgia, I had to call in a lot of favours to get a few days off,'' he said angrily. ''Why are you being like this?''

She stared at him. ''Why can't you accept our little romance is off?''

''It seemed like a big romance to me.''

He looked at her so queerly Georgia shifted uncomfortably.

"I'm sorry, Gavin. I really am. I don't want to hurt you, but I won't be harassed either."

"Harassed?" he cried, sounding genuinely shocked. "It's just *me*. I'm cool. Look, I realise I've made a few mistakes, but damn it all, Georgia, who's perfect? You've got *your* problems, and they haven't helped us, either. All that father-fixation stuff. Sometimes I think you actually *hate* men. And it's all because of your domineering old man. You know what they call him in the city—the mauler."

"Gavin, please." The mauler, that was new to her.

"Don't turn away from me, Georgia," he begged. "I don't think I could bear it."

"Oh, yes, you could." She lifted her chin. "You've survived a string of affairs. If we're naming names, when I first met you you were called loverboy. You'll survive me."

"I don't know." He shook his golden brown head. "I just don't know. You're different. I love you. Doesn't that mean anything at all?"

"It means you don't like losing, Gavin. That's all. Anyway, I told you I've found someone else."

He laughed breezily. "Not that round-shouldered guy with the ponytail and a kid in tow? What an insult."

"Friends of mine," Georgia burst out.

"You're *kidding*! He looks like a nutcase. All he needs is the round wire-rimmed glasses.

"Adam is a highly regarded composer."

"I can imagine." Gavin chortled. "No, it's too silly. I couldn't take *him* seriously at all. I thought I was talking to a girl who liked her guys exuding style, a hundred grand a year, a Merc or a Porsche."

"You've got it all wrong."

"I knew you weren't serious." He leant forward and kissed her cheek, his lips moving towards her mouth.

"Ah, Georgia, I was wondering where you were." A man's vibrant voice echoed down the gallery.

It wasn't going to be the day she had planned. She spun around to see Link walking towards them with that compelling inherent authority, his expression composed, his gaze diamond hard.

"This is the guy. Of course it is!" Gavin muttered. "Now it all adds up."

The two men exchanged glances. Important signals passed between them.

"Link, you don't know Gavin Underwood, do you?" Georgia said hastily, moving a few steps between them. "Link Robards, Gavin."

"Didn't we pass one another at the airport?" Gavin asked, in the awkward position of not having his hand taken.

"Yes," Link said crisply, "as it happens. I've heard a lot about you, Underwood."

Gavin considered that. "From Georgia?" he asked.

"Actually I've watched you in action in a court of law."

"Aha!" Gavin nodded with some satisfaction. "I knew I'd seen you before. Did I win?"

"You got the guilty party off," Link said in mock admiration.

Gavin flushed. "I give my clients the best legal representation I can."

"It must demand a very thick skin."

"I lost my innocence long ago." Gavin shrugged. "When you've seen what I've seen..."

"Gavin is here for a few days' relaxation," Georgia offered swiftly.

"Have you brought a friend with you?" Link asked.

Gavin stared at him. "No. I'm here to see Georgia."

"It was a long way to come."

"Have you any objection?"

Link looked at him coolly. "I'll go along with what Georgia wants."

"Peace," Georgia said instantly.

"It isn't all that easy to find," Link observed languidly.

"Then let's all pray." Georgia's tone was sharp.

"Actually I was more into taking a walk on the beach." Link turned to her. "I was hoping you'd come, too, so I can keep an eye on you."

She took a deep breath, resisting an impulse to retaliate. Keep an eye on her, indeed! "Fine. It's a beautiful day. Give me five minutes." Something had to convince Gavin their relationship was over. "See you, Gavin," she said pleasantly.

"What about lunch?" He looked angry and confused, his shapely mouth twisted.

"Sorry. I'm having lunch with friends. You know, the father and son in the lobby?"

"You can't *want* to," he said with a tight smile.

"She's entitled." Link's drawl had just the faintest edge.

"Then go ahead." Gavin turned, heading for the stairs. "I might do a bit of snorkelling."

''It's a wonderful day for it,'' Link called. ''Isn't life unfair,'' he observed when Gavin had disappeared on the central staircase. ''Just when we were having such a good time. I hope you didn't ask him?''

''Don't be absurd.'' She met his light glancing gaze.

''Just one question,'' he said suavely. ''You did make it perfectly plain your big romance was over?''

''I certainly did.''

''Very wise. I wouldn't want you mixed up with him at all.''

''Except *you* don't run my life,'' she said.

''Georgia, we had a pact, isn't that true?''

''I have to admit I need a *bit* of help,'' she conceded. ''Gavin won't take no for an answer.''

''Isn't that awful!'' he groaned. ''To think a barrister would harass a young woman.''

''Don't make too much of it, Link.'' She heard the steel behind the sarcasm. ''You were pretty rough with him.''

''Then eventually it will sink in. Incredibly, I heard all about that kiss in the lobby.''

''How? Who?'' Even to her own ears she sounded on the defensive.

''If you're that interested, it was Adam. He had a kind of Arnie Schwarzenegger look about him, too. He told me some ex-friend of yours had taken advantage of you in the lobby.''

''Keep it up,'' she said, surging ahead.

He caught her up easily with his long legs. ''That's how he described it. Leon said people clapped.''

''What a pity you missed it,'' she said acidly.

''I think maybe it was better that way. Even Adam

was quite perturbed, in his way. I'd say it was high time his wife arrived."

"No one would be happier than I." Georgia withdrew her door key from the pocket of her skirt and inserted it in the lock.

"Do me a favour, Georgie," he said.

"If I can, *James*." She spun to face him, her heart racing at his nearness.

"Don't be alone with Underwood if you can avoid it." His voice was serious, and he was watching her intently.

"No way he's going to hurt me," she assured him.

"He'd be very sorry about it if he did, but he's not the smooth charmer he looks."

"He's not a closet rapist, either," she protested.

He gave her a look spangled with cynicism. "For heaven's sake, did I suggest that? *Have* you slept with him?"

"I thought we'd settled that. Anyway, it's none of your business." The colour surged beneath her beautiful skin.

"I don't accept that," he said. "Let's go back over our little pact again, shall we?"

"No." Her resistance simply deserted her.

"Is that no, you won't, or no, you didn't sleep with him?"

"Both."

"You just saved his ass, do you know that?"

"Is this a joke?" Her velvety eyes stared up at him.

"No joke. I'm a man who makes seriousness a way of life."

"I think you're a man who likes to talk in riddles."

"That, too." He smiled for a moment. "Now pull

on a swimsuit and one of those alluring cover-ups that don't do the job at all. I want to be halfway to the point before Underwood hits the beach.''

At lunch Gavin chose a table close by.

He never gives up, Georgia thought, receiving the full force of his begruntled stare. She was considering changing places with Leon so she could present her back to him when two young female guests closed in on Gavin, having spotted him from afar. She heard the taller one, an attractive strawberry blonde in a shrunken top with low-slung pants perched snugly on her hips, ask if he minded if they share. On his mettle, he rose, seated them with a flourish beneath the yellow and white striped umbrella, the girls laughing, excited as though they'd been invited to a party.

Gavin was very good-looking in anyone's language. He never had the slightest difficulty attracting women. Holding onto them was another thing. Not every woman responded to being quizzed about her every movement.

In a radiant mood, Leon smiled at her. ''A hamburger and French fries sounds super to me. What are you having, Georgie?''

''Octopus,'' she joked, although baby octopus with fennel and green olives was indeed on the menu. ''On second thoughts, I think I'll settle for chicken breast stuffed with prawns and baked in pastry.''

''I'm actually hungry,'' Adam said, and smiled. ''It must be the sea air.''

Georgia left it until late afternoon to have her swim, heading out for the pontoon anchored inside the reef. This was the time she did her sunbathing, when the sun's rays were at their most gentle and caressing.

She hadn't been lying there for more than ten minutes when a head popped up beside the pontoon, thoroughly startling her. She hadn't heard anything but the terns and the warm crooning song of the sea.

She sat up quickly, trying to regain her composure.

"Hi, there!" Gavin put his long arms on the pontoon and hoisted himself up, his taut, slender body glistening with sea water. "The things I do for you. I'm a bit out of condition."

He *was* puffing slightly, but he was an excellent swimmer, as Georgia well knew.

She made no protest. Gavin was a guest at the resort. He was entitled to go where he liked.

"That's a great bikini!" He glanced down at her, his eyes following the singing lines of her body, the skin, smooth, golden, lustrous, delightfully on display. "New?"

"Yes, as it happens."

He looked at her narrowly. "For Robards's benefit?"

"Absolutely," she said firmly.

"You better wait until I tell you a few things," he said in a vehement voice, raking his hands through his thick hair.

"Oh, Gavin, please don't spoil the afternoon," she begged. "It's so beautiful. Can't you forget all about me and enjoy your few days off?"

"Sorry, doll. That's asking too much." He gave her a crooked grin.

"What happened to your friends from lunch?"

"I split. I was just filling in time. Come to that,

what do you see in that Caswell guy? Hell, I hate those sad, soulful guys. The wimpiest of wimps. And he's married with a kid."

"It's the little boy I like so much. He's been missing his mother. I'm filling in."

"Isn't that sweet?" Gavin said derisively. "You always were a sucker for kids. Don't overdo it, that's all. Wimps like Caswell are good at unloading their responsibilities. Where's the mother, anyway?"

"They're separated."

"I'm not surprised. And what's Robards's story? What's he doing up here? I wouldn't have thought Sunset was his scene."

"Oh? Let me tell you, he *loves* it."

"That could only be because he met you. I wouldn't have put it past him to change his plans midair. A high roller like that goes to Hayman or Bedarra or Lizard, like the Prince of Wales, not middle-of-the-road Sunset."

"He wanted privacy. Put that in your report."

Gavin smiled unpleasantly, lowering himself beside her. "If you think *that*, you haven't both oars in the water. You can bet our life it has something to do with business. The rumours have been flying since Dee died. The Robardses move in. They'd probably get Sunset for a good price, do the whole place up and turn it into an exclusive resort."

"It's not like that at all."

"Is that what he's telling you?" Gavin shook his head.

"Yes."

"Then he's just using you, sweetie. The father, Sam, would make your father look like a Scout leader. It's a hard old world out there, and Robards is one big, tough guy. A chip off the old block. I've managed to do some checking. Do you know he's involved with one Tania Harper?"

"No," Georgia said in a low, tight voice.

"Want me to tell you about it?"

"Put it on hold until he asks me to marry him."

"*Marry* him!" Gavin turned on his side to stare at her, his expression absolutely shocked.

"He's a great catch," Georgia went on.

"So am *I*. Admittedly I don't have his kind of money, but I happen to know you're no gold-digger."

"And I've got a rich father to begin with. Don't forget *that*. I'm quite sure it made me more attractive to you."

"Thanks a lot!"

"Gavin, you've never dated anybody who's not what you're pleased to call *somebody*," she scoffed.

"Correct. Anyway, they're always more interesting. Level with me, Georgia, what's *with* you and Robards?"

"I find him fascinating."

"Also I think a womaniser," Gavin said as though such a man should be jailed. "According to my informant he's broken a lot of hearts. I don't want yours to be one of them."

"Thank you, Gavin. I appreciate that." Georgia sat up. "Now I've had enough sun. I must go. Unless you want to race me to the beach?"

"You know I'd beat you."

"No doubt whatsoever, if I gave you a start."

She stood up smoothly, but he caught her around

the ankles, holding on. ''Georgia, how can you do this to me?'' he asked sorrowfully.

''Let go, Gavin.''

''How about dinner tonight?''

''I'm sorry, I'm booked.''

''All right! If that's the way you want it.'' He let go of her ankles and sprang up, slender but strong, an inch short of six feet.

''Kiss me.''

She stared into his eyes. ''Not by choice,'' she said in a steady voice.

''You used to love it.''

''I admit I did find it enjoyable.''

''It can be again.'' He drew her into his arms, holding her smooth, graceful body tightly to him.

''Gavin,'' she said, aware he was working himself up for a wrestle. ''I think you should know Link's swimming towards us.''

He laughed shortly. ''You're putting me on.'' Nevertheless he turned his head towards the shore, staring in some wonderment at the powerful male figure slicing through the water with the speed of a shark.

He thought for a moment, then said angrily, ''I'll pack up and be on my way. Two's company. Three's a crowd. I get bad vibes from that guy, anyway.''

''Maybe that's the way he wants it,'' Georgia replied, not that Gavin necessarily heard her as his blue-ribbon dive took him deeply underwater.

A few minutes more, and Link rose out of the water like some bronze sea god, springing black hair glistening like ebony, the water falling from his lean, powerful torso. He heaved himself up easily, sitting on the pontoon and staring at her.

"Pardon me if I think you nutty, but why in the world would you isolate yourself out here?"

Georgia sighed and lowered herself beside him, dangling her feet in the sparkling, shifting blues and greens of the water. "All I can say is, I was handling it."

"It didn't look like that to me," he said crisply.

She looked towards the shining beach, the stands of pandanus and the great soaring palms. "You must have been checking us out from the shore?"

"I was, too. I even borrowed a guy's binoculars."

She stared at their legs, his straight and so strong, hers almost fragile by comparison. "I'm sorry, Link. What should I say? I can't stop Gavin going where he likes on the island. He's a guest."

"I thought your intention was to avoid him." He was looking at her intently, his silvery gaze extraordinary in his tanned face.

"I didn't think he'd swim all the way out here," she said helplessly.

"Your big problem is you're not thinking at all."

"What?" she flared, turning her dark gaze on him.

"So what do you do when he's frantic to make love to you? Scream for help? Between the freshening breeze and the gulls it wouldn't have a lot of carrying power."

"Gavin has more sense than to force himself on me."

He made a kind of disgusted sound in his throat. "Do women ever *learn*? You can't lie around in some tiny bikini that leaves almost nothing to the imagination and think a guy like Underwood is going to keep his head. He's going to be out to prove something. You have to have people around for protection. That's the way it works. Unless Underwood means a whole lot more to you than you claim."

"He doesn't mean anything to me anymore. I keep assuring you of that." She tried to curb her rising agitation. Just to sit beside him, their hands barely touching, was to spark a fiery, sensual current.

"Then this might be the perfect time to prove it."

She turned her head inquiringly, only as their eyes met she forgot what she was going to say.

"A long, passionate kiss would look good," he suggested smoothly. "You can bet your life Underwood will have his sights fixed on the pontoon. Just give him time to get to the shore."

Georgia blushed. "I'm not taking part in any charade."

"Me, neither," he said in a dark, mocking voice.

"That's not what *I* hear."

"Oh, my!" He gave her a long gleaming stare. "Why do I have the feeling it was from Underwood?"

"Do you deny you have a few skeletons in the closet?" she challenged, holding his eyes.

His beautiful mouth quirked. "What are we talking about here? Hit and runs? I've never dated a woman who doesn't still speak to me."

"So you and all your ex-girlfriends are one big happy family?"

He laughed a little shortly. "Put it this way, Georgie, one or two are fairly bitchy to one another. You know, *women*. Now if you look towards the beach you'll see Underwood has finally made it. If he works a little harder he could be a damned good swimmer."

''But not a tiger shark like you.'' Why was she doing it? Out of sheer bloody-mindedness? He had swum all the way out to her in case she needed help.

''You're getting into dangerous territory, Georgia,'' he warned.

''All right, I'll shut up.''

''Well, there's one way to make sure of it.'' He rose to his feet in one beautifully coordinated movement, drawing her with him as though she weighed no more than a baby. ''And let's make it look good.''

She took a deep breath as if she were about to dive underwater, feeling his mouth come down over hers, covering it completely, the fresh clean taste of apples, salt water.

He kissed her until she was moaning softly, her arms clasped around his powerful body. His skin was like warm velvet, the mat of hair on his chest a delicious friction against the swell of her breasts. She had meant to keep this piece of theatre short, but in the end offered herself up to him like a sunflower to the sun. Even when they fell sideways into the water, their bodies and mouths remained fused, the two of them floating langorously in the blue water.

CHAPTER SIX

THAT evening Georgia chose a plain halter-necked top over a brilliantly patterned sarong skirt to wear to dinner. The aubergine of the top was repeated exactly in one of the floral swirls on the skirt. To add to the South Sea effect she wove a string of pearlescent sea-shells into her hair, forming a diadem. It all worked rather well. Dressing for dinner had become a big thrill, if only for the first moment when Link turned his silver-grey gaze on her.

Tonight her uncle was to join them, but when Georgia met up with the men in the foyer she thought he looked unusually flushed.

"Everything okay?" she asked quietly as they walked towards the dining room.

"Everything's fine, Georgia." He patted her arm. "Don't worry about me."

"But I *do*. You've never had a break. You've done nothing but work."

"Work has been my salvation," Robert Mowbray murmured a shade wearily.

"One can overdo it, Robert," Link pointed out, obviously sharing Georgia's concern. "You should take the opportunity to have a complete break when the renovations get underway."

"Georgia told you her design team will be handling it?" He looked from one to the other.

"Indeed she did." Link glanced at Georgia who

was walking between them. ''It's a tremendous coup for an up-and-coming young firm.''

''She's up to it, Link.'' Robert Mowbray looked at his niece proudly. ''Georgia's a very clever girl with quite a degree of her father's nous.''

The maître d' was on hand to meet them. They exchanged nods and smiles with guests at other tables. No sign of Gavin. He was probably brooding over room service or lining up with someone else. The island's three-piece group was playing soothing mood music, and tonight the table linen was the pale yellow Georgia thought most appropriate for the walls, with squat yellow candles glowing from a circlet of creamy, yellow-centred frangipani.

Dinner was a leisurely affair during which Georgia was pleased to see her uncle relaxing. Naturally they discussed the planned renovations. Link, when pressed, came up with options Georgia thought were brilliant. His training far exceeded hers, she was perfectly happy to concede. His answer to her cupola was a new pavilion entry of double height with glass curtain walls framing the breathtaking views of the gardens, the turquoise sea and the distant coral cays. Georgia had no difficulty seeing it in her mind's eye. White marble floor to echo the purity of the coral sands, lots of blue and white for the seating arrangements, one or two accent colours. A few strategically placed marble-topped consoles overhung by Gary Patterson's wonderful tropical paintings. Which reminded her, she would have to contact the artist as soon as possible. Maybe even take a trip to the mainland to arrange a visit to his rain forest home.

As they discussed various aspects of the proposed work, Robert Mowbray sat back, happy to see two clever and stimulating young people in animated conversation. Link was obviously master of his own field, but Georgia had an expertise all her own. It was no surprise to Robert Mowbray his niece had won so many awards. She had her father's business acumen and his sister's great gift for creating a beautiful and imaginative environment, a talent Dawson Bennett took very much for granted. Decoration of any kind was a woman's job, and as such unimportant.

"Between the two of you we're going to come up with some wonderful ideas to revitalise this tired old place," he said, over coffee.

"Keeping a hotel up to scratch isn't plain sailing," Link remarked. "It's an ongoing job."

"Georgia told me of your idea about changing the whole concept." Robert Mowbray took a long swallow of hot liquid.

"It was just that, Robert. An idea. My mind buzzes with them all the time."

"Of course, it would." Robert Mowbray nodded. "Georgie and I applaud the concept, but I have to work within my financial limits. I'm not a young man anymore. I don't have the borrowing power I used to have."

"You've never considered a partner?" Link asked almost casually.

"It's as I told you, Link," Georgia quickly intervened, "this is family."

Her uncle sighed. "I'm past it, I'm afraid. Losing Dee has changed everything. You could say I'm almost at the end of my career in the hotel business. I lack the time and the energy to start over."

"You wouldn't want to appoint a manager?" Link persisted, his eyes on Robert Mowbray's tired face.

"I'll have to consider it, Link, in a couple of years. Maybe earlier. First we have to make the existing place more attractive. You wouldn't care to act as our architect consultant, would you?"

Link shook his handsome head. "Renovations aren't my thing, Robert. My role is the total concept, and I'm fairly booked up, but I could recommend a very good firm who specialise in structural changes. Georgia would know them—Quadrant Architectural Services."

Georgia nodded. "They're excellent. As a matter of fact I handled the interior—" She broke off as her uncle leaned forward abruptly, his right hand beneath his jacket clutching at the area around his heart.

"Uncle Robert?" She stared at him in alarm. Link stood up, swiftly seeking out one of the guests, Dr. Lewis, who was dining that evening with his wife. The maître d' joined them, looking upset and flustered, but Georgia scarcely heard a word he was saying. She dropped to her knees, holding onto her uncle's arm. He was quite conscious, indeed he turned to reassure her, but it was obvious he was in pain and a certain state of dread.

Link's strong hands closed over Georgia's shoulders as he drew her to her feet. "It's the doctor, Georgia. We'll get out of his way."

The doctor, a specialist, lost no time making a quick on-the-spot examination before suggesting Robert Mowbray be moved to his room. The guests were looking upset. No one was eating.

In Robert Mowbray's private suite Dr. Lewis took another look at his patient, who was lying on his bed, looking all of a sudden much older and very vulnerable. The doctor's bag had been brought to him—he never travelled without it—and now he took Robert Mowbray's blood pressure, which was unacceptably high.

''What medication are you on?'' the doctor asked, removing his stethoscope and putting it into the bag. It was obvious he expected to hear one of the well-known drugs used to counteract hypertension.

Robert Mowbray supplied him with a trade name from the family of beta blockers, then with a sideways glance at Georgia admitted he'd run out of the prescription and hadn't had it renewed.

''Then you're a prime candidate for a heart attack or a stroke,'' the doctor told him bluntly. ''One can't cease medication abruptly. That's dangerous. I'll give you something for tonight, but tomorrow I'd recommend a trip to the mainland to see your own doctor, who I'm quite sure will want to do a few tests. In my opinion you're suffering from hypertension and an attack of tachycardia, probably stress-related. Did you have alcohol with your meal?''

''Two glasses of Riesling,'' Robert Mowbray, no drinker, murmured.

''Well, we can't exactly blame that. It would probably relax you more than anything else.''

''My uncle lost his wife just over a year ago,'' Georgia supplied, thinking it central to her uncle's condition. ''It was a great blow.''

''I see,'' the doctor said quietly, studying his patient from beneath bushy brows. ''Perhaps I could speak to your uncle alone for a few minutes, Miss Bennett?''

''Of course.'' She nodded and turned to go. ''We'll be in the sitting room.''

Link, who had been standing by the large plate

glass window, turned to face her, his expression sober.

Georgia drew near him, feeling enormously comforted by his presence. ''It seems nothing serious, thank God. Hypertension accompanied by a rapid heartbeat.''

Link nodded. ''That's probably what caused him to panic. The strong heart action. He's okay otherwise?''

''Dr. Lewis wants him to have tests on the mainland.'' Georgia realized she was clenching her hands. ''Tomorrow if possible. He's talking to Uncle Robert now. He was supposed to be taking medication for his condition but he let it slide.''

''That wasn't a good idea. Robert's in a low state. I know nothing can cure the source of his pain, but he badly needs a complete break.''

''I know.'' Georgia nibbled on her lip. ''Uncle Robert's been trying to keep on top of things, but his energies are at a low ebb. This is a warning, and it could change everything.''

Georgia was sitting quietly on the beach staring out at the turquoise lagoon when Link joined her. It was two days later, and Robert Mowbray had received a thorough medical checkup.

''Hi!'' Link lowered himself onto the white sand, studying Georgia's deeply pensive expression. ''You okay?''

''Sure.'' She tried to smile.

''Your stillness bothers me.''

Georgia clasped her arms around her knees. ''I'm all right, Link. I've just been sitting here thinking how dramatically life changes when ill health looms up.''

Link nodded gravely, reminded of his father's heart attack. ''Not that Robert's actually ill, thank the lord. But it's plain he can't continue the way he's going.''

''I should have known.'' Georgia bit her lip. ''I did know.''

''Georgia, you have nothing to blame yourself for. Losing one's wife is a tremendous pressure point in life. Robert should have taken a complete break. At least for a time. There's too much emotion, too many reminders.''

''Well, he's taking that break now.'' Georgia sighed. ''Doctor's orders. Mamma's got plans for them to spend a month or so at our place in the Blue Mountains. Dad never goes there.''

''And what does your father have to say to that?'' Link gave her an oblique look.

Georgia shrugged. ''Mamma didn't say, but for the first time she sounded like she didn't care. Dad always did do his utmost to keep them apart. Shows what the wrong man can do to families.''

''Wrong *person*, please,'' Link protested. ''Women have been known to do a lot of damage to relationships.''

''I suppose.'' Georgia's shoulders shrugged in a kind of despondency. She was more upset than she realised.

''Anyway, I've got a bit of good news for Robert,'' Link said in his positive way. ''I have the right man to step in as manager almost immediately, if Robert gives the okay. His name is Bernie Wilmot. He worked for us for over twenty years before he bought his own country pub, which he's turned over to his son. Bernie would jump at the chance of working up here.''

"That's great," Georgia said without enthusiasm.

"But you don't care?"

"Well, I can kiss off my plans. It seems selfish to be talking about them in the face of Uncle Robert's needs, but what's going to happen about the renovations? They desperately need doing."

"Maybe the answer is for your uncle to sell."

"To Robards Enterprises?" Her expression turned cynical.

He nodded rather curtly, responding to her tone. "Maybe. We have other options to consider."

"Oh, don't give me that!" Georgia burst out, her nerves stretched. "Sunset has a beautiful fringing reef. You've always been interested in it, Link. Probably you've been using me to get to my uncle."

She knew as soon as she said it that it was unforgivable.

His silver eyes froze. "That's a disgusting thing to say, and it smacks of your friend Underwood."

He was so right. "I'm sorry." Her voice was choked with the effort of saying it. "At least Gavin had enough pride to take himself off home."

"Hell, yes, after he unloaded a whole lot of malice."

His face was so taut and angry, Georgia felt the tears spring to her eyes. "It's worked out rather well for you all the same." She tried to get up but he stopped her and pulled her onto the sand.

"Listen, what's really eating you? Can't you tell me?"

"You're hurting me, Link," she said, trying to squirm free.

"You're hurting me, too, dammit. Anyone would think I've engineered all this."

"Well, I do know about manipulative men." She couldn't seem to stop.

"I'm not manipulative at all." He looked at her steadily. "If you've got problems, Georgia, you have to face them down. I can only repeat, I've been on the level from day one."

"Then there's nothing more to be said."

"Georgia, you're not crying?" Very gently he touched her wet lashes.

She blinked furiously. "And if I am? The past two days have been rough."

"Hey, don't you think I know that? Underwood upset you, too, with all his taunts."

"He did have a few things to say I didn't like."

"So how do you figure it?" he asked, eyes intent.

"Jealousy."

"That's for certain," he agreed. "So please don't go putting any labels on me. I'm not into control. I don't need any sweet dumb innocent woman to exploit. I want a woman who can stand on her own two feet. A woman who knows her own worth. You've got so much going for you in every department, yet you appear to believe you're going to make the same mistakes as your mother. Isn't that it?"

"Close." She managed a wry laugh. "I'm drawn to dynamos whether they're good for me or not."

He looked at her, both exasperated and amused. "Why shouldn't one of your so-called dynamos be a good guy?"

"If I find him I'll marry him."

"Then let's keep our fingers crossed." He held her chin and dropped a brief hard kiss on her mouth.

That evening Georgia and her uncle dined quietly in his suite and discussed the future.

"I must do as Link says and appoint a manager." Robert Mowbray stirred his coffee. "I'd dearly love to spend some time with your mother. Even take an overseas trip. This Wilmot chap must be a good man if Link is happy to vouch for him."

"I'm sure he is." Georgia nodded.

"In any event he'll be here next week for an interview."

"You've already decided to see him?"

"I couldn't let the offer go by, Georgie. Not in my position. The doctor insists on a complete change. Anyway Wilmot's only here on trial. Six months before we decide whether the job's going to be permanent or not. The renovations are the bother. They need doing, but I can't take on any more commitments at this time."

"Maybe your best idea, Uncle Robert, would be to sell," Georgia suggested, keeping her sadness well hidden.

Her uncle nodded, as if relieved by her answer. "It seems the best solution. But I've offered *you* the commission to refurbish it. That bothers me."

"Your health and well-being are my top priorities," Georgia said firmly. "There are other commissions. You're not to worry about it."

"Life changes overnight, doesn't it?" Her uncle sighed. "I suppose I knew my days on Sunset were numbered when I lost Dee. There's one more thing I was going to ask of you, Georgie." He paused and looked over the balcony at the romantically lit gardens.

"Anything."

"Do you think you can stay on for another week until Wilmot arrives and I can get away?"

"No problem," she said when it wasn't strictly true. "I've kept in touch with the shop. Everything's under control. Mamma said she was coming up for you."

"Insisted on it." Her uncle smiled. "You must have thrown a scare into her, Georgie."

"I simply told her what Dr. Cole had to say," Georgia answered quietly.

"I'll have a word with Link in the morning." Robert Mowbray settled more comfortably into his chair. "Sound him out. For all his gifts, he's such an easy person to talk to." He shot his niece a quick look. "It's a pleasure to see you two together."

"Don't start matchmaking now," Georgia warned.

"But you *are* getting on remarkably well?"

"Link's a remarkable man."

"And I suppose his being here lies at the heart of Gavin's speedy departure?"

Georgia sighed. "Gavin only had a few days, anyway. There was nothing to hold him."

"Just like him, too, to book under a false name," Robert Mowbray said disapprovingly. "I know it was supposed to be a surprise, but really! Gavin's smart and good-looking and all the rest of it, but I never did trust him, Georgie. It's a good thing Link made it so easy for you to get rid of him."

Within forty-eight hours of their conversation about the possibility of selling, Sam Robards flew into Sunset by helicopter from the mainland accompanied by a very glamorous dark-haired young woman who turned out to be Tania Harper, public relations manager for the Robards Belmont in Sydney.

Link had told Georgia his father would be arriving

to make his assessment of the island, but he made no mention of any ex-girlfriend hitching a lift.

It was Leon who spotted the helicopter as it whirred out of a brilliant blue sky.

"Look, Georgie," he cried, leaping up and going into a war dance. "That must be Link's dad."

"Very possibly," Georgia said, shading her eyes.

"So what's the matter?" Leon ran to her, going down on his knees and staring into her face. "Don't you like him?"

"I've never met him, Leon." She smiled into the endearing little face.

"But you don't want him to buy the island?"

"I've been coming here since I was not much older than you."

"But you can *still* come, Georgia. Link will let you."

"I mightn't want to, Leon. This was my special place."

"Yes, I know. I really love it here, too." Leon sank down on the sand, cupping handfuls and letting them go. "I told Mummy when I spoke to her last night."

Georgia looked at him in surprise. "You spoke to her, Leon? I'm so pleased."

"I told her all about you."

"Really? What did you say?" Georgia felt a whisper of concern.

"Oh, I told her how pretty you are. How much fun. I told her how you had my fringe cut so it wouldn't fall into my eyes and how you bought me my T-shirts and gym shoes for walking the reef. I told her about my swimming lessons and how we go everywhere together. I told her all about Link. I told her Daddy is writing his new symphonic poem all about a sea goddess who looks just like you.''

''You didn't tell Mummy he thought he might dedicate it to me?'' Georgia swallowed.

''Sure.'' Leon nodded. ''I did. We had a long talk. I told her all about the concert and how you and I played a duet. She was so interested in everything I said.''

''Did Daddy speak to her, too?'' Georgia asked.

''Daddy was taking his nap. Mummy said to say nothing about it.''

''The phone call?''

''It's all right, Georgie,'' Leon reassured her. ''She's going to ring again. She said she missed me terribly.''

''Of course she does. See how much she loves you?'' Georgia moved to squeeze his hand.

''I think she wanted to give Daddy a bit of a fright. I'd hate it if they split up. I know a kid whose parents are divorced. He says it's awful.''

''Yes.'' Georgia nodded, deeply sympathetic to Leon's fears. But sometimes it was even worse if two unhappy people stayed together.

Lunch was organised out on the terrace. The men rose to their feet at Georgia's approach, and Link made the introductions, keeping a light hand at Georgia's waist. Sam Robards came as something of a surprise. Although handsome in a big, bluff, vaguely rumpled way, with very sharp blue eyes, he was quite without his son's polish. His accent was broad, his manner breezy, the rough diamond her uncle had described, but a man who had battled innumerable obstacles, including a deprived childhood, to get to the top.

Link must have resembled his mother, because there was little physical resemblance so far as Georgia could see. Perhaps something about the heart-catching smile? Tania Harper looked up brightly, glamorous in a turquoise silk shirt with rather too many buttons undone and skin-tight hipsters.

"My son tells me you're in the interior design business, Georgia?" Sam Robards asked, looking at her in a very penetrating but kindly way.

"Georgia Bennett Interiors." She smiled.

"And you're Dawson Bennett's daughter?"

"You're not going to hold that against me?" Her velvet gaze was direct.

Sam Robards gave a great gusty laugh. "Came up against him once and came off the worse. He plays hard, even by my standards. I suppose he gave you a hand to start up your own business?"

"No." Georgia shook her head decisively. "Like the song, I did it my way."

"And you're very beautiful. That's a lot going for you. Beauty and talent."

It was an unusual sort of lunch. Most moments pleasant, others a touch awkward. Although it wasn't discussed, always in the background was the burning question. Did Sam Robards want the hotel? And if he did, was he going to turn into the notoriously tough negotiator right before their eyes? Link kept the conversation going smoothly. It was apparent his father regarded him with great pride mixed with an odd competitiveness, as though Sam Robards envied certain qualities in his own son.

"The coral trout was superb!" Tania Harper half closed her hazel eyes as she savoured her excellent Chardonnay. "In fact, everything's perfect. The view, the food, the wonderful sea air. And discovering such gardens! They're simply glorious.''

''My wife's creation,'' Robert Mowbray told her proudly. ''Nothing must ever threaten our gardens.''

Sam Robards looked at him for a full minute then nodded as though he totally understood. ''If you ask me, Bob, the whole place is full of love. You can breathe it in the air. What say us three guys discuss the island's future after lunch. The girls can toddle off for a swim.''

Georgia was silent, quietly simmering. *Toddle off.* It might have been her father talking.

''I don't believe I feel like a swim just yet. Not after that fabulous lunch,'' Tania said, touching Sam Robards's arm in rather familiar fashion, Georgia thought. ''I might have a siesta on the beach and wait for Link.''

Georgia was absolutely determined not to look in Link's direction. On the other hand, every time Tania Harper looked at him there was so much steam it was coming out her ears.

''Would you like me to sit in with you, Uncle Robert?'' she murmured as their party broke up. ''I could be some support.''

''That'd suit me, Georgie, but I don't think it's part of Sam's strategy.''

''I suppose not. In some ways he reminds me of Dad. Those sharp eyes!''

''I think he's a mite softer than your father.'' Robert Mowbray smiled. ''He idolizes Link. I like that.''

''And he's not the only one,'' Georgia said pointedly.

''No, indeed.'' Robert Mowbray pushed his glasses

up his nose. ''Miss Harper would appear to live in high hopes.''

''If she does, that makes Link a barefaced liar. He flatly denies any involvement.''

''Then if I were you, Georgia, I'd *believe* him. He doesn't strike me as any moral lightweight. You have to remember he must be one of the most eligible young men in the country. One can't blame Miss Harper for trying.''

''What's it to me, in any event?'' she asked flippantly.

''I'd say an awful lot.''

''Maybe you're right.'' Georgia smiled and kissed her uncle's cheek. ''Don't let them steamroller you.''

''I won't.'' He gave her a tight hug. ''This is a discussion. I'll make no decision without consulting with you.''

As they parted in the foyer Georgia caught sight of Link and Tania Harper having a conversation in one of the seating arrangements near the entrance. It was obvious Tania was a little upset about something. A lover's tiff? Such a fierceness of emotion overcame Georgia she put a hand to her heart. She was aware of an unfamiliar jealousy. Link had made no real commitment. She had fallen in love in this enchanted place. She had no one to blame but herself.

At that moment, as though at a signal, Link looked up. He waved a hand, and Tania Harper turned quickly to see who he was waving at. She was certainly an attractive young woman, Georgia had to admit. Full of confidence, informed, a good communicator, well able to hold her own. Georgia could see she'd be good at her job. Yet Georgia hadn't taken to her. It had little to do with Tania's connection to

Link, more a personality thing and her intuitive awareness that beneath Tania's practised charm of manner lurked someone else entirely. Georgia could easily see her as a tough opponent in the game of love. There was no way Georgia was going to intrude, so she returned the wave, keeping it casual. In her room she put through a call to the office before ringing her mother, who had asked for a daily report on her brother's condition. Her mother sounded stronger, more in charge, and Georgia privately mourned the fact it had taken so long. But then, as Link had reminded her, better late than never.

When she came out of the lagoon after a long, relaxing swim, Georgia found Tania Harper in a minuscule red bikini draped on one of the low featherweight recliners guests brought to the beach. Her dark curly hair was pinned into an artful looped arrangement, the expression in her hazel eyes hidden by a pair of expensive designer sunglasses.

"Hi, there!" she called in friendly fashion as Georgia approached. "You're some swimmer."

"Thanks. I love it." Georgia veered off to collect her towel and beach bag before joining the other woman. "I never feel so well as when I'm at the beach. I had a bad case of the flu a while back, but Sunset has worked wonders." Lightly she towelled herself, aware of Tania's close scrutiny. Probably looking for cellulite, the odd spider vein, something like that.

"Sit with me for a while," Tania invited. "This is a *glorious* place! The first time I've ever been here."

"I've been coming since I was a child," Georgia confided, running a wide-toothed comb through her long hair.

"Then you're going to miss it?" Tania flashed her a sympathetic smile.

"It's not a foregone conclusion a sale is in the offing."

Tania made a little scoffing sound. "What Sam Robards wants, Sam Robards gets."

"I wouldn't have thought he was into snap decisions."

"My dear, Link would have told him *plenty*," Tania said, putting a lot of weight into it.

"What are you implying?" Georgia was equally direct. "I understand Link was here for a holiday. Not a fact-finding mission."

This time Tania hooted. "Link's like his father. He's *never* off duty." She gave Georgia a wry glance. "Why, did he tell you that?"

"Absolutely. He said he wanted a quiet, private holiday somewhere he wasn't known."

"And you believed him?"

Georgia shrugged. "Why shouldn't I? It sounds perfectly reasonable."

"I think I'd be a tad more suspicious in your place."

"Maybe I was. At the beginning. But on closer scrutiny Link Robards strikes me as a man of integrity."

"Sounds like you're smitten." Tania gave her a look of jaded amusement.

"Link's an extraordinarily attractive man. I wouldn't have to tell *you* that."

Tania gave a hollow laugh. "I'd be lying in my teeth if I said no. Fact is, Link and I have been on and off for years. We both see other people but we keep coming back to each other. One of these days the whole darn thing has to be resolved. Neither of us is getting any younger.''

''So you're not absolutely dropped?''

''No *way*!'' Tania replied, banging her palms on the sides of the recliner so strongly it almost collapsed. ''Would *you* give up a guy like Link Robards? I'd be mad for him if he didn't have a dime!''

''So you followed him up here?''

''I had some time due to me. It was a sheer fluke I happened to speak to Sam. He was after my boss, but I answered the phone. We got talking. I begged a lift.''

''How long have you worked for the Robardses?'' Georgia continued her low-key interrogation, keeping calm through all Tania's revelations. She would have to confront them sometime. Preferably when she was in her room where she could scream into the pillow. Though Tania struck her as no novice in the dirty-tricks department.

''I've been with them for the best part of four years.'' Tania deliberately yawned. ''Not always at the top. My friendship with Link didn't hurt my career one bit. By the way, your uncle is a very nice man.''

''Indeed he is. I love him dearly. He wouldn't be thinking of selling at all only he lost his wife just over a year ago.''

''So Link told me.'' Tania scrunched up her dark curls. ''I'm so sorry. Weren't you going to handle the hotel's refurbishments?''

Georgia nodded. ''We'd made plans.''

''How very disappointing for you.'' Tania sounded sincere.

"It is, in a way," Georgia admitted. "But I care more about my uncle than a job."

"It's a shame all the same. Of course you'll have no chance when the Robardses acquire it. Sam is the big wheeler dealer, but Link has all the say when it comes to architectural concepts and interior design. He's the brilliant creative artist. Not Sam. And Sam knows it."

"So you're saying Link wouldn't consider my firm to handle the job?"

"Hey, Georgia!" Tania held up her hands. "Don't hold it against me. I wouldn't mind giving a talented young firm a go, but Link only works with the top professionals. People like himself."

"You mean you've discussed this?"

"Listen, hotels are my world," Tania said reasonably. "Of course we've discussed it. Link knows I'm very knowledgeable. He appreciates my input."

"I'm sure. By the same token I can't believe he told you Georgia Bennett Interiors couldn't bring the job off."

Tania's smooth forehead creased in a frown. "Look, I really shouldn't be discussing this, Georgia, if you don't mind. I've got a job to protect. I just wanted to warn you. That's all."

"Only I can't decide if it's about the job or Link."

Tania removed her sunglasses for the first time. "Maybe both," she said, the bright glitter of antagonism in her hazel eyes.

CHAPTER SEVEN

GEORGIA lost little time calling on her uncle. He opened the door and ushered her into his private quarters, a faint flush in his cheeks, scarcely able to control his excitement.

"Success?" Georgia asked brightly. She'd been bristling with anxiety. The very last thing she'd wanted was for her uncle to be put through the wringer by a master wheeler dealer.

"Sit down and let me tell you," her uncle urged.

"I'm dying to know."

"It's absolutely amazing." Robert Mowbray took a chair next to her. "I told Sam and Link I was going to speak to you before I gave my decision, but I don't think you're going to have any objection."

"Not me." Georgia shook her head. "What suits you suits me."

"Well, you *are* my heir, Georgia. Whatever I've got goes to you."

"You spend the lot," Georgia said firmly.

"Georgia, I *couldn't*." He named a figure that made Georgia sit straighter.

"Good lord, that's top dollar!" She blinked.

"It is, too." Robert Mowbray rubbed his hands in satisfaction. "I thought I'd start a bit high and come down. The usual old ploy. But they accepted almost at once. I couldn't believe it. I was led to believe Sam Robards was as tough as old boots. I knew Link didn't really want to haggle. He's got heart. But I thought Sam might drive a very hard bargain. After all I'm not in that good a position.''

''How perfectly extraordinary!'' Georgia breathed. ''I'm thrilled for you, Uncle Robert. Sad that we've lost Sunset, but we had so many wonderful years. Memories no one can take away from us.''

''But you haven't heard the rest.'' Robert Mowbray looked delightedly into her eyes. ''I'm to have my own holiday villa on the island as part of the deal. Link is going to design it for me specially.''

''He said that?'' Georgia leaned forward to grasp her uncle's wrist.

''He said it would give him the greatest pleasure.''

''How exceedingly generous!''

''As far as I'm concerned he has a heart of gold. And that's not all.''

Georgia drew a deep breath. ''Listen, I don't think I can take much more.''

''Georgia Bennett Interiors will be asked to submit proposals for the new concept.''

''You're joking!''

''I'm not!'' Robert Mowbray threw back his head and laughed.

''Are you sure you haven't been doing a little haggling yourself?'' Georgia felt a clutch of dismay.

''Well, I did think of it,'' he admitted, ''but as it happened I didn't have to say a word. It appears I'm not the only one who believes in you. Link does, too. From what I can make out Sam doesn't interfere in the creative side of things. That's Link's department. I'd say he'll keep you on your toes. There might even be a few clashes, but I'm confident between the two of you you'll come up with something marvellous. Something ideally suited to this environment. You both have a special feel for the place. Anyway, Link will be wanting to talk to you himself. I couldn't resist breaking the good news, though. You are my niece, after all.''

''And Mr. Robards had no objection? He must realise I've had no hotel experience.''

''But it's rather more like separate villas, isn't it, Georgia? Little houses. You'll handle that beautifully. The central complex might be more taxing, but you and Link will be working closely together. It could make you quite a name.''

''Dad might even have to take me seriously,'' Georgia said, feeling wonderfully elated. Little houses. Little jewels. Each one different. All keeping the magic. Above all, Link believed in her. All their discussions hadn't been for nothing.

''So do I tell them yes?'' Robert Mowbray asked gently.

Georgia went to her uncle and embraced him. ''I know what selling means to you, Uncle. There's no joy without sadness.''

''No. But life moves on, Georgia. Even if I hadn't lost Dee we'd have had to think of retiring some day. We'd planned a long overseas trip. Now I'll take it with your mother. We were so close when we were young.''

''You will be again. Mamma sounds much stronger in herself. So concerned about you. And you won't be losing your connection with Sunset. We can trust Link to keep all the magic. I'm so excited about *my* role I can scarcely take it in. I've so many ideas flowering in me. At least three distinct proposals, but of course I can't begin on anything until Link comes up with the new concept. It should be an exciting time.''

Robert Mowbray smiled at her enthusiasm. "Well, you seem to be on the same wavelength in more ways than one," he said meaningfully. "I've total confidence in you both to do what's best for Sunset. I never dreamed it would happen so quickly, that's all."

That night Georgia put on the prettiest dress she had to celebrate the deal that would make her uncle a rich man, free to travel and without the commitments that had been taking their toll. For her own part she couldn't believe in the good fortune she had learned first from her uncle and expected Link would discuss with her at some point in the evening. The Robards chain wasn't really risking anything. She was young, relatively inexperienced, but to quote the top people in the interior design business she had exceptional talent.

Not only that, she had a career, which she hoped could be successfully combined with marriage and a family. All she needed was the right man. A man who would not only excite her senses but tear at her heart and reside in her soul. A man she had already met. It was possible Link had had a passing affair with Tania. But Link impressed her as a man whose feelings went deep, not a player who entered into one relationship after the other, as Tania had implied. She felt sorry for the young woman, knowing her feelings. Indeed she felt a degree of caution. Some women would stop at nothing to maintain their position.

Her dress for the evening was a perfect showcase for shoulders, an organza halter neck with a small waist and full skirt. The material was beautiful. Pink, apricot and yellow lilies with a tracery of green on a soft cream ground. She'd found herself two perfect pink lilies to wear in her hair, pinning them just behind her ear. The sun had bleached the fine hair around her hairline, grading it with silver gilt. When she was completely ready she slipped into high-heeled pink sandals that were little more than a T bar. It was wonderful island dressing! She felt free to loom romantic, to wear flowers in her hair.

Tania was wearing a red hibiscus centre front of her piled-up dark curls. Pastels weren't her scene, or the soft romantic look. She was far more exuberant, wearing a tight-fitting red silk shantung dress, the skirt well above the knee showing shapely legs, and very chic gold evening sandals.

Sam Robards immediately took charge of Georgia, leading her towards the restaurant. "I expect your uncle's given you the good news?"

"Regarding the sale?" Even now Georgia wanted to make sure there hadn't been some mistake about her commission.

"Certainly, and the part you're going to play?"

Despite herself the blood rushed to Georgia's head. "I'm too thrilled for words, Mr. Robards. And very grateful you've considered me."

"Link's not a bad judge."

"I have no intention of letting him down."

Sam Robards bent his grizzled head closer. "What do you think of my son?" His big, powerful voice was barely above a murmur.

"I admire him immensely," Georgia said carefully.

"Fine. But that wasn't what I asked."

"What *did* you ask, Dad?" Link moved to join them, his hearing patently acute. Tania and Robert Mowbray trailed by some feet.

"I'm sorry. That's between Georgia and me."

"I'll get it out of her," Link promised, his glance gliding over Georgia's face and pale gold shoulders. "That's if I can ever get the chance."

"So what happened to the midnight stroll on the beach?" his father asked playfully. "This Robards Bennett venture will bring two very clever young people together." He turned his large, handsome head. "Come along, you two," he called to Tania and Robert Mowbray, who lagged behind in conversation. "I'm ready for a celebration. By the way, I thought we'd go game fishing tomorrow, Bob. I spent a bit of time with Lee Mason, the American actor, when he fished the reef. You'll remember him. A great fella."

"As a matter of fact I had to lend him a jacket and tie." Robert Mowbray joined them, leading Tania by the arm. "They wouldn't let him into one of the smart restaurants at Port Douglas."

"Is that a fact!" Sam Robards laughed. "I bet he didn't take too kindly to that."

"Actually he was charming."

Link turned to add a recollection of his own, leaving the two young women momentarily alone.

"That's a beautiful dress," Tania remarked, hazel eyes fixed on Georgia. "I like something with a bit more vitality myself, but I have to say the ladylike look suits you."

"Thank you." Georgia was determined to be pleasant. "You look very fetching yourself."

"I gather congratulations are in order." Tania leaned closer. "It's a good thing nepotism never goes out of style."

"You can't mean that?" Abruptly Georgia's tone changed.

"Oh, come off it!" Tania glanced quickly at the men. "Don't tell me your uncle didn't make you part of the deal. Not that I blame him. I just wish I had an uncle like that."

"I'm sorry, Tania, but you've got it all wrong," Georgia said firmly, at the same time unnerved.

"My dear, *you're* the one who hasn't got it right. Do you really think Link wants you for the job?"

Georgia considered briefly. "You don't have long to wait. Let's ask him."

"And cause everyone deep embarrassment?" Tania backed off. "Your uncle into the bargain? I daresay he told you you didn't figure in the deal because he wanted you to believe you'd won it on your own."

"What are you saying?" Georgia was feeling like settling this at once.

"Your uncle loves you. That's what. I wish someone cared that much about me. I came from a broken home."

"And you've been trying to break up other homes ever since?"

"Don't spar with me, Georgia," Tania said soberly. "You don't have a chance. Link tells me *everything* that's going on."

There was no time for Georgia to respond. Link finished his story to a burst of laughter then turned, eyes sparkling, to take her arm.

"What were you two whispering about?" he asked her, his expression sharpening as he picked up vibrations.

She had a split second in which to tell him, but decided against it. Not for anything was she going to upset her uncle.

"Georgia?" Link prompted her.

"Tania was saying how much she envied me for landing the job."

"Are you sure?" He spoke in a dry tone.

"Why would you doubt me?"

"You have that look about you," he returned crisply. The air was suddenly electric between them, though they spoke in undertones. "Besides, I've known Tania for years. I know all the signs. She's got her nose out of joint, but she's trying to cover it."

"Maybe she's been led to believe she had more importance in your life?"

"We'll leave that for now." He, in turn, was cool. "Actually I wanted to tell you about our plans myself, but Robert was so thrilled I suppose it was asking too much for him to keep it to himself. He regards you more as a daughter than a niece."

"That's true. I feel I ought to thank you," she added, trying to keep the seeds of doubt buried.

"You bet your life you should." He gave a short laugh.

"I didn't handle that well."

"No."

The maître d' had been watching for them and approached with a smile. He showed them to a table beside the floor-to-ceiling French doors open to the sea breeze and the star-studded night. Once Georgia was seated between Link and her uncle, her eyes dwelt on the table. It had been arranged beautifully with crystal, classic Royal Doulton, silver cutlery and silver candlesticks to enhance the scene. Exquisite dendrobium orchids, pure white with citron-yellow throats, formed a centrepiece, spilling out of an antique silver swan that had long been one of Dee's favourite table decorations.

Georgia turned to catch her uncle's eye. They exchanged a quiet look of understanding. Dee was represented at the table. Dee who had cared so much. Good manners and her own sensitivity demanded that Georgia pull herself together. This was supposed to be a celebration. Her uncle was looking happy and relaxed, and Sam Robards, too, was in high good spirits. The tension lay between Link, Tania and Georgia. It had to be seriously considered Tania had gone out of her way to destroy the feeling of accord. Her vivacious face never stopped smiling, but there was a concealed malevolence somewhere. Georgia was sure of it. Tania was jealous and deeply resentful, but she had the training to keep those feelings carefully under control.

Around them music, conversation, little bursts of laughter eddied. By the time the entrees arrived, oysters, prawns and shellfish prepared in various delicious ways, they had settled into a harmonious group. The food, as usual, was mouth-wateringly delicious, with coral trout, red emperor and succulent lobsters the catch of the day. Only Sam Robards found room for dessert, although Link, ever mindful of his father's heart attack, tried to jolly him out of it. He did in fact cause the order to be changed from a rich chocolate torte to tropical fruit salad with one scoop of ice cream and kiwi fruit coulis.

''He watches me like a hawk,'' Sam Robards told the others, trying to sound vexed when he was enormously pleased.

''We'd like you around as long as possible, Dad,'' Link cut in smoothly.

"You think he looks like me?" Sam Robards suddenly demanded of Georgia.

"One can see a resemblance."

"Really?" Sam seemed delighted by the notion, turning to stare at his son's stunning, fine-chiselled face.

"The same heart-catching smile," Georgia said.

Sam Robards went pink with pleasure. "That sounds fine to me, Georgia. His mother's always tried to tell me he has my smile, but when you see her you'll know who he's *really* like. She's a great beauty, right?" He again addressed his son.

Link's expression was indulgent. "She can still walk into a room and bring the conversation to a halt."

"Mrs. Robards is a very glamorous lady," Tania cooed, a trifle the worse for the wine.

They moved out onto the terrace for coffee, sweet, hot and strong. The conversation, which had ranged over many subjects, pleasant and entertaining, now turned to the new concept for the resort. Georgia, totally caught up in the discussion, wasn't sure at what point Tania's bright mood changed. One moment she was making rather frivolous suggestions that clearly irritated Sam, the next she stood up so hastily her chair scraped on the tiles.

"You'll all excuse me, won't you?" she said with a stiff, small smile. "I'm not really part of this. I've had a wonderful evening, but I could do with an early night."

She sounded brisk to the point of being brittle, giving Georgia the dismal feeling she cloaked some deep despair.

All three men were on their feet, and Sam Robards

glanced at his watch. ''I might call it a night, as well, What time do you reckon we could get away on our fishing trip, Bob?''

''I can organise for seven. If that suits you?''

''Fine. What about you, Link? Are you coming or not?''

''Not this time, Dad.''

''Other things on your mind?'' Tania gave a rather harsh laugh.

''I intend to walk all over the island,'' Link said, ignoring her remark.

''Want company?'' Tania leaned over the chair.

''It's a field trip, Tania. You'd be happier relaxing on the beach.''

''Wow!'' she said softly. ''Haven't you changed?''

Robert Mowbray solved the awkward moment by taking her arm. ''Let me escort you to your room, Tania.''

''Thank you, Robert. You're a gentleman.'' Tania wobbled just a little.

''She's upset about something,'' Georgia said when she and Link were alone.

''Unlike you, she doesn't stick to two drinks.''

''That's rather unkind.''

''It's the truth. What is this, the sisterhood thing?''

''I don't like seeing people unravel.''

''You're not on your own. Tania shouldn't have come here. Dad should have stopped her.''

''I expect she was very persuasive. Anyway, she's a free agent.''

''And a born troublemaker,'' Link said in a laconic voice.

''Surely that would affect her job? She's in the business of public relations, after all.''

"It's in her private relationships she likes to stir things up."

"And you've learned at first-hand?"

"I've learned to look out for Tania," Link drawled.

"Why not? You've been on and off for years."

"On and off?" Link gave her a look with a lot of glitter. "What the heck are you talking about, Georgia?"

"One wonders why you're so *angry*, James."

"So call me James. I'll learn to live with it, but I take objection to your implication."

"You're telling me you and Tania were never an item? I have it on good authority."

"I don't think I know what *an item* means."

"Does *lovers* help?"

"What is it you want? A full confession? Whatever happened between us, Georgia, was a long time ago."

"So you *did* have an affair?" Once started Georgia found she couldn't stop. So much for two drinks.

"Sure," Link responded. "It lasted about a week. Around the same time Tania was seeing a guy called Hadley. He was showering her with gifts."

"And you were heartbroken?"

"In a word, no. Tania was trying to move into what she called the big time. So tell me, why are you fretting about Tania?"

"I'm not fretting," Georgia protested. "I'm getting things straight. I have to agree, Tania's a stirrer."

Link fixed his eyes rather broodingly on her face. "So that's what your little discussion was about earlier in the evening?"

Georgia shook her head. "She implied I was given the commission because Uncle Robert forced the issue."

"And your immediate response was to believe her?" Link rose to his feet, grasping her wrist. "Let's get out of here."

"I detest forceful men," Georgia muttered, finding she meant the reverse.

"And who would take any notice of what a woman says?" Link retorted, in a taut voice.

"Well, on the issue of does no mean no, I mean yes."

"Would you mind running that past me again?"

"Link, *where* are we going?" she pleaded.

"To the villa. Where the hell else? It's about the only place I can get you to myself."

Excitement flowed. A great rush of sensation that was fabulous. She couldn't connect such radiance to the doubts that had assailed her. He had only to touch her for her flesh to melt.

The sky was limitless. Glittering with a billion stars, some of such brilliance they flashed tints of sapphire, ruby and gold. The Southern Cross hung above them, the great constellation of Orion, the mighty hunter, with his sparkling jewelled belt. There wasn't a cloud in the gleaming sky, the wind off the water fresh and cool on her heated skin.

Finally it all became too much. With a muted exclamation Link turned her masterfully into his arms. "You care about me, don't you?" His voice was low and urgent.

No answer. Which was a mystery even to Georgia, because she had fallen in love with him at first sight.

"Don't ruin it," Link warned her, giving her a slight shake.

"I won't," she whispered.

"You know you're the only person in this world. The *only* one."

His words were like music inside her head. "I want to believe you with all my heart."

"But you know it. Don't let Tania upset you. Or that nonsense she told you about Robert making you part of the deal. She knows nothing of our affairs."

"It's just that..." She struggled to explain.

"You're a real doubting Thomas, aren't you?" he said in a wry voice.

"I'm afraid of what I *feel* for you, Link. I couldn't bear betrayal. Not from *you*. It would leave me—"

"God, the things you say!" he interrupted. "You're so seemingly confident yet underneath you're so vulnerable."

"I think that happened when God created woman."

"He created the most beautiful creature on earth." His voice was both harsh and tender. He gathered a long coil of her hair and turned her face to his, a pale glimmer in the starlight.

"I *must* have you, Georgia. It's paradise and hell."

She understood *exactly* what he meant, opening her mouth to him and his exquisitely passionately kiss. He was so wonderfully familiar, yet so mysterious. She knew the scent of his skin. It was like some marvellous new aphrodisiac. He was irresistible to her, but at some level she felt a hot curl of panic, as if he could take her beyond herself to some place of dazzling light. A place where there were no guidelines, no borders, only sensual pleasure beyond her most exotic dreams.

When his hand shaped her breast so lovingly, caressingly, his thumb gently exciting the already erect nipple, she tensed slightly. Such a tender gesture, yet it was powerfully erotic, increasing his extraordinary power over her and her yearning, yielding body.

"Come with me, Georgia," he urged her, the faintest tremble in his lean, strong body. "We can't stay here."

Their footsteps fell away soundlessly as they made their way out of the grove of feathery tree ferns and tall golden canes. They were at the short flight of stairs that led to the veranda of his villa. Her hand was wrapped in his, her heart a live, leaping thing in her breast. She was a grown woman, but such desire was as terrifying as it was beautiful. She had only brushed with fire. Now it could devour her.

At first all they saw were shadows. Then one separated itself from the rest.

"I don't know that I can stand this. I don't honestly *know*!" a woman's voice cried out in anguish.

"Good grief, Tania!" Link's urgent passion dissolved into total exasperation. "What the devil are you doing here? Please keep your voice down."

"Didn't I tell you, Georgia?" Tania moved towards the railing, clinging blindly. "He's so *ruthless*."

"Ruthless enough to run you to your room." Link mounted the steps.

"Link!" Georgia went after him, disturbed and dismayed.

"This needn't concern you, Georgia," he told her.

"It should. You've been sleeping with her." Inexplicably, Tania laughed.

"Why don't we take her inside," Georgia suggested as a matter of urgency. "Poor thing. She's had too much to drink."

"I do that occasionally," Tania said.

''What do I want her inside for?'' Link demanded, emanating male irritation.

''I wonder if you realise how much your voices are carrying?''

''That's okay,'' said Tania. ''Why shouldn't everyone know?''

''That's it!'' Link said, but Georgia pushed Tania inside the door.

''You're sweet, Georgia. Do you know that?'' Tania laughed discordantly. ''I have to hand it to you. You're one sweet girl.'' She collapsed onto the sofa in a flurry of legs. ''So what do we do now, compare notes? I have to tell you he's the fieriest lover in the whole world. And I'd *know*!''

''Coffee,'' Georgia said staunchly. ''Strong black coffee. It might help.''

''They say *not*,'' Tania commented owlishly.

''What if I leave you two here and go back to the hotel for a stiff drink?'' Link asked sarcastically.

''Maybe we could talk about it,'' Georgia said. ''Tania obviously sees herself as a woman wronged.''

''We did have a good time, didn't we, Link?'' Tania demanded, hazel eyes glassy.

''You think I can remember back that far?''

''I've loved you more than anyone,'' Tania moaned. ''Much, much more than anyone. Beside you no one else counts.''

''Coffee, Link,'' Georgia urged, thinking Tania was about to dissolve into an old-fashioned crying jag.

''It's in the cupboard. Help yourself.''

''Listen, I make the coffee, then I'm out of here,'' Georgia said.

''Then Tania goes with you,'' Link retorted crisply.

''Throw us *both* out,'' Tania suggested, almost in triumph. ''He's got a cruel streak, Georgia.''

''I think I might have, too, in his place,'' Georgia said. She'd found a six-cup plunger, freshly ground coffee, cups and saucers. She set the electric kettle to boil.

''Isn't this cozy. A ménage à trois.'' Link pulled out a dining room chair and sat on it back to front. The wind had tousled his hair so that a crisp curl fell onto his dark copper forehead. He looked as highly mettled as a racehorse going into the stalls.

''Got the message, have you?'' Tania chortled. ''What happened between us, Link, hasn't finished.''

''Tania, you're suffering from delusions,'' he said bluntly.

''Be gentle with her, Link.''

''Gentle?'' His silver eyes glittered like crystals. ''What you don't understand, Georgia, she's revelling in this.''

''I *love* him, Georgia. I wouldn't lie to you.''

''Here, drink this,'' Georgia said soothingly, moving over to the sofa and putting the coffee into Tania's hand. ''I do believe you, Tania. You love Link, but sadly he doesn't love you.''

''He did before *you* turned up,'' Tania retorted so violently coffee splashed into the saucer.

''That's not true,'' Georgia continued in a quiet, soothing tone.

''I'll be damned!'' Link laughed. ''Trust at last.''

For once Georgia didn't go for her morning run. She slept late and breakfasted in her room. As might have been expected, once she and Link had walked Tania to the main building and deposited her in her room, their nerves were frayed to the point they had a short, sharp exchange themselves. With emotions so heightened Tania had scored a little victory, after all. Link had stalked off, the very picture of an outflanked outraged male, a bare second before Georgia decided to turn apologetic. It was all so exceedingly foolish. Tania Harper was one of those women with an obsessive streak. If she couldn't have Link herself, she deeply objected to anyone else having him.

That most definitely included Georgia.

Around mid-morning, when Georgia considered Link would be off on his field trip, she decided to venture out of her room, but when she opened her door a woman was standing directly outside. She was blonde, pretty, but so far as Georgia was concerned she had a hostile glitter in her eyes. ''Miss Bennett?''

''Yes?'' The eyes looked familiar.

''I'm Elizabeth Caswell.'' She might have been throwing down the gauntlet.

''Why, how lovely to meet you, Mrs. Caswell.'' Georgia smiled. ''This is a surprise!''

''Why do you say that?''

''I beg your pardon?'' Georgia looked back wide-eyed.

''Why is it a surprise?''

''I had no idea you were coming up.''

Elizabeth Caswell continued to stare at her. ''You *are* beautiful. Leon said you were.''

''Please don't hold it against me, Mrs. Caswell,'' Georgia said wryly. ''Leon is a delightful little boy. I've so enjoyed his company. Look, why don't we go and have a cup of coffee. We could talk for a while. That's if you're not doing anything else.''

''I think that would be a good idea,'' Elizabeth Caswell said firmly.

They had barely reached the end of the hallway before Link appeared at the top of the stairs. He looked stunningly handsome, full of a crackling energy that reached out for Georgia and warmed her. His diamond gaze swept over both women before he moved to join them, at the last minute gathering Georgia into a one-armed embrace and planting a brief, sizzling kiss on her mouth.

''Morning, darling,'' he murmured in a deep, sexy voice. ''I just wanted to tell you I'm off. I should be back around mid afternoon.'' He turned his dark head, looking expectantly at Elizabeth Caswell.

Now Elizabeth Caswell appeared bemused. She looked from one to the other with a slight frown between her delicate brows.

Somewhat dazed herself, Georgia made the introductions. That kiss was scorching. Her whole body vibrated.

Link was charming, saying all the right things about Leon and Adam and how they had all enjoyed their holiday acquaintance.

''I was about to ask Miss Bennett—Georgia—if she would join me for coffee,'' Elizabeth Caswell said in pink-faced confusion. ''She's been so kind to Leon. You, too, Mr. Robards. Leon told me. Perhaps one evening when you're free we could all have dinner together?''

''That would be lovely,'' Link said smoothly, his arm still clasped around Georgia's waist. ''Now I must be off. You won't mind if I have a quick word with Georgia, Mrs. Caswell?''

''Why, of course not,'' Elizabeth said. ''In fact,

Georgia, instead of coffee, could we meet for lunch? I actually should get back to my family.''

''I'm sure they're delighted you've arrived.'' Link smiled. ''Georgia and I have never seen such a lost pair!''

Elizabeth Caswell's pretty face lit with radiance. ''They *were* thrilled to see me,'' she confided. ''I really shouldn't have left them on their own. Both of them are my babies.''

''I'd say Leon was the older,'' Link muttered as Elizabeth disappeared down the hallway. ''At least that got *you* off the hook.''

''It's ridiculous,'' Georgia said. ''But I think she thought I was trying to take her husband off her.''

''I'd definitely say so,'' Link confirmed. ''See how dangerous it is to get mixed up with married men?''

''It's *too* silly,'' Georgia protested.

''Yes, but it brought her up here quick smart. All's well that ends well, I say.''

''I think she wants them to stay together as a family,'' Georgia said hopefully.

Link nodded. ''They were happy once. They can be again. They'll have to try harder. For Leon's sake.''

''If it means anything at all, thank you. The kiss was a great piece of strategy.''

''No strategy,'' he said lightly, ''but you can certainly thank me tonight.''

''There's one favor I'd like to ask.''

''Anything.''

''Don't invite Tania,'' Georgia teased.

''She said she couldn't remember a thing about it. Do you believe it?''

''Nope.''

"Me, either. Now I have to step on it. I want to make certain of every inch of this island. You can read over what I've written and look at my sketches when I get back."

"I'm wondering why you don't want me to come." Georgia lifted her velvety eyes to him.

"Georgia, I said I wanted to *work*."

"Really?" She laid a hand against his chest.

"You'd better believe it."

Lunch with the Caswells went off extremely well. With her worst fears banished, Elizabeth set out to be as charming as she knew how. She beamed on her son, constantly clutching his hand and giving it a little squeeze. Spurred on by his wife's warm, relaxed manner and her attentiveness to his every word, Adam showed a surprising wit and charm of his own. Both of them thanked Georgia profusely for being so kind to Leon and both expressed the earnest wish Georgia and Link would dine with them one evening soon. Adam confided his opus was going beautifully, but he intended to put work aside. There was talk of taking a few days' cruise around the many beautiful islands in the region, and if conditions were right visiting the outer reef.

"Isn't it great, Georgie?" Leon said to Georgia later. "They're not going to get a divorce after all."

"That's wonderful, Leon. I couldn't be more pleased for you." Georgia looked affectionately into the beautiful blue eyes. "You're going to need all the support you can get for your brilliant career."

"And we've got to stay friends."

They smacked hands.

With Leon happy and secure with his parents,

Georgia decided to make the canoeing trip to Tyron by herself.

As she was approaching the boathouse she met up with Tania, looking attractive in a matching cotton shirt and shorts with a bold floral print.

"Hi, there!" Georgia called pleasantly, wanting an awkward moment over.

"Oh, hello." Tania's voice was light and flat. "Listen, I'm sorry about last night." She stood in front of Georgia, almost blocking her way.

"It's forgotten," Georgia fibbed. "I don't like to see anyone upset."

"It was all true, you know." Tania's hazel eyes were dark and stormy.

"Tania!" Georgia held up a staying hand. "I don't want to discuss this further."

"You'd be wise to listen. Link is Sam Robards's heir and his mother's adored only son. There's not a woman alive good enough for him. Just wait until you meet her."

"Whether I meet her or not remains to be seen," Georgia said.

"You want Link, don't you?" Tania asked sharply.

"This is all private, Tania. I'm sorry." Georgia made to pass.

"Well, best of luck." Tania stood aside with an ironic salute. "Trying to hold onto a guy like Link is like trying to catch a tiger by the tail. Who knows, you might be like me and get badly mauled."

It was delivered like a parting salvo, and it found its mark. As much as she knew Tania was deeply jealous, the whole situation took the shine off Georgia's day. It was just as well the new manager was arriving, and she and Uncle Robert could get away.

By the time she reached the cay she was almost out of breath. For once the crossing had been like scaling a mountain, and she put it down to the fact Tania had upset her. She was human, after all, and very much in love. It seemed incredible to her her life had taken such an overwhelming change. It was difficult to deal with the suddenness and intensity of feeling.

Link had cut into her most profound being, but along with the wonder and desire there were needs and fears to be settled. She realized the traumas of childhood and adolescence still affected her. The old worry she might somehow be drawn to a man who would only make her suffer. Her mother had married such a man. It could be argued she was much stronger than her mother, much more independent, that Link bore no resemblance to her father beyond a certain male toughness. What she had to do was abandon the old emotional freight, to feel secure enough to totally let go.

Puffing a little, she pulled the canoe onto the shingle. She was looking forward to a quick cooling dip. How lovely it was here. The water looked wonderful, a jewel-like aquamarine. Several species of birds had their breeding grounds on Tyron. She watched as the gregarious little noddies and silver gulls came down to greet her, unconcerned by her presence. Green turtles also bred on the cay. A short distance away was the track where one of them had used its curious rowing action to slide into the water.

Years ago Dee had planted a line of coconut palms, and now Georgia sought their shade. One of them had been bent to an angle of forty-five degrees by the prevailing winds, and she leaned against it getting her breath. The vegetation on the cay was even more luxuriant than she remembered, thicker stands of pandanus with their prop roots and pineapple-like fruit, the taller pisonias with large pale green leaves, the feathery casuarinas. Long ribbons of yellow-flowering succulents decorated the low dunes and ran down onto the strand, their faces as bright as daisies. The view back to Sunset was beautiful, the shadings in the water incredible, the distinct tones as clearly defined as lines drawn across a painting. The light was so clear, so bright the horizon seemed to run on forever. How she loved her Treasure Island with all its memories.

After her swim Georgia visited all the old spots that were so special to her, gathering a few prettily marked shells for Leon before lying down in the shade. As always these days her thoughts turned to Link. Their relationship had moved with the speed of a lightning bolt. The *coup de foudre* of fiction. Except it really *had* happened. There had been no opportunity to ask her uncle if he had interceded on her behalf for the interior design commission. Now she decided she wouldn't. Who was she to trust, after all? Two men she loved, or foxy Tania Harper who had an agenda all her own?

Her mind tired, feeling faintly dizzy, Georgia dozed off. When she awoke some forty minutes later she realized the tide was coming in fast. It would be wise to paddle back now. She stood up quickly, but as she did so she reeled abruptly then fell back on the sand.

Vertigo. She suffered from it now and then, especially if she'd been diving. The only good thing was the sensation quickly passed.

Except this time it didn't. Georgia gave it a few minutes more, then tried to rise. Her head spun like a top. She felt a wave of nausea that had her lying prone. Keep calm, she thought. This will pass. It always does. She just needed stillness.

When Link returned to the hotel Georgia was nowhere to be found. She couldn't be on the beach. The sunset had come and gone in a blaze of glory, and the stars were coming out in their hundreds of thousands. No one at reception knew where she was. He spotted Tania in the lounge, enjoying a drink with a male guest. Trust Tania, he thought. He approached their table, asking if Tania had any idea where Georgia might be.

"Sorry." Tania looked up casually. "I met up with her once this afternoon. As far as I know she was just going down to the beach." She could have said *boathouse*, but why make it easy? Let him suffer. Under that controlled, super-confident facade she would have sworn Link Robards was fairly frantic.

It was Leon who remembered Georgia had said she was going over to Tryon. "She was going to take me, only Mummy arrived," he told Link. "Anyway, Miss Harper would know. They were talking near the boathouse. I saw them."

Link's face turned grim. He would follow up *that* piece of information later. He moved fast, taking out the dinghy he and Georgia used on their scuba diving expeditions, pointing it westward across the warm, sheltered waters. He couldn't think beyond getting to Tryon. Finding her. This was the worst dread he had ever known, yet he clung to the fact she was an excellent swimmer. She handled a boat extremely well.

He stared towards the adjacent cay, a dark silhouette against the radiant sky. A full moon rode high, exceptionally big and luminous, laying down a track like a silver blaze between the two islands. His vision was sharp, fully focused, his body full of power from the charge of adrenaline. Once he hit a current. The small craft rocked, then moved steadily forwards. The lights of Sunset were behind him. He could see nothing ahead but darkness against a pearlescent sky.

Nearing the beach, he felt a sudden intense fear. What if she weren't there? What if Leon had got it wrong? She hadn't gone diving. He had checked that out. Tryon was as close as he could get to solving the mystery. Georgia had often spoken about visiting the coral cay. She had wanted to take Leon, let him explore.

It was some comfort to realise she knew the cay well. There were no high places from which she could fall. No snakes. No venomous animals. The only threat came from the sea. Shark attacks were rarely heard of in these waters. There was the odd horror story about the worst scorpion fish, the stone fish, but all scorpion fish were sluggish bottom dwellers, living among the seaweed and coral rubble. Cone shells had caused serious injuries in the past but Georgia would know all about them. She had grown up in this world.

He beached the dinghy and looked around for some sign of a boat, some sign of life. There was a great knot inside him that was tightening its grip. He was gritting his teeth silently against the boundless anxiety.

He began to call her name, his voice amazingly clear on the still air. More than anything in the world he wanted to see her, to hold her, to assure himself of her safety.

There was a vague rustling from the line of trees. Just the singing of the leaves. Then she came at him like a gazelle. Her blonde hair flowed like a banner on the breeze. Her long, bare legs gleamed dully in the silvery light. He felt electrified, his mood suddenly turbulent. He ran to meet her, taking her roughly in his arms, kissing her, crushing her to him.

"What the devil do you mean giving me a fright like that?"

Such an extraordinary thing to hear the violence in his voice, but fear hadn't vanished without a trace. She felt small in his arms, slender, yet womanly, curved. Her own special fragrance clung to her. Clung to him.

"Link!" She rested her head against his chest, her long hair veiling her profile. "I'm so sorry you were worried."

"Worried?" He let out a long, whistling sigh. "I was nearly off my head."

"I had an attack of vertigo," she explained.

"Good God!" He held her away from him and stared into the pale oval of her face. "How are you now?"

"All right. The attack passed more than an hour ago. *After* the tide came in and collected my canoe. I couldn't stop it. I couldn't get it. I had to watch it float away."

"Why did you *do* this?" he groaned. "Why did you go by yourself?"

"I wasn't in any danger. There's nothing on the island to hurt me. I just had to sit it out. Besides, I had the certainty you'd come for me."

"To the ends of the earth," he said with a harshness born of emotion.

"You must love me."

"Beyond anything." He spoke with deep conviction. "I see such a future for us, Georgia. The promise of developing our careers together. I see children. A family."

"A *home*. Belonging," Georgia added shakily.

He kissed her forehead, her eyes, finally her mouth, feeling it open to him like an unfurling rose. "Georgia, they're not tears?" He caught a crystal drop on his tongue.

"It's perfectly normal for a woman to cry with happiness," she breathed.

"Where have you been all my life?"

"Waiting for you."

"No doubts?"

"None." A tide of emotion surged through her. "I'm fiercely proud of you. I love you." She lifted on tiptoes, making pecking little kisses all over his face.

"And I'll cherish you for the rest of your life." He bent to kiss her. "It would be *so* wonderful to stay here, but I must take you back. Everyone will be worrying about us."

"Yes, I know." Georgia clasped his hand, feeling such buoyancy she thought she could float back to Sunset. "I'm not dreaming all this, am I?"

"It's like a dream to me, too." He gave a deep elated laugh. "In fact I was beginning to wonder if I'd ever find my one perfect mate. The missing piece of my soul."

"We'll come back here, won't we?" Georgia asked.

"You *know* we will." He took her hand and kissed it. "This is where we declared our love."

EPILOGUE

Christmas Eve, eighteen months later

THE Christmas tree lofted almost to the high ceiling, festooned with the most beautiful ornaments Georgia could find, scarlet and green baubles, tiny boxes and drums lavishly decorated, sugary white and gold Christmas bells, heralding little angels in fine bisque porcelain dancing on golden threads, each winged cherub playing a different musical instrument. Sparkling tinsel cast a bright illumination, and dozens of fairy lights silhouetted each individual branch, causing the baubles to shimmer and glow and throw back a kaleidoscope of colours. At the very top of the tree was the glittering start of Bethlehem, the permanent symbol of peace, and just beneath it Noel, the angel of Christmas, with her exquisite porcelain face and rich raiment in the glorious colours of Christmas, ruby red and emerald trimmed with gold lamé to match her outstretched wings. The presents were piled high beneath the tree, as luxuriously wrapped and beribboned as Georgia knew how. She and Link had had a marvellous time decorating the tree, the house filled with their happy laughter and the golden voice of Dame Kiri Te Kanawa singing their favourite carols.

Looking around the beautiful home Link had designed and built for her, Georgia felt such an overflow of joy the tears rose to her eyes. This was a timeless moment. Soft and gleaming. A perfect moment in life when all her dreams were fulfilled. She would hold onto it for all time. The long skirt of her dress rustled as she began to move from living to dining room and out onto the plant-filled terrace that overlooked the fairytale glitter of night-time Sydney Harbour.

Her dress had been made from a gorgeous piece of green and gold embroidered silk her mother-in-law had given her. It seemed so right for Christmas. In the past year of her marriage she and Kate had become very close. Indeed, she had come to accept with gratitude Kate and Sam were far more caring, more involved and supportive than ever her parents were. It wasn't what she wanted, but it was the way her life had turned out. It was Kate who showed tremendous interest in Georgia's career. Kate who'd been so delighted with Georgia's total design concept for Sunset, travelling back and forth with Georgia as they made frequent trips to the island.

The new Sunset had reopened to considerable fanfare in late September, with extensive magazine coverage for Link and herself. It had been a breathless, scintillating time, her life in top gear, not without a few hassles and differences of opinion but with the give-and-take that was to characterise them. She and Link had always arrived at solutions that pleased them and eventually everyone else. Georgia was immensely proud of her husband. She felt she had blossomed under the warmth and brilliance of his influence.

They were supremely happy, and for that she thanked God every night of her life. It was with great joy and pride she carried their child, the greatest blessing a loving married couple could ever know. Her pregnancy had only just been confirmed.

She and Link had decided to announce their splendid news at midnight, when all the family was assembled. Kate and Sam would be thrilled out of their minds. They were intensely *family* people. Georgia's mother would be delighted. She thought her father would be happy, too. His first grandchild. There would be immediate talk of which schools *he* would go to. She and Link wanted no advance knowledge of the sex of their child. They were happy to wait for their wonderful little surprise package.

The house was filled with Christmas lilies, with great crystal bowls of her favourite long-stemmed red roses. She had even managed to find the time to make a decorative swag for the white marble mantelpiece, the dark evergreen foliage decorated with sumptuous little trinkets. It had been the greatest fun. She loved the graceful things in life. Even the standard ficus that stood in stone pots to flank the front door she had decorated with red and gold bows. Christmas wasn't just a festive season to her. Christmas really *meant* something. She touched a hand to her still flat stomach. Next Christmas, with the grace of God, she and Link would have their first beloved child. It was time of high emotion.

In another few minutes Link would join her. He had been delayed in town and had to rush to shower and dress. Tonight was for family. There would be around twenty at their celebration buffet. The hired trestle looked marvellous draped with dark green damask, golden tassels sweeping the parqueted floor of the dining room. She had used bright red highly polished apples for a centrepiece, interspersing the fruit with glossy camellia leaves. She thought it looked very effective surrounded by silver platters of smoked salmon rolls filled with a blend of crabmeat cream cheese and mayonnaise, lobster medallions, prawn barquettes and quail eggs, caviar and cream cheese on pastry, turkey and glazed ham, stuffed mushrooms, jubilee eggs with pesto. The two hot dishes, one beef, the other chicken sitting on a bed of rice, were in the kitchen waiting for gentle reheating. Three desserts were offered. A snowball of plum pudding, a magnificent chocolate log piled high with a chocolate caraque and served with crème chantilly, and especially for Sam a fresh fruit tart with the fruit arranged in concentric circles on a vanilla pastry cream.

They had planned a New Year's party for their friends and all the people who had been so supportive on the Sunset project. Uncle Robert was still abroad. He had met up with an old school chum in Moscow, of all places. The two of them intended to take in a few of the major European art galleries. Georgia would be speaking to him some time Christmas morning. She knew it would be emotional, what with all her news. That would bring him home.

''Darling?'' Link's dark head appeared over the gleaming banister of the gallery. He was fully dressed in black tie—they wanted to make of it a memorable occasion—so heartbreakingly handsome, so *dear*, she had the wonderful sensation of bright light within her.

It showed in her upturned face. ''Oh, you're dressed,'' she exclaimed radiantly. ''That's good. They should be here soon.''

''Not before I've given you my Christmas present. I'd like you to wear it.''

''What is it? Tell me.'' Link had never stopped showering her with presents, but she still got excited.

''Don't you *dare* run up the stairs.'' He met her

halfway, slipping an arm around her waist. "You're everything in the world to me, and don't you forget it."

She leaned her head against his shoulder. "And you to me, my love. You're so good to me when we've got the greatest Christmas gift we could ever wish for."

"That we have." He dropped a fervent kiss on the top of her shining head.

In their bedroom, Link slipped a pendant necklace around his wife's slender throat, holding her shoulders while they both studied the effect.

"It's absolutely lovely!" Georgia touched a hand to the pendant suspended from a gleaming gold chain. It was a beautifully designed sunburst in gold, at the centre a fully faceted Burmese ruby that seemed to glow with a life of its own. It complemented her skin and her dress perfectly.

"I designed it and had it made up. Gold for our happiness. Red for our love." He turned her to him, taking her face gently between his elegant hands. "This has been the most fulfilling year of my life, Georgia. Thank you with all my heart."

"And it's going to get better," Georgia promised, her dark eyes lustrous with the depth of her emotions.

They had barely arrived downstairs before the door chimes rang through the house.

"That's the family," Link said, in his vibrant voice. He took her hand as they walked down the hallway and opened the door on a cluster of bright, smiling faces.

He and Georgia stood silhouetted, hands clasped, their bodies leaning in to each other. In unity. The two of them. Three, really. Inside of Georgia a tiny heart was beating strongly.

Jessica Hart had a haphazard career before she began writing to finance a degree in history. Her experience ranged from waitress, theatre production assistant and outback cook to newsdesk secretary, expedition PA and English teacher, and she has worked in countries as different as France and Indonesia, Australia and Cameroon. She now lives in the north of England, where her hobbies are limited to eating and drinking and travelling when she can, preferably to places where she'll find good food or desert or tropical rain.

Look out for
ASSIGNMENT: BABY by Jessica Hart
In Tender Romance™, January 2002

OUTBACK BRIDE

by
Jessica Hart

CHAPTER ONE

'HELLO?' [illegible]
Copper peered inside [illegible] only a long
[illegible] corridor lined with boots, coats and an assortment of riding gear. 'Hello?' she called again. 'Is there anyone there?'

No response. She could hear her voice echoing in the empty house and glanced at her watch. Nearly four o'clock. You'd think there would be someone around. Her father had mentioned a housekeeper. Shouldn't she be here, keeping house instead of leaving it open for any passing stranger?

Not that there would be many passing strangers out here. Copper turned and looked out to where her car was parked in the full glare of an outback afternoon. A dusty track had brought her from beyond the horizon to this long, low homestead with its deep verandah and its corrugated iron roof that flashed in the sun, and here it stopped. This was the end of the road.

Still, this was just what their clients would want to see, Copper reminded herself, a gracious colonial homestead at the centre of a vast cattle station, accessible only by plane or fifty miles of dirt track.

Copper adjusted her sunglasses on her nose and looked around her with a touch of impatience. It was frustrating to have got this far and not be able to get straight down to business.

She paced up and down the verandah, wondering how long she would have to wait for Matthew Standish and

CHAPTER ONE

'HELLO?' The door stood open behind its fly screen. Copper peered through, but could make out only a long, dim corridor lined with boots, coats and an assortment of riding gear. 'Hello?' she called again. 'Is there anyone there?'

No response. She could hear her voice echoing in the empty house and glanced at her watch. Nearly four o'clock. You'd think there would be *someone* around. Her father had mentioned a housekeeper. Shouldn't she be here, keeping house instead of leaving it open for any passing stranger?

Not that there would be many passing strangers out here. Copper turned and looked out to where her car was parked in the full glare of an outback afternoon. A dusty track had brought her from beyond the horizon to this long, low homestead with its deep verandah and its corrugated iron roof that flashed in the sun, and here it stopped. Talk about the end of the road.

Still, this was just what their clients would want to see, Copper reassured herself: a gracious colonial homestead at the centre of a vast cattle station, accessible only by plane or fifty miles of dirt track.

Copper adjusted her sunglasses on her nose and looked around her with a touch of impatience. It was frustrating to have got this far and not be able to get straight down to business.

She paced up and down the verandah, wondering how long she would have to wait for Matthew Standish and what he would be like. Her father had just said that he was 'nobody's fool' and that she would have to handle him with care. Copper intended to. The future of Copley Travel depended on Matthew Standish agreeing to let them use Birraminda as a base for their new luxury camping tours, and she wasn't going to go home until she had that agreement signed and dated.

She looked at her watch again. Where was everybody? Copper hated hanging around waiting for things to happen; she liked to make them happen herself. Crossly, she sat down on the top step, very conscious of the silence settling around her, broken only by the mournful caw of a raven somewhere down by the creek. She would hate to live anywhere this quiet.

This was Mal's kind of country. She remembered how he had talked about the outback, about its stillness and its silence and its endless empty horizons. It was easy to imagine him out here, rangy and unhurried, beneath the pitiless blue sky.

Copper frowned. She wished she could forget about Mal. He belonged to the past, and she was a girl who liked to live in the present and look to the future. She had thought she had done a good job of filing his memory away as something secret and special, to be squirrelled away and taken out only when she was alone or down and wanted to remember that, however unromantic she might be, she too had had her moment of magic, but the long drive through the interior had inevitably reminded her of him. His image was out, like a genie from its lamp, and just as impossible to bottle up and ignore.

It wasn't even as if she had ever believed in love at first sight. Copper was the last person who had expected to meet a stranger's eyes and know that her life had changed for ever, and yet that was how it had been. Almost corny.

She had been at the centre of the crowd, as usual, and Mal had been on the edge, a solitary man but not a lonely one. He had a quality of quiet assurance that set him apart from everyone else on the beach, and when he had looked up, and their eyes had met, it was as if every love song ever composed had been written especially for her...

Copper sighed. Three warm Mediterranean nights, that was all they had had. Three nights, on the other side of the world, more than seven years ago. You would think she would have forgotten him by now.

Only he hadn't been the kind of man you could ever forget.

'Hello.'

Jerked out of the past by the unexpected voice behind her, Copper swivelled round from her seat on the steps. She found herself being regarded by a little girl who had come round the corner of the verandah and was staring at her with the frank, unsettling gaze of a child. She had a tangle of dark curls, huge blue eyes and a stubborn, wilful look. A beautiful child, Copper thought, or she would have been if she hadn't been quite so grubby. Her dungarees were torn and dirty and her small face was smeared with dust.

'You made me jump!' she said.

The little girl just carried on staring. 'What's your name?' she demanded.

'Copper,' said Copper.

The blue eyes darkened suspiciously. 'Copper's not a real name!'

'Well, no,' she admitted. 'It's a nickname—it's what

my friends call me.' Seeing that the child looked less than convinced, she added hastily, 'What's *your* name?'

'Megan. I'm four and a half.'

'I'm twenty seven and three quarters,' offered Copper.

Megan considered this, and then, as if satisfied, she came along the verandah and sat down on the top step next to Copper, who glanced down at the tousled head curiously. Her father hadn't mentioned anything about a child. Come to think of it, he had been so taken up with the beauty of the property that he hadn't said much at all about the people who lived there. All she knew was that Birraminda had a formidable owner. Perhaps it might be easier to start with the owner's wife?

'Is your mother around?' she asked Megan, hoping to find someone she could introduce herself to properly while she waited for Matthew Standish to appear.

Megan looked at her as if she was stupid. 'She's dead.'

'Oh, dear,' said Copper inadequately, thrown as much by the matter-of-fact little voice as by the information. What *did* you say to a child who had lost its mother? 'That's very sad. I'm sorry, Megan. Er...who looks after you?'

'Kim does.'

The housekeeper? 'Where's Kim now?' she asked.

'She's gone.'

'Gone?' echoed Copper, taken aback. What was this place, the *Marie Celeste*? 'Gone where?'

'I don't know,' Megan admitted. 'But Dad was cross with Uncle Brett because now there's no one to look after me.'

Copper's heart was wrung as she looked down at the oddly self-possessed little girl beside her. Poor little mite! Had she been abandoned entirely? She opened her mouth to ask the child if there was anyone who knew where she was when a voice called Megan's name, and the next moment a man came round the corner of the homestead from the direction of the old woolshed.

He was tall and lean, that much Copper could see, but in his stockman's hat, checked shirt, jeans and dusty boots he looked, at a distance, just like any other outback man. And yet there was something about him, something about the easy, unhurried way he moved, that clutched at Copper's throat. For a heart-stopping moment he reminded her so vividly of Mal that she felt quite breathless, and could only stare across the yard to where he had checked at the sight of her.

It couldn't be Mal, she told herself as she struggled to breathe normally. She was being ridiculous. Mal belonged to the past, to Turkey and a few star-shot nights. It was just the outback playing tricks with her mind. She had been thinking about him so much over the last few days that now she was going to imagine that every man she met was him. This man just happened to have the same air of quiet strength. It didn't mean he was Mal.

And then he moved out of the shadow of the house and came towards the steps to stand looking up at where she sat next to Megan, and Copper found herself getting shakily to her feet, her heart drumming in disbelief.

It couldn't be Mal, but it was...it *was*! No one else could have that quiet mouth or those unfathomable brown eyes, steady and watchful beneath the dark brows. No other man could have just that angle of cheek and jaw, or make her bones dissolve just by standing there.

Would he remember her as clearly as she remembered him? Oh, God, what if he did? Or would it be worse if he *didn't*?

Beneath his hat, Mal's eyes narrowed as he looked up

at Copper, clinging to the verandah post as if her legs were too weak to support her. She was wearing loose shorts and a matching short-sleeved linen jacket, an outfit she had chosen with care to impress the formidable Mr Standish. In the motel that morning it had seemed to strike the perfect balance between casual elegance and practicality, but the long, bumpy drive since then had left her looking instead hot, crumpled and ridiculously out of place, and the wavy brown hair that normally swung in a blunt cut to her jaw was dusty and limp.

All too conscious of the picture she must make, Copper was passionately grateful for the sunglasses that hid her eyes. Swallowing convulsively, she managed a weak 'hello', although her voice sounded so high and tight that she hardly recognised it as her own.

Before Mal had a chance to reply, Megan had launched herself down the steps towards him. 'Dad!'

Copper's mind, still spinning with shock, jarred to a sickening halt. *Dad?* All those times she had wondered about Mal and what he was doing, not once had she pictured him as a husband, as a father. And yet, why not? He must be thirty five by now, quite old enough to have settled down with a wife and child. It was just that he had been such a solitary man, Copper told herself, pretending that the hollow feeling in her stomach was due simply to surprise.

It was hard to imagine anyone so self-contained bogged down in a life of domesticity, that was all. Surely that was reason enough for her to feel as if someone had hit her very hard in the solar plexus? It had nothing whatsoever to do with any silly dreams that he might have stayed faithful to the memory of the few short days they had spent together. She hadn't, so why should he?

Mal had caught Megan instinctively as she hurtled

down the steps, and now swung her up into his arms. 'I thought I told you to stay on the fence where I could see you?' he said to her, but spoilt the stern effect by ruffling her dark curls before lowering her to the ground once more. Megan hung onto his hand as he turned his attention back to Copper, his expression quite unreadable.

'At last,' he said unexpectedly. 'I've been waiting for you.'

For one extraordinary moment Copper thought that he was telling her that he'd waited seven years for her after all. 'For—for *me*?' she stuttered, trying not to stare.

The angular face was just as she remembered, cool, rather quiet, but with strong, well-defined features and a mouth which could look almost stern in repose but which could relax too into an unexpected smile. Copper had never forgotten that smile, how it transformed his whole face and how the air had evaporated from her lungs the first time she had seen it.

He wasn't smiling now. The years had etched harsher lines around his mouth and there was a shuttered look to his eyes. Copper thought he looked tired, and her shock was punctured at last by shame as she remembered that Megan's mother was dead. It was no wonder that he looked harder, older than her memory.

'You're late,' Mal was saying, apparently unaware of her inner turmoil. 'I was expecting you at least four days ago.'

Had her father given him an exact date to expect her when he had written? Copper looked puzzled, but before she could ask him what he meant Megan had tugged at his hand. 'Her name's Copper.'

There was a tiny moment of silence. Surely he must remember her name, if nothing else, Copper thought wildly. She had sunglasses on and her hair was quite different now, but her name hadn't changed. She waited for Mal to turn, recognition and surprise lighting his face, but he was looking down at his daughter.

'Copper?' he repeated, his voice empty of all expression.

'It's not a proper name,' Megan informed him. 'It's a nickname.'

Mal did look at Copper then, but his brown eyes were quite unreadable. Could it be that he really *had* forgotten her? An obscure sense of pique sharpened Copper's voice.

'I'm Caroline Copley,' she said, relieved to hear that she sounded almost her old business-like self. At least her voice had lost that humiliating squeak. 'I was hoping to see Matthew Standish.'

'I'm Matthew Standish,' said Mal calmly, and all her newly recovered poise promptly deserted her as her jaw dropped.

'*You* are? But—' She broke off in embarrassment.

Mal lifted an eyebrow. 'But what?'

What could she say? She could hardly accuse him of not knowing his own name, and if she did she would have to explain how they had met before. Copper had her pride, and she was damned if she was going to remind a man that he had once made love to her!

She didn't remember telling him about her name, or asking him about his own. He might have told her his surname, but if he had, she hadn't remembered it. She remembered only his slow, sure hands on her skin and the strange sense of coming home as she had walked barefoot across the sand towards him.

'But what?' said Mal again. He didn't remember her. *He* wasn't racked by memories. His heart wasn't booming in his ears at the thought of what they had once shared. He was just standing there with that inscrutable look on his face, waiting for a flustered stranger to answer his question.

'Nothing,' said Copper. Realising that she was still clinging to the verandah post, she let it go hurriedly. 'I mean, I...I was expecting an older man, that's all.'

'I'm sorry to disappoint you.' Was that an undercurrent of amusement in his voice? 'If it's any comfort, you're not exactly what I was expecting either.'

His face didn't change, there wasn't even a suspicion of a smile about his mouth, but somehow Copper got the feeling that he was laughing at her. Confused, uncertain whether to feel hurt or relieved that Mal didn't remember her, she stuck her chin out. 'Oh?' she said almost belligerently. 'What were you expecting me to be like?'

Mal studied her with a disconcerting lack of haste, from her flushed face, tense and vivid beneath her sunglasses, down over the slender figure in the crumpled suit, down slim, brown legs to the leather sandals which showed off deep red toenails. Still standing nervously at the top of the steps, Copper managed to look tired and vibrant and completely out of place.

'Let's say that I was expecting someone a little more...practical,' he said at last.

'I'm very practical,' snapped Copper, burningly aware of his scrutiny.

Mal said nothing, but his eyes rested on her toenails and she had to resist the urge to curl up her feet. He obviously thought she was just a city girl who had no idea about life in the outback. City girl she might be, but impractical she wasn't. She was a professional businesswoman and it was about time she behaved like one, instead of stuttering and stammering like a schoolgirl just because she had come face to face with a man she had met briefly more than seven years ago. It was a surprise, a coincidence, but no more than that.

Mal's unspoken disbelief helped Copper pull herself together. 'I realise I don't look quite as efficient as I usually do,' she said coldly, 'but it was a longer drive than I anticipated, and your track is in very poor condition.'

'You should have come in the bus,' said Mal, with a disparaging glance across to where her car sat, looking as citified and inappropriate as she did. 'I'd have sent someone to pick you up.'

Copper eyed him in some puzzlement. Her father had written to say that his daughter would be coming to Birraminda to negotiate the deal in his stead, but she certainly hadn't had the impression that Matthew Standish had been so enthusiastic about their plan that he would go to the trouble of collecting her. Still, perhaps her father had misjudged his interest?

'I thought it would be better for me to be independent,' she said loftily, unprepared for the look of distaste that swept across Mal's face.

'We've had enough independent types at Birraminda,' he said in a flat voice. 'And it's not as if you're going to need a car while you're here.' His mouth twisted with sudden bitterness. 'I'm reliably informed that there's nowhere to go.'

Looking out at the empty horizon, Copper could believe it. 'Well, no,' she agreed. 'But I wasn't planning on staying for ever!'

An odd look flickered in Mal's eyes and then was gone. 'I realise that,' he said expressionlessly. He looked down at the child leaning trustfully against his leg, and rested his hand on the small head. 'I can't say I'm not glad to see you, anyway,' he added as if he had just reminded himself of something. 'Megan, run along and tell Uncle Brett to finish off without me, will you?'

Megan nodded importantly and scampered off. Mal looked after her, his expression unguarded for a moment, and, watching him, Copper felt something twist inside her. He had looked at her like that once. She suppressed a sigh as he turned back to her, his face closed once more. She might as well forget all about their brief affair right now. Mal obviously had.

'You'd better come inside,' he said, climbing up the steps towards her and Copper found herself taking a quick step back in case he brushed against her.

Her instinctive movement didn't go unnoticed by Mal. He made no comment, and his eyes were as inscrutable as ever, but Copper was convinced there was subtle mockery in the way he held the screen door open for her, as if he knew just how confused she was, how terrified that his slightest touch would bring back an avalanche of memories.

Head held high, she walked past him into the house. Inside, all was dim and cool and quiet. The homestead was much bigger than Copper had imagined from outside, with several corridors leading off from the long entrance hall, and it had a kind of dusty charm that she had somehow not expected to find this far from any kind of civilisation.

Mal led the way along to a very large, very untidy kitchen with a door onto the back verandah. Through the window, Copper could see a dusty yard shaded by a gnarled old gum and surrounded by a collection of outbuildings, a tall windmill and two enormous iron water tanks. To one side lay the creek, where cockatoos wheeled out of the trees and galahs darted over the water, turning in flashes of pink and grey, and in the distance an irrigated paddock looked extraordinarily green and lush compared to the expanse of bare holding yards that stretched out of sight. Copper could just make out some cattle milling around in the pens, lifting clouds of red dust with their hooves.

Tossing his hat onto the table, Mal crossed over to the sink and filled up the kettle. 'Tea?'

'Er…yes…thank you.' Copper took off her sunglasses and sank down into a chair. She felt very odd.

At times, perhaps more often than she wanted to admit, she had dreamt about meeting Mal again. Her fantasies had usually involved them catching sight of each other unexpectedly, their faces lighting up with instant recognition. Sometimes she had pictured him shouldering his way through crowds towards her, reaching for her hands, surrendering to the same electric attraction that had brought them together the first night they met. Or she had let herself imagine him looking deep into her eyes and explaining how he had lost her address and spent the last seven years scouring England and Australia to find her again.

What she *hadn't* imagined was that he would behave as if he had never seen her before in his life and calmly offer her a cup of tea!

Copper sighed inwardly. Perhaps it was just as well. She mustn't forget that she was here to set up a vital deal, and trying to negotiate with a man who remembered the past as clearly as she did would have been more than a little awkward.

Her clear green eyes rested on Mal's back as he made tea in a battered enamel pot. The sureness of his every gesture tugged at her heart. Her gaze drifted from the broad shoulders down to lean hips, and she was suddenly swamped with the memory of how it had felt to run her hands over him. It was as if she could still feel the texture of his skin beneath her fingers, still trace the outline of his spine and feel his muscles flex in response to her touch.

Memory pulsated like pain in her fingertips, and Copper drew a sharp breath and squeezed her eyes shut. She opened them just as Mal turned round, and across the kitchen their gazes locked.

Copper wanted to look away, to make a light comment and laugh, but she couldn't move. She was riveted by the current of awareness that leapt to life between them, held by those deep, deep brown eyes while her heart began to boom and thud in her ears. Why had she taken her sunglasses off? She felt naked and vulnerable without them. Her eyes had always been embarrassingly transparent. One look into them and Mal would know that her hands were still tingling with the memory of his body, that all those years, when he had forgotten her, his kisses had continued to haunt her dreams.

Then Mal moved forward and set the teapot down on the table, and Copper jerked her eyes away with a tiny gasp. He looked at her narrowly. 'Are you all right?'

'I'm fine,' said Copper, horribly conscious of how high and tight her voice sounded. She could feel the telltale colour blotching her throat and willed it to fade. 'I'm just a bit tired, that's all.'

Mal pulled out a chair and sat down opposite her. 'You wouldn't be tired if you'd taken the bus,' he said, pouring the tea into two mugs.

Copper sat up straighter at the implied criticism. She had, in fact, looked into doing the journey on the bus in case they wanted to offer it as option to their clients, but it would have taken forty-eight hours just to get to the nearest town—hardly a recipe for arriving fresh as a daisy! 'Oh, wouldn't I?' she retorted. 'How long is it since *you've* been on a bus?'

'Not for years.' An intriguing half-smile dented the corners of Mal's mouth as he acknowledged her point. 'Now you come to mention it, I don't think I've been on a bus since I was travelling in Europe—a long time ago now.'

Seven years. For one awful moment, Copper thought she had spoken aloud, but a covert look at Mal showed that he was calmly drinking his tea. He looked cool and self-contained, a little watchful, perhaps, but certainly not like a man who had suddenly been brought face to face with embarrassment from the past. What would he say if she told him that she knew exactly when he had been in Europe? Oh, yes, she could have said. I remember you then. We spent three days making love on a beach.

Great way to impress him with her professionalism.

'Oh,' she said weakly instead.

She risked another glance at Mal, who was looking thoughtfully down into his tea, dark brows drawn together as if pondering an insuperable problem. Copper could see the lines of strain around his eyes and she wondered how long ago his wife had died. What had she been like, the woman who had shared his life and borne his child? All at once Copper was ashamed of herself for worrying about the past and whether Mal remembered her or not. He had more important things to think about than a girl he had met on a beach seven years ago.

And, really, wasn't that all it had been? A chance encounter, ships passing in the night? It had felt much more than that at the time, but it was all so long ago and they were different people now. Mal had changed and so had she. All she had to do was forget about that brief, magical interlude and pretend that he was a complete stranger.

Easy.

It didn't stop her heart lurching when Mal looked up suddenly from his tea and found her watching him, but at least this time she was able to look away. 'What… what a nice kitchen,' she said brightly. It was the first thing that came into her head, but when she looked at it, it *was* a nice kitchen, cool and spacious and beautifully designed, although most of the equipment was hidden beneath a clutter of packets and jars, papers and unwashed dishes.

'I'm sorry about the mess,' said Mal, as if he had read her mind. He looked ruefully around him. 'This is a busy time on the station and everything's got out of control in the house since Kim left. We really need a good housekeeper to sort everything out.'

'I can see that,' said Copper with feeling, averting her eyes from the dirty dishes piled high in the sink. She wasn't obsessively tidy herself, but her business brain deplored the inefficiency.

'Have you spent any time in the outback before?' asked Mal abruptly, and Copper set down her mug. She had a feeling that some kind of interview was just beginning.

'Not really,' she said cautiously. Her father had warned her that Mal had been unimpressed by the idea of a city firm setting up luxury camping trips, so it would be up to her to convince him that they knew what they were doing. 'A couple of camping trips in the Flinders Ranges, that's all.'

Mal sighed. 'In other words, you don't have any relevant experience?'

'I wouldn't say that,' said Copper rather coldly. There was no need for him to write her off just yet! She had been organising tours for more than five years and it wasn't as if she was going to be leading the groups herself. Her role was strictly administrative. 'I don't need to be Crocodile Dundee, do I?' she added with a challenging look. 'I've got more than enough experience to do my job, and it's not as if I'm going to be roping bulls or doing any of that kind of stuff myself!'

'True,' said Mal. 'But you do need to have some understanding of what we do, or you'll just get in the way.'

'I realise that,' she said a little stiffly. 'It's one of the reasons I'm here, after all. I want to learn as much as I can about how things work out here.'

There was a flicker of surprise in Mal's eyes. 'You may find it pretty boring,' he warned.

'I'm never bored,' said Copper firmly.

It wasn't strictly true. She was a believer in living life to the full, and crammed as much as possible into every day, but on the few occasions when she found herself with nothing to do, her zest quickly degenerated into restlessness and she would end up inventing jobs for herself.

'I hope you're right,' said Mal, but not as if he believed it very much.

'I am.' Copper decided it was time to start steering the conversation towards business. 'I'm looking forward to seeing as much of Birraminda as I can,' she said, rather pleased with her brisk tone. Now that she had got over the initial shock, it was easy to treat him as a stranger—a colleague, perhaps, or just someone to do business with.

'I'll see what we can do,' he said, but he was looking at her so strangely that Copper rubbed a surreptitious finger under her eyes in case her mascara had smudged. 'Anyway,' he went on, 'you're here now, so we'll just have to make the best of it. If you're prepared to put up with the state of things, then I'm sure we can work something out.'

It didn't sound *that* encouraging, but at least he hadn't refused to have anything to do with her, and Copper refused to be disheartened. 'That's fine by me,' she said heartily.

Mal stared at her for a moment, his expression quite impenetrable, and then all at once he seemed to relax. 'Good,' he said, and then, just when she was least expecting it, he smiled and Copper's heart flipped over.

It was only a smile, she told herself desperately, trying not to notice how the creases deepened at the corners of his mouth and eyes, how the cool, watchful look dissolved into warmth and devastating charm, how white his teeth were against his tan. Trying not to notice the way his smile reverberated the length of her spine and tingled down to her toes.

'I'm sorry I haven't been very welcoming,' he was saying. 'We've had so many girls who come for a few weeks and then rush home because they can't cope with the life out here that I've got too cynical, but if you really do want to get to know Birraminda, and aren't afraid of hard work, then we're glad to have you.' He looked across at Copper and something stirred in the depths of his eyes. 'Very glad,' he amended softly, and held out his hand.

Copper wasn't listening. She was still concentrating on breathing, in and out, very carefully. This was business, remember? she castigated herself. She would never convince Mal that she was a professional if she went to pieces every time he smiled. It was only two lips curving, a mere twitch of the facial muscles; it was absolutely stupid to let it affect her like this, especially when she had just decided to put her memories of Mal in a mental locker firmly marked 'Forgotten'. She was being worse than stupid; she was being pathetic.

Her gaze focused suddenly on Mal, who was watching her, one eyebrow lifted in faint surprise at her expression, and her heart sank as her eyes dropped belatedly to the hand stretched out to her across the table. She could hardly ignore it. Now she would have to cope with touching him as well! That was all she needed!

Bracing herself, Copper seized his hand before she had a chance to lose her nerve. This is a business contact, she chanted inwardly through gritted teeth. Business, business, business.

Mal's long brown fingers closed around hers in a firm clasp, and in spite of all her efforts to resist Copper felt her senses magically sharpen. It *was* a sort of magic, she thought incoherently. How else could she be so excruciatingly aware of everything? She could feel each line on his palm, each crease in his fingers, and his face was lit with a new clarity so that she could see every tiny detail: the thickness of his lashes, the way his hair grew, the faint scar just above his jaw. Copper could remember tracing its line with her fingers, could remember Mal telling her how it had happened, could remember exactly how it had felt to touch her lips to the warm, male-rough skin and tickle the pale line with her tongue...

CHAPTER TWO

'AHA! Holding hands already!'

So much for her senses being heightened! Copper hadn't even heard the clatter of boots on the verandah steps, and when the kitchen door burst open she jerked her hand out of Mal's as if she had been caught in the most passionate of clinches, her cheeks burning.

One of the most handsome men she had ever seen stood in the doorway. He was as tall as Mal, but much fairer, with sun-streaked hair, merry blue eyes and an air of almost tangible charm. Laughing, he tossed Megan up in his arms.

'You see what happens when you leave your father alone with a pretty girl!'

'Brett!' An expression of weary resignation and something else Copper couldn't quite identify swept across Mal's face. 'Have you finished those cattle?'

'The boys can finish them,' said Brett carelessly, apparently oblivious to Mal's frown. 'When Megan told me Dad had got a beautiful girl all to himself, I had to come and see for myself.' The dancing blue eyes studied Copper approvingly as he let his niece down, and his gaiety was so infectious that she found herself smiling back at him.

'This is my brother, Brett,' said Mal. His face was wiped of all expression, but there was a rigid set to his jaw and a muscle jumped in his cheek. 'Brett, this is Copper—' He stopped, obviously trying to remember her surname.

'Copley,' she said helpfully. 'I know it sounds silly, but there was another Caroline at school so I used to get called by my surname. Somehow Copley became Copper, and then I was stuck with it. Nobody calls me Caroline now, except my family, and I think some of my friends don't even realise that Copper's not my real name.'

'Sounds like Mal,' said Brett, ignoring Mal's warning look and pulling out the chair next to Copper's. 'He was lumbered with three names—Matthew Anthony Langland Standish—so we always shortened it to Mal when we were kids, and now only business people call him Matthew.'

'Perhaps I'd better call you Matthew, then,' said Copper, turning to Mal. It seemed like a good opportunity to establish the appropriate relations.

Mal frowned slightly. 'I hardly think that's necessary,' he said. 'If you're going to be living here as a member of the family, there's no need to be formal.'

'Absolutely not,' Brett agreed, running a lazily appreciative eye over Copper as he shook her hand with mock solemnity. 'We're going to use your nickname, so we can all be informal together. Copper suits you,' he added, reaching out a hand to touch her hair. 'Beautiful name…it sounds warm and burnished, like your hair.'

Copper's lips twitched. He was obviously a terrible flirt. She glanced at Mal from under her lashes. He was watching them with a dour expression, looking dark and stern in contrast to Brett's golden, laughing presence. It was odd that the less handsome brother should be so much more intriguing. Brett was easily the better-looking, but he lacked Mal's air of quiet, coiled strength, and when he touched her hand she felt no jolt of awareness, no tingling of the nerves, no clutch at the heart as she did just looking at Mal.

She could sense his displeasure coming in waves across the table, and it was enough to make her smile charmingly back at Brett. After all, what did she care what he thought of her? Hadn't she already decided that he meant no more than any other stranger? 'Don't tell me!' she said. 'Next you'll be saying that all I need is a good rub to make me all bright and shiny!'

Brett laughed. 'I think you're quite bright and shiny enough already,' he said.

Mal's mouth was turned down at the corner. 'I think you should go back and keep an eye on the jackaroos,' he said pointedly to his brother.

'They'll be fine.' Brett waved a dismissive hand. 'It's more important for me to be here to welcome the new housekeeper.'

'Oh?' said Copper, not sorry to divert Mal's attention in spite of her bravado. 'Are you expecting someone else today?'

There was a short silence. Mal and Brett both looked at her. 'Just you,' said Mal, but there was an ominous note in his voice.

Copper glanced from one to the other, sensing that something was wrong. 'When's the new housekeeper coming, then?'

'What new housekeeper?' said Brett in surprise. '*You're* the new housekeeper!'

She goggled at him. 'Me?'

Mal's brows had snapped together. 'Do you mean to tell us that you're *not* here to replace Kim?'

'Of course not!' said Copper indignantly. 'Do I look like a housekeeper?'

'Why do you think I was surprised to see you in a

suit?' he retorted with a trace of weariness, and pinched the bridge of his nose. 'The agency in Brisbane said they were sending a new girl out from there nearly a week ago, so I just assumed that's who you were.'

'Well, that explains why you thought I should have come on the bus, anyway,' she said.

'It doesn't explain what you're doing here, though, does it?' There was a slight edge to Mal's words and Copper found herself sitting up straighter.

'I thought you'd had my father's letter,' she said, not very clearly.

A hint of impatience was beginning to crack Mal's imperturbable mask. 'What letter?'

'The letter he wrote you a couple of weeks ago, telling you that he'd had a heart attack and that I'd be coming up in his place.' Copper looked at him expectantly, but Mal was obviously none the wiser and only holding onto his temper with difficulty. 'Dan Copley? Copley Travel?' she hurried on, hoping to jog his memory. He might not remember what had happened seven years ago, but surely he could manage a matter of weeks? 'He was here two or three months ago. He came to talk to you about the possibility of using Birraminda as a site for the new tours we're planning.'

Recognition dawned at last in Mal's eyes. 'Oh, yes, I remember,' he said. 'But what's that got to do with you turning up here?'

'I've come to negotiate a deal with you, of course,' said Copper, surprised.

'Deal?' Mal brought his hand down flat on the table and leant forward. 'What *deal*?' he asked. He didn't raise his voice but something in his expression made her lean warily back into her chair. 'I never agreed to any deal!'

'I know.' Copper stiffened her spine. She had dealt with worse people than Mal Standish. 'But you did agree to let Dad come back when he had a viable financial plan. You said you'd be prepared to discuss terms if he could convince you then that the project would work.'

Rather to her relief, he sat back and the dangerous look faded from his face. 'I might have said that,' he admitted. 'But I can't say I ever thought he would put a plan together. The whole idea seemed mad to me!'

'It's not a mad idea,' said Copper coldly. 'It's an extremely good idea. Lots of people would like to experience the outback in style. They don't want to sit on buses or stay in hotels, but they don't necessarily want to crawl around in a tiny tent either. We're going to offer permanent safari tents with camp beds and a bathroom, as well as fine cooking and specialist leaders for the different groups—expert artists, ornithologists, people like that,' she finished, with an airy wave of the hand.

'It sounds good to me,' enthused Brett. 'Especially if they're prepared to pay pots of money for the privilege of getting squawked at by treefuls of cockatoos!'

'Well, money is certainly something we'd have to discuss,' said Copper carefully.

'Right now we're not going to discuss anything,' said Mal with an air of flat finality. 'I'm sorry that your father's been ill, but, frankly, you couldn't have picked a worse time. If I'd realised you were coming, I could have told you not to bother.'

'But my father wrote to you,' she protested. 'That's why I thought you were expecting me. You must have had the letter!'

'I may have.' He shrugged his indifference. 'There's been so much to do here recently, and things have been so chaotic since Kim left that any paperwork that's not absolutely urgent has just had to wait.'

Copper eyed him with growing resentment. It might not have been urgent to him, but if he'd bothered to read the letter he could have saved her a three-day drive from Adelaide!

'I'm here now,' she pointed out. 'Couldn't you at least listen to our proposals?'

'No,' said Mal flatly. 'I've got too many other things on my mind at the moment, especially since you're not anything useful like a housekeeper. I need one of those more than I need a crackpot scheme that sounds like nothing but trouble from start to finish. I've got no one to look after the house, I've got no one to look after my daughter and I've got no rain.' Picking up his hat, he got to his feet. 'What I *have* got is eighty thousand head of cattle, and a thousand of them are out there in the holding yards right now, so you'll have to excuse us.' He jerked his head towards the door. 'That "us" includes you, Brett. We've still got work to do.'

Settling his hat on his head, Mal looked down at Copper. Her chin was set at a stubborn angle and the green eyes were mutinous. She was still seething over the way he had dismissed their cherished project. Her father had invested everything in the success of these tours. The whole future of Copley Travel was at stake and all Mal could say was that it sounded a crackpot scheme!

'You can stay tonight, of course,' he said to her. 'But I can tell you now that we won't be doing any discussing.'

Behind Mal's back, Brett gave Copper a sympathetic grin. 'I'm sure we'll be able to find something else to do,' he said meaningfully, and winked at her.

Mal's mouth tightened. 'Come on, Brett,' he snapped. 'We've wasted enough time today as it is.'

Charming! Copper glared after them. All those years of dreaming about Mal and what it would be like to meet him again, and all she turned out to be was a waste of his time!

In a way she was glad that he had been so objectionable. It made it much easier to ignore the way her heart had leapt at the sight of him, the treacherous way her body had responded to one brief smile. Now she really could put the past behind her.

Copper's eyes narrowed as she remembered how Mal had refused even to listen to her proposals. She had driven a file full of proposals all the way from Adelaide, and if he thought she was going to meekly turn around and go home tomorrow, he was very much mistaken!

Worry over the future of Copley Travel had almost killed her father, and the prospect of restoring their fortunes by investing in a project that would appeal to the quality end of the market was all that was keeping him going. The company had been Dan Copley's life, and the luxury outback tours a long-held dream. While he had been in hospital, Copper had taken over the project, working all hours of the day and night to get to the stage where they could confidently approach Matthew Standish again. And Mal had refused to listen just because he didn't have anyone to wash up for him!

Well, he would soon learn that Copper had no intention of taking no for an answer! If politely asking wouldn't make Mal listen, then she would have to find some other way of convincing him that she meant business!

When Mal came back, much later, Copper was sitting on the verandah outside the kitchen door, looking out over the creek. Megan sat beside her in a clean nightie, chattering about life on the station. Her face sparkled and her dusky curls had been brushed until they shone. 'There's Dad!' she interrupted herself suddenly, pointing, and Copper's heart promptly jumped to her throat, where it lodged, fluttering wildly in spite of all her stern attempts to subdue it.

Grateful for the fading light, she watched Mal walking towards them through the dusk. There was a lithe, unconscious grace about the way he moved, an ease and assurance in his stride that stirred something in the pit of Copper's stomach. Megan was dancing barefoot at the top of the steps.

'Dad, Dad, we've got a surprise for you!'

Copper forced herself not to notice as Mal smiled down at his daughter and lifted her up into his arms.

'You've had a bath,' he said as Megan hugged her arms around his neck.

'Copper bathed me, and she sang a funny song.'

'Did she now?' Shifting Megan onto his hip, Mal looked over to where Copper sat in a low wicker chair. She had showered and changed into a sleeveless white shirt and narrow trousers. Her shiny brown hair was still wet, and her tilted lashes clung damply together, but she hoped she looked cool and comfortable and suitably dressed at last.

Tilting her chin in unconscious challenge, she looked back at him. 'You don't mind, do you?'

'Of course not.' There was an odd note in his voice, but before Copper could speculate as to what it might mean Megan was wriggling to be let down.

'Can I show you the surprise now?'

'I thought the surprise was you being bathed and

ready for bed?' he teased, but Megan shook her head solemnly.

'No, this is a proper surprise.'

Mal lifted his brows in silent enquiry at Copper, but she just smiled blandly. She was saving the real surprise until later.

Megan dragged her father into the kitchen. Through the screen, Copper could hear the counterpoint between the two voices, one high and excited, the other calm and deep, and she smiled to herself as she listened, content for once to sit quietly and watch the sunset. It had been a long day and tiredness was buzzing along her bones.

It was some time before Mal reappeared, carrying two bottles of beer. He handed one to Copper and the wicker creaked as he sat down on the chair next to hers. The beer was so cold that condensation ran down the outside and Copper had to keep shifting it from hand to hand.

'Where's Megan?' she asked.

'In bed.'

'And Brett?'

'Having a shower.' Mal had showered too. His hair was damp and she could smell the soap on his clean skin as he leant forward, resting his arms on his knees, and turning the beer bottle thoughtfully between his hands.

Copper found herself watching them as if mesmerised. She had loved Mal's hands. They were strong and brown, with long, deft fingers that had traced slow patterns of fire over her skin. They had curved around her breast and smoothed the long length of her thigh, possessing her with a sureness and a hunger that had left her gasping his name.

Wrenching her eyes away, Copper took a desperate pull of beer and forced the memories back into that box labelled 'Forgotten'. She was not going to think about his hands or his mouth or anything about him at all. She was going to think business.

It had grown dark while Mal had been inside, and the only light came from the blue lamp that was set below the verandah to attract flying insects. At regular intervals it would fizz and crackle as one got too close and was zapped out of existence. Copper watched it in silence and tried to think how to bring the conversation round to her new proposal.

In the end it was Mal who spoke first. 'You've been busy,' he said. 'It must have taken you a long time to clean that kitchen.'

Copper shrugged. 'Megan helped me.' In fact, Megan had been more of a hindrance than a help, but she had been so thrilled to be in on the surprise that Copper hadn't had the heart to discourage her. Together they had tidied the clutter off the table and washed the huge pile of dishes. Then they had swept the floor and wiped the surfaces until everything gleamed. There had been no time to clean the fridge or sort out the cupboards, but Copper felt that the contrast with the earlier mess would be enough to make an impact.

Mal was still turning the bottle slowly between his hands. 'I don't want you to think I don't appreciate it,' he said, 'but a clean kitchen isn't enough to make me change my mind.'

'I'm not asking you to,' said Copper, and his gaze narrowed as he looked at her.

'You're not expecting me to believe that you did all that out of the goodness of your heart? You must want something!'

'I do,' she said evenly. 'I want you to give me a job.'

Mal's fingers stilled abruptly and he sat up in surprise. 'What kind of job?'

'You need a housekeeper, don't you? I'm suggesting that you let me take over until this girl from the agency turns up.'

Copper was pleased with how cool and business-like she sounded, but Mal didn't seem particularly impressed. 'What do you know about being a housekeeper?' he asked suspiciously.

He could have sounded a bit more grateful! 'What is there to know?' said Copper. 'You don't need any qualifications to clean a house—or do you only take girls with higher degrees in vacuuming and washing dishes?'

Mal ignored her sarcasm. 'Perhaps I should have asked why you suddenly want to be a housekeeper,' he said. 'You looked pretty offended at being mistaken for one earlier on.'

'I don't want to be a housekeeper,' she said, 'but I do want to stay at Birraminda. And if it means spending a few days working as hard as I did this afternoon, then I'm prepared to do that.'

'And in return I have to agree to let you and your father set up this mad scheme of yours?' Mal set his beer on the floor and shook his head. 'I can't deny I need a housekeeper, but I don't want one badly enough to commit Birraminda to an enterprise that could involve us in a lot of disruption and hassle. Even if it's a wild success, the financial return isn't likely to be enough to make it worth our while.'

Copper took a steadying breath. This was not the time to prove to Mal that he had quite the wrong idea about the project. 'I'm not asking you to agree,' she said. 'At least, not yet. All I'm asking is for you to put aside some time to just listen to our proposals before I leave. I'm sure that if I showed you our plans I'd be able to convince you that they could be good for you as well as for us, but I'd rather wait until you can give them your full attention. In the meantime, I'll keep house for you.'

She glanced at him, wishing that she could read the expression on his face. 'It's a good offer,' she assured him. 'An hour of your time in return for free housekeeping.'

'You mean you wouldn't expect any payment?' Mal raised his brows in disbelief.

'All I'd ask is a chance to see a bit more of Birraminda. There are still a lot of practical details we have to sort out and I really need to see the sites my father chose for myself.'

There was a pause. Mal picked up his beer again and took a pull, his eyes on the crackling blue light. 'This eagerness to stay wouldn't be anything to do with my brother, would it?' he asked at last.

'With Brett?' Copper stared at him. 'What would it have to do with him?'

Mal shrugged. 'He can be very charming.'

'I realise that, but if you think I'd be prepared to spend my days cooking and cleaning just to be near him, you must be out of your mind!'

'You wouldn't say that if you'd seen as many girls make fools of themselves over him as I have.' Mal rubbed a weary hand over his face. 'Brett, as you've probably gathered, is physically incapable of being in the same room as a woman without flirting with her. He doesn't take it seriously—Brett doesn't take anything seriously—but the agency keeps sending us girls who think they're the only one he's ever kissed. They fall madly in love with him, he gets bored after a week or so, and it all ends in tears. The next thing I know, they're on the bus back to Brisbane. Once the passionate affair is over, there isn't any way of avoiding each other out here,' he added in a dry voice.

Was that some kind of hint? Copper looked at him sharply. She had the best of reasons for knowing that it was true, but did Mal realise? Not for the first time, she cursed the impossibility of ever knowing just what he was thinking.

'I can imagine it's rather difficult,' she said after a moment. Her voice held a slight chill. If Mal remembered their own passionate affair, he could come right out and say so. *She* certainly wasn't going to mention it! 'Why don't you ask the agency to send an older woman?'

'Do you think I haven't thought of that?' Mal sighed. 'It isn't that easy. There aren't many middle-aged women who are prepared to give up comfortable lives to come and live somewhere like this. It's not exactly a career opportunity. Even the younger girls will only come out on short contracts. There isn't anything for them to do and they get bored, so none of them are going to stay permanently, but they might stay a bit longer if it wasn't for Brett.'

'Can't you ask him to leave them alone?'

Mal smiled but there was no humour in it. 'Sure—and I could ask him to stop breathing while I'm at it!'

'It must make it very difficult for Megan with all these girls coming and going,' said Copper, and he frowned.

'I know, but what can I do?'

'If Brett won't stop flirting, you could always tell him to leave,' she suggested.

'And go where?' Mal got irritably to his feet and walked over to lean against the rail. 'Brett grew up at Birraminda and it's part of his inheritance. Oh, I know he can be absolutely infuriating at times, but I can't just turn him off. He's my brother.'

'Doesn't he realise how difficult he's making things for you?' asked Copper curiously.

At the rail, Mal shrugged. 'He's always sorry when I explain why yet another housekeeper has left, but you've seen what he's like. Criticism just runs off his back, and somehow it's impossible to stay cross with him for very long. He's nearly ten years younger than me, so he was always the baby of the family. That's probably why he's never learnt any responsibility.'

Turning round to face Copper once more, he leant back against the rail and crossed his ankles. 'It doesn't help that I run things here at Birraminda. Brett would soon learn responsibility if he had his own property to run, but property doesn't come cheap, and we've been working flat out to make enough to invest in more land. That's one of the reasons I was prepared to listen to your father when he was here. I'd hoped that there might be some money for us in his project, but once I heard what he was planning I soon gave that idea up!'

'Well, maybe I'll be able to change your mind about that,' said Copper with a tight smile. 'I won't try and persuade you now, though. I'll wait until you let me have that hour—if you accept my offer, of course.' She lifted her chin at him. 'I think I can safely promise you that I won't fall in love with Brett!'

'You seem very sure of that,' said Mal, eyeing her speculatively.

'I am. I like your brother very much, but he's really not my type. Besides,' she hurried on, before Mal decided to ask her just what her type *was*, 'I happen to already be in love with someone else.'

Mal didn't move, and his expression didn't change,

but Copper had the feeling that the air had tightened somehow. 'Someone in Adelaide?' he said, without any inflection in his voice at all.

'Yes.' Mentally she crossed her fingers, thinking of Glyn who had been her boyfriend until a month ago. They had had some good times together, and in spite of the way it had ended Copper knew that she would always be fond of him. She wasn't in love with him now, but there was no need to tell Mal that. All Mal needed to know was that she was serious about staying at Birraminda until she had had a chance to convince him that Copley Travel meant business.

'I see,' said Mal.

'So, do we have a deal?' she asked with forced brightness.

'It'll be hard work,' he warned. 'This won't be like working in an office. You and your father seem to have some romantic ideas about the outback, but it's a tough life. The days are long and hot and dusty, and at the end of them there's nowhere to go and no one else to see. You'll have the most boring jobs to do and no one to help you. It won't be at all romantic.'

'I'm not in the slightest bit romantic,' said Copper icily.

It was true. Copper liked life as it was, and didn't believe in dreaming about the way things might be. Her friends would fall about with laughter if they knew she had been accused of being romantic, but then, she hadn't told any of them about the three days she had spent with Mal in Turkey. That had been stepping out of time and out of character. For Copper, it had been too special to share with anyone else. Mal had been her secret, her aberration, her one brief encounter with romance.

'That must be very disappointing for your boyfriend,' said Mal, with something of a sneer.

Looking back, Copper thought that it probably *had* been disappointing for Glyn, but she had no intention of admitting as much to Mal.

'It depends what you mean by romantic, doesn't it?' she challenged him. 'I prefer to get on with things rather than mope around wishing they were different.'

Oh, yes? said an inner voice. So why did you never quite manage to forget about Mal, no matter how hard you tried? Why were you so hurt when he didn't remember you?

'Anyway,' Copper went on, firmly squashing the voice, 'all you need to know is that I'll work hard and I won't waste my time dreaming about your brother. As far as I'm concerned Birraminda is business, and I'm not interested in anything else up here.'

Mal studied her in silence for a moment. Copper would have given anything to know what he was thinking, but as usual he kept his reactions to himself. 'OK,' he said at last, straightening from the rail. 'You can stay on as housekeeper—but only until the girl from the agency turns up. She should be here any day.'

'That's all right,' said Copper, getting to her feet in relief at having passed the first hurdle. At least she wouldn't have to drive back to Adelaide tomorrow! 'And you will give me an opportunity to show you our proposal?'

'As long as you don't mention it the rest of the time,' said Mal stringently. 'I don't want you nagging at me. You can bring out your financial plan and your proposals, but you're only getting one chance to talk me round.'

Copper smiled. 'One will be enough,' she said.

CHAPTER THREE

BY LUNCHTIME the next day, Copper was exhausted. Mal hadn't been wrong about the hard work. She had been up at five to cook breakfast for Mal and Brett, as well as the three jackaroos, and she seemed to have spent the whole morning since then running between the cookhouse and the homestead.

She had washed and wiped, swept and scrubbed. She had fed chickens and dogs and six men who had appeared for morning smoko and now lunch, and in the middle of it all she had had to deal with a lively and strong-willed four-year-old.

It hadn't helped that she had spent most of the night lying awake and thinking about Mal—the one thing she had sworn not to do. Her body had craved sleep, but her mind had refused to settle. It had turned Mal's image round and round, testing it from all angles, disconcerted to find him at once so familiar and yet a stranger. Did he really not remember? Had he forgotten touching her, tasting her with his tongue, tangling his fingers in her hair as they surrendered to the wild beat of their bodies?

Copper had struggled to bury the memories. She was at Birraminda on business, she'd told herself fiercely, gritting her teeth as she worked doggedly through the morning. It was the business that mattered now, and she had better not forget it.

She had had lunch with the jackaroos and all the other men except Bill in the cookhouse. It was a long, wooden building that didn't look as if it had been decorated since the days when sixty thousand sheep had grazed at Birraminda and whole teams of men had moved in at shearing time and had to be fed at the two huge tables. Bill was an older man who was known as the ''married man''. While the jackaroos slept in quarters he had his own house a mile or so from the homestead, and he went home at lunchtime. His wife, Naomi, prepared a meal for the men in the evenings, so that was one job she wouldn't have to do, Copper thought. Dinner for three ought to be a cinch after all she had done this morning!

Mal had told her that cold meat and bread were all that the men wanted at lunchtime, so that had not been too difficult to get ready. Now Copper ticked 'lunch' off her list and studied her remaining chores, wondering if she would have time to explore around the homestead. She would need to take photographs and get the feel of the place if she was to put together an inspiring brochure.

'What are you doing?' asked Mal, craning his head to see as she pencilled times against 'prepare vegetables' and 'bath Megan'. He raised his eyebrows derisively when he saw what she had written. 'I never met anyone who had to have a timetable just to get through the day before!'

'I like to be organised,' said Copper, instantly on the defensive. 'Otherwise nothing ever gets done.'

'I hope you've given yourself time for breathing.' Mal wasn't actually smiling but she knew perfectly well that he was laughing at her.

'I need to with this much to do!' she retorted, more ruffled than she cared to admit by the amusement gleaming in the depths of his brown eyes. 'I hadn't realised slavery was still legal in the outback!'

Brett twitched the list out of her hand. 'You've been

working much too hard,' he agreed. He had greeted the news that Copper was to stay with flattering enthusiasm, and now he edged along the bench towards her. 'You deserve a break this afternoon,' he went on, echoing Copper's own thoughts. 'Why don't I take you out and show you the waterhole your father had in mind for a site?'

'Possibly because you've remembered that you're going to check those bores this afternoon,' Mal interrupted, before Copper had a chance to accept. His voice was quiet but implacable. 'Megan and I will take Copper out.'

Megan looked up, suddenly alert. 'Are we going to ride?'

Mal glanced at Copper. She was more practically dressed today, in jeans and a fresh, mint-coloured shirt, but there was still something indefinably citified about her. Over lunch, all the talk had been about the forthcoming rodeo, and the expressive green eyes had been appalled at the thought of wrestling a steer to the ground, or trying to cling onto a bucking bronco.

'I think Copper would probably prefer to go in the car,' he said, but a smile lurked around his mouth.

Copper stiffened, well aware of how out of place she looked. 'Not at all,' she said, lifting her chin. She wasn't going to give Mal the excuse of dismissing her proposals just because he thought she couldn't cope in the outback! So what if she had never ridden before? It couldn't be that difficult. 'I'd like to ride.'

She regretted her bravado as soon as she laid eyes on the horse that Mal led towards her. It looked enormous, and as Copper edged closer it rolled its eyes and shook the flies off its mane with a snort. Backing rapidly away, she clutched her wallet file nervously to her chest. Maybe the car would be a better idea.

Mal nodded at the file. 'What have you got there?'

'Just a few things I want to check—Dad's plan of the site, the measurements of the tent, that kind of thing—and I'm bound to need to take some notes.'

'Where are you going to put it?' he asked in exasperation. 'Or were you planning to ride one-handed?'

Copper hadn't even thought about it until that moment. 'Isn't there a saddle-bag or something?'

Mal sighed. 'Here, give it to me. I'll hold it while you get on.'

'Right.' She blew out a breath and squared her shoulders. 'Right.'

The horse tossed its head up and down impatiently as Copper seized the reins. She had seen this lots of times on television. All she had to do was put one foot in the stirrup and throw her other leg over. There was nothing to it.

On television, though, the horses stood obligingly still. *This* horse danced sideways as soon as she got her foot into the stirrup, and she ended up hopping around the yard while the three jackaroos sitting on the fence watched with broad grins. Tipping their hats back, they had the air of settling down for a rare afternoon's entertainment.

Cursing the horse under her breath, Copper clenched her teeth and hopped harder. Mal shook his head with a mixture of amusement and exasperation. 'Would it help if I held him?' he asked, the very politeness of his voice a humiliation. He took hold of the bridle, and the horse, sensing the hand of a master, stopped dead.

'Thank you,' said Copper grittily. Gathering the reins more firmly in her hand, she tried again, but with no more success than before, and in the end Mal had to take her foot and boost her unceremoniously up into the saddle where she landed with a bump.

'Oh, my God,' she muttered, horrified to find herself so far from the ground. She would need a parachute to get down again! Too nervous to notice the resigned expression on Mal's face, she stared straight ahead as he let the horse go and stepped back.

Flicking its ears at the delay, the horse immediately set off. 'Whoa!' squawked Copper in alarm, and yanked at the reins, but it only seemed to take that as encouragement and broke into a brisk trot around the yard. Copper's feet bumped out of the stirrups and she bounced hopelessly around in the saddle, bawling at the horse to stop. Somewhere in the background, she could hear the sound of heartless laughter. At least someone was enjoying themselves!

The horse was heading straight for the gate into the paddock. Oh, God, what if it decided to jump? 'Who-oo-oo-oa!' yelled Copper, pulling frantically at the reins, and the horse turned smartly, sending her lurching sideways before it discovered Mal barring its way and stopped dead. Unprepared, Copper pitched forward, slithered down its neck and landed on her bottom in an undignified heap at Mal's feet.

He was grinning callously. 'Are you OK?' he asked, not even bothering to conceal his amusement as Megan squealed with laughter and the jackaroos hooted and whistled from the fence.

Without waiting for an answer, Mal reached down and put a firm hand beneath her arm to lift her easily to her feet. Copper was very conscious of the strength in his fingers and the whiteness of his teeth against his brown skin as he grinned. She jerked her arm away and made a great show of brushing the dust off the seat of her jeans. 'I think so,' she said a little sulkily. Much he would have cared if she had broken her leg! That would have been *really* funny, wouldn't it?

'Why didn't you tell me you couldn't ride?' Mal asked, his voice still warm with amusement.

'I didn't think you'd put me on a beastly wild horse!' snapped Copper, almost disappointed to discover that the only injury was to her pride. It would have served him right if she had had to be stretchered back to Adelaide!

Mal only laughed. 'Wild? Old Duke here is the laziest horse we've got. I picked him specially for you.'

'Sweet of you,' she said between her teeth. 'Remind me never to ask you for anything else special!'

'How did you think you were going to manage with a file under your arm when you'd never ridden before?' He shook his head. 'Wish I'd seen it, though! It would have made quite a story to keep us going in the wet!'

'Perhaps I'll just take a notebook,' said Copper coldly. 'I can put it in my shirt pocket—or is that too bizarre for you?'

'You want to have another go?'

Copper looked over at the grinning jackaroos. The youngest cupped his hands around his mouth. 'Hey, Copper!' he shouted. 'We're going to enter you for the bucking bronco at the rodeo! Better get in some more practice!'

'Why not?' she said. 'I'd hate to deprive you all of such good entertainment!'

'Good girl.' Mal smiled at her and turned to send one of the boys for a leading rein. 'We'll keep good hold of you this time,' he said, and gave her a leg up back into the saddle. 'Look, you hold the reins like this.' He looked up at her and her heart seemed to stop. She saw his face in sudden and startling detail: the grooves at either side of his mouth, the smile crinkling his eyes, the prickle of stubble along his jaw. 'Relax!' he said, giving the strap a final tug to secure it and slapping Duke's rump affectionately.

Copper smiled weakly and managed to look away. 'I think I've got altitude sickness!' she said. That would account for the queer feeling in the pit of her stomach, anyway.

Mal rolled his eyes, but his smile burned behind her eyelids as he swung himself easily onto an enormous chestnut horse with a star on its forehead. The jackaroo attached a leading rein to Duke's bridle and handed the end up to Mal, who moved his horse up beside her. 'Ready?'

'Yes.' Copper cleared her throat. 'Yes,' she said again, more firmly this time.

Megan was already on her pony, trotting it around in circles with humiliating ease. The gate was swung open. Mal touched his heels to his horse's flanks, clicked his tongue behind his teeth to urge Duke forward, and Copper found herself riding.

They took it very slowly at first. Megan trotted ahead on her pony, but the two horses ambled contentedly together. The lack of speed didn't seem to bother Mal, but then it wouldn't, Copper thought. He was never hurried, never flustered, never nervous. She was very conscious of him sitting relaxed in the saddle, his eyes creased as he scanned the horizon instinctively and his outline uncannily distinct in the fierce outback light.

Copper felt very safe knowing that he could control her horse as well as his own, and after a while she, too, began to relax and look around her. They were following the line of the creek, picking their way through the spindly gums that spread out from the watercourse. It was very quiet. In the heat of the afternoon the birds were mostly silent, and there was just the creak of the saddles and the rustle of leaves beneath the horses' hooves as they kicked up a distinctive dry fragrance. Copper breathed it in as it mingled with the smell of leather in her hands.

She was very aware of Mal, overwhelmingly solid beside her. Unlike her, he wore no sunglasses, but the brim of his hat threw a shadow that divided his face in two. Above, his eyes were hidden, but below, his mouth was very clear, cool and firm and peculiarly exciting.

It was just a mouth, just two lips. Copper stared desperately ahead between Duke's ears, but it tugged irresistibly at the corner of her vision and her eyes kept skittering sideways in spite of herself. Every time they rested on his mouth, the breath would dry in her throat and she would look quickly away.

She was so taken up with keeping her eyes under control that she didn't notice at first that Mal had brought the horses to a halt in a clearing beside the creek. He swung himself off his horse and looped its reins around the branch of a fallen tree before lifting Megan off her pony. She ran happily down to the water's edge, where there was a tiny sandy beach, and Mal turned to Copper, who was wondering how she was going to get off. Perhaps she should just try falling off like before?

'Take your foot out of the stirrup,' he said. 'Then swing your leg over the saddle. I'll catch you.'

He held his arms up as he spoke but a paralysing shyness had Copper in its grip once more and she could only stare helplessly down at him and wish that he had never been married, that the last seven years would simply dissolve and leave them as they had been then, a man and a girl bound briefly by magic.

'Come on,' said Mal as she hesitated still. 'You're going to have to get off some time!'

Somehow Copper managed to wriggle one leg over the saddle, and the next thing she knew she was slithering clumsily to the ground, Mal's hands hard at her waist. He held her for a moment and she stood with her hands resting on his shoulders for support, struggling against the overwhelming temptation to slide them round his neck and lean against him.

'Thank you,' she muttered, unable to meet his eyes in case he read the longing in her own, and after a tiny moment he let her go.

'This is where your father wanted to put the camp,' said Mal, looking around him at the tranquil scene.

'It looks perfect.' Copper cleared her throat and moved away from him in what she hoped would look a casual way. 'Well, I...I'd better take some notes.'

She threw herself into looking busy. She paced out the site and stopped to make notes, but her mind wasn't on siting tents or camp kitchens. It was on Mal, leading the horses down to the creek to drink before he tethered them in the shade. He looked tough and self-contained and somehow *right*, she thought, watching him move through the splintered light beneath the trees with his deliberate, unhurried tread. There was something uncompromising about him that belonged with this unrelenting landscape.

Then Mal turned to see her watching him, and Copper hurriedly bent her head back over her notebook. She couldn't take notes for ever, though, and when she thought she had impressed him enough with the fact that she only cared about business, she went to join him on the fallen tree.

Mal moved along to make room for her. There was an ironic look about his mouth as she put her notebook away. He made no comment but Copper had the feeling that he knew perfectly well that all her rushing around had just been for show, and she avoided his eye as she sat down beside him.

For a while they sat without speaking, watching Megan who was busily scooping water from the creek for some unseen project that seemed to involve a good deal of mess and mud. Behind them, the horses shifted their legs and blew softly. Slowly the peace settled around Copper, and some of the tension went out of her shoulders.

'It's a beautiful place,' she said at last.

'Yes.' Mal looked around him, and then at her. 'It wouldn't be so beautiful with a clutter of tents and a busload of tourists, though, would it?'

Copper met his eyes squarely, her own green and direct. 'Everything would be in keeping with the landscape,' she said. 'I think you'd be surprised at how beautiful it will all still be, but I'm not going to try and convince you now.' She smiled. 'I haven't forgotten what we agreed and I'm not going to waste my one chance!'

'Oh, yes, talking of our agreement...' Mal tipped his hat and resettled it on his head. 'I rang the agency at lunchtime to find out what had happened to my new housekeeper. Apparently she got offered a job as a waitress in town at the last minute and decided to take that instead.'

Copper looked at the trees reflected in the glassy water and wondered why anyone would choose to work in a restaurant when they could be somewhere like this. Then she thought about the chores she had slogged through that morning and decided that the girl, whoever she was, might have made a sensible decision.

'Are they going to send someone else?'

'They haven't got anyone immediately available, so they're going to have to advertise. It'll be at least a week before I get someone else, maybe longer.' Mal glanced at her. 'Think you can stand it for that long?'

'Of course,' said Copper, secretly relieved. She wasn't ready to go back to Adelaide yet, but nor was she ready to enquire too closely into the reasons for her reluctance to leave Birraminda. 'I said I'd stay until you got a proper housekeeper, and I will.'

'What about your commitments at home?'

'That's not a problem,' she said with some surprise. 'We got someone in to help out at the office so that I could concentrate on our plans for here, and Dad can keep an eye on things. It's not a very busy time of year, anyway.'

'I was thinking more of personal commitments,' said Mal dryly. 'Isn't anyone going to miss you?'

Would anyone miss her? She had plenty of friends who would wonder aloud where she was and wish that she was around to get a party going, but they were as busy as she was and their lives wouldn't stop without her.

'No,' said Copper with a sad smile. 'I don't think anyone will miss me very much.'

'What about this man you're so in love with?'

She had forgotten that she had told him about Glyn. 'I don't think he'll notice much difference.' She sighed and stirred some curls of dried bark in the dust with her foot. 'He was always complaining that I was never at home, anyway. I have to travel a lot, and when I'm in Adelaide there's so much paperwork to catch up with at the office. I can't be home at four o'clock every day, just waiting for him to come home.'

'You could get a different job,' said Mal.

'You sound like Glyn,' she said bitterly. 'Quite apart from the fact that Dad needs me now, I love my job. Why should I give it up?'

'No reason, if your job is more important to you than your boyfriend.'

'Why does it always have to be a choice between them?' Copper burst out in remembered frustration. 'I was perfectly happy with the way things were. Glyn knew what I was like. Why did I have to be the one to make all the compromises?'

'It doesn't sound as if you were prepared to make any compromises,' commented Mal, with an unexpectedly harsh note in his voice, and Copper's angry resentment collapsed abruptly.

'That's what Glyn said.' She took off her hat and combed her fingers dispiritedly through her hair. 'Anyway, it doesn't matter any more. I'd been in Singapore for ten days, and when I got back Glyn said he wanted to talk to me. I made a joke about it at first, said I'd have to consult my diary to see if I could arrange an appointment, but he was dead serious. He said he was fed up with coming home to an empty house and that he didn't feel there was any point in us pretending to be a couple any longer when he spent most of his time on his own. And then he said that he'd been seeing a lot of Ellie, who's a good friend of mine. Her husband left her earlier this year, and they were both lonely, and...'

Copper tried to shrug carelessly but the memory still hurt. 'Well, in the end he said he was going to move in with her. It was all very amicable. Glyn has always been one of my friends and so has Ellie. We're all part of the same crowd. I couldn't avoid seeing either of them if I wanted to keep my friends, so we were very civilised and talked it through together.'

'And you had your job to comfort you,' Mal reminded her ironically.

'Yes, I had my job,' she said in a flat voice. What had she expected? That he would be sympathetic?

Mal leant forward, linking his fingers loosely between his knees. 'So when you said you were in love with this Glyn yesterday, you weren't telling the truth?'

'Oh, I don't know...' Copper turned her hat listlessly between her hands. 'I do love Glyn. He's a great person. We even talked about getting married once, but we never got round to it. *I* never got round to it,' she corrected herself. 'There was always too much else to do. And now I think it was all for the best. Copley Travel is too important to me to give up, and if it's meant giving up Glyn instead, well, I think he probably didn't really love me either, if he wanted me to change that much.'

Mal said nothing. It was impossible to tell whether his silence was sympathetic or contemptuous. 'Anyway,' she went on brightly after a while, 'at least you know now why I'm not in any hurry to go back to Adelaide. I really don't mind seeing Glyn and Ellie together, but it seems to make everybody else feel awkward when we're all together. If I'm away for a while, it'll give everyone a chance to get used to the situation.'

'It sounds to me as if this Glyn had a lucky escape.' Mal was watching his daughter playing happily in the sand, but his mouth was twisted as if with bitter remembrance. 'It must have been a shock for him to realise that you were prepared to put your business before everything else.

'My wife was like you,' he went on after a moment. 'She thought she could have everything. When I met her, she had her own chain of shops in Brisbane. I never thought she'd be prepared to give it all up to live out here, but Lisa liked the idea of being mistress of a huge outback station. She always thought big, and Birraminda was that all right. Of course, I made sure that she spent some time out here before we were married, so that she could see exactly what was involved, but no! Lisa knew what she wanted—and what Lisa wanted, Lisa got.'

'Why did you marry her if she was like that?' asked Copper, more sharply than she had intended. She had been prepared to be jealous of Mal's dead wife, but she hadn't expected to resent being compared to her!

'I didn't realise what she was like until it was too late,' he said. 'And she was very beautiful...' He trailed off, as if conjuring up an image. 'You'd have to have known her to understand what she was like,' he went on finally. 'She could charm the birds off the trees when she wanted to, but she had a will of iron and she never had any doubt where her priorities lay. At first she thought she could run her business from out here, so I paid a fortune to equip a special office for her.

'You should go in there some time,' he added, with a glance at Copper. 'It's got telephones, a computer, a fax machine, a photocopier—everything you need to run a business. But it wasn't enough for Lisa. She wasn't interested in cooking or cleaning, although I had a whole new kitchen put in for her as well, to help her adjust, and she was easily bored if she didn't have anything she wanted to do, so she was always nagging at me to fly her to Brisbane so that she could check up on the accounts or visit designers or negotiate some special deal or other. Oh, she was an astute businesswoman, all right.'

Why did he have to make it sound like an insult? wondered Copper, who was recognising more of herself in Lisa than she really wanted to. What was wrong with being energetic and intelligent?

'If she was that astute, she wouldn't have married you unless she really wanted to be with you,' she said after a moment.

Mal shook his head. 'That was what I thought. Of course, I had what you would call a stupidly romantic idea about marriage, but Lisa's attitude was much more practical. Marriage to me gave her a sort of position, an image of someone equally at home in the outback as in the city, but she never really liked it out here and she ended up spending more and more time back in Brisbane.'

'But what about Megan?'

'Megan was the result of a doomed attempt to save a doomed marriage,' said Mal stonily. 'It didn't work, of course. Lisa saw pregnancy as an excuse to escape permanently to the city. She said that she needed to be near a hospital, that Birraminda was no place for a baby, so she went to Brisbane and she never came back. She didn't even ring me until after the baby was born.' His mouth set in a bitter line. 'She told me her labour came on unexpectedly and that there hadn't been time to call me and tell me to come to the hospital, but it wasn't true. I was supposed to be grateful that she even let me see my own child.'

His voice was very controlled but Copper could see the rigidity in his jaw. She understood now what had put that shuttered look in his eyes and carved sternness into his face. No wonder Mal had changed. The birth of his daughter ought to have been a joyful occasion, but instead he had been excluded, rejected, denied the emotional intensity of seeing his child come into the world.

Copper wished she knew how to offer him sympathy. If she had been another girl she might have been able to take his hand, or put her arms around him, but she wasn't another girl. She had condemned herself as a girl who put her job first, just like his wife, and she was afraid that Mal would flinch from her touch.

So she only clenched her hands around the rim of her hat and said nothing.

After a while Mal went on, as if the words were being forced out of him but he needed to finish the story. 'We both knew that there was no point in pretending that the marriage was going to work after that,' he said. 'It was a relief in a way, but the divorce settlement crippled me financially. All my money's in land, and I'm still struggling to get back to the way things were before. The worst thing was leaving Megan behind, but everyone said she needed to be with her mother.'

His expression was closed, refusing pity. 'I believed it myself until I saw how she was handed over to a succession of nannies while Lisa went back to working fifteen-hour days in her business. I flew down to see her as often as I could, but the child had no chance to get to know me. When Lisa was killed in a car accident and I went to bring Megan home, she was terrified. She was only two and it must have seemed as if she was being handed over to a complete stranger.'

Copper's eyes rested on Megan, squatting by the water. Her hands were full of mud, her face grubby and absorbed, and she was chattering away to herself, oblivious to the two adults watching her. 'She seems happy enough now.'

'I think so too, when I see her like this, but she's too used to playing on her own.' Mal sighed. 'She doesn't remember much about Lisa, but she misses having a mother. It might be different if I could get a housekeeper to come out here and stay for a year or so, but these girls who come and go are just unsettling for her. She needs some security.'

'You're her security,' said Copper gently, but he shook his head.

'I'm not enough,' he said. 'I can't be around the homestead the whole time. Megan needs more attention than I can give her. Too often she has to sit on a fence where I can see her and keep out of the way. She's learning plenty about how to run a cattle station but she isn't learning enough about being a child.'

Mal's eyes rested on the curve of his daughter's back. 'Of course, what I really need is a new wife,' he said with a mirthless smile. 'But I don't think I can go through another marriage like that again.'

Copper hesitated. 'It doesn't need to be like that,' she said quietly. You didn't need to be a romantic to believe that marriage didn't have to be a battleground of conflicting interests, as Mal's had been.

'Doesn't it?' said Mal. 'Where am I going to find a woman who'd be prepared to give up everything and come and live out here? No friends, no shops, no restaurants, no interesting job—just heat and dust and hard work.'

It would be hard, Copper thought. There was no doubt about it. And yet Mal's wife would have other things. She would have the creek and the gums and the diamond bright air. She would be able to reach out and touch Mal whenever she wanted. His lean, brown body would be as familiar to her as her own. She'd have long, sweet nights in his arms, and when she went to sleep she would know that he would be there in the morning when she woke. What kind of woman had Lisa been to walk away from all that?

A woman like her? Something cold touched Copper's heart. 'None of that would matter if she loved you,' she said, in a voice that was not quite steady.

'If there's one thing I learnt from my marriage, it's that love isn't enough,' said Mal bleakly. 'Lisa loved me—or she said she did—and look where that got me. And look at you. You love Glyn, but not enough to give up the things that really matter to you. Why should it be any different for the next woman I marry? Always supposing I could find one wandering around the bush! No,' he said, getting to his feet and beginning to untether Megan's pony, 'I'm not getting married again. Megan will be all right if I can find a decent housekeeper. All I can do is keep hoping that one will turn up sooner or later.'

He glanced over his shoulder at his daughter. 'Come on, Megan. We're going home.'

CHAPTER FOUR

'I'M NOT getting married again.' Again and again, over the next few days, Copper found herself brooding over Mal's words, although she could never satisfactorily explain to herself why they grated in her memory so much.

After all, Mal and his daughter weren't her business. It was a shame that his marriage had been such a disaster, of course, but Copper couldn't help resenting the way he had lumped her in the same category as Lisa. *She* hadn't walked out on a marriage, or deprived a father of his child. Glyn was the one who had walked out on her. All she had done was care about the work she did. What was so wrong with that?

At least she understood now the guarded way Mal treated her. He was polite but watchful, and, although he patently found her amusing in an exasperating kind of way, he rarely smiled—and if he did it was as if the smile had been surprised out of him against his will. Sometimes Copper felt his eyes resting on her with an expression that she could never identify, but which made her edgy and nervous, and she wanted to shout at him and tell him that she wasn't like Lisa.

At times, Copper hated Lisa for turning the intriguing man she remembered into this cool, reserved stranger. And at other times, like now, lying awake in the dark, she was disgusted to find herself envying her. Lisa had been beautiful, Mal had said. He must have loved her very much. He had married her and brought her to

Birraminda and done everything he could to make her stay.

Which meant that it hadn't taken long for him to forget *her*. Megan was four and a half now, so he must have married Lisa at least five years ago, six if one took into account the fact that the marriage had gone wrong long before the baby was conceived. And *that* meant that a year after their idyllic encounter on that Mediterranean beach Mal had dismissed her from his mind and married someone else.

Copper turned over irritably. The knowledge that he had so quickly forgotten left her feeling a fool for having remembered him so clearly, even when all hope of ever seeing him again had gone. It was just that the three days they had spent together had felt so utterly right that it was impossible to believe that it hadn't been meant to last for ever. She had used to invent endless excuses as to why Mal had never got in touch with her in London, as he had promised, but never once had she thought that he would simply carry straight on and fall in love with someone else.

Perhaps he had never really been in love with her at all. Perhaps she had just been another girl on another beach. The thought twisted in Copper like a knife.

At least it made it easier for her to pretend that she didn't care about the fact that Mal had obviously dismissed her as an obsessive career woman. Copper told herself that if he wanted to waste his life being suspicious of every woman he met, that was his loss. She just had to persuade him to let Copley Travel use Birraminda as their base and then she would be more than happy to go back to Adelaide and forget him properly this time!

But as the days passed, and a week turned into ten days, Copper began to almost forget why she had come to Birraminda in the first place. She had rung her father to explain that she would be staying on to argue their case properly, but she had stuck to her word and hadn't tried to tackle Mal on the subject.

Most afternoons he took her and Megan for a ride or a drive to more distant parts of the station. For the first few days she rushed around with a clipboard, taking notes and measurements and inspecting the landing strip where Mal kept a small plane, but after a while there seemed to be too much else important to do.

Without daily contact with her office, the business had become increasingly unreal. Real was the dazzling outback light and Megan's face screwed up in concentration. It was the sound of the birds squabbling in the trees and the sway of the saddle and the way Mal creased up his eyes as he scanned the wide, empty horizon.

Copper hated getting up early, and couldn't say that she had learnt to love housework, but she did enjoy being with Megan. She taught her how to write her name and she read her stories and played endless imaginary games, and slowly the little girl began to blossom. It was not all plain sailing, of course. Megan was a bright, funny child, but she had a wilful streak and was prone to tantrums if crossed. She soon discovered, though, that Copper's will was even stronger than her own, and that she could only go so far. Every night Copper would tuck her into bed and kiss her goodnight before Mal came in, and Megan's arms would hug her neck, and that was enough for Copper to feel that the long, exhausting day had been worthwhile.

'Look, Dad, I'm having my hair washed!' Megan stood up in the bath one evening to show off her halo of shampoo and waved her hands excitedly at her father.

Copper had been crouching by the bath, but at that

she jerked round, annoyed to find that after ten days her heart still hadn't learnt not to cartwheel crazily whenever Mal appeared unexpectedly. She had been entertaining Megan by singing with a plastic beaker clamped over her nose, and she was so busy trying to get her breathing under control that she forgot all about it until Mal lifted an enquiring eyebrow. Flushing ridiculously, she snatched the beaker off her face. Why was it that when she tried so hard to be cool and business-like Mal always seemed to find her making a fool of herself?

'You're early,' she said, almost truculently.

'I know,' said Mal with infuriating calmness. 'I thought this might be a good time for you to put your case for a campsite.'

'Oh.' Copper sat back on her heels and pushed her tousled hair behind her ears. Her sleeves were pushed up to her elbows and the beaker had left a faint red mark across the bridge of her nose. 'Now?'

'I'll just have a shower and then I can finish putting Megan to bed while you get your papers together. We could have a talk after that.'

'Fine.' Trust Mal to wait until she had forgotten all her carefully rehearsed arguments and then expect her to convince him with just half an hour's notice!

Well, if he was going to have a shower, she was going to have one too. There was no way Copper was going to face him looking hot and crumpled after a day running round after a four-year-old. This was her big chance and she mustn't blow it.

Copper stood under the streaming water and tried to gear herself back into executive mode. She thought about her father, anxiously awaiting news of Mal's decision, and she thought about Copley Travel's falling bookings. They badly needed a successful new idea to capture people's imagination, and the Birraminda tours could put them back as market leaders in exclusive holidays. There were other properties they could try if Mal refused to be convinced, but her father had his heart set on Birraminda—and anyway, it would take too long to go back to square one at this stage. Mal *had* to say yes!

Copper dressed carefully in a soft cream-coloured outfit made up of a swirling panelled skirt and a neat, cropped top. When she looked at herself in the mirror she thought she looked cool and business-like, more like herself, somehow, but not too smart to alienate Mal before she started. She could hear him putting Megan to bed next door as she left her room with her files under one arm. That meant there would be time for her to go and check the roast.

'You look stunning!' Brett came whistling into the kitchen as she bent down to put the beef back in the oven.

It was impossible not to like Brett. He was selfish and careless and irresponsible, but he flirted outrageously and made Copper laugh even when she most wanted to disapprove. Every time she saw him she was struck by how handsome he was, but his sudden appearance never had the slightest effect on her breathing, and her heart just kept placidly beating—which was strange, considering the ridiculous way it behaved whenever she saw Mal.

Next to Brett, he looked austere and understated, as if deliberately underplaying the warmth and humour that Copper remembered so well from Turkey, and yet there was no doubt who held the authority. Brett might tease his brother, or grumble at his orders, but he never challenged him, and when the men rode out in a group there was something indefinable about Mal that marked him out as leader, although he was never loud or aggressive, nor did he make any effort to draw attention to himself.

Shutting the oven door now, she turned to smile a welcome at Brett, her hands still in the mitts. 'Busy day?'

'Frantic,' said Brett lazily. 'Mal doesn't seem to appreciate that there are only so many hours in one day.' He strolled over to the cooker and lifted the lid of a saucepan to sniff appreciatively. 'Where is the old slave-driver, anyway?'

'He's just putting Megan to bed.'

'Oh, good, so he's out of the way for a bit.' Brett brightened and slid an arm around Copper's waist. 'I never seem to get a chance to talk to you on your own. Mal's always hanging around and watching disapprovingly if I go anywhere near you. Have you noticed?'

Copper had. She noticed everything about Mal. He had made a point of never leaving her alone with Brett, although it must have been obvious that she was in no danger of taking his brother seriously. In another man, his behaviour might have looked like jealousy, but Copper had the nasty feeling that she was the last woman Mal would care about. She was too like Lisa for him to be jealous. He made no effort to charm her, as Brett did, and his eyes when they rested on her held no warmth but only an odd, speculative expression.

'He's got a lot on his mind,' she told Brett, even as she marvelled to find herself defending Mal.

'So have I,' said Brett. 'A pair of gorgeous green eyes that do terrible things to a man's blood pressure.' His hold tightened. 'Has anyone ever told you what an enchanting smile you've got, Copper?'

If Mal had put his arm round her, Copper would have been strumming with nerves, but she didn't even bother to move away from Brett as she laughed up at him. 'Now, why do I get the feeling that you've used that line before?'

Brett grinned. 'I've never meant it before, though! I swear, you're the prettiest girl we've ever had out here and I'm madly in love with you. Why won't you love me back?'

'I've just got no taste,' said Copper, shaking her head in mock sorrow. 'Sad, isn't it?'

'It does seem a waste,' agreed Brett, blue eyes dancing. 'A beautiful girl like you should be in love with someone. You haven't done anything silly like falling in love with Mal, have you? He's a hardened case, and you'd have much more fun with me!'

It was obvious that he was joking, but Copper sprang away from him as if he had jabbed her with a hot poker. 'In love with *Mal*?' she spluttered, with quite unnecessary vehemence. 'What a ridiculous idea! Of course I'm not in love with Mal!'

'Now that we've cleared that up, do you think you could come and say goodnight to Megan?' Mal's cool voice from the doorway made Copper spin round, her cheeks aflame. 'Then, if you're ready, we could have that talk—or are you and Brett busy?'

'No—no, of course not,' stammered Copper, but Brett only grinned.

'Yes, we are,' he said gaily. 'I'm extremely busy trying to persuade Copper to fall in love with me, but so far we've only established that she's not in love with you!'

Mal's expression was unreadable. 'So I heard.'

'I'll—um— I'll just say goodnight to Megan,' said Copper hurriedly. She tried to gather up her files from the kitchen table, but she was so flustered that she managed to drop most of them on the floor, and then had to scrabble around picking them up again.

Mal held the door open for her with ironic courtesy. 'I'll be in my office,' he said.

What did it matter if he had heard her tell Brett that she wasn't in love with him? Copper asked herself as she bent down to kiss Megan. It was perfectly true. OK, there had been Turkey, but that had been youthful infatuation, and anyway, he had been different then. He wasn't in love with her now and she wasn't in love with him.

Absolutely, definitely not.

So why are you lurking in here as if you don't want to face him? an inner voice enquired. Copper drew a deep breath. The whole future of Copley Travel was at stake while she was dithering in here. Stop being pathetic, she told herself. Just go out there and show Mal what you're made of!

'Come in,' said Mal as she knocked at the open door with an assumption of confidence. He came round his desk to shut the door behind her. 'Sit down.'

The formality was a little disconcerting, but Copper took it as encouragement. Mal was just making it clear that this was a business meeting like any other. Trying to ignore the undertow of tension in the room, she opened a file and drew out the plan of the waterhole site that her father had drawn and a sheaf of artists' impressions of what the camp would look like.

She talked for nearly an hour. And all the time she was excruciatingly aware of Mal leaning over the plans, of the taut power of his body close to hers, the brown finger running down a list of figures and the hard, exciting line of his cheek tugging at the edge of her vision.

At length Copper talked herself to a standstill. She

had done the best she could and now all she could do was wait for Mal's decision. 'I'm not sure that there's anything else I can tell you at this stage,' she said carefully as she began to stack the papers back together. 'Obviously there are still a lot of details to be worked out, but at this stage we'd really just like to reach an agreement with you in principle.'

There was no way of telling what he thought of her arguments. His face gave nothing away as he straightened from the desk and walked over to the window. 'This project means a great deal to you, doesn't it?' he said, turning back to face her at last.

'Yes, it does,' she said honestly.

'I'm just wondering how much you're prepared to do to get me to agree to it.'

'Well, the figure I suggested is open to negotiation,' Copper began with caution, but Mal waved that idea aside.

'I'm not talking about money. I'm talking about what you personally are prepared to do.'

'Personally?' What was he driving at? Copper gave a rather uncertain laugh. 'I guess it rather depends on the sort of thing you've got in mind.'

'Let's say marriage, for instance.'

She froze in the middle of shoving papers back into their file, wondering if she had misheard. '*Marriage*? Whose marriage?'

'Yours and mine,' said Mal calmly.

Copper had the oddest feeling that the floor had tipped beneath her feet, and she sat down abruptly on her chair, still clutching the file. 'Is this some kind of joke?' she asked, in a voice that sounded quite unlike her own.

'Believe me, I've never felt less like joking,' said Mal. 'I'm offering you a straight deal. Here it is: you can use the waterhole to do whatever you want with your tourists if you agree to marry me. I'm not talking about a lifetime commitment,' he went on when Copper just gaped at him. 'I'm thinking of an agreed period of three years—but that figure is open to negotiation, as you would say.'

Copper moistened her lips surreptitiously. She couldn't get rid of the feeling that she had blundered into a play to discover that she had no idea of her own lines. 'But—but this is crazy!' she stuttered. 'You don't even want to get married. You said so!'

'I don't *want* to, but I will. I need a wife.' Mal picked up a fax message from a pile on his desk. 'I got this from the agency today. They've found a girl who's prepared to come out on a short-term contract, but I can see already what's going to happen. She'll be keen for a week or so and then she'll get bored, and Brett will think it's his duty to entertain her, and before we know where we are she'll be in tears and booking herself on the first bus back to Brisbane. Meanwhile Megan is left, abandoned by yet another stranger just when she's got used to her.'

He dropped the fax wearily back onto the desk. 'I've been thinking about what you said at the waterhole that day, and I've decided that you're right.'

'Something *I* said?' echoed Copper, surprise helping her to find her voice. 'What did I say?'

'You said that marriage didn't have to be the way it was with Lisa, and the more I think about it, the more I think you're right. A business arrangement where both sides know quite clearly what's involved would be a different sort of marriage altogether.'

'That wasn't exactly the different kind of marriage I had in mind,' she said with a tiny sigh, but Mal wasn't listening.

'It makes sense,' he said, getting up to prowl around the room as he ticked the advantages off on his fingers. 'Even Brett would draw the line at seducing his brother's wife, so I get a permanent housekeeper and Megan gets a mother figure. Three years isn't ideal, but it's more security than she gets at the moment, and—who knows?—the marriage might be a success and we could renegotiate terms for a longer period.'

'I don't believe this!' said Copper incredulously. 'You're not seriously asking me to marry you just to solve your housekeeping problems?'

'Why not? You're perfect.' Mal stopped striding and came to prop himself against the desk beside her so that he could study her dispassionately. 'The first and most important thing is that you're good with Megan and she likes you.'

'I'm not being asked to marry Megan, though, am I?'

'Second,' he said, ignoring her sarcastic interruption, 'you don't seem to take Brett too seriously. And third, as you were so busy telling Brett, you're not in love with me.'

Copper looked down at the file in her lap. She was very aware of the soft material of her skirt hanging against her bare legs and there was a cold knot gathering deep inside her. 'Most husbands would think of that as a disadvantage,' she said, amazed that she could sound so composed when her blood was still booming at the shock of his proposal.

'It's not as far as I'm concerned,' said Mal. 'I've had one wife who said she loved me, and I don't want another. No, you've told me that you're not romantic, and that suits me fine. I want someone who'll treat the marriage like a business deal, with no messy emotions or false expectations of what it'll be like.'

'And what do I get out of this *deal*?'

He looked at her in surprise. 'I would have thought that was obvious. You get the chance to run your business at Birraminda. You can say what you like about group leaders and logistical operations, but when it comes down to it, a project that size is going to have to have someone permanently on the spot. Just organising supplies is going to be a full-time job, and who's going to deal with your people when they turn up at Birraminda wanting gas or a telephone or someone to mend a tyre? You can't do any of that from Adelaide, so you might as well be up here yourself, keeping an eye on everything.'

'It's a big step from administrator to wife,' Copper pointed out, still hardly able to credit that they were actually *talking* about the crazy idea.

'You can look on it as doing two jobs at the same time,' said Mal. 'It's not even as if I'm asking you to choose between your husband and your business, am I?' He folded his arms across his chest, about at Copper's eye level, and she found herself staring at the dark hairs on his forearms where his blue checked shirt was rolled up from his wrists.

'Look,' he went on, as if talking about the most reasonable thing in the world, 'I wouldn't have thought of suggesting it if you hadn't told me how things were in Adelaide. As it is, you're alone, your boyfriend's gone off with someone else and your friends are feeling uncomfortable. Marrying me would be the perfect excuse to move away for a while.'

'You don't think marriage is rather an extreme solution to a bit of awkwardness?' Copper asked, her tone edged with irony. 'I could get a job in another state if I was that desperate to get away.'

'I'm offering you that job,' he said. 'You don't have to be madly in love to work successfully with someone.'

'No, but it helps when you're married to them!'

'Not in my experience.' The corners of Mal's mouth turned down. 'You've said that all you're really interested in is your business. Well, that's fine by me—I'm offering you the chance to prove it. You can stay here as my wife and make sure that your project is a success or you can find some other station owner willing to put up with all the hassle. Either way, I'd bet that you're going to spend most of your time sorting out problems on site, so you might as well be here at Birraminda where you'd have a lot more influence.'

Copper sat bolt upright. 'Can we get this quite clear?' she said coldly. 'You'll let Copley Travel use Birraminda if I agree to marry you, but if not, the whole project's off?'

'That's it,' he agreed, as if pleased with her quick comprehension.

'But that's blackmail!'

Mal shrugged. 'I prefer to look on it as a question of priorities. I've already decided mine—Megan. All you have to do is decide what yours is.'

It was a challenge. Angry green eyes stared into impassive brown in an almost audible clash of wills, while the air between them jangled with tension. Copper didn't know whether she wanted to laugh or cry or simply haul off and hit him for standing there so coolly while she felt as if the whole world was reeling. All she knew was that if her father's dreams weren't to fall apart there and then, she couldn't throw Mal's offer back in his face with the contempt it deserved and stalk out of the room.

Her gaze dropped and she lurched to her feet. 'I—I'll

have to think about it,' she said, gathering the rest of her files from the desk with fumbling fingers.

'All right.' Mal levered himself upright as well and walked over to open the door for her. 'Let me know when you've made a decision,' he said, and shut the door behind her.

That was it? Copper stared incredulously at the closed door, her files clutched in her arms. No word of encouragement, no suggestion of reassurance, no attempt at persuasion. Would it have killed him to show a little more interest in her? Mal was obviously never going to declare undying love after his first marriage, but he could have said that he found her attractive or that he liked her, or even just that he felt they would get on together. That would have been better than nothing. At least it wouldn't have left her feeling as if her most important attributes in his eyes were availability and a susceptibility to blackmail!

Anyway, the whole idea was ridiculous. She would say no, of course. Of course she would.

Copper was distracted through dinner, oblivious to Brett's teasing comments about what she and Mal had been up to in the office for so long, and aware only of Mal sitting at the head of the table. If he was worried about her decision, he gave absolutely no sign of it. He must have known that she would still be reeling after his extraordinary proposal, but did he make the slightest effort to make her feel as if he cared one way or the other? A smile, a reassuring look, even an effort to include her in the conversation was all it would take, but no! He just sat there and talked about *cows*. She wasn't even going to *think* about marrying him!

The trouble was that she *was* thinking about it, Copper realised as she tossed and turned in futile search of sleep that night. On her way to bed, she had checked automatically on Megan. A restless sleeper, she always ended up sprawled half-in and half-out of bed. Copper straightened her and tucked the bedclothes around her, stroking the soft curls away from the child's face. Megan mumbled in her sleep and sighed and Copper felt her heart contract. Maybe there were worse ways to spend three years than in making sure that a child was loved and secure.

She had thought, too, about going back to England to work for a couple of years once the Birraminda project was up and running. They had recently recruited a promising new member of staff to run the agency office, so she would hardly be abandoning her father. It would give her a break from Adelaide and the humiliating sympathy of friends. Why shouldn't she spend those years at Birraminda instead? What difference would it make?

Mal would make the difference. The very thought of marrying him clutched at the base of Copper's spine. You couldn't live with someone for three years and not become part of their life. 'A business arrangement', Mal had said, but just how business-like did he intend their marriage to be? Would they calmly go off to their separate rooms at night, as they did now, or would they share a room? Would he expect her to go to sleep lying next to him every night, to wake up next to him every morning? That was what a real wife would do—but then, Mal didn't want a real wife, Copper remembered bleakly.

Or did he? Housekeeper or wife—which did he really want? And which could she bear to be?

Copper fell into an exhausted sleep at last, surprised to find when she woke that she felt much calmer. She was even able to have a cool discussion with Mal about what time they would be back from the muster that evening and whether or not Naomi would provide sandwiches for their lunch. The really important issue, she had woken up realising, was not whether Mal would sleep with her or not, but the effect on her father if she refused to marry him and he carried out his threat to deny them access to Birraminda.

Dan would be bitterly disappointed at losing what he considered the perfect site. He would be frustrated at the delay in getting the project off the ground, and depressed at the thought of starting again and finding somewhere else. Already desperately worried about the future of Copley Travel if they couldn't break into a new market, the last thing her father needed at the moment was the additional stress of seeing his beloved project crumbling before his eyes. If she went home without Mal's agreement, Copper would feel that she had failed him miserably, and she already knew what that felt like.

Once before, fresh out of college, she had had a choice between spending two years working and travelling in Europe, or helping her father out at the agency during a particularly difficult period. Dan had urged Copper to go while she had the chance, and it had been the best time of her life, but her father had soldiered on alone and when he had had his first heart attack everyone had been surprised that it hadn't happened sooner. Copper, though, just back from England, had never forgiven herself. It wouldn't have killed her to have put off her trip for a few months, but it had nearly killed her father, who had loved her and protected her and cared for her, just as Mal did his own daughter.

No, she had failed her father once, but she wouldn't do it again.

Megan was ensconced at the kitchen table, breathing heavily over a work of art provisionally entitled 'Two

Horses in a Paddock'. An identical scribble, which Copper had assumed was a third horse, was scornfully described by the artist as 'a house—no, a crocodile—no, it's Dad', which just went to show how much Copper knew.

Copper couldn't help thinking that a house or even a crocodile would be a lot easier to deal with than the particular dad in question as she dialled her parents' number on her mobile phone. She wasn't going to ask their advice—they would be appalled if they knew what she was considering—but she needed to talk to them before she made up her mind one way or the other.

'Dad's *much* better,' said Jill Copley in answer to Copper's determinedly casual enquiry. She lowered her voice so that Dan couldn't hear from the bedroom, where he was resting. 'You know what a worrier he is, and he'd been fretting about what would happen if you didn't manage to set up this deal with Matthew Standish, but ever since you rang and told us you were staying on up there for a while he's been so much more relaxed. He seemed to think that it was a good sign and he's been driving me mad with plans for once the site's agreed. I haven't seen him this positive for a long time,' she confided. 'It's done him so much good and we're both so grateful to you, dear.'

'Mal—Mr Standish—hasn't committed himself to any definite agreement yet,' Copper said. She felt she had to warn her, but her mother was apparently in as confident a mood as her father.

'He'd hardly say no when you've been up there nearly two weeks, would he? What's he like, anyway?' she went on, before Copper could answer. 'Your father's not much help. He just says he's no fool. Is he nice?'

An image of Mal burned behind Copper's eyelids: the

stern angles of his face, the impenetrable brown eyes, the corners of his mouth that dented into something that was almost but not quite a smile, the way he picked up his daughter, the way he rode his horse, the way he settled his hat on his head. 'He can be.'

'Is he married?'

Copper hesitated. 'No.'

'Ah.' Her mother managed to invest it with at least six syllables, not to mention a question mark and an exclamation mark.

'Don't be silly, Mum,' said Copper, a little too sharply. 'Is Dad there?'

Dan was delighted to hear from her, and was bubbling over with so many plans that Copper had a hard time getting a word in edgeways. 'Now, how are you getting on with Matthew Standish?' he asked buoyantly at last. 'Have we got to the stage where we can start drawing up a contract yet?'

Copper looked at Megan's dark head bent over her picture, and then at the phone in her hand. 'Just one or two details to sort out, Dad,' she said slowly, 'and then we'll be ready to sign.'

'Good girl!' Dan was bursting with pride and excitement. 'I knew you wouldn't let me down.'

'No,' said Copper almost to herself as she pressed the button to cut the connection. 'I won't let you down, Dad.' Very carefully, she pushed the antenna back into place and laid the phone on the table.

It looked as if her decision was made.

CHAPTER FIVE

COPPER edged warily around the holding yards, eyeing the milling cattle with distinct nervousness. She had watched, awed, from the verandah as they had come pounding in a cloud of snorting, stamping red dust. It was hard to believe that so many animals could be controlled by a mere six men on horses, but now, a couple of hours later, they were all firmly corralled and the noise and confusion had slowly subsided to an occasional aggrieved bellow.

Two of the jackaroos were perched laconically on a fence, enjoying a smoke with the satisfaction of a job well done. 'Have you seen Mal?' she asked.

'Last time I saw him, he was heading towards the paddock,' said one out of the corner of his mouth.

So he *was* back. Copper's mouth tightened. It was two days since Mal's proposal—or rather, his ultimatum—and since then he had made no effort to get her on her own. Copper had been gripped by a kind of nervous energy after making her decision, and all she'd wanted was to tell Mal so that she could stop thinking about whether it was the right one or not. But they had been out mustering in the far paddocks yesterday and had slept in their swags under the stars. This was her first chance to talk to him.

Copper had been tense all day, waiting for him to come home, and since she had heard them come in her nerves had reached snapping point. But Mal, it seemed, was in no hurry to find out what she had decided, and in the end she had come in search of him herself, unable to bear the waiting any longer.

The paddock where the horses were kept was irrigated, and in the late afternoon light, it looked peaceful and still and very green in contrast to the red dust around it. Copper could see Duke grazing in the shade, flicking his tail against the inevitable flies, and she called his name, absurdly gratified to see his head come up. He gazed at her for a moment with liquid brown eyes and then calmly resumed his placid chewing, having obviously decided that it wasn't worth the bother of coming over to say hello.

He and Mal had a lot in common, thought Copper with an inward sigh, and turned away from the fence only to see Mal himself coming round the corner of the paddock on his great chestnut, Red.

The paddock, the yards, the dusty track beneath her feet all dropped abruptly into nothingness, and there was only Mal, very distinct against the blue outback sky. Copper felt oddly weightless, suspended in thin air, and something clutched at her heart as the nerves that had buoyed her up all day collapsed into sudden shyness. Two whole days she had been waiting to talk to him, and now that he was here, she couldn't think of anything to say.

'Hello,' was all she managed, shading her eyes against the glare with one hand as he brought Red to a halt in front of her.

High up on the horse, Mal seemed impossibly remote and unapproachable as he looked down at Copper, standing slender in jeans and a pale, long-sleeved T-shirt. The sunlight glanced off her thick brown hair, turning it to bronze, and tipped her lashes with gold. Very conscious of his scrutiny, Copper found that she couldn't look back at him. Instead she stroked Red's nose and fiddled with his bridle.

'Where's Megan?' asked Mal after a moment.

'I left her with Naomi.' Bill, the "married man", and his wife had two toddlers and another baby on the way, and when Copper had seen how tired Naomi looked she had felt rather guilty about asking her if she could keep an eye on Megan for a few minutes. 'I...I wanted to talk to you on our own.'

'About our marriage?'

'Yes.'

Without a word, Mal swung easily off the horse and led it into the paddock. Copper had to wait and watch as he took off the bridle and hung the saddle over the fence. The men were notoriously unsentimental about the animals they worked with, but she was oddly touched to see that Mal fed Red something from his shirt pocket and let the big horse nuzzle his arm before he gave it a final pat and a slap on the rump to send it cantering off into the field.

Only then did he close the gate behind him and join Copper where she stood watching the way Red kicked up his heels and revelled in his freedom. He leant his arms on the fence and glanced at her from under his dusty hat.

'Well?' he said.

'There's no need to sound so anxious to find out what I've decided,' snapped Copper, whose nerves had snarled up again as soon as Mal came near her.

Mal sighed. 'What would be the point of me getting in a state about it?' he asked. 'Nothing I can do is going to change your mind, whatever you've decided.'

'That's good coming from a man who wrapped up a proposal of marriage in a neat bit of blackmail!'

'It wasn't blackmail,' said Mal evenly. 'It's your choice whether you marry me or not.'

'Some choice!' muttered Copper.

His eyes rested on the grazing horses beneath the trees. 'Are you trying to tell me that your answer's no?'

'Are you sure you can be bothered to hear the answer?' she retorted, and he frowned.

'What do you mean by that?'

'You make me a bizarre offer of marriage and then ignore me for the next two days,' she accused him. 'Hardly the action of a man who's particularly interested one way or another!'

Mal's jaw tightened ominously. 'I've been mustering for the last two days,' he pointed out. 'How could I ignore you when I wasn't even here?'

'You ignored me all evening before you left,' Copper countered sullenly. '*And* this afternoon! You've been back for hours but you never even tried to find me!'

'I've been back just over half an hour,' said Mal, tight-lipped. 'I brought in the stragglers at the rear, so I've only just got them in and finished checking the others. That hasn't left me much time to ignore you, but, since you ask, even if I'd got back with the others I wouldn't have rushed straight up to the homestead to demand an answer only to be accused of pressurising you! I reckoned you needed time to think things through and I was prepared to wait until you were ready to tell me what you'd decided.' His voice acquired a certain steel. 'Now that you *are* ready—presumably—perhaps you could tell me what you've decided. Or am I expected to guess?'

'Under the circumstances, that shouldn't be too hard,' she snapped back without thinking.

At least she had the satisfaction of provoking Mal to

exasperation. 'Look, Copper, why don't you just give me your answer?' He sighed. 'Are you going to marry me or not? Yes or no?'

There was a pause. This wasn't how the conversation had been meant to go, Copper thought desperately. She had intended to be cool and crisply business-like and look what had happened! She had ended up sounding like a petulant child instead.

She scuffed one foot against the bottom rail of the fence. 'Yes,' she muttered. Oh, God, she still sounded like Megan after a tantrum. She cleared her throat. 'Yes, I will marry you,' she said more clearly. 'But only if you sign a formal agreement allowing Copley Travel access and control over the site.'

'Fine,' said Mal.

Copper waited for more, but apparently that was it. 'Fine?' she repeated, her voice rising in outrage. '*Fine*? Is that all you can say?'

'What else do you want me to say? I've got no objection to a formal agreement—quite the opposite. I suggest that before we get married we get a legal contract drawn up that specifies the conditions that we've both agreed to in advance. I'm not risking another divorce settlement like last time, so when we agree a date to end the marriage, we can agree the financial implications as well.'

'I don't want your money,' said Copper with distaste. 'All I'll want is assurance that Copley Travel can continue to use Birraminda after the marriage is over.'

'That's something that can be discussed when we draw up the contract,' said Mal indifferently. 'All I'm saying is that we should know exactly where we stand before we get married. I'm sure a woman of your business acumen will see the sense in a legal contract.'

The prospect of reducing a marriage to a number of clauses in a contract chilled Copper to the bone, but, having brought up the idea of a written agreement, she was hardly in a position to object. 'Right now I think we've got more important things to discuss than a pre-nuptial contract,' she said.

'Like what?'

'Like…well, like *everything*!' said Copper in frustration. She lifted her arms and then let them drop helplessly to her sides. 'For a start, what are we going to tell everybody?'

Mal turned so that he was leaning back against the fence and considered her. 'We just tell them we're getting married,' he said, and Copper hugged her arms together edgily.

'We'll need to do more than that to convince my parents that I'm serious about going to live with a perfect stranger! They'd be horrified if they knew why we're getting married,' she pointed out. 'I'll only marry you on the condition that they never, ever guess what I'm doing—and that means convincing them that we're a genuine couple.'

'What's a *genuine* couple?' asked Mal with a sardonic look. 'Every marriage is different, so why should we be any less genuine than the others?'

'You know what I mean!' said Copper crossly. 'My parents need to believe that we're getting married because we're madly in love, not because we've agreed some cold-blooded business deal.'

Mal hooked his thumbs into the pockets of his dust-encrusted jeans. 'That's not a problem, is it?'

How could he sound so casual about it? Copper eyed him resentfully. 'No, but I'm wondering how good your acting is!'

'We're both going to have to get used to acting,' said Mal, unperturbed. 'There's no point to the whole exercise unless everyone believes that you're a suitably loving wife—particularly Brett. Do you think you'll be able to convince him that you're more interested in me than you are in your business?'

'That depends on whether you'll be able to convince him that *you're* a suitably loving husband,' she said tartly.

'I expect I can manage that.'

Copper was stung by his laconic attitude. They might have been discussing the chances of rain—although, come to think of it, Mal would probably get a lot more excited about *that*! 'There's a bit more to marriage than just behaving affectionately in front of other people, you know! I think we should establish now just how ''married'' we're going to be. Real wives aren't just housekeepers with rings on their fingers,' she went on with some difficulty. 'They share things with their husbands in private as well as in public...like bedrooms, for instance.'

'We're not likely to persuade Brett that you belong with me unless we share a bedroom,' Mal agreed dryly. 'And a bed.' He glanced at Copper, who was picking a splinter of wood out of the fence post, her face averted. 'Or is that the problem?'

'It's not a *problem*,' Copper said, flustered now that she had finally come to the point. She pushed her hair awkwardly behind her ears. 'It's just...well, yes, I think we should decide now whether...you know, whether you...whether *we*...'

She could hear herself floundering and risked a peep at Mal. There was the faintest suggestion of a smile bracketing his mouth. That meant he knew exactly what she was trying to say but wasn't going to make it any easier for her. He was just leaning back against the rail, looking cool and calm and completely relaxed and watching her with those infuriatingly unreadable brown eyes. A spurt of real anger helped Copper pull herself together and she turned to face him directly.

'What I'm trying to ask,' she said icily, 'is whether you're expecting us to sleep together?'

'Why not?' said Mal with the same aggravating calmness.

'Well, we…we hardly know each other.'

'That didn't stop us before, did it?'

There was a long, long silence. Copper froze and then, very slowly, she turned her head to look at him. 'So you do remember!'

'Did you think I'd forgotten?' There was an enigmatic look in Mal's brown eyes, and a faint smile touched his mouth.

'Why didn't you say anything before?' she asked huskily. She felt very peculiar, as if the past and the present had suddenly collapsed together into a jumble of conflicting emotions where nothing was certain any more.

'You didn't.' With a shrug Mal turned back to watch the horses. 'I wasn't sure at first. I recognised your name as soon as Megan told me, but you looked so different,' he said slowly, as if visualising the Copper who had stood clutching the verandah post and comparing her with the girl who had walked out of the crowd towards him across the sand.

Her hair had been longer then, dishevelled from the sea and streaked with sunshine, and like almost everyone else on her tour she had worn shorts and a faded sleeveless top. Only her smile had marked her out from the ordinary—her smile and the clear green eyes that had looked so directly into his.

'Your hair's shorter now—smarter, I suppose,' he went on after a moment. 'You had sunglasses on, you were wearing a suit, for God's sake, and I simply wasn't expecting you. It hardly seemed possible that you could be the same girl. And then you took off your sunglasses and I saw your eyes and I realised that it really was you. By then…'

Mal paused, lifting his shoulders as if searching for the best way to explain. 'Well, by then it was clear that even if you had recognised me, you weren't going to acknowledge it. I don't know—I thought you might feel awkward, even embarrassed about working for me if I raised the subject, and since I was assuming that you'd come as a new housekeeper it just seemed easier to follow your lead and pretend that you were a stranger.' He glanced sideways at Copper. 'It's been seven years, after all,' he added. 'There was no reason why you should have remembered me.'

No reason? Copper thought about his lips against her skin, about the mastery of his hands and the sleek, supple strength of his body. She thought about the way he had made her senses sing and the breathtaking passion they had shared.

She wanted to look at the horses, at the fence, at her hands, at anything other than Mal, but an irresistible force was dragging her gaze round and against her will she found herself looking into his eyes, drowning in the brown depths that sucked her into the past, sending her spinning back seven years to the moment when she had looked up, laughing, from the crowd and seen him watching her.

Mal had been travelling on his own, Copper with a

group due to move on in three days, but none of that had mattered at the time. They had been more than just fellow Australians far from home; they had been two halves of a whole, clicking naturally into place. Being together had seemed utterly right, as if it had been somehow inevitable that they should meet that way. It was like a compass swinging to north, like an arrow heading straight for its target, like walking through a door and knowing that you had come home without even realising that you had been away.

It had been time out of time. For three days they had talked and laughed. They had swum in the turquoise sea. Droplets of water had glistened on Mal's shoulders as he surfaced and he had smiled as he shook the wet hair out of his eyes and reached for her. They had climbed the hill to the ruined fort overlooking the beach and watched the sunset, and when the soft night had closed around them making love had been the most natural thing in the world. Afterwards they had walked down to the sea again, to sink into the cool, dark water, and the phosphorescence had glimmered around their entwined bodies.

'Stay,' Mal had said on the last night, but Copper had been part of an overland tour making its way back to London, where friends were expecting her. It hadn't seemed so bad saying goodbye when he had her contact address there and promised to ring her as soon as he got there himself. She had been so sure that they had been meant for each other. How was she to have known that it would be seven years before she saw him again?

No reason to remember him? With an effort, Copper wrenched her eyes from Mal and back to the present. The beach snapped into a dirt track, the warm Mediterranean night into the fierce glare of an outback afternoon, and she was left feeling jarred and disorientated by the abrupt transition. 'Of course I remembered,' she said in a low voice.

'Why didn't *you* say anything?'

'The same sort of reasons, I suppose,' she said weakly. 'I didn't think you remembered *me*. All I knew was that you'd been married and that your wife had died, so it didn't seem very appropriate to remind you that we'd met before. And there didn't seem much point. It was just a holiday romance,' she added, trying to convince herself.

'Was it?' said Mal, without looking at her.

'You never got in touch,' Copper reminded him. She wanted to sound casual, as if she hadn't really cared one way or the other, but her voice came out flat, accusing.

'I rang you,' he said.

Surprise made her swing round. 'No, you didn't!'

'I did,' he insisted. Linking his hands loosely together, he leant on the top rail once more. Copper could see the dust on his skin, the pulse beating below his ear. 'I'd spent that year working as an agricultural consultant in East Africa. I'd waited until Brett had finished school and could help Dad while I was away and knew I would never have a better chance to travel than when my contract was finished. I was making the most of that chance in Turkey because I knew that once I got back there wouldn't be many opportunities like it, but it meant that I was out of contact for a couple of months.'

Mal's voice lost all expression. 'When I got to London there was a message saying that my father had died suddenly over a month before. Brett was too young to manage on his own so I had to get the first plane home.' He hesitated. 'I rang you from the airport. One of your friends answered the phone. She said you were at a party but that she'd give you the message. Didn't you get it?'

'No,' said Copper slowly, thinking how differently she might have felt if she had known that Mal had tried to contact her. 'No, I never got a message.'

'I even tried to ring you from here when I got back,' Mal went on after a moment. 'But you were out again and…oh, I don't know.' He stopped, narrowing his eyes at the distant horizon. 'I suppose there didn't seem much point, just like you said. You were on the other side of the world and obviously having a good time. I remembered what you'd said about your life in Adelaide, about the parties and the clubs and the sailing weekends, and I couldn't see you giving all that up for the kind of life I could offer you out here. I had other things on my mind as well, trying to get Birraminda back together after my father's death.'

He paused again and brought his eyes back to Copper's face. 'You'd seemed like the kind of girl who would enjoy herself whatever she was doing, so I didn't think you would waste much time wondering what had happened to me.'

Only seven years. 'No,' said Copper.

'Anyway,' Mal finished, 'it doesn't matter now. It's all in the past.'

'Yes,' said Copper.

There was an uncomfortable silence. At least *she* found it uncomfortable. Mal didn't look as if it bothered him in the least. It ought to be so easy now that each knew that the other remembered. It ought to be easy to relax, to laugh, to say 'Do you remember?' or 'We had a good time, didn't we?' But somehow it wasn't easy at all. Memories shimmered in the air between them, so close that Copper felt as if she could reach out and push them apart with her hands.

'It's...er...quite a coincidence, isn't it?' she managed at last, moving a few surreptitious inches away from Mal. 'Ending up together again after all this time, I mean.'

'Does it make any difference?' he asked coolly, and she knew that he wasn't thinking of the past but of the present, of Megan and his determination to provide her with stability for as long as he could.

'No,' said Copper awkwardly. She ought to be thinking of the present too, of the future and what this marriage would gain for Copley Travel. 'No, of course not.'

Mal's eyes rested on her standing rigidly away from him, her arms hugged together in an unconsciously defensive posture. 'As far as I'm concerned, as long as you behave like a wife in public after we're married, how you behave in private is your decision. My feeling is that we're both adults, and we've found each other attractive in the past, so we might as well make the most of the time we're going to spend together in bed as well as out of it. We did before.'

'It was different then,' she said with a touch of desperation. '*We're* different. You hadn't been married then; I hadn't met Glyn. It can't ever be the same as it was then.'

Mal's eyes flickered at the mention of Glyn. 'I'm not saying it would be the same,' he said a little impatiently. 'I'm just suggesting that since we're going to be sharing a bed for three years we should enjoy a physical as well as a business relationship, but it's entirely up to you. I won't lay a finger on you in private unless invited. All you have to do is ask...nicely, of course!'

Copper tensed at the undercurrent of mockery in his

voice. 'Will I have to put in a formal request?' she snapped, wishing she had never raised the subject in the first place.

'I'm sure you'll know just what to say if the occasion arises,' said Mal, but when she only scowled at the horses standing companionably nose to tail in the shade, he sighed. 'Look, I can see you don't like the idea. Fine. I respect that. We can even put it in the contract, if that makes you feel any better. As far as I'm concerned, the matter's closed, but if you change your mind, you only have to say so. Until you do, there's no need for you to feel nervous about climbing into bed beside me. Is that clear enough for you?'

'Yes,' said Copper stiltedly. 'Thank you.' Mal's assurance that he wouldn't touch her unless she asked should have been reassuring, but somehow it only made her feel worse. She could hardly object to his willingness to make the choice hers, but he hadn't sounded as if he cared much one way or the other. Did he really expect her to coolly ask him to make love to her?

Copper tried to imagine herself putting in a casual request. Oh, by the way, Mal, I want you to make love to me tonight. Or maybe he had an unspoken invitation in mind? Perhaps he expected her to roll over to his side of the bed and trail her fingers suggestively over his body?

And what would Mal do then? He hadn't exactly fallen over himself to persuade her that they would be as good together as they had been before. He might sigh and shake her off, or—worse—turn over with a martyred air and apply himself to the tedious business of satisfying her. Copper burned with humiliation at the thought. She would never be able to do it! But how could she spend three years sleeping beside him and never touching him while their memories made a taunting third in the bed?

'So,' said Mal, settling his hat on his head as he straightened. 'Do we have a deal?'

Three years keeping house or driving home to tell her father that she had failed him again? Three years with Mal or the rest of her life without him? 'Yes,' she said after a tiny pause. 'We have a deal.'

Mal hadn't missed that moment of hesitation. 'Your business must mean a lot to you,' he commented with a sardonic look, and she knew that he was thinking of Lisa, who had also put business first.

Well, what did it matter if he thought she was just like his wife? Wasn't that better than letting him know that she was afraid of the treacherous clamour of her own body more than anything he might do? 'It does,' she said, gathering the vestiges of her pride around her and with only a trace of huskiness in her voice. 'I would hardly have agreed to marry you if it didn't, would I?'

'No,' he said. 'I suppose you wouldn't.'

Another painful pause. Couldn't he see how desperate she was for reassurance? Why couldn't he put his arms around her and tell her that everything would work out all right? How could he just stand there and *look* like that when all she wanted was to take two steps and burrow into his hard strength?

'Come on,' said Mal, suddenly brusque. He took off his hat, ran his fingers through his hair and then put it back on. 'There's no point in standing here all evening.'

They turned and began walking along the track in the direction of the homestead, keeping a careful distance between them. Mal walked with a kind of loose-jointed ease, so tall and strong that the impulse to scuttle over and clamp herself to his side like iron to a magnet was almost irresistible. Copper felt as if she was having to lean away from him in order to walk upright at all.

'When shall we get married?' she asked with a brittle smile, as much to distract herself as anything else.

'The sooner the better, as far as I'm concerned,' said Mal. 'You don't want to make a fuss about the wedding, do you?'

'I wouldn't if it was up to me, but I'm going to have to convince my parents that we're marrying for love, and I think a proper wedding would help. We can keep it small, of course, but they would think it looked suspicious if I didn't get married from home.'

'I suppose it would be more convincing,' he admitted without enthusiasm. 'You're not thinking of long white dresses and veils or anything like that, are you?'

'Of course not.' Copper gritted her teeth at his lack of interest. 'I'm sure I'll be able to find something appropriate to wear. Megan might like to be a bridesmaid, too. I'm just talking about going through the motions, that's all.'

'Well, I'll leave that side of it up to you,' said Mal casually. 'Just tell me when and where I have to turn up.'

'It's nice to know that our wedding is going to mean so much to you,' she said with heavy sarcasm. 'Nobody's going to think that our marriage is genuine if that's going to be your attitude!'

'Oh, don't worry, I'll be suitably loving when required,' he promised.

Copper glanced at him and then away. The sky was flushed with an unearthly pink light as the sun dropped behind the ghost gums lining the creek. 'Do you think anyone will believe that we're really getting married?'

she asked abruptly, as if the words had been forced out of her.

'Why shouldn't they?'

'Well...I've only been up here two weeks. It might all seem a bit sudden.'

'We'll just have to persuade them that we fell in love at first sight, then, won't we?'

We did before. Mal didn't actually say it, but the words hung unspoken in the air between them. They seemed to whisper down Copper's spine and echo in her brain, and in spite of herself a slow, hot flush seeped upwards from her toes.

'Brett's not going to believe that,' she said, keeping her eyes fixed firmly on the sunset. 'He's been with us all the time and he must know quite well that we *haven't* fallen in love. I even told him so the other night.'

'I remember,' said Mal in a dry voice. 'But he didn't believe you. He told me that you were protesting too much.'

Copper stopped dead in the middle of the track. 'Oh, did he?' she said wrathfully.

'Judging by the remarks he was dropping after we'd spent so long in the office that evening, I'd say that he's almost expecting it,' Mal went on calmly. 'All you need to do is go in now looking as if you've just been thoroughly kissed.'

'And how am I supposed to do that?' demanded Copper, distinctly ruffled. 'It's not that easy!'

'Oh, I don't know.' Mal's eyes lit with a sudden speculative gleam and he reached out with one hand, letting his fingers drift tantalisingly down her cheek to curve below her jaw and slide beneath her soft hair. 'I don't think it should be that difficult.'

Copper's heart stilled and she forgot to breathe. She

had emptied of awkwardness, of anger, of any feeling at all except the deep, low thrill that went through her in response to his touch, so that instead of stepping back, or pushing his hand away, she could only stand, her eyes wide and unfocused with a terrible longing. And when Mal put out his other hand to draw her slowly towards him, she went, unresisting.

'In my experience, the simplest solution is usually the best,' he murmured. 'And the simplest way to look kissed is to be kissed,' he added very softly, and then, bending his head, he kissed her at last.

At the first touch of his mouth, a tiny sigh of release escaped Copper, and her lips parted as past and present arrowed into a piercing recognition that this was what she had thought about ever since Mal had walked around the woolshed and back into her life. It was like coming home. His tongue was so enticing, his lips as warm and persuasive as she remembered, but this time the unbearable sweetness that had lingered in her memory for seven long years was swamped almost at once by a great, rolling wave of explosive excitement that caught her unprepared and swept her up into a turbulent tide of desire.

Helpless against it, almost panic-stricken by the sheer force of her response, Copper clutched at Mal's shirt as if trying to anchor herself to the solid security of his body. The dust and the light, the very earth beneath her feet had vanished, leaving her weightless, adrift in a world where nothing existed but Mal—the taste of his mouth, the touch of his hands and the searing intensity of his kiss.

Her body was pounding, her head whirling, and when Mal let go of her face to gather her more closely into his arms she didn't even think to protest. Instead her fingers released their frantic grip on his shirt and crept around his waist, spreading over his back as if impelled by a force of their own.

Their kisses were deep, breathless, almost desperate as the doubts and confusion of the last two weeks swirled away, and all that mattered was the feel of Mal's hands, hard and possessive against her, and his taut male strength, gloriously *real* again after so many years of mere memories. Copper was lost, but she didn't care. She cared only that his arms were around her and that he was kissing her and that she never wanted him to let her go.

CHAPTER SIX

'MAL? Are you—?' Brett's voice broke through the dizzying pleasure that had them in its thrall. It stopped abruptly as he took in the scene. 'Uh-oh!' he said, and, even lost in a different world as she was, Copper could hear him grinning.

Mal didn't even tense. Without haste, he lifted his head and looked at his brother. 'What is it?' he asked, with not so much as a tremor in his voice.

Copper, dazed and shaken, almost fell as he made to release her, and if he hadn't tightened one arm around her once more she was sure that she would simply have collapsed in a heap on the track. Her legs were trembling uncontrollably and her cheeks burned. She couldn't have spoken if she had tried.

'I was coming to see if you were ready for a beer,' said Brett, still grinning broadly. 'But I can see that you're busy!'

'We were until you interrupted us,' said Mal. How could he sound so normal? Copper's heart was pounding, her head spinning, her body aroused and gasping for air, and he wasn't even out of breath!

Brett refused to take the hint. 'I thought it was my job to kiss the housekeepers,' he said, pretending to sound aggrieved.

'Not this housekeeper.' Mal glanced down at Copper, who was still struggling to adjust to the abrupt return to reality. 'This one's mine.'

He looked back at his brother and his voice held a

distinct note of warning. 'Copper's going to marry me, so you'll just have to count her as the one that got away.'

'I knew it!' Brett gave a shout of laughter and bounded forward to slap his brother on the shoulder and sweep Copper into an exuberant hug. 'I knew it! Mal thinks I can't read that poker face of his, but I could tell how he felt about you right from the start!'

'Really?' she croaked. When he set her back down on the ground, her knees were so weak that she clutched instinctively at Mal, who drew her back against the hard security of his body.

'I didn't realise you were so observant, Brett,' he said, and Copper wondered if the sarcastic edge was as obvious to Brett as it was to her.

Apparently not. Brett was nodding vigorously. 'I notice more than you think. You pretended to ignore each other but I could tell by the way you watched each other when you thought the other wasn't looking that it was real love!'

'What would you know about real love?' asked Mal, not even bothering to hide the edge to his voice this time.

'Not much,' his brother admitted. 'But I can recognise it when I see it all right, and I think you're both lucky.' The blue eyes sobered briefly. 'Very lucky,' he added seriously, and then grinned. 'Come on, let's celebrate!'

'I—' Copper was appalled to hear the squeak that came out when she opened her mouth, and cleared her throat in a desperate attempt to pull herself together. She couldn't stand here clutching Mal for ever. 'I'd better go and fetch Megan.' She tried again, not that she sounded much better second time around. But how could she be expected to sound normal when the world was still rocking around her and that wonderful, glorious, heart-stopping kiss was still strumming over her skin?

'I'll come with you,' said Mal easily.

'I'll go and make sure the beer's cold,' Brett offered. 'Don't be too long.'

'Let's hope everyone's as easy to convince as he is,' muttered Mal as his brother strode off towards the homestead. He looked down at Copper, who was leaning against him and trying to work up the determination to move away. 'Are you all right now?'

The concern in his voice snapped her upright. The last thing she wanted was for Mal to think that that kiss had meant any more to her than it had to him! 'I'm fine,' she said sharply, pushing her hair defensively behind her ears.

She set off down the track at a cracking pace, but as Mal refused to hurry, and she could hardly walk the whole way with him a ridiculous ten paces behind, she was forced to stop until he caught up and then carry on more slowly. The silence was agonising.

'Fancy Brett thinking we were in love all along!' said Copper at last, with a nervous laugh.

'Fancy,' Mal agreed expressionlessly, and she wished that she had kept her mouth shut.

The evening deepened as they walked back to the homestead with Megan. She skipped along between them, full of how naughty one of Naomi's toddlers had been and delighted to have been able to look down on his behaviour from the lofty heights of four and a half years. Copper was very aware of Mal, bending his head to listen gravely to his daughter's chatter. His gentleness with the little girl, somehow unexpected in such a strong, silent man, always wrenched at her heart. He must love

Megan very much if he was prepared to marry a woman he didn't love just for her sake.

The thought steadied Copper's nerves. The future might be an unknown quantity, her own feelings for Mal confused and uncertain, but for now it was enough to walk beside him through the hush of evening and smell the dryness of the gums drifting up from the creek.

Megan released their hands to run ahead, legs and arms completely uncoordinated. Stampeding up the steps, she disappeared into the kitchen and let the screen door clatter behind her.

'Are you going to tell her tonight?' Copper asked, worry beginning to seep back. Megan was used to having her father to herself; what if she was jealous?

'I may as well,' said Mal.

At the bottom of the verandah steps Copper faltered. The brief moment of serenity had dissolved, leaving her once more with all her doubts and uncertainties about the marriage and what it would mean. Once they had told Megan there would be no going back. They were going to walk up these steps and into a new life. For the next three years they would both be playing a part, deceiving everyone except each other.

'Do you really think we can carry it off?' she asked, abruptly apprehensive.

Mal had stopped beside her, and he turned now to look down into her troubled eyes. 'Of course we can,' he said, taking both her hands in a compelling clasp. 'I'll remember Megan and you remember your project, and we'll make it work together.' Strength seemed to flow through his hands, and Copper's fingers curled instinctively around his as she felt herself steadied.

They stood like that in the dusk, and the air between them shortened with a new intensity. Mal's grip on her hands tightened. 'It will be all right,' he promised quietly and slowly, very slowly, he bent his head and touched his lips to hers. The giddy excitement of before dissolved into tenderness and warmth and infinite reassurance, and Copper relaxed, leaning into his kiss for one enticing moment before Mal lifted his head.

Fingers entwined, they looked at each other in silence, as if dazzled by that unexpected glimpse of sweetness, and then Brett was banging through the screen door and calling to them to hurry up.

'Hey, break it up!' he ordered after one look at the tableau below him. 'You're not alone and the beer's getting warm!'

Inside, the kitchen seemed very bright, and Copper avoided Mal's eyes. She didn't know what to do with her hands. They felt very conspicuous, as if branded with the imprint of his fingers, and her lips tingled still with that brief, sweet kiss. Had he meant to kiss her? Had he been caught unawares, as she had, or had he just been trying to reassure her? Or had he heard Brett coming out from the kitchen and forced himself into his new role?

Megan was puzzled by the atmosphere until Mal took her on his knee and explained that he and Copper were going to be married so that Copper could stay with them all at Birraminda. 'Would you like that?'

Megan wasn't prepared to commit herself yet. 'How long will she stay?'

'A long time.'

The big blue eyes looked at Copper with unnerving directness. 'For ever?' she insisted, and Copper's smile went a little awry. Her eyes met Mal's for a fleeting moment over the small head.

'I hope so, Megan,' she said. By the time she left

Megan would be seven, nearly eight. That would seem like for ever to a child of four.

Megan seemed to take that as the end of the discussion. Copper had somehow envisioned the child rushing into her open arms, but Megan had seen too many strangers come and go to put her trust in anyone immediately. She simply slid off her father's knee and carried on with what she had been doing before, but when she was tucked up in bed, and Copper bent down to kiss her goodnight, two small arms shot up to cling around her neck.

'I love you,' said Megan fervently, and Copper's eyes stung with tears.

'I love you too, sweetheart.'

'I'm glad you're going to marry Dad,' she confided in a small voice.

'So am I,' whispered Copper, only to look up and see Mal watching them from the doorway.

'So is Dad,' he said.

'I can see him!' Megan tugged at Copper's hand, dancing up and down with excitement as she spotted Mal's lean, rangy figure appear through a door at the other side of the terminal, Brett close behind him. They paused for a moment, searching the crowd with their eyes.

Copper saw Mal at the same moment as Megan. Two weeks she and the child had been in Adelaide and now suddenly he was here, looking as quiet and as cool and as self-contained as ever, and all the careful composure that she had practised had crumbled at the mere sight of him. She wished she could be like Megan, running towards her father, confident in the knowledge that he would reach for her and smile and catch her up in his arms.

Pride forced Copper to follow more decorously, although her heart was hammering and her breathing uneven. 'Hello,' she said with a wavering smile as she reached them, and Mal stilled as he saw her at last.

She was wearing a summer dress in a faded yellow print, with a scoop neck and a soft swirl of skirt, and she was carrying a simple straw hat in her hands. Mal drew a long breath. 'Copper,' he said, and then stopped as if uncertain how to go on. His voice sounded odd, almost strained as they looked at each other.

Then he shifted Megan into one arm and reached slowly for Copper with the other, drawing her into his side, and she found herself lifting her face quite naturally for his kiss, her own arm creeping instinctively around his waist so that she could cling to him for the reassurance she hadn't even known she craved until then.

The touch of his mouth was electrifyingly brief. 'I've missed you,' he said as he raised his head.

Did he mean it, or was it just an act for Brett, who was watching them indulgently? 'I've missed you too,' she said huskily.

In her case it was true. She had brought Megan down to Adelaide over two weeks ago, and she had missed Mal more than she had thought possible. She had got used to him being there, used to the way he'd smile when he came in every evening. There had been times when she had almost forgotten that it was all a pretence.

Sometimes, when Mal had taken her riding along the creek, or when they'd sat on the verandah and watched the moon rise, it had seemed utterly natural that they should be together, talking easily about the day. It was only when their eyes had met unexpectedly that the tension would seep back into the atmosphere and Copper would remember that they weren't really in love. They were just pretending.

It wasn't as if Mal hadn't made his position absolutely clear. Judging by his ostentatious absence every night, Brett had no doubts about their relationship, but Copper had been all too conscious of the fact that she and Mal said a polite goodnight in the corridor and retired to their separate rooms.

'I suppose he thinks he's being tactful,' Mal had sighed that first evening, when Brett had taken himself off with much nodding and winking.

'You realise he's expecting us to fall into bed the moment the door closes behind him?' said Copper. She tried to sound amused but it didn't quite work.

'Of course he does.'

Copper fidgeted by the sink. 'Do you want...do you want to start now? Sharing a room, I mean,' she said awkwardly. 'Do you think it'll look odd if we don't?'

'Let Brett think we're making the most of it while he's out,' said Mal, unconcerned. 'It won't be long until we're married, and there'll be plenty of time for you to get used to sharing then.'

Copper should have felt relieved, but instead was left faintly disgruntled. In the face of such indifference she could hardly insist on dragging him to bed, could she?

During the day there was so much to do that it was easy to forget, but at night the knowledge that Mal didn't really want her was a constant reminder of the reality of the deal they had made, and as the weeks went by the contrast between the way things seemed and the way they were left Copper feeling increasingly edgy and irritable.

In the end, it was a relief when Mal flew her to Brisbane with Megan and put them on a plane to

Adelaide to organise the wedding, but being apart hadn't done anything to lessen the knot of mingled apprehension and anticipation inside her. It was permanently lodged somewhere in her stomach, and it tightened whenever she thought about Mal. As the prospect of marrying him drew nearer she grew more and more tense, until she felt hollow with nerves that looped and dived inside her. Now, in the busy airport building, she could feel them still, quivering distractingly just beneath her skin.

Things had been so busy at Birraminda that Mal and Brett had left it until now, two days before the wedding, before flying down in the small six-seater plane that sat on the landing strip. When they all flew back together afterwards, Copper would be Mal's wife. At the thought, a slow shiver snaked down her spine, and her shoulders flexed in response.

'Hey, Megan!' called Brett. 'Come and give me a hug so that Dad can say hello to Copper properly!'

Mal put his daughter down and she ran happily over to her uncle, who swung her up and tickled her until she squealed. Copper hardly heard. Mal had turned back to her, a smile lurking in the depths of his brown eyes, and the gentle trembling inside her erupted into a frantic flutter at the knowledge that he was going to kiss her again.

Only because Brett had reminded him that a brief touch of the lips wasn't enough for lovers who had been apart for two weeks, she told herself feverishly as Mal took both her hands and tugged her gently towards him. Her head struggled to hang onto the shreds of her pride and be the business-like Copper he expected her to be while her heart urged her to stop fighting the longing that unwound itself inside her. She had promised to act as if she was in love with him, instinct reasoned, and instinct won, allowing her to relax against Mal with a tiny sigh. It was only pretending, after all.

They were standing very close, marooned together in a hushed circle of awareness. The hustle and bustle of the airport faded into insignificance and there was only Mal, sliding his hands up her bare arms to her shoulders to cup her throat and tilt her face up to his. Very slowly he lowered his head, until his mouth was just brushing hers. Poised on the brink of release, Copper closed her eyes in delicious anticipation, and then the terrible, tantalising waiting was over. Mal secured her against him, his lips possessing hers in a kiss that was fierce and hard and yet achingly sweet.

Copper felt all her doubts dissolve in a golden rush of enchantment. Her hands crept up his chest and coiled around his neck as she abandoned herself to the swirl of sensation that carried her up out of time. It was bliss to feel his arms around her, to cling to the hard strength of his body and let the warmth of his mouth vanquish any last, lingering thoughts of resistance so utterly that when she sensed Mal begin to draw away, she couldn't prevent a murmur of protest. He stopped it with another kiss, softer this time and briefer, and then another, briefer still, until the green eyes opened languorously and Copper found herself back on earth.

Mal smiled at her dazzled expression. 'Hello,' he said, obedient to Brett's instructions.

'Dad, I've got a pink dress!' Megan tugged at his shirt, bored by the way they were just standing there looking at each other. She had much more exciting things to report.

Copper blinked and gave a rather shaky laugh, certain that she ought to be grateful for Megan's interruption. Take it lightly, she told herself frantically. It wasn't a real kiss. Mal had just been pretending because Brett was there. *She* had just been pretending too.

Hadn't she?

Her legs felt as if they belonged to another body entirely, and, acting or not, she was pathetically glad when Mal took her hand again. His clasp was calming, invigorating, indescribably reassuring.

'A *pink* dress?' he was saying to Megan, holding out his other hand to her. 'That sounds very smart.'

'Yes, and I've got a friend called Kathryn,' Megan informed him importantly. She skipped along beside them as Brett followed with the bags. 'I'm going to play with her this afternoon.'

'I hope you don't mind?' Copper moistened her lips, amazed to find that she sounded quite normal. 'I know you haven't seen Megan for a while, but she's had such a lovely time playing with my cousin's little girl.'

'No, I don't mind,' said Mal as they reached the car that Copper had borrowed from her father. 'I'm going to be taking Megan out tomorrow, while you and your mother do whatever it is women do before weddings, so I was hoping for a chance to get you on your own today.'

'Oh?' Hoping she didn't sound too pleased, Copper concentrated on digging into her bag for the car key.

Megan had run around the side of the car to pull on a doorhandle. Mal glanced back at Brett, who had been diverted by a pretty girl who wanted directions, and lowered his voice. 'I've arranged for a legal office here to draw up a contract for us,' he said, and Copper's fingers clenched around the key. 'Today will be our only chance to sign it before the wedding.'

'Fine,' said Copper in a tight voice, feeling a fool for allowing herself even a moment's dream that he might want to see her for herself. Well, what had she expected?

That one kiss would make any difference to Mal? He could hardly have found a better way of reminding her that their marriage was strictly business as far as he was concerned.

Megan chattered excitedly all the way back to the house and Copper was glad to concentrate on driving and on fighting down the wash of bitter disappointment. She was nervous, too, about Mal's first meeting with her mother, who had always been very fond of Glyn and who was less convinced than her father that Copper wasn't making a terrible mistake.

But she had forgotten how charming Mal could be when he tried. In a remarkably short space of time her mother was treating the two brothers like the sons she had never had, and by the time she had embarked on the most embarrassing stories from Copper's childhood Copper decided that she would prefer signing the contract after all.

Dan Copley, correctly interpreting her anguished glance, hastened to change the subject. 'I'm afraid that you're going to have to face a family party this evening, but we thought you and Caroline might like some time alone together this afternoon as you haven't seen each other for some time.'

'Sounds good to me,' said Mal. Glancing at his watch, he got to his feet. 'Brett and I are booked into a hotel in the city centre, so we'd better go and check in. Why don't you come with us, Copper, and I'll take you out to lunch?'

Copper smiled stiffly, knowing that as soon as he had got rid of Brett Mal would be whisking her off not to a romantic restaurant but to a lawyer's office, where they would sign three years of their lives away to a loveless marriage.

It didn't take long. Briefed by Mal from Birraminda, the admirably discreet lawyer had drawn up a concise document setting out exactly the terms of the cold-blooded deal they had agreed. Copper bent her head over the contract, pretending to read it through, but her eyes were shimmering with tears and when she signed her name it seemed to waver over the page.

'Here's your copy,' said Mal as they left. 'You'd better keep it safe.'

The day seemed hot and very bright after the air-conditioned cool of the office building, and Copper was glad of the excuse to hide her eyes with sunglasses. 'Can you keep mine until after the wedding?' she asked, rejoicing at the coolness in her voice. 'I don't want Mum or Dad finding it by mistake and knowing just what price I'm paying for our business to succeed.'

'If that's what you want.' Mal's face closed and he tucked the two contracts into his top pocket. 'Well, shall we go and have some lunch, since that's what we're supposed to be doing?'

They walked in strained silence down to the Torrens and along to a restaurant that overlooked the river, its tables shaded beneath a vine-covered pergola. Mal had changed at the hotel, and now, in light moleskin trousers and a pale blue washed cotton shirt, he looked casual and stylish and somehow unfamiliar. Copper had expected him to look out of place in the city, and it was oddly disconcerting to find him instead as at home in this cosmopolitan setting as he was riding Red under the huge outback sky.

Mal took the contracts out of his pocket and laid them on the table between them, where they lay taunting Copper in their pristine white envelopes. She tried not to look at them and fiddled with her fork as Mal dealt with the waiters, only lifting her head in surprise when he closed the wine list and coolly ordered a bottle of the best champagne.

'We *are* getting married the day after tomorrow,' he explained, in answer to her unspoken question.

'I know, but...well, we don't need to pretend when we're on our own, do we?' said Copper with some difficulty.

'No, but your parents might well ask you about your lunch, and I think they would expect us to have champagne, don't you?'

'I don't think they need any more convincing,' she said, concentrating on crumbling a roll between her fingers. 'Mum thought it was a bit sudden at first, but it helped that Dad had already met you, and he didn't seem to think there was anything odd about it at all. And they've both loved having Megan, so they feel as if you're part of the family already.' There were crumbs all over the tablecloth by now, and she brushed them into a careful pile. 'I don't think it's even occurred to them that we're not exactly what we're pretending to be.'

'Brett's the same,' said Mal. 'He's accepted the whole idea without question.'

Copper smiled painfully. 'We must be better actors than we think we are.'

There was a tiny pause. Was Mal remembering that kiss at the airport this morning? Or was he thinking of the contract, with its brisk specification that they should both behave in an appropriate manner whenever they were with other people?

'I suppose we must be,' he said at last.

The wine waiter was hovering, opening the champagne with a flourish. Copper could see the other diners smiling at the scene, obviously thinking that they were lovers, and she wanted to stand up and shout at them that it wasn't true, Mal didn't love her, it was all just for show and it meant nothing, *nothing*!

But she couldn't do that. She watched the bubbles fizzing in her glass and reminded herself about the successful business she would run and how happy her father was to know that his beloved project was going ahead. Her mind skittered to Mal, to the warmth of his mouth and the hardness of his hands, before she forced it back to the agreement they had made.

'Well…' She smiled bravely and lifted her glass. 'To our deal!'

Mal hesitated a moment, then touched his glass to hers. 'To our deal,' he said evenly.

There was a jarring silence as their eyes met and held, and then Copper managed to look away. She put her glass down on the white tablecloth rather unsteadily and tried desperately to think of something to say, but all she wanted to do was to snatch up those contracts lying there so mockingly and tear them into tiny pieces.

It was Mal who spoke first, anyway. 'So,' he said, 'how's it been going?'

'Not too badly.' Copper seized on the subject. Anything was better than that awful, jangling silence. 'I'm afraid the wedding's going to be bigger than we wanted, though. My mother's spent the last twenty-seven years looking forward to my wedding, and she's not going to be done out of it now.' She sighed. 'I kept telling her that we both wanted the ceremony to be simple, with just a quiet party afterwards, but every time I turn round she's invited someone else and the celebrations are getting more and more elaborate.'

'I'd have thought all the organisation would have appealed to someone with your business instincts,' said Mal indifferently. Nobody would guess that they were discussing his own wedding, Copper thought with a flash of resentment.

She turned the stem of her glass between her fingers. A couple were strolling along the riverbank opposite, hand in hand, absorbed in each other. Copper watched them with wistful green eyes. It had been a difficult two weeks. The strain of trying to keep her mother's plans under control had been bad enough, but far worse had been the effort of acting the part of the happiest girl in the world the whole time.

'I wouldn't have minded if it had been for a real wedding,' she said. 'But all the pretence gets tiring after a while, and it seems stupid to go to so much effort when you and I know the whole thing's just a charade.'

Mal's eyes were shuttered, expressionless. 'It'll soon be over,' was all he said.

'It won't be over for another three years,' said Copper bleakly, and he put down his glass.

'Are you trying to tell me that you're having second thoughts?'

She looked deliberately down at the contracts. 'It's too late for that now, isn't it? We've signed on the dotted line.'

'We're not married yet,' Mal pointed out impassively. 'It's not too late for you to change your mind.'

'And find somewhere else to set up the project? No.' Copper shook her head, avoiding his eye. How could she change her mind now, when her father was better, when Megan was thrilled at the prospect of being a bridesmaid? When cancelling the wedding would mean saying goodbye to Mal and never seeing Birraminda again? She smoothed the cloth over the table. 'No, don't take any notice of me. I'm just…'

'Nervous?' he suggested.

'Nervous?' she tried to scoff. 'Of course I'm not nervous!' She picked up her glass and made to drain it, only to discover that it was empty. Feeling foolish, she set it back on the table and tried to meet Mal's gaze confidently, but her defiance collapsed at one look from those shrewd brown eyes. 'Oh, all right, I *am* nervous!' she admitted crossly. 'If you must know, I'm absolutely terrified!'

'About the wedding?'

'About everything! We hardly know each other and yet in two days' time we're going to be married.' She flicked the white envelopes with her hand. 'It's all very well to talk about contracts, but a piece of paper isn't going to help us live together, is it?'

'At least you know what to expect out of the marriage,' said Mal, watching her over the rim of his glass.

'I know which jobs you'll expect me to do every day, yes, but I don't know how we're going to get on, or whether I'll be able to cope living in the outback, or what it will be like suddenly becoming mother to a four-year-old…or *anything*!' Copper finished despairingly.

'You've been living in the outback with Megan for nearly two months,' said Mal reasonably. 'And as for us getting on…well, we've got on in the past and I don't see any reason why we shouldn't do the same again—particularly as neither of us has any illusions about the other or any false expectations about what the other one really wants. And if it's a disaster at least you'll know that you're not trapped and that your life isn't going to change for ever. When three years is up, you'll have established your new business. You'll be able to come home to Adelaide, sit back and reap the benefits, and simply carry on as you were before.'

Copper tried to imagine walking away from Birraminda, from Megan, from Mal, and trying to pretend that they had never existed. She couldn't do it now. How would she be able to do it in three years' time? 'Somehow I don't think things will be the same,' she said sadly.

The first course arrived just then, immaculately presented on huge white plates, and as if at a signal the tension was broken. For the rest of the meal they kept the conversation carefully impersonal, and Copper was even able to relax slightly as she listened to the news from Birraminda and told Mal in her turn how excited Megan had been with everything she had seen and done.

It was only when they were drinking coffee that Mal brought the conversation back to their marriage. 'By the way,' he said casually, 'I've booked a hotel in the hills for Saturday night.'

Copper put her cup down into its saucer and looked at him blankly. 'What for?'

He raised an eyebrow. 'For our honeymoon, of course.'

'But…I thought we would be going straight back to Birraminda!'

'The wedding's not until five o'clock,' Mal pointed out patiently. 'By the time we get away it'll be much too late to fly back that night. We'll pick up Megan and Brett in the morning and go then. It's not a problem, is it?'

'No,' said Copper quickly. 'No, of course not.' Stupidly, she had never thought about a honeymoon. She had somehow assumed that they would spend their first night at Birraminda, where it would be so much easier to remember just why they were married. 'I just thought… Aren't you very busy at the moment?'

'One night isn't going to make much difference,' said Mal with a dry look.

It might not make a difference to him, but Copper knew that it was going to make a big difference to her! It was the night she was going to share a bed with Mal for the first time, the night she had to decide whether to lie stiffly by his side or to swallow her pride and succumb to the desire that seeped through her body whenever she thought about it. Copper had no idea whether she would ever find the courage to ask him to make love to her. Perhaps Mal would make things easy for her, she thought hopefully. He might take her in his arms and let passion sweep them up to a place where pride counted for nothing and no words were necessary…

Or he might get out his contract and check for the relevant clause, Copper amended with a bitter smile as she got dressed for the party that night. She was dreading the evening ahead. All the uncles and aunts and cousins and close family friends had been invited to meet Mal and Brett before the wedding, and she knew that she would have to spend the night being bright and cheerful and deliriously happy at the prospect of marrying a man who would expect her to put in a formal request before he would lay a finger on her!

The party was even worse than Copper had feared. Tense and jaded and headachy from too much champagne in the middle of the day, she had to endure endless teasing about her unsuitability for the outback. People kept kissing her and telling her what a lucky girl she was.

Copper's smile grew more and more brittle. Everyone seemed to be having a good time except her. Mal was relaxed and charming, unbothered by the fact that he was the centre of attention, while Brett had wasted no time at all in cornering her prettiest cousin and was meeting with plenty of encouragement. Her parents were delighted with their prospective son-in-law and all the relatives were entering into the party spirit with gusto.

That left Copper, inwardly cursing the day she had ever acquired a reputation for being good fun at any party. Why couldn't she have been so quiet and shy that nobody would notice if she sat in a corner by herself all evening? Better still, why couldn't she have been born without any family at all?

The party wore on and Copper's smile grew more desperate. She was listening to an elderly aunt tell her how fortunate she was to have found such a husband when she looked up to find Mal watching her from across the room. He was a still, steady focus in the hubbub, and all at once the thought of Birraminda hit Copper with the force of a blow.

The creek, the trees, the white blur of cockatoos wheeling in the sky and Mal, strong and sure beside her as the evening hush settled slowly around them... The longing to be there was so acute that Copper almost reeled. When someone stepped away and blocked Mal from sight, and she found herself back in the middle of the hot, noisy party, she felt almost sick with disappointment.

With disappointment and the heart-stopping realisation that she at least had no need to pretend. It was no use denying it any longer. She had fallen in love with him all over again.

CHAPTER SEVEN

WHY had it taken her so long to accept that she loved him? This time she couldn't tell herself that it was just a holiday romance, a passing passion for a stranger. This time it was for real.

Copper looked at her reflection in the long mirror. It was her wedding day. She was wearing a simple Twenties-style dress in ecru silk, with a drop waist, slender satin straps and a gossamer-fine top which whispered over her bare shoulders and floated ethereally with her slightest movement. Pearl drops trembled in her ears and there was frangipani in her hair. Her eyes were wide and dark and very green.

She ought to be happy. In a few minutes' time she would walk into the garden and marry the man she loved, surrounded by family and friends. She would be Mal's wife and he would take her back to Birraminda where she would have the challenge of setting up a project that would ensure her father's future and keep her busy and stimulated. What more could she want?

She wanted Mal to love her too. She wanted him to need her the way she needed him, to ache for her when she wasn't there, to feel that the world would stop turning without her.

But that hadn't been in the agreement, had it? Copper turned sadly away from the mirror and pulled the ribbon from her bouquet through her fingers as she remembered his words. 'I've had one wife who said that she loved me, and I don't want another.' Mal didn't want his life cluttered up with messy emotions. He wanted a practical wife, a business-like wife who would stick to the terms of the contract they had signed, and that was the kind of wife she would have to be.

'Dad's here!' Megan rushed in, trembling with excitement and still thrilled with the way the hairdresser had tied up her dusky curls with the palest pink ribbon to match her dress. 'Do you think he'll like my dress?'

'He'll think you're the prettiest little girl in the world,' Copper assured her, although her heart had started to do crazy somersaults and it was suddenly hard to breathe.

She hadn't been alone with Mal since that dreadful party. He had taken Megan out the next day while she had been swept into a whirl of activity by friends determined to celebrate her romantic marriage, and she had spent that evening quietly with her parents.

The knowledge of how much she loved him had held Copper in thrall for two days. She felt as if she were trapped in a strange dream-like state where she could walk and talk but everyone else was vaguely blurred. Nothing seemed real except her feelings for Mal, and now it was five o'clock and he was here and they were going to be married. Copper swallowed.

'You look beautiful.' Her father appeared behind her, turning her to hold her at arm's length so that he could admire her properly. 'This is the proudest day of my life,' he told her, his smile crooked with emotion. 'You're marrying a fine man, Caroline. We're going to miss you, but I know you'll be very happy together.'

Would they? Copper blinked back sudden tears. 'Thank you, Dad,' she said huskily, and kissed him on the cheek. 'Thank you for everything.'

Dan held her tightly for a moment, and then smiled

almost fiercely as he offered her his arm. 'Are you ready?'

'Are we ready, Megan?'

Megan nodded vigorously. She had been ready all day.

Copper drew a deep breath and took her father's arm. 'We're ready,' she said.

Together they walked through the house where Copper had grown up and out under the pergola at the back. The garden was decorated with white and gold balloons, and there were vases of yellow and white flowers on every table beneath wide white sunshades. Frangipani flowers floated in the pool and the air was sweet with their scent.

When Copper appeared, a hush fell over the guests grouped in a semi-circle around the celebrant, who stood with Mal and Brett, and they all turned to watch her walk across the grass. Copper noticed none of them. There was only Mal, waiting for her in a white dinner jacket that emphasised the darkness of his hair and the tanned, angular planes of his face, but which did nothing to detract from his distinctive air of quiet, tough assurance.

He turned too, as she approached, and as their eyes met Copper's world steadied miraculously. The dreamy haze that had enveloped her for the last two days snapped into focus and she was suddenly acutely aware of every detail: the gossamer touch of silk against her skin, the heady scent of the flowers in her hand, the feel of her father's arm and the concentration on Megan's face as she tried to remember her part.

And Mal, watching her with a smile that made her heart turn over.

Suddenly she was beside him. Her father squeezed her

hand, lifted it and kissed it before he stepped away, and Copper remembered to hand her flowers down to Megan, who peeped a smile at her as she took them very carefully. Then Mal was holding out his hand. She put hers into it and felt his fingers close around hers in a warm, strong clasp. Everything else ceased to exist.

Copper never knew how she got through the ceremony, but somehow she must have made the right responses in the right places, for Mal was sliding the ring onto her finger. She looked down at the gold band that linked her to him: they were married. Wonderingly, Copper lifted her eyes to his.

Mal's smile was oddly twisted as he looked down at her for a moment before cradling her face in his hands and bending his head very gently to kiss her. The touch of his mouth was enough to drench Copper in a golden, honeyed enchantment that spilled through her like a rush of light. The terms of the contract they had agreed, the watching crowd, the knowledge that Mal would never love her as she loved him, none of these mattered as their lips caught and clung and sweetness spun an invisible web around them, enclosing them in their own private world where time lost its meaning and a kiss could stretch into infinity and yet end much, much too soon.

A sentimental sigh gusted through the guests as Mal lifted his head and let Copper drift gently back to earth. Her eyes were still dark and dazed, but she managed a tremulous smile which seemed to be the signal for the garden to erupt into laughter and cheers.

Megan was clutching her flowers, wide-eyed and a little bewildered by the sudden noise. Copper crouched down to hug her and then lifted her up so that Mal could take her and hold her high and safe in his arms. Reassured that she was included in the magic that she had sensed between the two of them, Megan's face cleared, and she released her vice-like grip on her father's neck, smiling and ready to be let down so that she could run off and boast to her little friend about her part in the ceremony.

Copper's mother was weeping, and her father looked as if he had something hard and tight stuck in his throat. Copper just had time to kiss them both before she and Mal were surrounded and swamped in a tide of congratulations and kisses. At first Mal kept a tight, reassuring grip on her hand, but it wasn't long before they were separated and Copper was borne apart by friends who were meeting him for the first time and wanted to tell her how lucky she was.

'He's gorgeous!' they sighed enviously. 'And just right for you, Copper. It's all so romantic!' Then they would pause and add casually, 'His brother seems nice too. Is he married?'

Romantic was the one thing her marriage wasn't, Copper thought wistfully as she nodded and smiled and agreed that everything had worked out perfectly. Even seeing Glyn again wasn't enough to distract her from the gleam of gold on her finger that kept catching at the corner of her vision. I'm married, she kept telling herself disbelievingly. I'm Mal's wife.

Mal's housekeeper, she corrected herself sadly. 'To our deal,' Mal had toasted her, and the last, lingering enchantment of his kiss seeped away at the memory. A few kisses wouldn't change anything for Mal.

Unaware of the wistful look on her face as she hugged Glyn and turned away, Copper suddenly found Mal beside her. 'Come and dance,' he said, taking a possessive hold of her waist and drawing her over to the paved area under the pergola before anyone had a chance to intercept them with more congratulations.

It had grown dark as the party wore on and someone had lit the candle lanterns that were hung around the garden. They cast a flickering glow over Mal's face as he swung Copper into his arms. It was obvious that everyone had been waiting for them to start the dancing, for a suitably romantic song was playing and others soon joined them in the soft candlelight.

Mal's hand was warm and strong in the small of her back as he held her close, and Copper was overwhelmingly aware of him as she rested her head against his shoulder. To anyone else they must look as if they were madly in love, she thought. Out of the corner of her eye she could see the pulse beating in his throat, tantalisingly close. If she was a real bride, dancing with her new husband, she could turn her head and touch it with her lips. She could lift her face up to his and know that he would kiss her. She could whisper that she wished they were alone and let her pulse leap at the thought of the night to come.

But she wasn't a real bride, and she couldn't do any of the things she wanted to do. She could only lean a little closer and pretend that she was just acting, and wish that it could be true.

They were married. Copper succumbed to temptation and rested her face against Mal's throat, breathing in the clean, male scent of his skin. She felt boneless, weak with desire. Some time tonight they would say goodbye to everybody and drive up into the hills to the hotel and the door would shut behind them and they would be alone in their room. And what then? Would Mal really wait for her to ask before he touched her? Or would he take her hand and draw her down onto the bed and let the excitement that leapt between them whenever they kissed take its course? Copper's skin clenched at the thought and she shivered as anticipation beat a wild tattoo down her spine.

They danced in silence, holding each other like lovers. Copper was so absorbed in her dreams that it was a shock when Mal spoke at last. 'Who was that you were kissing?' he asked, as if the words had been wrenched out of him.

'Kissing?' Copper pulled slightly away, disorientated by the contrast between his cool voice and the intimacy of his hold. 'When?' she asked vaguely. Surely she had kissed everybody that evening?

'Just now.'

'Oh…' She made an effort to remember who she had been talking to before Mal had appeared at her side. 'That was Glyn.'

Mal's grip on her tightened almost painfully. '*Glyn*?' he echoed. 'Wasn't he the one who walked out on you? Who asked him to the wedding?'

'I did,' she said. 'Glyn was always a good friend. I couldn't not invite him.'

'I don't see why not,' said Mal disagreeably. 'I wouldn't have thought you'd have wanted to see him at all.'

'I don't hold any grudge against Glyn,' said Copper, a little puzzled by his attitude. If she hadn't known better, she might have thought Mal was jealous. 'If anything, we get on better now than we did before.'

It was true. The news of her engagement to Mal had dissolved the last vestiges of constraint between them and she had been able to talk to Glyn quite naturally as an old friend. And seeing him here tonight had made her realise just how differently she felt about Mal. Her relationship with Glyn had been warm and comfortable, but a tame thing compared to what she felt for the man who was holding her in his arms right now.

'You mean you've seen him before this evening?' Mal asked incredulously.

'A couple of times, yes.'

'And what about the so-called friend he left you for?' he went on in a harsh voice. 'Was she at those cosy reunions?'

Copper's face saddened, remembering how upset Glyn had been. 'No, Ellie's husband came back a couple of weeks ago, and Ellie feels that she owes it to him to give the marriage one last chance. So she and Glyn have agreed that they won't see each other for a while.'

'So he's free now,' Mal goaded her. 'You must be sorry you didn't wait for him a bit longer!'

He swung her round as he spoke. His arms were close around her, his head bent down to hers, for all the world a doting bridegroom. Sudden bitterness at the falsity of the picture sharpened Copper's tongue. 'I wouldn't have been able to set up business at Birraminda then, would I?' she said in a brief spurt of exasperation at his blindness. Couldn't he *see* how she felt? Wasn't it obvious whenever he kissed her?

She regretted the words as soon as they were spoken. The mention of business had been enough to harden Mal's expression, and it didn't take much to guess that he was thinking of his first wife who had also put business first.

'Reminding me of why you married me?' he asked, and Copper turned her face away into his shoulder.

'I don't think I need to do that,' she said in a low voice. Mal never forgot the real reasons for their marriage, and neither should she.

And yet, much later, when they finally managed to slip away from the party, Copper could think of nothing but the night to come. The tension of their exchange about Glyn had faded as the evening wore on, to be replaced by a new and very different kind of tension as the moment when they would be alone at last drew nearer.

The silence jangled between them as they drove through the wide, tree-lined streets and up into the hills, and Copper was gripped by such a strait-jacket of shyness that she would even have welcomed another argument to take her mind off the terrible, nameless longing that was drumming through her.

Mal was an overwhelming figure beside her in the darkness. Copper tried not to look at him, but her eyes kept flickering back to his profile, to the unyielding line of his jaw and the way the faint greenish light from the dashboard glanced over his lips. Every time her gaze fell on his mouth the knot of nerves would twist painfully inside her, and she would jerk her eyes away with a suppressed gasp, only to find herself staring at the strong, competent hands on the steering wheel and remembering how they had once felt against her body instead. It was all too easy to forget just why she had married him when desire tightened like a mesh over her skin.

By the time they reached the hotel Copper was vibrating with awareness, and her throat was so tight that she could hardly speak. It was Mal who checked in, Mal who replied to the hotel manager's discreet congratulations and Mal who closed the door to their room at last, leaving Copper standing nervelessly in the middle of the carpet.

'Thank God that's over,' he sighed, dropping into one

of the armchairs and wrenching at his bow tie until it dangled around his neck.

'Yes,' was all she could manage. She watched as Mal undid the top button of his shirt and closed his eyes, leaning his head back against the chair and pushing his hands through his dark hair. Her breath shortened.

'It went all right, though, didn't it?'

'Yes,' she said on a gasp.

He looked tired. She wanted to go over to him, to stand behind him and massage his shoulders, to lean down and drop tiny kisses over his face until he smiled and forgot his exhaustion. The longing was so acute that Copper's bones dissolved. Her legs gave way abruptly and she collapsed onto the edge of the chair opposite his.

There was something hard and tight inside her, strangling the air in her lungs and making her heart boom and thud in her ears. Copper forced herself to concentrate on breathing. Inflate the lungs, hold it a moment, breathe out. It was easy when you tried.

Then Mal opened his eyes without warning and all her effort was wasted as the air evaporated around her, leaving her stranded, suspended in mid-breath, unable to speak or move or even think. The deep brown gaze held her transfixed for what seemed like an eternity before Copper was able to stumble to her feet with a cross between a gasp and a gulp. 'I—I think I'll have a shower,' she stammered, and fled to the bathroom.

Her body pounded as she stood under the shower and images from the past slid over her, as physical as the streaming water but infinitely more disturbing. She wanted to coil herself around him, just as she had done before. She wanted to kiss his throat and taste his skin and listen to his heart beating. She wanted to spread her hands over his back and glory in the hardness of his body.

Copper's hands were shaking as she wrapped a towelling robe around her, and when she looked in the mirror her eyes were a bright, almost feverish green. Her skin felt as if it were pulsating with a life of its own, twitching and rippling and aching for Mal and the way things had once been between them.

'All you have to do is ask…' Mal's words reverberated down her spine and Copper welcomed the suddenly invigorating surge of anger that accompanied the memory. It wasn't fair of him to make her beg him to make love to her. What did he expect her to say? Oh, by the way, Mal, I would like to sleep with you after all?

Copper stared at her reflection. She couldn't do it…could she?

Mal had been quite straightforward, after all. He hadn't seen any reason why they shouldn't have a satisfying physical relationship. The only thing he didn't want was to get emotionally involved, but she didn't have to tell him that she was in love with him. Surely anything would be better than spending three years racked by this terrible yearning?

'Have you fallen asleep in there?'

Copper started as Mal's shout broke through her fevered speculation. 'No, no…I'm just coming.' Drawing a deep breath, she tied her robe more securely. It was now or never.

When she opened the door, Mal was sitting bare-chested on the side of the bed, taking off his shoes and socks. 'I was beginning to wonder if you were planning to spend the night in there,' he said, without looking up.

'Sorry.' Copper's voice came out as a pathetic squeak. This was the moment. All she had to do was cross the room and sit down next to him. All she had to do was lay her hand on the warm, bare skin of his back. Make love to me, Mal—that was all she had to say. It wouldn't be so hard, she told herself. But her feet wouldn't move and the words stuck in her throat, and then Mal was standing up and heading for the bathroom in his turn and the moment had passed.

Sick with disappointment and despising herself for her lack of courage, Copper pushed open the door onto the balcony and let the night air cool her burning cheeks. Far below her she could see the lights of Adelaide, strung in spangled lines across the plain between the hills and the sea. Somewhere down there amongst them all her family and friends were still celebrating her marriage, perhaps imagining her up here with Mal, blissfully happy, in love, confidently facing a lifetime together instead of three years of tension and frustration.

'What are you doing out there?' Mal stopped as he came out of the bathroom and saw Copper still standing on the balcony, barefoot and half hidden in the shadows. After a moment's hesitation he stepped out onto the balcony as well, and leant on the rail a couple of feet away from her. He had taken off his trousers and was wearing only his boxer shorts, and his body was lean and powerful and tantalisingly close.

'I was thinking,' Copper answered him at last. A light breeze rustled through the trees and lifted her hair. She clutched the robe at her throat with both hands, as if she were cold.

'What about?'

'Oh…just that this isn't what I imagined my wedding night would be like,' she said, keeping her eyes firmly on the city lights below.

'What did you imagine?' asked Mal quietly from the shadows, and Copper swallowed.

'A room like this, perhaps,' she said painfully. 'A view like this. A night like this. I thought it might be all these things but I never thought that everything else would be so different.'

'I saw the way you looked when you were talking to Glyn this evening.' Mal's voice was flat, rather harsh. 'I suppose you imagined you would be with him.'

Copper clutched her robe tighter. 'I just imagined that I would be with someone I loved, with someone who loved me,' she said with difficulty. 'That's all.'

There was a long, airless silence. Copper was excruciatingly aware of the beat of her own heart, of the soft towelling next to her skin, of Mal's powerful frame and the unbearable gap between them.

'Mal?' she said, suddenly urgent.

'Yes?'

'I—I know it's not like that for us, but…' Copper's voice petered out in despair as her nerve began to fail. 'But I've been thinking about what you said…' she struggled on desperately, before she lost it altogether.

She felt rather than saw Mal straighten, suddenly alert. 'What did I say?' he asked softly.

'You—you said that you wouldn't touch me unless I asked you to,' said Copper in a rush. She was still staring down at the distant lights that winked and glimmered as if mocking her stammered attempts to explain. 'And…and I wondered if…well, if we could pretend—just for tonight—that…that it was all how I'd imagined it after all, and that we'd just got married because… because we loved each other and not because of some deal we've made?'

She trailed off, unable to look at Mal but miserably

aware of his silence. 'I mean…you don't have to. It's probably not a good idea, anyway,' she said desperately. 'It's been a long day and we're both tired and—'

The rest of the sentence died in her throat as Mal closed the gap between them and very gently turned her towards him. 'I'm not tired,' he said softly, sliding his hand around her throat to tilt her face with his thumb so that she had to meet his eyes. 'Are you?'

Copper's heart stopped at the expression in his eyes. 'N-no,' she whispered.

'Shall we pretend, then?' Mal's thumb was drifting along her jaw, feathering down her throat, the merest graze of his fingers enough to send sparks fizzling through her veins.

'J-just for tonight,' stammered Copper. It was suddenly terribly important that Mal didn't think that she was changing the rules already. Let him believe that she was just regretting what might have been instead of feeling weak with need for him. Let him think anything as long as he kissed her soon.

'Just for tonight,' Mal confirmed gravely, but there was a smile gleaming at the back of his eyes and his hand was sliding around to stroke the nape of her neck. 'How shall we begin?'

The caress of his fingers sent tiny shudders of desire down Copper's spine, and all at once it was easy. 'We-ell…' She pretended to consider. 'If I were in love with you, I wouldn't be at all shy. I might step a bit closer—like this,' she said, lifting her hands to his chest and spreading them over his bare skin with a wonderful sense of release. 'And then I *might* kiss you—just here.' She touched her lips tantalisingly to the pulse in his throat before kissing her way slowly, deliciously, up to the angle of his jaw and then the lobe of his ear. 'Or maybe here,' she whispered as she went. 'Or here…or here…'

Mal had stilled at her first touch, but as her kisses grew more provocative he tangled his fingers in the softness of her hair and tipped her head back almost fiercely. 'If *I* were in love with you,' he said, looking down into her face, 'I'd tell you that you looked beautiful today.' His voice was deep and very low. 'I'd tell you what it felt like to watch you and know that you were mine at last.' Slowly, very slowly, he lowered his head until his lips were just brushing hers. 'I might even tell you that I'd spent all day thinking about this,' he murmured, and then the waiting was over and his mouth came down on hers.

Copper's mouth opened like a flower to the sun. Her arms slid up to his shoulders and locked around his neck as she kissed him back, giddy with the pleasure of being able to touch him and taste him, of knowing that he was real and that whatever happened tomorrow, tonight was theirs.

Mal had released her head only to gather her hard against him, his hands insistent through the towelling robe, and Copper gasped with excitement as his lips left hers. 'I *think*,' he murmured wickedly against her throat, 'we would make ourselves more comfortable, don't you? If we were in love, that is,' he added, brushing the robe apart to tease kisses along her shoulder.

'I'm sure we would,' she said unsteadily.

Inside, Mal switched off the overhead light, and for a long moment they just looked at each other in the warm glow cast by the bedside lamps, both held by the knowledge of what was to come. Copper's body strummed with anticipation as Mal took off his boxer shorts and then, very deliberately, reached out at last and loosened the belt of her robe so that he could slide the towelling off her shoulders and down her arms until it fell in a soft heap at her feet.

Her skin was luminous in the soft light and Mal drew an uneven breath, his hands unsteady as they spanned her waist. 'Copper,' was all he said, but he made her name a caress, and Copper's every sense snarled at the desire in his voice and the expression in his eyes and the hard promise of his hands. Not daring to breathe in case she broke the spell and woke to find that this was all a dream, Copper waited, poised breathless on the brink, and then Mal smiled and secured her against him as he drew her down onto the soft bed, and the world shattered into a thousand spinning fragments of delight.

The thrill of skin meeting skin was so intense that Copper gave something between a gasp and a sob. Her hands were impatient over him, exploring the texture of taut flesh over muscles, loving his sleekness and his strength as her body clamoured for his possession, but Mal was in no hurry.

He stretched her beside him and swept his hand luxuriously up from the gentle curve of her hip. 'If we were in love,' he whispered as he reached her breast, 'I'd tell you that I'd dreamed about you, about touching you like this...' His fingers circled and teased, searing Copper's senses until she arched beneath him, and when he bent his head to allow his lips to follow their scorching progress she could only sob his name, afire with a nameless, electrifying hunger.

He explored every inch of her without haste, lingering possessively over each bewitching curve, treasuring each dip and hollow, ravishing, exploring, smiling against her skin. Mal's hands were as slow and sure as Copper remembered, his mouth as enticing, but her need for him was greater, much greater than before. His body was like tempered steel, unyielding and yet warm and supple and gloriously exciting.

Intoxicated by it, she tumbled over him, running her hands down his flank and trailing kisses from his chest down to his flat stomach, tickling him with her tongue and her tousled hair until Mal groaned and swung her back roughly beneath him. He punished her with long, slow kisses, deliberately prolonging her torment, and it was only when Copper begged for release, her words tumbling incoherently over each other, that he gave himself up to the urgency that was spiralling out of control.

Copper cried out at the feel of him inside her. Wrapping herself around him, she sobbed his name, and Mal responded instinctively to her unspoken appeal, taking her with him through the wild, clamorous, spinning hunger until the insistent plunging rhythm of their bodies bore them out of it and onto the edge of eternity.

There they paused for one dazzling, timeless moment before a great, unstoppable surge of feeling broke over them, sweeping them out over the abyss, swirling them onwards and upwards and onwards again. Awed, abandoned, Mal and Copper clung together, calling each other's names for reassurance, and then, just when it seemed that they would shatter like glass, they exploded into sheer ecstasy that blotted out anything but each other and let them spiral slowly downwards through the afterglow at last.

Aeons later, Copper opened her eyes languorously and was amazed to find that the room was still there, looking quite unchanged. They had left the door to the balcony open and the breeze was billowing the curtains but otherwise all was still, as if time itself had stopped. She could hear the sound of their ragged breathing, but it seemed to come from a long way away. Copper's real self seemed to be still spinning through the stars and she felt curiously disembodied, able to look down on herself lying tangled with Mal in drowsy limbo.

She lay contentedly, her hands smoothing lovingly over his back, savouring the warm, compact body lying relaxed and heavy on hers, and listened to their breathing as it slowed and steadied. Mal stirred then and lifted himself up slightly to smile down at Copper and smooth the hair tenderly away from her face.

'I know we're pretending,' he said very softly, 'but if I was in love with you, I would tell you how much I loved you now.'

The truth trembled on Copper's tongue but she held it back. If she told him that she was really in love with him he might feel irritated or embarrassed, or feel that she expected him to say it back, and she wanted nothing to spoil this magical night. Instead she wound her arms around his neck and pulled his head down to blot out reality with a kiss.

'And I would say I loved you too.'

CHAPTER EIGHT

WHEN Copper woke the next morning, Mal was already up and dressed. He was standing by the dressing table, but as she stirred he looked across at her. Her hair was tumbled, her eyes green and sleepy, her mouth dreamily curved as she stretched languidly, and something blazed in his eyes before the old guarded look clanged back into place.

Only half-awake, but instinctively sensing the change in him, Copper pulled herself up onto the pillows and clutched the sheet over her breasts. 'Good morning,' she said, ridiculously shy after all they had shared the night before.

'Good morning.' Mal was pleasant but distant, as if he had withdrawn behind some invisible barrier.

Copper's throat tightened. What had happened? Last night he had made love to her with a passion that was beyond words. How could he be standing there now, looking so cool, so quiet, so utterly unreachable? Then her gaze dropped and she saw what he was holding in his hands.

The contract.

Mal dropped it onto the dressing table, where it landed with a faint slap. 'That's your copy,' he said, his face blank of all expression. 'You'd better keep it safe.'

The last lingering traces of enchantment cracked and splintered, falling in icy shards around Copper and leaving her cold and bereft. He could hardly have made it clearer that last night had indeed been a pretence as far as he was concerned. She turned her face away on the pillow. 'I will,' she said dully.

She was silent and strained as they drove back down the winding road to the city to pick up Megan. The whole day had taken on a nightmarish atmosphere. Over breakfast Mal had behaved as if absolutely nothing had happened between them. He'd talked about taking the opportunity to stock up on fresh fruit and vegetables and about what time he had arranged to meet Brett at the hotel for the return trip, but he'd said nothing at all about the long, sweet hours they had held each other in the darkness.

She had asked him to pretend to be in love with her, and he had pretended. That was all there was to it.

Copper clung to the thought of the night to come. The contract belonged to the harsh light of day, but surely once darkness fell, and they closed the bedroom door, they could recreate the tenderness and joy once more. She wouldn't even mind that Mal was pretending, Copper told herself, as long as he would take her in his arms again.

She longed to be back at Birraminda, but the day seemed perversely long. Stores had to be bought, Megan had to be picked up, goodbyes had to be said, and then Brett was late meeting them at the hotel so they had to hang around for over an hour before he turned up.

It was a long flight back to Birraminda in the tiny plane. Everyone was tired and on edge. Mal scowled at the controls, Brett was sullen and Megan fractious, and Copper just wanted to shut herself in a dark room and be left alone to enjoy a good cry.

When they touched down on the rough landing strip it was nearly dark, and they still had to pack the fruit and vegetables and everything else Copper had brought with her into the pick-up truck and then out again at the homestead. Megan had to be fed and bathed and put to bed, but she was over-tired and over-excited after all the attention of the last couple of weeks and the whole process culminated in a shattering tantrum. Copper just wished that she could do the same. Her head was aching and her eyes felt gritty with unshed tears.

By the time she and Mal were able to go to bed, the night before seemed like a lifetime ago and Copper was too tired even to think about the plans she had made to rediscover the sense of magic they had shared. 'I'm exhausted!' she sighed, sinking down onto the edge of the bed as Mal closed the door.

'There's no need to start dropping hints,' he snarled, and she stared at him, surprised out of her lethargy.

'What do you mean?'

Irritably, Mal began to strip off his shirt. 'I mean you don't have to think up an excuse every night to avoid sleeping with me. You made yourself clear enough last night.'

'But...but I wasn't hinting,' stammered Copper. 'I was just saying that I was tired!'

'Fine,' said Mal, chucking his shirt onto the back of a chair and reaching for a towel. 'You're tired, I'm tired, so let's just get some sleep.'

When he came back from the bathroom, Copper was lying stiffly under the sheet with her back turned to the light. Her eyes were squeezed shut and she was pretending to be asleep, but she was vibrating with awareness. She could sense Mal moving around the room, hear the clunk of his boots hitting the floor and the sound of the zip as he undid his trousers, and she could picture him so clearly that she might as well have had her eyes wide open.

Then he clicked off the light and the bed dipped as he got in beside her. Copper held her breath in the sudden darkness. If he turned to her now, if he spoke, everything might still be all right. She would meet him halfway and burrow into the comfort of his arms and they would laugh together over the tensions and misunderstandings of the day.

But Mal didn't turn. He didn't even say goodnight. He simply settled himself down and went calmly to sleep.

Aching with disappointment, Copper edged onto her back. Had he just been indulging her the night before? The thought made her burn with humiliation. If Mal thought she was going to beg him to make love to her every night, he had another think coming. She had asked once, and she was damned if she was going to ask again! He could make the first move next time.

In the dark hours of the morning Copper came to a decision. It was easy to make angry resolutions, but it didn't change the fact that she still loved him. Somehow she was just going to have to make him fall in love with her as well. If Mal wanted a practical, unromantic wife, that was the kind of wife she would be. She would play her part and she wouldn't ask anything of him, and perhaps, in time, he would realise that she was nothing like Lisa and decide that he wanted a wife who loved him after all.

Over the next few weeks, Copper worked really hard at being what Mal wanted her to be. Most of her time she spent with Megan, starting her on elementary lessons with the books that she had bought in Adelaide. She gave Megan the security of knowing that she would be firmly disciplined if she was naughty, comforted if she was hurt and loved whatever happened.

When she wasn't with Megan, Copper cleaned and tidied and scrubbed and polished, and gradually the homestead lost the faintly neglected air it had worn when she arrived. She sorted out the storerooms and reorganised the office and even offered to help Mal with all the paperwork. There was the camp site to be established too. Copper threw herself into the project, setting aside time every day to study tenders for the construction work or redraft their plans in the light of everything that she was learning about real life in the outback.

She was so busy that it was easy to get through the days, but the nights were much harder. It wasn't too difficult to talk normally together during the day, but every night when they went to bed they lay carefully apart and didn't talk at all. Copper made no demands on Mal, but as it became obvious that her careful strategy wasn't working she became increasingly crotchety and frustrated.

She was trying her best to be a good outback wife but it obviously wasn't enough. She couldn't brand a cow or ride a horse very well, and nothing else seemed to count with Mal. She got no credit for keeping the house or noticing that one of the jackaroos wasn't feeling well or discovering that Naomi was deeply unhappy. What thanks did she get for caring for his daughter and ensuring that they all got three square meals a day? None!

The more Copper brooded, the more her resentment grew—until she had almost convinced herself that she wasn't really in love with Mal at all. How could she be in love with a man who barely acknowledged her existence?

As the weeks passed, so the tension grew, until it shimmered like the heat haze over the scrub and the air between them twanged and whined, and finally snapped.

She was in the office one day, working on some figures, when Mal strode in and informed her that the men would need sandwiches for lunch as he was sending them out to check the fences.

Copper laid down her pen, a dangerous look in her green eyes. 'Why didn't you tell me this at breakfast?'

'I didn't know at breakfast,' said Mal, with a touch of impatience. 'I thought it would take them most of the day to finish off what they started yesterday, but they've made good time and it's worth them making a start on those fences this morning.'

'If they're making such good time, they can make their own sandwiches,' said Copper, and picked up her pen again.

There was an ominous silence. 'Why can't you make them?' asked Mal in a glacial voice.

'Because I'm busy,' she snapped, and her lip curled dismissively.

'You're not busy; you're just playing around with that precious project of yours!'

Copper looked up furiously. 'I am not *playing around*! I'm working out the cheapest way to bring in supplies for the tour groups and how we can calculate that into our costs. I think that's a bit more important than making a few sandwiches that you are all more than capable of making yourselves!'

'Of course, you would think that was more important,' said Mal contemptuously. 'You're obsessed with your business. You're always in here, fussing over your files. The rest of Birraminda could fall to pieces as far as you're concerned, as long as your camp site survives to keep your business going!'

'Do you want to know what I've done so far this morning, Mal?' said Copper, hanging onto the shreds of her temper with difficulty. 'I've cooked breakfast for you and your men, I've washed your dishes afterwards and put everything away, and I've swept your floor and cleaned your units. I've made your bed and washed your clothes and scrubbed out your shower.

'And in the middle of it all,' she swept on, without giving Mal a chance to speak, 'I've fed your dogs and your hens and made a meatloaf for your lunch and two apple pies for your dinner, not to mention some ice-cream for the freezer. I've washed and dressed your daughter and kept her entertained, and now that I've got a few minutes to myself, I'm working out how to run a profitable business that will bring some much needed cash into your property, judging by your accounts—which I have also kept up to date. And you *dare* to suggest that I don't do anything for Birraminda!'

'I'm not accusing you of sitting around all day,' said Mal, unmoved by her tirade. 'But you're only doing what any housekeeper would do, and you knew exactly what you were taking on when you signed that contract.'

'I didn't realise that I was signing up to three years' slavery!' she said bitterly.

'If you've got so much to do, why did you take over the evening cooking for the men?' he demanded. 'Naomi was perfectly happy doing it.'

'Naomi was *not* happy doing it!' Copper flared. 'If you had eyes to see anything beyond your stupid cows, you'd know that.' Pushing back her chair, she walked edgily over to the window, clutching her arms together defensively. 'I found Naomi in tears one day,' she said, swinging round to face Mal accusingly once more. 'She's got two small children and another one on the way, Bill's out all day, and she can't cope with the cooking on top of everything else. When I spoke to her she was so miserable that she was ready to take the children and go back to her mother in Brisbane. If I hadn't listened to her and tried to make her life a little easier, by taking over the cooking and looking after the children when I can, she'd be there now.'

Copper paused angrily, then swept on. 'Bill's not a demonstrative type, but anyone can see that he adores his wife, and if she'd gone he'd have followed her, and you'd have been left short of a man. And since you've spent the last few weeks telling me how busy you are, I assumed that you would prefer it if I could persuade Naomi to stay. But are you grateful?' She flung her arms out in a furious gesture. 'No! You think you can just walk in here and snap your fingers and I'll drop everything to make a few sandwiches. And when I object, you start quoting the terms of the contract to me!

'Well, I'm a good businesswoman, Mal,' she went on, green eyes flashing, 'and I read that contract before I signed it. There was nothing in it about making sandwiches on your say-so. What there *was* was an agreement that I would spend part of my time setting up the project which was the only reason I married you in the first place, in case you've forgotten!'

'I hadn't forgotten,' said Mal icily. There was a white look about his mouth and he was as angry as she was. 'You never give me a chance to forget.'

'That's good coming from you!' Copper retorted, too angry now to care what she said. 'You hardly ever open your mouth except to quote that agreement at me! If you had your way I'd spend all day at your beck and call. Perhaps I should be grateful you let me sleep at night?'

'There's no question about you doing anything else at night, is there?' he said savagely, and turned on his heel. 'You're not as essential as you think you are, Copper.

We managed perfectly well before you came, and we'll manage again whether you're here or not.' He paused with his hand on the door and looked back at where she stood, rigid with temper, by the window. 'I'll make the sandwiches myself—I wouldn't want to drag you away from your important business!'

The door slammed behind him and Copper was left alone to grind her teeth and find the only outlet for her feelings in throwing a stapler across the room to where Mal had been. She had worked her fingers to the bone for him and all he could do was quote the contract at her and demand sandwiches! How had she ever thought she was in love with him? He was arrogant, selfish and a bully, and she hated him!

Too angry to sit still, Copper paced around the office. So Mal thought she was obsessed with business, did he? He hadn't seen anything yet! All that was left to her out of the whole wretched business of her marriage was the chance to create a superlative new tourist location. Copper vowed to prove to Mal that "playing around" would produce the best tours in the country! She would show him just how obsessive she could be!

The atmosphere that evening was tight-lipped. Copper talked exclusively to Brett and was careful to say nothing that was not in some way concerned with the project. Mal himself hardly said a word, except to announce that he was flying to Brisbane the next morning and wouldn't be back until the following day.

Copper told herself that she was glad to see him go, and was furious with herself for listening for his step on the verandah all day, or noticing how empty the doorway seemed without him. That evening she and Brett sat in the creaky wicker chairs and drank a beer together, and the very air seemed to echo with Mal's absence.

Brett glanced at her shadowed face. 'Have you and Mal had an argument?'

'What makes you think that?' said Copper, not without some sarcasm. It must have been obvious that she and Mal were hardly talking to each other.

'Mal walked around looking like a thundercloud all yesterday and when I showed a bit of brotherly concern, and asked what was the matter, he bit my head off,' said Brett ruefully. 'Talk about bears and sore heads!'

It was no use pretending that nothing was wrong, Copper thought, and it wasn't as if real couples never had arguments. 'If you must know, he's being impossible!' she confided, and was comforted to find Brett such a sympathetic listener.

'I know,' he said with feeling. 'I've been doing my best to avoid him for weeks! I'm not saying he isn't a great bloke, but when he's like that the only thing to do is take cover. You should have heard him when I forgot to check the jackaroos had finished the fencing the other day! He tore me into little pieces and threw me all over the paddock.'

Brett grimaced at the recollection and then shrugged it off. 'If you think it's hard being his wife, you should try being his brother sometimes,' he said. 'At least he's in love with you.'

'Is he?' Copper was unable to prevent the bitter note in her voice. She couldn't tell Brett the truth about her relationship with Mal, but she didn't see why she should pretend that it was roses all the way either. 'You'd never have guessed it if you'd heard him yesterday.'

'He's not very good at showing his feelings, that's all.' Brett shifted a little uncomfortably in his chair. 'I haven't said anything before, but he had a bad time with Lisa. I hated her,' he said with sudden vehemence. 'She was the most beautiful woman I've ever seen, but she destroyed something in Mal. She made him hard and bitter and he was never the same again.'

Brett sighed and shook his head as he took a pull of his beer. 'That's why I was so glad when he married you—apart from my own bitter disappointment, of course!' he interposed with a grin. 'You're good for him, Copper. He shut himself off for too long, as if he didn't have any emotions at all. It's a good sign that he can get angry again.'

'I'll remember that the next time we have an argument,' said Copper with a rather twisted smile, and Brett put his beer down on the verandah.

'Tell you what, let's have a bottle of wine with our meal tonight,' he suggested. 'We deserve a treat. Mal's snug in some hotel, so the least we can do is show that we can have a good time without him!'

In the end they had two bottles, and Copper felt decidedly fragile the next day. There was no word from Mal as to when he would be back, and when Brett came in that evening, also very much the worse for wear, she asked if she ought to ring the hotel and find out what had happened to him. 'Do you think he's all right?' she said, despising the anxious note in her voice.

'Of course he is,' said Brett. 'He must have decided to stay another night, that's all.'

'Wouldn't he have let me know?'

'Perhaps he forgot,' Brett said casually, sinking down onto a chair and clutching his head. 'God, I feel awful!'

Copper ignored the state of his head. Mal would come back when he was good and ready, and not before, but it wouldn't kill him to let her know when to expect him, would it? He had probably written into his wretched contract that she was to wait dutifully and be prepared to serve him a meal whenever he deigned to appear!

She banged the oven door shut crossly and went to sit down at the kitchen table next to Brett. 'Do you think another bottle of wine would make us feel better?' he said.

'Would Mal approve?' she asked, and he grinned.

'No.'

Copper smiled brilliantly back at him. 'In that case, I'll get the corkscrew!'

They had just started on their first glass when they heard the sound of the plane overhead, and they exchanged glances of ludicrous dismay. 'Hadn't you better go and meet him?' she suggested, but Brett said that he was feeling brave.

'He's got the pick-up truck at the landing strip,' he pointed out. 'Let's brazen it out!'

'You're right.' Copper straightened her shoulders. 'There's no reason why we shouldn't have some wine if we feel like it, is there?'

'Absolutely not.'

The situation was so ridiculous that they both began to giggle nervously like naughty children, egging each other on with their bravado. When Mal walked in, it was to find his wife and his brother sitting at the kitchen table, convulsed with laughter.

Copper's giggles stuck in her throat as soon as she saw Mal, and her heart constricted inexplicably. Her first impulse was to throw herself into his arms and beg him not to go away and leave her again, but somehow she forced her voice to a nonchalance she was far from feeling. *She* wasn't the one who had swanned off to the city without bothering to let anyone know when she would return, was she?

'Oh, you're back.'

'Yes, I'm back.' Mal looked grimly from one to the other. 'What do you two think you're doing?'

'We've been consoling each other for your absence,' said Copper acidly.

'Well, I didn't mind you not being here,' Brett put in, 'but I thought it was my duty to comfort Copper.'

'It doesn't look to me as if she's in much need of comfort,' Mal bit out. 'If I'd known you were going to be like this, I would have come back on my own.'

'What do you mean?' she said, puzzled. 'You are on your own.'

'No, I'm not. I've brought you a housekeeper. Although I don't think she's going to be very impressed when she sees what kind of state you get into as soon as I leave you alone!'

Copper exchanged a baffled glance with Brett. 'You've brought a *what*?' she said stupidly.

'A housekeeper,' Mal confirmed, and then turned at the light step on the verandah outside. 'Here she is now.'

Even as he spoke a very slender, very neat girl with honey-coloured hair and intensely blue eyes stepped into the kitchen and smiled at Brett and Copper, who were staring at her, slack-jawed with surprise. 'Hi,' she said.

'This is Georgia,' said Mal.

Copper could hardly wait for Mal to close the bedroom door before she rounded on him. 'How dare you bring that girl here without consulting me?' she stormed. 'I thought you were going to Brisbane on business?'

Mal's jaw tightened ominously. 'I was.'

'And you just happened to find a pretty girl to bring home with you, is that it?'

'I explained all this when I introduced Georgia,' he

said impatiently. 'I had to go and see our accountant, who's an old friend. He told me about a friend of his daughter's who was looking for a job in the outback and asked me if I knew of anyone who might need someone.'

'So you said you did?' said Copper with a withering look, and he clenched his teeth, keeping his temper with difficulty.

'No, I said *you* did. You were the one who was complaining that you had too much to do. It seemed a good opportunity to find a girl to help you, if only to prevent any more accusations of treating you like a slave! And Georgia's an outback girl. She should be really useful.'

'Oh, yes, she's ideal,' said Copper jealously.

Over dinner, Georgia had told them that her father had been manager of a station very similar to Birraminda, so she had grown up in the outback. Once he had retired, she had gone to the city to find work, but she hadn't been happy and had jumped at the chance to come back. She was friendly and pretty and obviously competent, judging by the way she had rescued the disaster Copper had made of dinner, and the more she had talked, the more inadequate Copper had felt. Georgia could ride and lasso a calf and fly a plane…*and* she was a good five years younger than Copper.

'What a pity you didn't visit your accountant before I turned up here,' she added nastily as she began to get undressed. Mal was stripping off his clothes too, both of them too angry to feel any of the awkwardness that had existed in the past.

'Look, what's the problem?' he demanded. 'You said you had too much work to do and I've found someone to help you. Georgia was free this afternoon, so it made sense to bring her back straight away. I thought you'd be grateful!'

'We do have a phone,' snapped Copper, stepping out of her jeans. 'You might have asked me if I wanted some help!'

Mal swore under his breath as he tossed his shirt aside. 'It never occurred to me that you'd be this unreasonable!'

'I would have liked to have been consulted,' she said stubbornly. 'I *am* supposed to be your wife.'

'Only when you feel like it!'

'Only when *I* feel like it?' Copper echoed incredulously. 'You're the one that treats me like a housekeeper, and not a very satisfactory one at that!'

He restrained himself with an effort. 'I wouldn't have gone to such lengths to find a housekeeper if I thought that's all you were, would I?'

'I don't know.' She peeled off her top and shook her hair irritably out of her eyes. 'It doesn't leave me much to do as a wife, does it? I don't even get to be a wife in bed.'

'And whose fault is that?' said Mal unpleasantly. 'You made it very plain at the time that you only wanted me for that one night. I agreed that I wouldn't touch you unless you asked me to, and you certainly haven't done any asking.'

'A real wife wouldn't have to put in a request,' said Copper, unclipping her bra and reaching for her nightdress. 'Why can't we just behave normally?'

'All right.' Mal walked naked round the bed and twitched the nightdress from her fingers. 'Let's go to bed.'

'What?'

'Let's go to bed,' he repeated. 'You want us to be a normal couple. Normal couples make up in bed.'

'Don't be ridiculous,' said Copper tightly, and tried to snatch back the nightdress.

'Oh, no!' said Mal, chucking it out of reach and sweeping her up into his arms to carry her over to the bed, where he dumped her unceremoniously.

The electric shock of his bare flesh against hers had momentarily deprived Copper of speech, and she could only sprawl there as she struggled for breath. Before she could roll away, Mal had pinned her beneath him, her arms outstretched and her green eyes stormy.

'You're the one who wants to be normal,' he reminded her. 'I'll start, shall I?'

The feel of his flesh was indescribably exciting, and Copper's feeble attempts to wriggle out from underneath him only snarled her further in a treacherous tangle of desire. Mal must have felt the instant response of her body, for he released her arms and lifted one of her hands to his mouth instead.

'A normal husband would apologise with a kiss,' he murmured, planting a warm kiss in her palm and then letting his lips move lovingly to her wrist. 'I'm sorry I didn't consult you about employing a new housekeeper,' he went on as his mouth traced a delicious path over the soft skin of her inner arm, nuzzling into the shadow of her elbow before drifting on along her shoulder, lingering at the wildly beating pulse at the base of her throat and reaching her lips at last. 'I'm very sorry,' he breathed against them, and then he had captured her mouth with his own and there was no more need for words as everything exploded into intoxicating delight.

Copper had forgotten that she had meant to resist. She had forgotten the anger and the jealousy and the terrible tension of the last few weeks. Nothing mattered now but the fire that sparked along her veins and gathered into a flame that melted her bones and ravished her senses, consuming everything but the hunger. She wound her arms around Mal's neck and her lips opened to the sinfully seductive exploration of his tongue as she stretched voluptuously beneath him.

'Now it's your turn,' Mal whispered, smiling against her skin.

It was so wonderful to be able to touch him again, to run her hands over the powerful muscles and luxuriate in the warm, taut flesh. Copper's eyes gleamed greenly and she rolled onto him, exhilarated by her own power over the lean, brown body that lay deceptively quiescent beneath her. 'I'm sorry for being so grumpy and ungrateful,' she said obediently as she began to tease kisses along his jaw.

'How sorry?' said Mal indistinctly.

Her lips moved lower and she smiled. 'I'll show you.'

CHAPTER NINE

COPPER shaded her eyes with her hand and squinted across the yard. Yes, there they were, Megan bobbing up and down beside her father, her small face animated, and Mal, head bent to listen to her, slowing his rangy stride to her short little legs. His expression was hidden beneath his hat but, as if sensing Copper's presence, he glanced up and saw her standing there, and their eyes met with an instinctive smile. He was too far away for Copper to hear what he said, but he must have pointed her out to Megan, who spotted her with a cry of pleasure and came running towards her. Mal followed, still smiling, and Copper's heart turned over as she caught the little girl in a hug.

The last few days had been good ones. The terrible tension between her and Mal had crumbled in the face of the mutual need that had set them afire the night he had brought Georgia home. By day, Mal was as coolly self-contained as ever, but something in him had relaxed and, although he rarely touched Copper in front of the others, when the door closed behind them at night the quiet reserve dropped and he would pull her into his arms and make love to her with a tenderness and a passion that left her vibrant and glowing with joy.

He hadn't said that he loved her, but for the time being Copper was content to leave things as they were. It was hard to believe that Mal could make love to her like that without feeling anything, and she saw no need to force a commitment out of him that he was not ready to give. He had three years to fall in love with her, after all, and if the nights passed as the last ten had done, then he must surely find it hard to resist. Copper was still tingling with the memory of the previous night and her mouth curved in a reminiscent smile as she set Megan down.

'You look very pleased with yourself,' said Mal with mock suspicion. 'What are you thinking about?'

Copper's eyes shone warm and green as she smiled at him. 'Tonight,' she said honestly, and rejoiced to see the blaze of response in his face.

'You're a bad woman,' he said softly, but he smiled too as he drew her towards him for a kiss that was warm and sweet with promise.

It was such a natural gesture that Copper's heart cracked with love for him. Could he be coming to love her already? She felt almost giddy with happiness. Everything was working out perfectly. Mal might not love her yet, but he would, and Megan was blooming into a happy, loving child.

Even Georgia was enjoying her new life. The resentment that Copper had felt at the other girl's arrival had been quickly replaced by real liking. Georgia was natural and friendly and a hard worker. She cheerfully took on the cooking and the more humdrum household tasks, which left Copper more time to spend with Megan or working in the office. She still had plenty to do on the project, but she was waiting for the contractors to set a date, and in the meantime she had taken on more and more of Mal's paperwork. Her business experience stood her in good stead and at least she felt that she was being useful.

Only Brett seemed discontented. Oddly, he had made no attempt to flirt with Georgia, and even seemed to actively dislike her. 'She's too perfect,' he told Copper a few days later when she found him sitting moodily alone on the verandah.

'I thought you'd like her,' said Copper, trying to cajole him out of his mood. 'We're worried about you, Brett! A pretty girl with no attachments and you've hardly said a word to her!'

Brett hunched a shoulder. 'She's not that pretty,' he said sullenly. 'I don't like those cool, competent types.'

'Georgia may be competent, but nobody could call her cool,' Copper objected. 'She's a nice, warm, friendly girl, and I wouldn't blame her if she felt hurt at the way you ignore her. It's not as if there are lots of other people out here for her to talk to.'

'She's the one who's ignoring me,' said Brett. 'She always makes me feel as if I've crawled out from under a stone.' He brooded silently for a moment. 'I don't want her approval anyway,' he went on unconvincingly, but with a flicker of his old self. 'She's not nearly as much fun as you, Copper. And have you noticed how chummy she and Mal are?'

After that, of course, Copper *did* notice. Georgia behaved quite naturally, but Copper's jealous eye discerned rather too much approval in Mal's expression when he looked at the other girl. Georgia's knowledge of station life meant that she always knew what Mal was talking about, too, and she could discuss station matters and breaking horses. She knew about musters and how to make billy tea. She could castrate a calf and rope a cow as easily as she could cook a perfect roast, and it wasn't long before Copper began to feel excluded from their conversations. All *she* could talk about was settling invoices and checking accounts, and nobody was interested in that.

Unable to compete when it came to discussing the day, Copper turned more and more to Brett, who kept pointedly aloof from such station conversation and was more than willing to flirt outrageously with Copper instead. Once or twice Copper caught him watching Georgia with an expression that made her suspect that he had been protesting too much about his dislike of the other girl. She was pretty sure that Brett was harder hit than he wanted to admit. His flirting had a desperate edge that she recognised from her own doomed attempts to disguise how she felt about Mal, and a sense of fellow feeling drew them increasingly together.

Mal didn't say anything at first, but as the evenings passed, and the division between the conversations grew more and more obvious, his jaw acquired a set look, and whenever he glanced at Brett and Copper his mouth turned disapprovingly down at the corners. Copper pretended not to notice. Who was Mal to complain about the way she laughed with Brett, when he spent his whole time monopolising Georgia?

Copper could never put her finger on the moment when the warmth and the fire in her relationship with Mal faded. One day it seemed as if they fell laughing into bed together every night, and the next that the following three years would be spent undressing in tense silence.

'Why are you encouraging Brett to make such a fool of himself over you?' Mal asked one night, after Brett had been particularly obstreperous. They were lying stiffly apart in the dark and the words sounded as if they had been forced out of him.

'I'm not *encouraging* him,' said Copper. 'I'm just talking to him, which is more than you and Georgia ever do.'

Mal snorted. 'You call that display "just talking", do you? It doesn't look much like talking to me!'

'I'm surprised you notice,' Copper snapped back. 'You're always nose to nose with Georgia. I thought you'd forgotten who you were married to!'

'*I'm* not the one who seems to have forgotten,' he said grimly. 'You and Brett are the ones who have decided that you needn't bother about a little thing like a wedding ring!'

Exasperated by his obtuseness, Copper struggled up into a sitting position and snapped on the bedside light. If they were going to argue—as they obviously were—they might as well be able to see each other! 'Brett's not interested in me,' she said. 'It's perfectly obvious that he's in love with Georgia.'

'Brett?' Mal sat up too, at that, and turned to her incredulously. 'Brett's never been in love in his life!'

She gritted her teeth and tried not to let the sight of his bare chest distract her. 'I think he is now.'

'And I suppose being in love with Georgia explains why he spends his whole time hanging over you?' he said, not bothering to hide his sarcasm.

'Of course it does,' said Copper impatiently. 'Georgia hasn't shown any interest in him, so Brett doesn't want her to think that he cares about her, that's all.'

'All this amateur psychology doesn't sound very convincing to me,' sneered Mal. 'What makes you such an expert on love suddenly?'

'I know more than you, anyway,' she retorted. 'You wouldn't recognise love if it got up and punched you in the face!'

'Whereas you have all your experience with Glyn to go on!' he snapped back.

'Yes, I do,' said Copper defiantly. 'It's more than you have, anyway! Glyn and I loved each other.'

'Some love when he couldn't wait to dump you for someone else!'

'At least Glyn was honest about what he felt,' she said furiously. 'He's kind and he cares about me, which is more than I can say for you!'

'Why didn't you fight for him if he was so great?' sneered Mal, and Copper's green eyes flashed.

'I wish I had!'

'Just think,' he taunted her, 'if you'd waited a few more weeks, you could have had him back!'

'It's not too late,' Copper pointed out, so angry by now that she hardly knew or cared what she was saying. 'Ellie's still with her husband.'

Mal's brows snapped together. 'How do you know that?'

'There is a world outside Birraminda, you know,' she said sarcastically, 'and I still communicate with it occasionally!'

'You've been in touch with Glyn?' Mal shot out a hand to grasp Copper's arm and pull her round, but she jerked herself out of his grip, terrified in case the mere touch of his fingers against her skin should be enough to defuse her anger. After the numb misery of those endless tense, silent nights, it was oddly invigorating to feel the fury churning through her.

'What if I have? It's none of your business, anyway!'

'None of my business if my wife rings up her ex-lover for cosy little chats? Of course it's my business!'

'We agreed what sort of marriage we were going to have,' she said with a resentful glance, ostentatiously rubbing her arm where he had gripped her with his hard fingers. 'It was to be a purely practical arrangement. There was nothing in the contract about giving up all contact with the outside world!'

'We *agreed* that we would do our best to make sure that everyone thought that we were genuinely married,' said Mal savagely. 'You married me, Copper, and I think it's time you did a better job of acting like my wife than you've done so far—and for a start you can forget all about Glyn until your three years is up!'

Copper shook her hair angrily away from her face. 'Careful, Mal!' she said provocatively. 'You're sounding almost jealous, and you don't want that, do you? Jealousy is one of those ''messy'' emotions, like love or need, and we all know how you feel about those!'

'What would you know about emotions?' he said unpleasantly. 'All you care about is business.'

'That's good coming from a man who had to resort to blackmail to get a wife!'

'Then I got what I deserved, didn't I?' said Mal with dislike. 'A woman prepared to sell herself just to be able to pitch a few tents and make people pay through the nose for the privilege of sleeping in them!'

Copper's hands clenched around the sheet. 'If that's what you think of me, I think we'd better put an end to this farce right now,' she said, in a voice that shook with fury. 'There's no point in us carrying on like this. All you wanted was a housekeeper, and you've got Georgia now. It's pretty obvious that you think she's doing a much better job than I ever could, so I might as well leave you both to it and go back to Adelaide.'

'What, and give up on your precious project?' Mal mocked. 'You'd never do that, would you, Copper? No, you signed a contract that committed you to staying here for three years, and three years you're going to stay. You can't tear up our agreement just because you've got the chance to go running back to Glyn.'

'It might be worth losing the project to live with a man who appreciated me!' said Copper wildly.

There was a dangerous pause. '*I'd* appreciate you if you'd just stick to your part of our agreement and act like a proper wife,' said Mal, in a voice of cold control. 'And leave Brett alone, of course.'

Back to square one! Copper blew out a hopeless sigh and put her head between her hands. It might have felt good to let off steam, but the argument wasn't going anywhere. 'Look, I keep trying to tell you,' she said grittily. 'Brett only flirts with me because he's jealous of you.

'*Brett's* jealous of *me*?' Mal gave a mirthless laugh. 'That's a good one! How do you work that out?'

'He never gets a chance to impress Georgia because you're always there.' She lifted her head from her hands and tried to explain. 'You're the one who runs everything. You're the one who decides what should be done. You're the one who monopolises Georgia every night. How can Brett compete with you?'

'He's never found any difficulty before!'

'I know, but it's different now. This time Brett's in love.'

'Which he shows by behaving as if he's infatuated with my wife?' Mal suggested sardonically.

Copper gave a despairing gesture. 'It's all aimed at Georgia,' she insisted. 'Surely you can see that?'

'The only thing I can see is you making big green eyes at him every night,' he said in a biting voice as he lay down again and punched his pillow savagely into shape. 'If you left him alone, he might have a chance to fall in love with Georgia, but as it is you're just causing trouble. It's embarrassing for me and extremely awkward for Georgia to see the way you and Brett carry on.'

'Oh, and we can't have *Georgia* feeling awkward, can we?' flared Copper, wrenching the sheet over to her side of the bed before throwing herself angrily down onto her pillow with her back to Mal.

Mal pulled the sheet back. 'I'm warning you, Copper,' he said dangerously. 'You leave Brett alone. I won't stand by and watch you screw my brother up.'

Copper was so enraged that she jerked round to face him. 'All I've done to your brother is to offer him a bit of sympathy and understanding, which is more than he ever gets from you. You're so pig-headed and arrogant that you can't even see what's going on under your own nose!'

'You're not here to understand Brett,' said Mal callously. 'You're here to behave as my wife whenever anybody else is present, and that means not making an exhibition of yourself with my brother—or anyone else. I'd be grateful if you'd remember that in future.'

'You needn't worry,' said Copper in a voice that shook. 'I've got no intention of forgetting why I married you!' Oh, God, the light was still on! Scowling furiously to stop herself from crying, she heaved herself up once more to click it off and then pointedly turned her back. There was a pause, then with a short, exasperated sigh he did the same, and although she lay tensely awake for hours he made no move to touch her again.

It was such a stupid argument, Copper thought wearily the next day. It wouldn't have been too difficult to make up in each other's arms as they had done before. All she had needed to do was to roll over and whisper his name, but part of her had rebelled. Why should she grovel to Mal when she had nothing to apologise for? She wasn't the one being stubborn and blind and completely unreasonable, was she?

'We'll be out mustering all day,' Mal said brusquely at breakfast. 'I need Georgia to spot the strays from the plane, so you'll have to forget your business for once and keep an eye on Megan for a change.'

He clearly thought that was all she was good for, thought Copper, too weary after a sleepless night even to object to his implication that she didn't spend almost all of her time with Megan anyway while Georgia dealt with more of the household chores. She couldn't fly a plane, like Georgia, or ride out with the stockmen, cracking whips and chivvying the cattle along with piercing yells. As far as Mal was concerned, she was useful only for staying at home and keeping out of the way. It was amazing that he hadn't jumped at her suggestion that she go back to Adelaide. After last night, she would have thought he would be glad to be rid of her.

The homestead felt horribly empty when Georgia and the men had gone and Copper was left alone with Megan. Miserably, she began clearing up the kitchen, but the silence was oppressive and accusing and in the end she could bear it no longer. 'Let's have a picnic,' she said to Megan, wanting only to get away from the house with its taunting memories of Mal: Mal climbing the verandah steps, Mal turning his head, Mal closing the bedroom door with a smile in his eyes. 'We'll take my car and go somewhere different for a change.'

Copper hadn't used her car since she had driven up from Adelaide all those weeks ago, and it felt strange getting into it again. The last time she had sat behind the wheel Mal had been just a treasured memory, no more than an image from the past or a vague regret, and now…now he was so much part of her life that it was hard to imagine a time when she had existed without him. To Copper it seemed as if her whole life had been directed to the moment when she had driven up along the track and parked in front of the homestead. It was odd, looking back, to think that she had sat down to wait on the verandah steps without an inkling that Mal would walk around the corner of the woolshed and change her life again for ever.

She thought about how much had changed since then as she drove out along the rough track that led towards a wild, rocky area that she had never seen for herself. Mal had pointed it out once on one of their afternoon rides. It had been too far for them to go on horseback, but he had told her about the eerie red rocks and the spindly gums and the huge termite hills that gave the place its own special atmosphere.

Just remembering those rides made Copper's heart ache for the way things had been then. He had sat on his horse, relaxed and still, and the huge, empty horizon and the dazzling light had focused around him. Then, everything had seemed possible. She hadn't known how contemptuous his eyes could be, or how savage his tongue. Had she changed, or had he?

It took much longer than she had expected to coax

the car along the track, but they made it eventually and ate their picnic in the shade of an overhanging rock. It was a strange, wild place, that echoed with age and silence, but Copper was glad that she had come. Idly, she watched Megan playing house amongst the weirdly shaped stones. The stillness seemed to seep through her, calming her jagged nerves, and she was able to think clearly at last.

She and Mal had been happy before, and they could be happy again. There was no point in hanging onto her pride if it just made her miserable. She would talk to Mal tonight and tell him that she loved him. He might recoil, but at least it would be the truth. Copper didn't think she could bear the thought of spending three years pretending that she cared more for her business than she did for him.

She had to do *something*, anyway. They couldn't go on like this, letting stupid misunderstandings tangle themselves up into bitter arguments. The desire they had felt together was too strong, surely, to fall apart in a matter of days. Copper thought about the way Mal had kissed her and hope twisted inside her. If they could just have a night alone together everything would be all right again. It had to be.

Suddenly eager to get back and tell Mal exactly how she felt, Copper got to her feet and stretched. 'Come on, Megan, let's go home.'

It took a little while to persuade Megan to leave the little house she had created, but at last she was in the car, the picnic was packed away, and she settled herself behind the wheel. Her mind on Mal and what she would say when she saw him, Copper didn't register at first that the engine was wheezing and coughing. When she did, she frowned irritably and tried turning the ignition key again. Nothing happened.

Copper tried again—and again, exasperated, then angry, and at last afraid. Trying to conceal her sinking heart, she got out of the car to open the bonnet and peer helplessly at the engine. She had no idea where to start finding out what was wrong, let alone how to fix it.

The heat bounced off the metal and glared into her eyes. 'I'm hot!' Megan complained.

Biting her lip, Copper opened the door. 'Play in the shade for a while,' she suggested, and went back to the engine. Nothing seemed to be broken. She checked the water and the oil, more for something to do than anything else, and then went to try the ignition again in the wild hope that wishful thinking was enough to do the trick.

It wasn't, of course. Copper wiped her brow with the back of her arm and told herself there was no need to worry. When the muster got back, Mal would realise they were missing and come and find them. He won't know where to look, a cold voice whispered, and ice trickled down Copper's spine before she clamped down on the thought. Mal would find them. All she had to do was sit tight and keep Megan safe.

Megan. Copper got out of the car. Where *was* Megan? Around her were rocks and trees and utter, utter quiet, but no little girl. 'Megan?' Her voice bounced eerily off the stones and her heart seemed to freeze in her chest. 'Megan?'

All at once the afternoon had taken on a nightmarish quality. It was as if she had turned round and found herself on a different time plane, where nothing made any sense. Megan had been there only a minute ago. How could she be gone?

Copper forced herself to breathe deeply and slowly. The one thing she must not do was panic. Calling Megan's name, she began making systematic circles around the car, spreading a little wider every time, until a cry, abruptly cut off, sent her stumbling through the trees in its direction, her heart pounding with dread. Copper found that she was praying as she looked desperately around her for any sign of the child, but she made herself work steadily between the trees until she came out into a sort of clearing and saw Megan, lying sprawled and much, much too still, beneath a weathered red boulder.

'Megan!' Copper fell frantically to her knees beside her. The world had gone suddenly black. 'Please, no… please, no…please, no…' She could hear a voice muttering incoherently, and it was some time before she realised that it was her own and could fight her way back through the darkness to feel for Megan's pulse—a feeble beat that told her the child was unconscious but alive.

'Oh, thank God!' The tears streamed unheeded down Copper's face as Megan stirred and moaned.

'My foot hurts!'

Copper's first reaction was one of relief that it was only her foot. Very gently, she checked Megan all over. One ankle was badly swollen, but she didn't know enough to tell whether it was broken or just sprained. 'What happened, Megan?' she asked.

'I heard you calling, and I was going to hide up on the rocks, but I fell.' Megan began to cry. 'My head hurts as well,' she wept.

She must have hit it as she fell onto the hard ground.

Looking up at the smooth surface of the boulder, Copper went cold. It was quite a drop, and she could have been much more badly hurt. 'It's all right,' she soothed the child, gathering her into her arms without jarring the sore ankle.

Why, why, why had she never learnt any first aid? Megan didn't seem to have hurt anything other than her foot, but who knew what damage the fall might have done to her head? 'Shh,' she murmured into the dark curls, rocking her gently for comfort. She suspected that Megan was more shocked by her fall than anything else, but she might so easily be wrong.

Never had Copper felt more inadequate. Pretending that she knew what she was doing, she ripped up part of her shirt to make a bandage and tied it around Megan's ankle, but the slightest touch was enough to make Megan cry out in pain. 'I want to go home,' she sobbed.

It was only then that Copper remembered the car. 'We can't go home just yet, sweetheart,' she said with difficulty. 'But I'll carry you back to the car and we'll get you some water.'

'I don't want any water. I want to go home!'

'I know, I know.' Copper laid Megan down in the shade near the car and used another piece of her shirt to clean the dust from her face. At least she had thought to bring some water with her. It was the only sensible thing she had done today.

All the time she kept up a flow of cheerful talk, so that Megan wouldn't guess how desperately afraid she was, but inside she was desperately trying to calculate how long it would take Mal to realise that they were missing and organise a search. They were mustering in the far paddocks. What if they didn't get back to the homestead until it was almost dark and it was too late to look for them? She didn't want to think what it would be like to spend a night alone out here, with Megan frightened and hurt and only one bottle of water to see them through.

For what seemed like a lifetime, Copper sat in the shade, cradling Megan on her lap and distracting her by crooning to her softly or telling her stories until she fell into an exhausted sleep. After that there was nothing to do but wait and watch the minute hand of her watch crawl slowly round. The silence gathered weight with every second that passed. Copper could feel it squeezing the air around her, crushing her until she felt so deafened by it that when she heard the plane at last she thought she was hallucinating.

Lying the sleeping child gently on the ground, she struggled out from under the rock. Yes, there was the plane, flying low over the trees but still some distance away. Copper's first impulse was to shout, until she realised that she would only wake Megan needlessly, so she scrambled into the car instead, to begin frenziedly flashing the headlights.

With an excruciating lack of speed, the plane banked and flew towards her, low enough for Copper to see Georgia gesturing from the cockpit as she talked into the radio. Desperately, Copper pointed to the lifted bonnet of the car to show that it had broken down. Georgia nodded and gave Copper the thumbs-up sign for encouragement. Then she dipped her wings and headed back for the homestead.

For a full minute Copper just stared after her, unable to believe that Georgia had just gone and left them there.

Then reason returned and she realised that there was nowhere for the plane to land among all the rocks. Georgia must have been radioing their position back to Mal. The relief was so overwhelming that Copper had to hold onto the car door for support.

Making her way back to their shelter beneath the rock, she gathered the sleepily whimpering Megan back into her lap. 'It's all right now,' she murmured. 'Dad's coming.'

CHAPTER TEN

THE silence was so complete that Copper heard the crunch of changing gears long before she saw Mal's four-wheel drive, but the light was rapidly fading before the vehicle swung into the clearing, its headlights raking across Copper's useless car. By then she was too stiff and weary to move, and she could only sit helplessly as Mal leapt out and looked anxiously around him.

'We're here,' she tried to call, but her mouth was so dry that it came out as no more than a whisper. It was enough, though, for Mal to swing round and see them huddled beneath their rock.

After that everything was a blur for Copper, interspersed with sudden flashes of terrible clarity—like the look on Megan's face when she saw her father or the way Mal's arms tightened round his daughter with a sort of desperation. Too clear was the whiteness of fear around his mouth, the stony expression in his eyes when he looked at Copper and the terrible silence as he drove them home.

'The explanations can wait,' he said curtly, when she tried to tell him what had happened.

Back at the homestead, Georgia was waiting to help them inside. It was Georgia who knew about first aid and could bandage Megan's ankle properly, Georgia who helped Mal to soothe her and wash her and put her to bed. Copper was left to limp stiffly along to the bedroom, too sick at heart to do anything but sit numbly on the side of the bed with the remnants of her shirt in her hands. It was all her fault. She should never have taken Megan out there, should never have taken her eyes off her.

Her sense of guilt was so great that Copper didn't even try and defend herself when Mal came into the room, shutting the door behind him with an ominous click. 'You realise you could have killed my daughter this afternoon?' he said, dangerously quiet.

Copper flinched as if from a blow, but all she could do was turn her head away. She felt Mal's eyes boring into her as he moved into the room. 'You put her in a car that's not fit to drive outside a city and took her out to the most dangerous part of the property,' he said. He didn't raise his voice, but every word was like a lash from a whip. 'And then you let her wander off on her own and hurt herself badly falling off a rock. You might as well have pushed her off yourself!'

'I'm sorry,' whispered Copper, linking her hands together to stop them shaking.

'Sorry? What's the use of being sorry?' Mal was white with fury. 'How dared you take a risk like that with my daughter's life? You didn't even think to leave a note to say where you were going! If Georgia hadn't come back early and found you missing, you could have been out there all night. If she hadn't radioed me straight away it would have been too late for me to get back to a car. As it was she only just spotted you in time. We could all have spent the night driving around in the dark looking for you!'

'I didn't know the car was going to break down,' said Copper painfully.

'It wasn't broken down,' he said with withering contempt. 'Brett's brought it back already. Anyone with the most basic knowledge of mechanics could have fixed it.'

'I don't know anything about mechanics,' she muttered, looking down at her hands.

'Of course you don't!' She could hear Mal striding savagely around the room. 'You don't know about anything useful and you haven't made any attempt to learn. All you've done is push bits of paper around and make a fool out of me!'

Stung out of her guilt and misery, Copper looked up at last. 'That's not true!'

'Isn't it?' Mal's mouth twisted with distaste. 'God, you'd think I'd have learnt my lesson about unsuitable women, wouldn't you? Lisa was just as useless as you, but even she didn't behave as irresponsibly. She might not have spent much time with Megan, but at least she never exposed her to the kind of danger you did today!'

'Why do you keep marrying unsuitable women, then?' Copper leapt to her feet and flung the torn shirt aside, too hurt and bitter to keep still any longer. 'Have you ever thought that when things go wrong it might be something to do with you? No, of course you haven't!' She answered her own question.

'You'll never find a woman who satisfies you, Mal, because you think marriage is something that can be organised by some stupid contract. You accuse me of being obsessed with business, but you're the one who looks at everything in terms of a deal. You always think about what you're going to get out of a marriage and never about what you're going to share. You never give anything of yourself, do you?' She was shaking as she swept on, green eyes blazing with the injustice of his remarks. 'I used to think that it was because you'd been hurt by Lisa, but now I think it's because you've got nothing *to* give—and even if you had, it wouldn't be worth having!'

Mal took a sharp step towards her, and for a moment she thought he was actually going to hit her, but then he had turned on his heel and was at the door. At the last moment he glanced back at Copper with eyes like ice and a voice that dripped with contempt. 'The reason I don't give anything to you, Copper, is that there's nothing I want from you in return.' And he went out, pulling the door behind him with a final, terrible click.

'Copper, you look awful!' Georgia exclaimed in concern when she saw Copper the next morning. Her face was pinched with exhaustion and the green eyes were blank with misery.

'I'm all right.' Copper managed a wavering smile in spite of the fact that there was an agonising pounding behind her eyes and her heart felt as if it was gripped by talons of ice.

She had spent the night curled in a foetal position on the bed, staring numbly at the wall and too despairing even to cry while Mal's words jeered and echoed remorselessly in her brain. Useless. Irresponsible. Worse than Lisa. She hadn't seen him since he had walked out of the room, but she didn't need to. She knew now exactly what he thought of her, and her belief that they would be able to resolve all their differences in bed seemed hopelessly naïve.

Mal would never forgive her for endangering Megan, and the more Copper thought about it the more she thought he was right. She *was* useless here at Birraminda. She didn't belong and she never would. Mal needed a wife like Georgia, who was everything Copper wasn't. The realisation turned Copper's heart to stone, but she knew what she had to do.

She tried to ignore the other girl's worried look. 'How's Megan?'

'She seems fine apart from her ankle,' said Georgia. 'Children are pretty resilient, but we thought she ought to spend the day in bed, anyway, in case there were any after effects from that bump on the head.'

Copper flinched at that 'we'. She knew that it was unintentional, but Georgia's calm good sense only seemed to reinforce her own uselessness. 'I'll go and see her,' she said dully.

Megan was propped up against a pile of pillows, looking more bored than ill, but her face brightened when she saw Copper, and she was anxious to show off her bandaged foot. 'I've got a sprained ankle,' she said proudly, and then, barely pausing for breath, 'Can you read me a story?'

'Not today, sweetheart.' Copper sat down on the edge of the bed, her throat so tight that it was painful to swallow. 'I've got to go to Adelaide.'

'Can I come?' said Megan eagerly.

She shook her head. 'You've got to stay and look after Dad.'

'When are you coming back?'

Copper hesitated. She had been going to tell Megan that she would only be away a week or so, but wasn't that more cruel than telling her the truth? 'I—I'm not coming back, Megan.' It was one of the hardest things she had ever had to say.

Megan stared at her, blue eyes huge as understanding dawned painfully through her confusion. 'You can't go.' Copper had dreaded this moment, but the look in the child's eyes was worse than anything she could have imagined. 'Dad said you'd stay.' Her voice rose to a wail and then broke as she began to cry.

'Oh, Megan…' Copper pulled the sobbing child into her arms and rocked her, her own tears pouring down her face and into the soft curls buried into her throat. 'I'm so sorry,' she whispered, knowing that for a little girl like Megan being sorry was not enough. 'But Georgia's here to look after you now, and you like her, don't you?'

'I don't want Georgia,' wept Megan. 'I want you! You said you'd stay for ever!'

'Megan, I—' She broke off, her voice suspended in tears. 'I don't want to go.' She tried again. 'I wish I could stay with you for always.'

'Then why are you going?'

How could she explain to a child of four? 'Megan, you love Dad, don't you?' The dark head nodded mutely and Copper struggled to go on. 'So do I, but he doesn't love me.'

'He does! He does!'

Copper tried to close her ears to the anguish in the child's voice. 'Sometimes, when you love someone, you want them to be happy even if it makes you unhappy, and that's what it's like for me. I think Dad would be happier if I went away.'

'No!' sobbed Megan. 'He wants you to stay!'

Copper held her tightly, kissing the dark curls. 'I don't belong here, Megan,' she said brokenly through her tears. 'But I want you to know that I love you very much. I always will.' She swallowed painfully. 'You'll be a good girl for Dad, won't you?'

Megan didn't answer, only clung to her in desperation as Copper tried to lay her back down in the bed, and in the end Copper had to sit there, crooning softly, until she was so worn out by crying that she fell asleep.

Gently Copper covered Megan with a sheet and smoothed the curls away from the flushed, tearstained little face. She stood looking down at her for a long time while her heart splintered inside her, and then she walked quietly away and closed the door behind her.

'You can't go!' Georgia was aghast when Copper told her she was leaving. 'You're in no state to drive anywhere.'

'I have to.' Copper's face felt numb and she was moving stiffly, like an old woman.

Georgia was obviously distressed. 'Copper, I know you and Mal had an argument last night,' she said awkwardly. 'I saw him come out of your room, and he looked as if the world had just ended. But it was such an awful day, and you were both upset. I'm sure if you could just talk about it you'd be able to work everything out.'

'Mal and I have done enough talking,' said Copper. She felt very weary, although it wasn't yet nine o'clock. 'I don't belong here, Georgia. I can't ride a horse or fix a car or strap up an ankle, and after yesterday it's obvious that I'm not even any good at looking after Megan.'

'None of those things matter,' said Georgia urgently. 'The only thing that matters is that you and Mal love each other. Please stay and talk to him tonight!'

'I can't.' Copper's face was ravaged by tears. She couldn't stand to see the disgust in Mal's eyes again. 'I just can't!'

'But what will I tell Mal when he asks why you've gone?'

Copper picked up her case. She had torn her copy of the contract into two and left the pieces on her pillow. 'You won't need to tell him anything. He'll know why I've gone.'

Georgia was crying as she followed her out to the car. 'I wish you wouldn't go,' she wept as Copper turned to hug her goodbye.

'It'll be better for everyone this way.' Copper choked back her own tears. 'Look after Megan for me, Georgia, and tell Mal…tell him I'm sorry…about everything.'

'I'll put a brochure in the post tonight.' Copper put down the phone and rubbed her aching neck. Had she really used to love working in an office?

Over the last ten days she had struggled to pick up the threads of her old life, but she felt trapped in a dull sense of unreality where only the pain inside her seemed less than a blur. Every day seemed interminable, and when she got to the end of each one, like now, there was only the evening stretching bleakly ahead. In the past Copper had thrived on a frenetic lifestyle, but now she hated everything about the city. She hated the tarmac roads and the smell of cars. She hated the endlessly ringing phone and the hours spent making bookings or stuffing brochures into envelopes.

Copper lifted a pile of booking forms and then dropped them listlessly back onto her desk. All she was doing was pushing pieces of paper around, just as Mal had said. Once the very sound of exotic destinations like Quito or Kampala or Rangoon had been enough to thrill her, but now there was only one place she wanted to be.

Birraminda. Copper wanted the empty outback sky, the sharp light and the space and the scent of dust and dry leaves along the creek. She wanted the cockatoos squawking and screeching in the trees and the horses grazing peacefully in the paddock. She wanted the clatter of the screen door and the glare of the sun on the corrugated iron roof and Megan snuggling into her side for a story.

And Mal.

Copper ached with the need to hear his footsteps on the verandah, to watch him settle his hat on his head. She craved the lean, muscled grace of his body and his slow, sure hands on her skin. Most of all she wanted him to fold her in his arms and tell her that he loved her, to melt the ice around her heart and let her live again.

It had taken some time to persuade her parents that she really had left Mal. 'But we were so sure that you were right for each other,' her mother had said, bewildered when Copper had arrived, grey with misery and exhaustion.

'It was all just a pretence,' said Copper bitterly. 'We were just acting.'

Dan Copley snorted. 'If that was acting, you should both be in Hollywood!'

In the end, she had to tell them about the deal she had made with Mal. Her father's face darkened as he heard her story, and Copper felt crushed by guilt at the knowledge that she had thrown his dream away.

'I'm sorry, Dad,' she stammered. 'I know how much you wanted the project at Birraminda, but I'm sure I'll be able to find somewhere else if I—'

'The project!' Dan dismissed his dream with an angry gesture. 'What does the project matter? All I care about is you! I've a good mind to ring that Mal up right now and give him a piece of my mind! How could he have blackmailed my daughter!'

Seeing that he was working himself up into a state, Copper clutched at his arm and tried to calm him before he put too much strain on his heart. 'Dad, don't! It wasn't blackmail. I chose to marry Mal.'

'He must have forced you. How could you have chosen to marry a man you were only pretending to love?'

Copper's face twisted. 'But I wasn't pretending, Dad. That was the trouble.'

Although still doubtful, her parents had eventually accepted her decision to come home and Copper had thrown herself into work at the office. Anything was better than sitting at home waiting for the phone to ring, or for a knock at the door that would mean Mal had come to find her. He must realise that she had gone back to her parents, but he had made no effort to get in touch with her. This time he had no excuse for not knowing where to find her.

If Mal had loved her, he would have come straight down to Adelaide to fetch her back. At the very least he would have rung to check that she was safe and hadn't broken down again in the middle of the outback. But there had been no word from him at all. That meant that Copper was just going to have to learn to live without him. She had got over Mal once before, she tried to tell herself, and she would again.

With a sigh, Copper pushed back her chair. Six o'clock. Her father would be here any minute. Her car was in for a service and he had promised to come and pick her up. Dully, she switched on the answering machine and straightened the papers on her desk before running her hands wearily through her hair. The vitality that had always been so much a part of her had been drained by despair, and she didn't need to look in the mirror to know that her terrible sense of desolation could be read in her thin face and the green eyes that were smudged with exhaustion.

Outside the window, Copper saw her father's car slide to a halt and she raised a hand in acknowledgement. Locking the door behind her, she went over and got into the car, summoning a smile as she turned to thank her father.

But he wasn't there.

Mal was.

Copper's heart stopped and all the air went whooshing from her lungs as the world tilted alarmingly around her. Mal was *there*, quiet and contained and unbelievably real. He was wearing his moleskin trousers and a dark green shirt open at the throat, and there was an expression in his eyes that Copper had never seen there before. She might even have thought that it was anxiety if her gaze hadn't dropped to the piece of paper sticking out of his shirt pocket.

Copper recognised that paper all too well, and cold, cruel reality wiped out that first dazzling moment of joy with a brutality that clutched agonisingly at her throat. Mal had brought the contract with him and was going to try and force her to its terms.

Bitterness closed around her. There had been times when she had thought that it would be enough just to see him again, but she hadn't wanted it to be like this. 'What are you doing in Dad's car?' she asked him through stiff lips. It was the first thing that came into her head, and even as she asked the question she thought how irrelevant it was.

'He lent it to me.' Calmly, Mal put on his indicator, glanced over his shoulder and pulled out into the traffic. 'Did you think I had stolen it?'

'You've been to see my parents?'

He was concentrating on driving, not looking at her. 'I got here earlier this afternoon. I had to endure an unpleasant session with your father, but once I'd had a chance to explain what I was doing here he gave me the car and told me to come and pick you up myself.'

'And what *are* you doing here?' Copper cast a bitter glance at the contract. 'As if I don't know!'

'I would have thought it would be obvious, yes,' said Mal. 'We need to talk.'

She looked out of the window. How could he sit there, coolly manoeuvring through the traffic, when her world was reeling? 'We've said everything we had to say,' she said bleakly.

'I haven't,' he said.

'Well, I have!'

'That's all right,' said Mal. 'You can listen.'

He drove her to the beach and parked the car facing the sea. Copper felt curiously detached, too shaken by Mal's unexpected appearance even to wonder how he knew the way. It had been a sunny day, but not particularly warm for late summer, and the beach was almost empty—except for an occasional jogger and a few seagulls squabbling over scraps, their cries drifting on the sea breeze.

For a while they sat there without speaking, watching the waves rippling against the sand. Mal seemed to have forgotten that he wanted to talk to her. He was staring through the windscreen, his hands resting on the steering wheel and his shoulders tense.

'Well?' said Copper eventually. 'What is it that you want to say?'

'I wanted to know why you left without saying goodbye.'

'You must know why I left,' she said bitterly. 'You made it very clear what you thought of me the night before and I thought you'd be glad to find that I'd gone.'

Mal turned at that. 'You thought I'd be glad to come home and find that my wife had walked out on me?'

'But I wasn't ever really your wife, was I, Mal?' said Copper. 'Oh, I know we went through a ceremony, and said all the right words in the right places, but it takes more than that to be married. I was only ever a housekeeper as far as you were concerned, and I knew you'd replaced plenty of those before. You didn't even have to go to the trouble of ringing up the agency when you had Georgia there, on the spot, ready to take my place. Why don't you try and blackmail *her* into marrying you? She'd be a far better wife than I ever was!'

Mal half smiled. 'She's certainly ideal—' he began, but Copper couldn't bear to hear any more. She jumped out of the car, blinded by tears, and began to stumble towards the beach. But Mal was cutting her off from the other side.

'Don't you walk away from me again!' he shouted. 'Why do you think I came down here to find you?'

'I don't know!' She tried to brush the tears angrily from her eyes but they kept spilling over. 'I suppose you're going to try waving that contract at me. What are you going to do, sue me for breach of promise?'

'No.' Mal pulled it from his pocket. 'I did bring the contract with me, though. Look, here it is,' he said, and then, very deliberately, he tore it into tiny pieces. The lightest of breezes lifting off the sea caught them and they fluttered away, to be pounced on by a seagull who carried it away, screeching in triumph.

Copper stared blankly across the bonnet, her tears forgotten. 'That was the contract!' she said stupidly.

'Not any more.'

'But...don't you want it?'

'I never wanted it,' he said.

'But you insisted on it! You only ever opened your mouth to quote it at me! Why would you do that if you didn't want it?'

'God, wasn't it obvious?' cried Mal in sudden despair.

'I did it because it was the only way I could make you stay!'

The words rang between them, echoing in the sudden silence. Copper couldn't move. She could only gaze at Mal in disbelief as he walked round the front of the car to take her very gently by the elbows.

'I never wanted the contract, Copper,' he said. 'I only ever wanted you.'

'Y-you wanted a housekeeper,' she corrected him. She was trembling, terrified of facing the bitterness of disillusion again but incapable of ignoring the hope that was flickering into life against all the odds.

'I told myself that, but it was only an excuse. I'd been looking for one ever since I looked across the yard and saw you sitting on the steps next to Megan.' His thumbs moved tantalisingly over her inner arms, caressing the soft skin. 'It was like a miracle, to find you again after seven years.'

'I didn't think you even remembered me,' said Copper unsteadily. 'You can't tell me that you'd been waiting for me all that time!'

'I hadn't been waiting, no,' said Mal, 'but I had been regretting. I'd accepted that I would never see you again, and then I met Lisa. I wanted her to make me feel the way you had done, but she could never be you and the marriage was a disaster from the start. I can't tell you how many times I'd find myself thinking about you, about the way you smiled, the way you closed your eyes when I kissed you, the way you felt in my arms.'

He paused, looking down into Copper's face, and the expression in his eyes made her heart beat faster. 'I used to wonder what my life would have been like if my father hadn't died just then, or if you'd been in when I called, but I knew there was no point in wishing that things had been different, so I tried my best to forget you. And then, just when I thought I'd managed to push you to the back of my mind, suddenly there you were.'

'Why didn't you tell me this then?' she asked uncertainly, and Mal's fingers tightened around her arms.

'I wasn't sure that the time we'd spent together in Turkey had meant the same thing to you. You'd obviously got on with enjoying your life and you didn't seem to have any regrets.' His mouth twisted. 'And Lisa taught me to be wary. It was a blow to realise that you were so determined about your business, but I thought that if I could just get you to stay a little longer we'd have a chance to get to know each other again. When you offered to stay on as housekeeper it seemed too good to be true, but it wasn't long before I realised that wasn't going to be enough. You'd made it clear that your business was your priority, and I knew you wouldn't stay just because I asked you.'

'So you thought you'd try a spot of blackmail?' said Copper, with the beginnings of a smile.

Mal grimaced. 'It was all I could think of, but it just made things worse. I felt guilty at having forced you into a marriage that you didn't want, and the very fact that you'd agreed made it obvious that your business meant far more to you than I ever could.'

Could he really have been so blind? 'Did it seem like I was thinking of business on our wedding night?' she asked, and he slid his hands slowly up her arms.

'I wasn't sure,' he confessed. 'When I made love to you, I was sure that you had to feel the same, but I'd watched you with Glyn at the wedding, and I remembered what you'd said about still loving him. I was afraid you'd just been trying to forget him, and when I woke up the next morning and saw the contracts I realised what an impossible situation I'd put us both in. I knew that I'd no right to touch you unless you asked, because that's what I'd agreed, but you've no idea how hard it was to lie next to you night after night.'

'Don't I?'

She smiled at him as she spoke and Mal gripped her shoulders. 'Copper,' he said with sudden urgency. 'I've said a lot of stupid things about love. I pretended that I didn't want anything more to do with it after Lisa, when all the time I was just afraid to tell you how much I loved you. I came down because I knew I had to apologise for the way I treated you, but all I really want is to ask you to come back.'

He hesitated, and Copper marvelled at the uncertainty in his expression. 'I've got no right to ask you, I know, but Birraminda isn't the same without you. It isn't like before. You're not just a special memory any more. I *need* you now, and Megan needs you too.' He gestured at the scattered pieces of paper. 'The contract doesn't exist any more. I want you to come back because *you* want to, not because some lawyer says you have to.'

His hands cupped her face lovingly and his voice was very low. '*Will* you come back, Copper? Not as a housekeeper, not as a wife—not as anything but yourself?'

Copper slipped her arms around his waist and smiled up at him with shining eyes. 'It depends how long you want me to stay this time.'

'Nothing less than for ever will do,' said Mal.

'For ever it is, then,' she said, and melted joyously into his kiss. He crushed her against him, kissing her with a deep, desperate hunger, and Copper clung to him, dizzy with pleasure and almost aching with the happiness of knowing that he loved her.

'Are you sure you want me back?' she asked much later, struck by sudden doubt as they walked slowly along the beach together. 'I'm so hopeless at everything. I can't do any of the things your wife should be able to do. You need someone who knows what they're doing and—'

Mal stopped her with another long kiss before she could say any more. 'I need *you*,' he said against her mouth. 'Only you.'

Deeply satisfied, Copper wound her arms around his neck and nibbled tiny, tantalising kisses along his jaw. 'But I thought Georgia was your ideal wife,' she murmured provocatively into his ear.

'*If* you'd let me finish,' said Mal, 'you'd have heard me say that Georgia was the ideal wife for Brett.' He pretended to sound stern, but she could feel his cheek crease into a smile beneath her lips. 'You were right about that too, which just goes to show how useful you're going to be.'

'Georgia and Brett are getting married?' Copper pulled back at the news, delighted. 'When did that happen?'

'After you left. Trying to cope with me brought them together—I think it made them realise how they'd feel if one of them left.'

'I knew Brett was in love, but I didn't realise Georgia

felt anything for him!' Copper tucked herself into Mal's side as they resumed their walk.

'I don't think she wanted to be just another girl for him, so she held off as long as she could,' Mal told her. 'She's certainly the only girl Brett's ever taken seriously, and I think she'll be good for him. He's steadier already. I've been so taken up with running around after you that he's had to take over a lot of the work on the station, and it's done him the world of good. There's a nice property up for sale not too far away, and together they should make a success of it.' He smiled down at Copper. 'They're just waiting for you to come back so that they can get married.'

Copper flashed him a demure look from beneath her lashes. 'So you're not jealous of Brett any more?'

'Not now,' said Mal with a rueful smile. 'I was, though. But not nearly as jealous as I was of Glyn. I kept thinking about the things you'd said about him—how he was kind and honest and a good friend—and I was terrified that you'd decide to go back to him. And later, when I thought about the things I'd said to you, I didn't think I could blame you.'

His arms tightened. 'I said some unforgivable things to you that last night, Copper,' he confessed. 'I've never been as scared as I was when I heard that you and Megan were missing, but I was still angry after that argument the night before and I took it all out on you. It didn't help, though, and I felt so bad the next day that I turned back halfway out to the muster. I was going to tell you that I was sorry, and hadn't meant what I'd said, but when I got back Georgia had to tell me you'd gone.'

The memory made Mal crush her so hard against him

that she could hardly breathe, but Copper didn't mind. 'It was the worst moment of my life,' he said. 'Georgia was crying, Megan was inconsolable, Brett kept telling me what a bloody fool I'd been—but all I could think was that you'd decided to try and work things out with Glyn after all. I remembered what you'd said about it not being too late now that Ellie was back with her husband, and I was so desperate and angry at first that I refused to go after you. I've spent the last ten days in hell, imagining you with him, and this morning I couldn't stand it any longer. I flew down and went straight to your parents', but you weren't there. Your father tore a strip off me for making you so unhappy, but when I told him that my life just wasn't going to be worth living unless I could persuade you to come back and try again, he took pity on me and tossed me the car keys!'

'Mal?' Copper held herself slightly away from him so that she could look deep into his eyes. 'Have I told you that I love you?'

He smiled at her in a way that made her heart sing. 'Now that you come to mention it, I don't think you have,' he said.

'I do,' said Copper, and kissed him—a long, warm, inexpressibly sweet kiss that thrilled with the promise of the years to come.

Later, much later, they took off their shoes and walked barefoot along the sand. It was cool and soft between Copper's toes and reminded her of the beach they had walked along seven years ago, hand in hand as now but knowing nothing then of the long road that would bring them back together again.

'We don't have to get married again now that we've torn up our contracts, do we?' she murmured, nuzzling Mal's throat as they halted for yet another kiss.

'We don't need another wedding, but I think we might have another honeymoon, don't you?' said Mal. 'Why don't we tell your parents that the project's on again, and then take ourselves back to that hotel in the hills? We could have a real honeymoon now that we don't need to pretend any more.' His lips drifted along Copper's jaw to linger at her mouth. 'How does that sound?'

Copper heaved an ecstatic sigh as they turned towards the car. 'It sounds like heaven!'

Three days later, the little plane flew over the creek and touched down at Birraminda. 'Welcome home,' said Mal, leaning over to kiss Copper as they came to a bumpy halt.

Brett and Georgia were waiting together on the edge of the landing strip, restraining an impatient Megan with difficulty until the propeller had spun to a stop. But as Mal lifted Copper down, his hands hard and possessive at her waist, she came flying over the dust towards them.

'Copper, Copper!' she called, and flung herself into Copper's waiting arms. 'You came home!'

Copper lifted her up in a tight hug, and the green eyes that met Mal's over the small head shone with love. 'Yes,' she said. 'I'm home now.'

Modern Romance™
...seduction and passion guaranteed

Tender Romance™
...love affairs that last a lifetime

Sensual Romance™
...sassy, sexy and seductive

Blaze™
...sultry days and steamy nights

Medical Romance™
...medical drama on the pulse

Historical Romance™
...rich, vivid and passionate

29 new titles every month.

With all kinds of Romance for every kind of mood...

MAT4

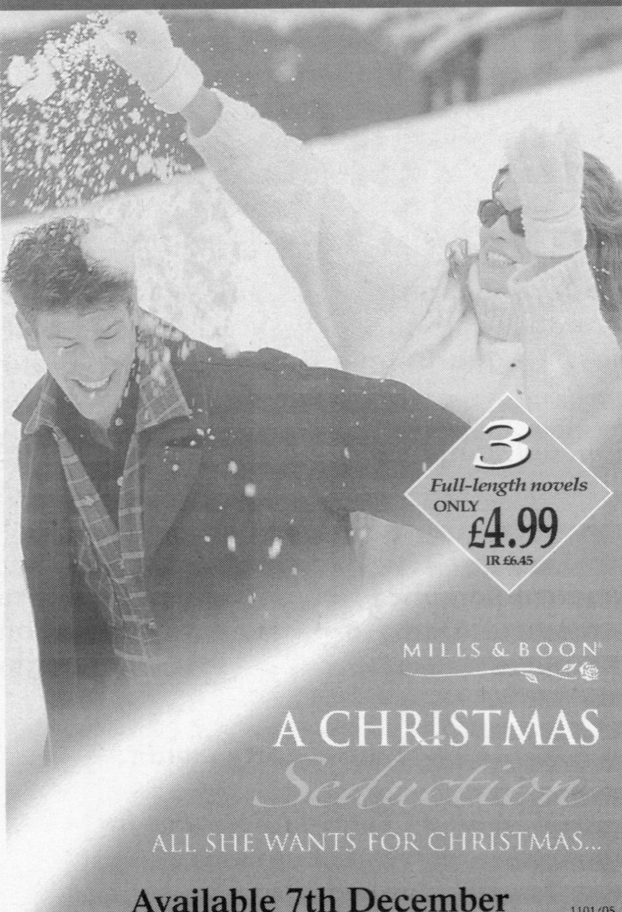

Available at most branches of WH Smith, Tesco, Martins, Borders, Eason, Sainsbury's, and most good paperback bookshops.

Christmas with a Latin Lover

Three brand-new stories

Lynne Graham
Penny Jordan
Lucy Gordon

Published 19th October

Available at most branches of WH Smith, Tesco, Martins, Borders, Eason, Sainsbury's, and most good paperback bookshops.

The perfect gift this Christmas from

MILLS & BOON®

3 brand new romance novels and a FREE French manicure set

for just £7.99

featuring best selling authors

Betty Neels,

Kim Lawrence and Nicola Cornick

Available from 19th October

Available at most branches of WH Smith, Tesco, Martins, Borders, Eason, Sainsbury's, and most good paperback bookshops.

1101/94/MB28

0801/123/MB19

OTHER NOVELS BY

PENNY JORDAN

POWER GAMES

POWER PLAY

CRUEL LEGACY

TO LOVE, HONOUR & BETRAY

THE HIDDEN YEARS

THE PERFECT SINNER

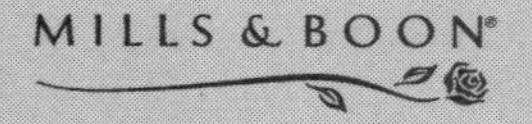

MILLS & BOON

FOREIGN AFFAIRS

A captivating 12 book collection of sun-kissed seductions.
Enjoy romance around the world

DON'T MISS BOOK 2

french kiss–
Proposals Parisian style

Available from 2nd November

Available at most branches of WH Smith, Tesco, Martins, Borders, Eason, Sainsbury's, and most good paperback bookshops.

FA/RTL/2

Sensual Romance™

Men of Chance

Come and meet the three strong
and sexy Chance brothers—be seduced!

October 2001
PURE CHANCE
by Julie Elizabeth Leto

November 2001
HER ONLY CHANCE
by Cheryl Anne Porter

December 2001
CHANCE ENCOUNTER
by Jill Shalvis

Chance—

It's not just a name, it's the family motto!

0901/21/LC04

Modern Romance™

Eight brand new titles each month

...seduction and passion guaranteed

Available at most branches of WH Smith, Tesco, Martins, Borders, Eason, Sainsbury's, and most good paperback bookshops.

GEN/01/RTL5

Tender Romance™

Four brand new titles each month

...love affairs that last a lifetime.

Available at most branches of WH Smith, Tesco, Martins, Borders, Eason, Sainsbury's, and most good paperback bookshops.

GEN/02/RTL5

Medical Romance™

Six brand new titles each month

...medical drama
on the pulse.

*Available at most branches of WH Smith,
Tesco, Martins, Borders, Eason, Sainsbury's,
and most good paperback bookshops.*

GEN/03/RTL5

Historical Romance™

Two brand new titles each month

...rich, vivid and passionate.

Available at most branches of WH Smith, Tesco, Martins, Borders, Eason, Sainsbury's, and most good paperback bookshops.

GEN/04/RTL5

Sensual Romance™

Four brand new titles each month

...sassy, sexy and seductive.

Available at most branches of WH Smith, Tesco, Martins, Borders, Eason, Sainsbury's, and most good paperback bookshops.

GEN/21/RTL5